Desire and Delusion

Arthur Schnitzler

Desire and Delusion

THREE NOVELLAS

Selected and Translated from the German by
Margret Schaefer

IVAN R. DEE

Chicago

DESIRE AND DELUSION. Three Novellas by Arthur Schnitzler. English
translation copyright © 2003 by Margret Schaefer. All rights reserved, including
the right to reproduce this book or portions thereof in any form. For information,
address: Ivan R. Dee, Publisher, 1332 North Halsted Street, Chicago 60622.
Manufactured in the United States of America and printed on acid-free paper.

The paperback edition of this book carries the ISBN 1-56663-603-5.

Library of Congress Cataloging-in-Publication Data:
Schnitzler, Arthur, 1862–1931.
    [Short stories. English. Selections]
    Desire and delusion : three novellas / Arthur Schnitzler ; selected and
translated from the German by Margret Schaefer.
        p. cm.
    Contents: Flight into darkness — Dying — Fräulein Else.
    ISBN 1-56663-542-X (alk. paper)
    1. Schnitzler, Arthur, 1862–1931—Translations into English. I. Schaefer,
Margret. II. Title.

PT2638.N5A22 2003
833'.8—dc21   2003053165

Contents

Foreword

"EVERY ARTIST," wrote Arthur Schnitzler, "is at once a realist and an idealist, an impressionist and an expressionist, a naturalist and a symbolist—as far as he is an artist." Although perhaps not true of every artist, it is a good description of Schnitzler. His ability to combine these seemingly contradictory approaches is his major strength.

For one thing, he was a doctor as well as a writer, the son of a highly respected Viennese laryngologist and professor of medicine. After studying medicine in Vienna, in 1886, at the age of twenty-four, Schnitzler was appointed assistant doctor in the psychiatric clinic of Theodore Meynert, where Freud also trained. He wrote in his diaries at the time, "Medicine and poetry are fighting a battle in my so-called soul," and later largely gave up the practice of medicine in favor of writing. But he also observed that "one can stop being many things—a doctor never." By virtue of family background and training, Schnitzler was thus more exposed to the natural sciences than most of the writers of his time. Perhaps this is what gave his writing the capacity for an unflinching realism, almost a naturalism.

His special interest was, like Freud's, psychology—the strange and convoluted byways of human emotions. His first piece of writing was a medical paper describing the psychology of aphonia (loss of voice). Freud thought so highly of it that he cited the work in his description of Dora in his famous "Fragments of an Analysis of a Case of Hysteria." As a writer, Schnitzler had a lyrical and poetic side that always remained anchored in the concrete and corporeal. He managed to meld a scientific objectivity with the empathic expressiveness and imagination of a writer.

Only a writer who was also a doctor could have written the novellas collected in this volume. All of them are stories of illness, mostly of the emotional and mental kind. Schnitzler was at home in what Susan Sontag has called "the country of the sick." So clinically accurate are these novellas in their portrayals of the psychology of emotionally distressed people, traumatized by their society or by illness or by their own obsessions, that they could be seen as "case studies." But Schnitzler's remarkable empathic ability to express in literary form his characters' subjectivity makes us feel the immediacy of their pain and the depths of their longings and fears. *Flight into Darkness, Dying,* and *Fräulein Else,* like the stories and novellas translated in the earlier collection *Night Games,* feature a Schnitzler quite different from the internationally famous author of risqué and cynical plays like *Reigen* (the basis of Max Ophuls's *La Ronde*), *Anatol,* and *Flirtation.* The longer prose fictions collected here reveal the other side of those egotistical, womanizing roués who dominate most of his plays—a darker, more troubled, more vulnerable side that lends credence to the old saw that behind the hedonistic cynic is a man who seeks to quiet his fear of death by losing himself in a whirlwind of sexual intoxication.

Acknowledged masterpieces of psychological realism, these longer prose works, newly translated here, span Schnitzler's career from 1892 to 1931, the year of his death. They show his development of a narrative technique new at the time: the stream-of-consciousness interior monologue, which enables him to immerse his readers directly in his characters' subjectivity while emphasizing their essential apartness and loneliness. For his theme is often the dissociation and disjunction between the inner self and the outer self, between the self and its social masks, between the self and others, and—reaching even deeper—between parts of the self in conflict with one another. His main characters are often surprised by aspects of themselves they do not know and do not want to know. They are continually asking themselves, Why did I do that? Why did I say that? How could I feel this? Even, as Else of *Fräulein Else* asks: Is this really my voice, my smile, my look? Interior monologue of this kind allows Schnitzler to express the enigmatic aspects of his character's personal identity and experience. He asks not only which of our often contradictory selves is real but whether we can speak of such a thing as a self at all. If there is a self, is it revealed more in our actions or in our thoughts? And if the latter, what, the stories ask, is to save us from losing touch with the world around us, from becoming solipsistic—from going mad? Explored most directly in *Flight into Darkness*, this question underlies all three of the novellas that follow.

Dying was Schnitzler's first venture into longer fiction. Initially titled *Imminent Death* and written in a few months in 1892, it became his first real success as a writer. True, the publisher to whom he first sent it turned it down as "too grim" for his magazine audience, though he recognized its quality by comparing it to Tolstoy's masterpiece *The Death of Ivan Ilych*. As its title bluntly announces, *Dying* is about a man who believes he is dying. Schnitzler focuses on both the psychology of the presumably dying man and on the reactions of his devoted lover to a doctor's prognosis that Felix has only a year to live. Felix and Marie are not middle-aged bourgeois stuck in an unsatisfying marriage and a conventional, boring, and meaningless life, like Ivan Ilych and his wife in Tolstoy's novella. They are very much in love, though Felix seems to be one of those well-to-do men about town who appear so often in Schnitzler's plays, and Marie, his lover, seems at first glance to be one of those compliant, totally devoted "sweet girls" that Schnitzler's plays made a cliché.

Schnitzler's aim in this novella is nothing less than to tell the truth about the reality of dying. For, as Felix bitterly observes, "We don't really understand the psychology of the dying. . . . Our understanding of the psychology of the dying is wrong because all of the greats of world history—the ones whose deaths we know about—felt an obligation to put on an act for posterity. . . . The poor devil who walks up to the gallows with composure, the great sage who utters aphorisms after he's emptied the cup of hemlock, and the captured freedom fighter who smiles when he sees the rifles aimed at his chest—they're all hypocrites, I know that their composure, their smiles, are all a charade, for they're all terrified, hideously afraid, of death."

Although the symptoms that Schnitzler describes in the course of the story suggest that Felix has tuberculosis, the disease is not named, and its exact nature doesn't matter. If Schnitzler had written the story in 1992 instead of 1892 he might have given his protagonist cancer or AIDS. Schnitzler is not squeamish and does not flinch at describing the physical symptoms and detritus of illness—no doubt his experience as a doctor dealing with dying patients has helped him here—but what really interests him are the psychological consequences of the awful verdict: you have a year left to live. He details the seesaw of belief and disbelief, despair and hope, anger and denial, fear and boredom, desperation and love, grief and euphoria, ennui and desire that it creates for each of the two lovers.

Schnitzler pares the story to its essence: there are no other characters in this novella except for one male friend. No family, no circle of friends, no social life, nothing except Felix and Marie, who are cut off from everyone else as they leave Vienna to travel first to the mountains, then "south" seeking a cure. Narrowing his focus in this way and using interior monologue, Schnitzler is able to explore the details of the ever-changing, momentary, unspoken, hidden, and often unacceptable thoughts and feelings that underlie the couple's mostly uneventful daily routine.

Schnitzler wrote *Dying* when he was barely thirty. A strange topic for such a young man? Perhaps not for a "nervous" man in a "nervous" century in the "most nervous" city of Europe, as Frederick Morton has called Vienna. If Schnitzler was obsessed with death, suicide, and love-deaths, so was all of Vienna. The city at the time was notorious for its extravagant, baroque cult of death. This cult, with its florid funerals, complete with professional mourners; its many luxuriant cemeteries, overflowing with crowds not only on All Saints Day but every Sunday; its long periods of proscribed mourning with every article of dress detailed down to the last black glove, flourished particularly around the turn of the century. One of the goals of the Viennese was to become a *schöne Leich'*, or beautiful corpse. A peculiar fascination with suicide was part of this cult. Stories of all sorts of imaginative suicides were detailed in Viennese newspapers of the time and found an avid audience. The number of suicides was double the average in Europe. Most astounding is the number of eminent and distinguished *haute bourgeois* Viennese who took their own lives around this time, including the writers Adalbert Stifter and Georg Trakl; the philosopher Otto Weininger; the double agent Colonel Alfred Redl; the brother of Gustav Mahler; not just one but three brothers of Ludwig Wittgenstein, sons of one of the wealthiest families in Austria; the son of Hugo von Hofmannsthal—and, tragically, Schnitzler's own daughter Lily at the age of eighteen, a few years before his own death.

Just a few years before Schnitzler wrote *Dying*, the cult of death and the romantic fantasy of a *Liebestod* (love-death) had fatefully converged in one catastrophic event: on January 30, 1889, Crown Prince Archduke Rudolf, the handsome, much admired, wildly popular son of the beloved emperor Franz Joseph, took his own life in his hunting lodge at Mayerling in the serene Vienna Woods along with that of his seventeen-year-old mistress of a few weeks, Mary Vetsera. Rudolf was heir to the throne of the vast Austro-Hungarian Empire as well as a married man with a four-year-old daughter. To say that his double suicide with Mary (an assumed, fashionably English name; her real name was Marie) preoccupied the empire for months and shook Vienna to its foundation is an understatement. No one in Vienna at the time could have remained unaware of the tragedy and of the extravagant funeral of the crown prince, a sensational and flamboyant event even by Viennese standards, comparable in the emotion it aroused to that of Princess Diana's in our own day.

The young archduke's double suicide spurred a wave of suicides in Vienna, as Goethe's *The Sorrows of Young Werther* had done in the eighteenth century. Although Schnitzler too was taken with the presumed romantic nature of this famous double suicide, his death-oriented and dark Dionysian self was tempered by his more rational "doctor" self. Thus *Dying* begins with a vow of a *Liebestod* but ends by exposing its reality and horror—though Schnitzler understands better than most what drives people to such a brink.

Flight into Darkness is also the story of an illness—this time a purely mental one, though one no less catastrophic for being so. Schnitzler began this chilling novella about personal disintegration in 1909 and said it was inspired by his own fear of madness, of giving in to his obsessions—mostly of a jealous nature—and going insane. Here he meticulously and relentlessly recounts a forty-three-year-old man's gradual descent into a maelstrom of obsessions and delusions. This is an astonishingly accurate clinical understanding of the unfolding of a mental illness. Schnitzler's interior monologue technique permits us to "hear" Robert's mostly unspoken emotions, thoughts, dreams, fantasies, and perceptions as though from the inside, and thus to share his agonizing doubts about whether his perceptions are fantasies or realities, whether what he perceives originates from the external world or from within himself. When Robert feels he is being "observed," is this an accurate perception on his part, or is he imagining it? Are others trying to decide whether he is insane and should be placed in an asylum—or is he? We feel what it's like to become obsessed by an idea, to rationalize a "crazy" thought so that it seems incontrovertibly true.

Flight into Darkness is played out mostly in terms of a relationship between two brothers. Robert's comments on the importance of the tie of brother-to-brother may seem extravagant, to say the least. But 1909 was not the first time Schnitzler had portrayed such a relationship as a particularly profound and life-sustaining one. In one of his early works, a short story entitled "Geronimo and His Brother," published in 1900 (translated in *Night Games*), Schnitzler had also taken up the subject of an intense brother relationship marked by love and identification as well as ambivalence, mistrust, hatred, fear, and guilt. *Flight into Darkness* is darker than "Geronimo." And from what Schnitzler himself said, indications are that Robert was a self-portrait.

As Oscar Wilde has said, "All art is autobiography"—but this is a matter of degree. Schnitzler worked on *Flight into Darkness* for a longer time than any of his other works and was reluctant to publish it. He worked and reworked it for twenty years; it did not appear in print until the year of his death, 1931. His "obsession" with it probably has to do with its barely disguised autobiographical character. Schnitzler himself was obviously not clinically "mad" or paranoid—he couldn't have written about it so masterfully if he were. But he gave Robert many of his own traits and symptoms.

Like Robert in the story, Schnitzler suffered from obsessive ideas, hypochondriacal symptoms, anxiety attacks, intrusive thoughts, a narcissistic vulnerability to criticism, often misplaced suspicion, and a pathological jealousy that ruined many of his relationships, as he was well aware. Like Robert, who is something of a musician, Schnitzler was an artist interested in dreams and fantasies. Like Robert, he had a brother who was a doctor and had a wife and children, to whom he went for advice about his various complaints, including his anxiety attacks. Schnitzler admired and loved his brother Julius, just as Robert loves Otto, but he also envied him and often felt a peculiar "inhibition" with him, as he notes in his diaries.

Yet Otto, Robert's brother in the story, is no less a self-portrait than Robert. Like Otto, Schnitzler felt he could and should control his obsessions and hypochondriacal symptoms by not "indulging" his anxieties, by "choosing" sanity over insanity. Like Otto, he believed in looking reality in the eye, in not losing himself in fantasies and dreams, in the usefulness of a daily discipline of work to help contain anxiety. Otto represents the healthier side of Schnitzler; Robert the less healthy but more imaginative side which Schnitzler valued because he felt it opened him to artistic inspiration, but also feared. He valued his Otto side because, among other things, it enabled him to give artistic form to his frightening fantasies and wayward thoughts.

Fräulein Else is also a story of illness, though it is much more than that. There is no question of Fräulein Else's actually being "mad"—or if she is mad, so is her society. Schnitzler's use in *Fräulein Else* of the more radical form of interior monologue, stream of consciousness, allows him to give us a searing, seemingly unmediated glimpse into the interior life of a young woman. Schnitzler had used the stream-of-consciousness technique once before to reveal a character's inner reality. *Lieutenant Gustl*, published in 1900, is a vivid portrait "from the inside" of an Austrian army officer, revealed by his own musings as a vain, hypersensitive, insecure, and self-deluded boor. This story was path-breaking—it was the first systematic use of the stream-of-consciousness technique in European literature, twenty years before Joyce and Virginia Woolf used it.

In August 1921, just before he began writing *Fräulein Else*, Schnitzler noted in his diaries his intention of writing a story "in the technique of Lt. Gustl." In *Fräulein Else*, however, unlike in *Lieutenant Gustl*, Schnitzler uses stream of consciousness to create a sympathetic portrayal, this time of a woman. His Else joins the Molly of *Ulysses* and the Mrs. Dalloway of Virginia Woolf's novel as one of the most compelling literary portraits of a woman "from the inside." By making audible the thoughts of a nineteen-year-old girl, Schnitzler reveals what she dare not and does not say—and what society does not wish to hear—by showing what she feels but cannot say. She has no public voice, yet we hear her. Interestingly, in contrast to Joyce's Molly, the woman who famously says yes to life and love, Else is a girl at the brink of womanhood who says no— though she wants to say yes. She is as vital, as high spirited, as sensual, and as ready to embrace life as Molly. But she is more self-aware, and her sexuality is more complicated. After all, she's Viennese.

Among many other things, Else is a brilliant portrait of the classic adolescent female hysteric that turn-of-the-century Vienna was evidently so good at producing, the kind of patient that set Freud on the road to psychoanalysis. No doubt alluding even in its title to Freud's case histories of teenage hysterics (e.g., "Fr. Elisabeth von R . . ."), *Fräulein Else* is a comment on them, most particularly on Dora, the subject of Freud's "Fragment of an Analysis of a Case of Hysteria." But Schnitzler understands Else better than Freud understood Dora.

There are many similarities between Dora and Else. Both are

adolescent girls at the brink of womanhood, intelligent and gifted;
both are being used by older men as objects of exchange. Both try to
rebel—in one sense both are early feminists. Freud, however, keeps
Dora at arm's length in his very manner of telling her story, and never
transcends the male point of view. He was in fact acting in complicity
with Dora's father, who had hired Freud to—in essence—convince
her to take up with the husband of the married woman who was his
mistress. Schnitzler's stream-of-consciousness technique, in contrast,
succeeds in placing us so empathically within Else's subjectivity that
we hear her inner voice seemingly unmediated.

And unlike Freud, whose history of Dora has more than an
overtone of blaming the victim, Schnitzler clearly places the weight
of blame on the shoulders of Else's father and the other men in her
world. In fact, Schnitzler admits his own complicity in the patriarchal social system by making both Herr von Dorsday and Else's father self-portraits. In his earlier years, Schnitzler had large gambling
debts—he told someone that it would not have been out of the question for him to have run up a debt of thirty thousand gulden—and he
was certainly a roué like Herr von Dorsday. Years after Dora
slammed the door on him, Freud, to his credit, realized his "mistake" in her analysis. What he called "counter-transference," however, was exactly his own complicity with the patriarchal use and
control of women—a complicity he never quite acknowledged.

What motivated the sixty-one-year-old Schnitzler, an aging
Casanova, to create such a complex and sympathetic portrait of a
girl of nineteen? Of course the reasons are over-determined, as
Freudians like to say. One of Schnitzler's friends claimed that the
author told him the novella was inspired by memories of "debts in
his youth, and seeing a woman with such a low back décolletage
that she seemed naked to him, while an old man watched the scene
cynically." In 1925, shortly after the novella appeared in book form,

Schnitzler told another friend that he had known many women like Else. He had had a cousin named Else whose family circumstances were strikingly similar to those of his character: her father had had to flee Vienna because he was being sought for embezzling trust funds. And Schnitzler had been present at an incident in which his aunt, Dora (!), had approached an "art dealer" who had once wooed her for money to help her wayward husband.

Closer to the time he wrote the story, Schnitzler was a close friend of a young woman named Stephanie Bachrach, who he feared was "unbalanced" and who indeed later committed suicide with an overdose of Veronal and morphine. Her father too had committed suicide after losing all his money in a stock market speculation, following which Stefi and her mother had had to live in much reduced circumstances. There is another fascinating detail in this episode: Schnitzler noted in his diaries that he felt Stefi's being premenstrual was one of the causes of her suicide. In *Fräulein Else*, Else makes a point of noticing her own premenstrual symptoms, including cramps—a detail of the story evidently considered so shocking that the only existing English translation, done in 1931, completely omits all parts of the text in which Else clearly indicates her concern with her imminent period.

When he wrote *Fräulein Else*, Schnitzler was raising his adolescent daughter Lily. She was twelve when he began the story and sixteen when he published it. Lily lived alone with him after his divorce from his wife Olga in 1921. Ten days after beginning the story, Schnitzler wrote in his diary, "Lily says approximately the same things I just dictated." Lily appears to have been unstable. Schnitzler hospitalized her briefly for anorexia and later once diagnosed her as "hebephrenic"—a now outmoded psychiatric diagnosis for a type of schizophrenia, which in Schnitzler's use appears simply to mean that she exhibited inappropriate behavior. Did Schnitzler fear that the teenage Lily would follow the path of Fräulein Else? Uncannily and tragically, she did. At the age of sixteen, while on vacation in Venice, she fell in love with an Italian fascist twenty years her senior—exactly the sort of "Roman head" and *filou* that Else dreams about and desires. Lily badgered her father until he agreed to her marriage with the Italian when she was only seventeen. Married and living in Venice, she committed suicide a year later—a trauma from which Schnitzler never recovered. We can imagine what he felt when on the way home from her funeral he saw a woman reading *Fräulein Else* on the train and overheard someone else comment, "No wonder she committed suicide, when her father writes such books!"

Fräulein Else is one of Schnitzler's most celebrated works. It also became his most popular, selling seventy thousand copies in 1929 alone after it appeared as a silent film with the famous Elisabeth Bergner. Hugo von Hofmannsthal called it a masterpiece of German literature, in "a genre of its own," and most critics of the time shared his judgment. It was technically innovative not only in its use of the stream-of-consciousness technique but—perhaps less successfully—in its use of parts of a musical score to intensify and underline those of Else's feelings she never becomes conscious of. Schnitzler uses sections from a Schumann score during the climactic scene. Obviously he must have assumed that most of his readers could read music and thus "hear" the music in the right places—a skill that the average educated reader in our time may not have. (Psychoanalytic critics have made much of the fact that one of the three pieces of score is from a section of *Carneval* entitled *Reconnaissance*, or *Reminiscences*, pointing out that Freud had famously said that the hysteric "suffers from reminiscences.")

So vivid and dramatic is Schnitzler's *Fräulein Else* that it has been dramatized and filmed many times. Schnitzler realized its potential as a piece of theatre from the beginning, and discussed a dramatization of it as a monologue with Elisabeth Bergner soon after its publication in 1924. Although no such version appeared in his lifetime, Elisabeth Bergner did make a silent film of it in 1929. Schnitzler, who did not have a hand in the screenplay, claimed to like the film, though he took exception to the ending and observed that the film's Else, while impressive, was "not my Else."

The first dramatic version of *Fräulein Else* was not staged in Vienna until 1936, five years after Schnitzler's death. Ernst Lothar, who adapted and directed it, turned the novella into a conventional society play in which Else's stream of consciousness becomes a series of conversations she has with other characters. The story is conveyed by means of "confidences" she has with her aunt instead of in the monologue form that Schnitzler envisioned. Not only does this lose the sense of access to Else's inner life we have in the novella, but it changes the meaning of the work in a major way—if Else could talk and confide in others, she would not be as isolated and as lonely as she is. The play compounds the distortion by explicitly exonerating Else's father and making her mother the villain responsible for the outrageous demand that Else rescue her father. This version of *Fräulein Else*, though it is still being played today in Vienna's Burgtheater as well as in other German-speaking cities, is obviously not Schnitzler's Else either. A dramatic version in English, staged in London in 1932 by T. Komisarevsky, turns Else's stream of consciousness into a monologue spoken to the audience, as Schnitzler envisioned it, and is a much more faithful adaptation of the novella than Lothar's. Recently, *Fräulein Else* was again successfully adapted and acted by Francesca Faridany at the Berkeley Repertory Theater. Faridany's adaptation of the novella as a simultaneous monologue and drama is a brilliant evocation of Else that Schnitzler might well acknowledge as "his Else."

Else is one of the great female portraits in literature. She feels
so real and multi-dimensional that she has been seen in a variety of
identities: a hysteric; a daughter trapped in an incestuous attachment
to her father; an early childhood sexual abuse victim; a Jewish girl
who mirrors the problem of Jewish identity in early-twentieth-
century Vienna; a narcissist; a *femme fatale*; and an early feminist.
She is all of these things at once. She is Salome—in an earlier version of the novella she asks Dorsday, "Shall I dance for you, too?"
and he answers, "With whose head on the platter"?—and an incarnation of one of Klimt's erotic *Jugendstil* paintings; but at the same
time she is Goethe's Gretchen and even the Virgin Mary.

Each of these three novellas seamlessly meshes fantasy and reality, dream and experience, desire and delusion, and with artistic
skill creates a world of experience that, in the reading, becomes our
own. Only a writer who was an intuitive depth psychologist as well
as a skilled literary artist could have written these novellas that combine—just as Schnitzler hoped to do—realism and idealism, impres-
sionism and expressionism, naturalism and symbolism. Schnitzler
is not an archaeologist, digging up and re-creating a "lost world"
buried almost a century ago, as was sometimes alleged—to his ag-
gravation—even in his lifetime. As much as Else may be the arche-
typical early-twentieth-century Viennese hysteric, she, as Schnitzler
insisted, is not tied to a single time or place: "There are always new
Elses born," he wrote to a friend in the late 1920s, "mankind hasn't
changed since the war." Many women today will recognize an as-
pect of themselves in Else. Nor have the mistrust and suspiciousness
that Schnitzler finds in Robert vanished. And the psychology of
dying that Schnitzler set out to delineate in *Dying* is as accurate
today as it was when he wrote it. Schnitzler is not merely a regional
Viennese writer, a chronicler of a lost *fin-de-siècle* world, but one
whose profound explorations of subjectivity have as much to say to

us at the beginning of the twenty-first century as to his contemporaries at the beginning of the twentieth.

MARGRET SCHAEFER

Berkeley, California
May 2003

Desire and Delusion

Flight into Darkness

THERE WAS A KNOCK on the door. The commissioner awoke, and in response to his absentminded "Come in," a waiter abruptly appeared at the door with his breakfast, which he had ordered as usual for eight o'clock. Robert's first thought was that he must have forgotten to lock the door again last night. But he hardly had time to indulge his irritation at this latest evidence of his absentmindedness—the morning mail stacked on the breakfast tray next to the teapot, butter, and honey caught his attention. Beneath the usual mail he found a letter from his brother expressing his pleasure in the anticipation of Robert's upcoming visit. And, after a report of trivial family matters, he reported with studied casualness his recent appointment to the rank of associate professor. Robert dashed off a telegram of hearty congratulations and had it rushed to the telegraph office. Even if professional duties and other circumstances often kept the two brothers apart for days and weeks at a time, something always came up which, precisely because of its relative insignificance, made them both feel the unquestionable and indissoluble nature of their bond. Such occasions made the younger Robert feel that all of his other past and present relationships were of lesser importance—even his early marriage to a charming woman, now long deceased. More and more he was starting to believe that the sibling relationship of brother to brother was not only the best and most precious prize of his own life, but was generally the only relationship that was by nature ultimately lasting—more lasting than the relationship of child to parent, which was destined all too soon to be lost to age and death, and more lasting than that of parents to children, which—though Robert, to be sure, had no experience of this himself—was destined to be lost, if not to others, then surely to youth itself. Most particularly, it remained at all times free from those ominous clouds which, rising unexpectedly from the dark depth of the soul, commonly threatened the relationship between husband and wife.

So Robert regarded his brother's letter, arriving as it did now, on the day of his departure, as a favorable omen. He felt wonderfully strengthened in his hopes for a future that would inaugurate a new epoch of his life after this period of unrest.

The sun was already high in the sky when Robert finished packing and left his room. At this hour most of the guests were either out swimming or taking a walk and therefore it was very quiet in the vicinity of the hotel. Robert walked out on the wide stone pier that stretched far into the water and had a bright little steamer taking its afternoon siesta tethered against it. He looked at the almost-motionless white, yellow, and red sails that glistened in the canal; finally he let his gaze wander northward, where the gradually widening straits hinted at the open sea. Baring his head to the direct rays of sun, he breathed in deeply with open mouth to taste the tang of salt on his tongue, and he luxuriated in the balmy air that brought this southern island a summer warmth even on such late October days. Gradually the feeling crept over him that the moment he was experiencing now was really a moment long past; that he himself, as he stood here on the landing, hat in hand and lips parted, was a blurry image of his own remembering. He wished he could hold on to this feeling, which came over him now and not for the first time, and which he experienced not as frightening but as liberating. But the feeling disappeared in the very act of his wishing it to continue. And suddenly he felt at odds with the world around him: sky, sea, and air had become alien, cold, and distant. The glorious moment had faded away into insignificance.

Robert left the pier and took one of the narrow, seldom-used trails that led to the interior of the island through tangled underbrush growing beneath pines and oaks. Yet this landscape too now seemed to him odorless and dry, stripped of its usual charm. Suddenly he was glad that the hour of his departure was drawing near, and lively visions of urban winter pleasures surfaced in his mind, pleasures he had long ago ceased to care about. He saw himself at the theatre, in a comfortable armchair in a loge, engrossed in a light comedy; he saw himself strolling along crowded, brightly illuminated streets, between tempting window displays of precious jewels and leather goods; and finally he saw his own figure, somewhat refreshed and rejuvenated, in the quiet corner of a comfortable, elegant café alongside a feminine creature to whom his imagination involuntarily gave the charming features of Alberta. For the first time since their parting he thought of her now with some regret. He asked himself if it had indeed been wise of him to step aside in favor of the young American whom she would certainly have forgotten in a few days once she left his dangerous presence. And he wondered if in that evening conversation in the woods by Lake Lucerne, it had not been his duty to warn her against, rather than advise her to accept, a proposal of marriage that, despite all the passion involved, had to be viewed with some suspicion since it resulted from an acquaintance of only a few days. But Robert did not fool himself—he knew that his momentary discomfort was due less to belated reproaches of conscience than to the reawakening of his senses. And he was grateful for this, however painful it was at the moment.

Having come back to the hotel somewhat later than he had intended, he had his lunch alone in front of one of the wide bay windows in the dining room with a view of the sea, as was his custom. Afterward he made his polite farewells to some of his spa acquaintances and finally sat down for a few minutes at the table of the two Rolf ladies who were having their afternoon coffee on the beach terrace. Fräulein Paula, to whom Robert had paid no particular attention during his stay on the island (the society of unmarried ladies of good family having little attraction for him), regarded him today with an interest that made him thoughtful. When, as he took his leave, he kissed the hand not only of the still beautiful, somewhat haughty mother, but also—contrary to his usual custom—that of the daughter, he felt on his brow the warm glow of an intimate, friendly glance that intensified as it encountered his.

He went into the music room and struck a few chords on the badly out-of-tune piano, but soon, oppressed by the stuffiness of the room, whose drawn blinds trapped the heat of the sultry afternoon sun, he left the room. Walking back and forth on the gleaming white gravel beachfront, he felt painfully the unfathomable emptiness of the wasted hours before a scheduled departure. So he decided that instead of waiting around until evening for the regular steamer, he would make the short trip across the channel to the mainland train station now, while there was still full daylight, in one of the small motorboats. There, until just before the departure of the train, he strolled about the winding, hilly streets of the seaport whose notable sites he had meant to visit every day but had postponed just as often until now, the last hours of his stay. As he stood on the top step of the ruined Roman arena, surrounded by the fading light of day, the evening seemed to rise up to him from the depths of the immense bowl like a dark admonition.

II

As the train left the station, Robert tarried at the window of his compartment and took a last unemotional look at the island shrouded in a pale, reddish grey mist, and at the sea, where the violet afterglow of the setting sun floated in distant waves. The train coughed slowly upward between scraggly vineyards toward the limestone plateau near Trieste, then darted through a long tunnel into a twilight landscape of rocky bluffs where the horizon contained a suggestion, but no longer a view, of the sea. Only now did Robert stretch out on his bunk, exhausted by his wandering through the uneven and ill-paved streets of the old seaport. He sought to recapture the pleasant feeling of anticipation which, as recently as this morning during his walk, had moved and almost heartened him. What he found, however, was no longer delight but rather a strange anxiety, as though he were being carried toward a crisis involving a significant, serious decision. Was it the nearness of his homeland that made itself felt in such an undesirable way? Was he destined to return home just as disconsolate as he had left? Would he now, after the many restful and easy moments of the last few months, be overcome once more by that incomprehensible something that could hardly be captured in thought—let alone in words—and that seemed ominously to threaten something worse?

Had the doctors been mistaken or had they deliberately deceived him when they claimed that six months of distracting travel would completely cure him? True, Dr. Leinbach, his friend from boyhood, was always inclined to take his patients' symptoms lightly; and it was hardly reassuring that he claimed to have had them all himself. But it was out of the question that Otto would have taken on the responsibility of sending his only brother away all by himself for half a year if he had believed him to be seriously ill. At the same time, however, Robert had to ask himself—and not for the first time—whether he had really fully revealed himself to his brother; or whether he had, even in that last consultation with him, under the constraint of a peculiar inhibition, painted his condition as less dangerous than he really felt it to be, in the unconscious hope of getting a lighter judgment by doing so.

Judgment. That was the word that forced itself upon his mind, and it was the appropriate one. Because from childhood on he had, in spite of his superficially more brilliant qualities, felt himself to be of less value than his brother; and he could not conceal from himself the fact that Otto viewed his way of life with indulgence, perhaps, but also with impatience and disapproval. And Robert understood completely. Otto's heavy responsibilities, the seriousness of his profession, in which matters of life and death were at stake, his steady and almost self-denying, quiet family life—all of this so exalted him in Robert's eyes that his own existence, by contrast, even though confined by the obligations of his office, often appeared to him to be without real honor or deeper meaning.

To be wholeheartedly welcomed by his brother as cured, perhaps even as healthier than before, seemed to him the best welcome that home could offer. That this eager anticipation of a happy reunion had transformed itself gradually into an ever-more-restless anxiety had to have hidden causes—causes that Robert found himself unable to resist exploring. He felt a memory dully yet irresistibly rising from the depths of his soul, as though it were no longer content to remain in its deceptive sleep of many years; and a word began to resound in him that at first did not dare reveal its meaning. He deliberately whispered the word once, twice, then fifty times over, as if in this way he could rob it of its meaning and its power. And indeed it gradually became more and more empty and meaningless, until in the end it was nothing more than a random sequence of letters, arbitrarily strung together and no more meaningful than the rumble of the wheels beneath the homeward-rushing train where the sound of it mingled and was finally lost completely as he sank gradually into sleep.

III

When Robert climbed into a carriage at the train station in pouring rain, he first gave the coachman the address of his former apartment, which he had given up before leaving on his trip. Only then, remembering, did he name the old hotel where he had reserved a room. Hidden behind a church in the city center, between tall, gloomy buildings, it didn't have the friendly and festive appearance with which the newer hotels greeted the traveler. But Robert had chosen this hotel not only because his means, though still sufficient for necessities, didn't permit a lengthy stay in one of the modern hotels, but also because it was here, in a room on the fourth floor, where he had long ago spent many happy hours in the company of a long-dead friend whose mistress had lived here. His memory, strangely enough, had preserved an image of this hotel as a small, antique *palais*; but now he looked in vain for traces of the faded splendor that would have induced (or at least favored) such an illusion back then. He found neither the artistic decorations on the iron banisters nor the baroque reliefs he expected to find on the corridor ceilings; and the stair carpet, thin and tattered, now shimmered a faded and shabby purple red. But the room he was shown, with its high vaulted ceiling and its two wide windows, comfortably furnished, with a view of the green, patina-covered cupola of the church directly opposite, compensated for his first bleak impression. He had his luggage brought up and at once set about giving the hotel room a little touch of hominess with the help of a few trifles he always carried with him on trips—a briefcase, a letter holder, a paper knife, an ashtray, and the like. Afterward he went into the bathroom, which be-

trayed all too obviously that it had been converted to its present purpose only as a reluctant concession to the demands of a new age. A
yellowish lamp attached to the ceiling spread a wan light in the win-
dowless room, and the oval mirror that hung on the wall in a pol-
ished, gilded frame had a crack running from top to bottom. As was
his custom, Robert remained in the bathtub for a rather long time;
then, with the rough white robe slung over his shoulders, he walked
over to the mirror and found his beardless, narrow face quite refreshed, even young looking for his forty-three years. He was just
about to turn away satisfied when an alien eye seemed to regard him
enigmatically from the cloudy glass. He bent over and thought he
noticed that his left eyelid drooped lower than his right. He was a little shocked; he examined it with his fingers; he blinked, pressed his
eyelids tightly shut, and opened them again. But the difference between the two eyes remained. He hastily dressed himself, walked up
to the larger mirror on the wall between the two windows, opened
his eyelids as wide as he could, and was forced to admit that his left
eyelid didn't obey his will as quickly as his right. But there was
nothing wrong with the eye itself, and the pupil responded to light;
and since Robert then remembered that he had slept the entire
night on his left side, he felt he had found a sufficient reason for the
weakness of his eyelid. Nevertheless he decided to consult Dr. Leinbach or Otto tomorrow. Or better still, he would wait to see if his
brother noticed the dissimilarity between his eyelids without being
prompted. At the same time this resolution became suffused with an
indefinable anxiety, almost as though he had committed a wrong and
had to expect at least a reprimand, if not a punishment. At first he
strove not to understand this emotion; then, stretching out both arms
as though fending off an approaching enemy, he retreated from
his mirror image and walked over to the window now splattered
with heavy raindrops. His eyes fell upon the marble statue of the

holy St. Christopher which stood in a niche in the wall of the church opposite, exactly as it had twenty years before. Only now did he realize that he occupied the very same room that his friend Höhnburg's mistress had lived in so many years ago. But the furniture was new, and instead of the heavy, plush crimson drapes, a light, flowered cretonne curtain in a color that harmonized with that of the new carpet now fell in soft folds from the brass rod of the alcove. Should he consider this change toward brightness and friendliness a good omen? He tried to but couldn't. With horrifying clarity he remembered that long-ago spring evening, that evening in which not only his friend's fate but, he recalled with a profound shudder, perhaps his own fate too had mysteriously been announced. And he relived that evening.

With his brother Otto, Lt. Höhnburg, and other good friends, he had gone to a crowded Prater nightspot after attending the horse races in the Freudenau. Höhnburg had been the loudest and gayest of them all, more boisterous and exuberant even than usual, and it didn't strike anyone as particularly odd when he gave a waiter a vastly exaggerated tip. But on the way home, Otto had taken his brother aside and told him confidentially that their mutual friend Höhnburg had become incurably insane and would be dead and buried within three years at the outside. No one suspected it yet, but as a physician he was absolutely certain of it, and had been for some time.

At first Robert refused to believe that the young cavalry officer, his friend, the very picture of robust health, could be a marked, a condemned man. But by the end of the evening, yielding to his brother's professional knowledge, he began to find his friend's personality and behavior, indeed, everything about him, more and more strange. He avoided speaking to him; indeed, he was terrified that his friend might turn to him and perhaps try to link arms with him.

So he had disappeared from the company without saying goodbye to anyone. Only a few days later, Höhnburg had indeed suffered a fit of stark, raving madness, and had to be consigned to an institution.

The next time he saw Otto, he had demanded—without intend-ing to, but on a sudden, irresistible impulse—that if his brother ever at any time, tomorrow or in the remote future, should detect in him the signs of a mental illness, he should without further ado help him end his life in a quick and painless way, as Otto, being a physician, could easily do. At first Otto had derided him as an incorrigible hypochondriac, but Robert had not given up; he had declared that brotherly love could not, must not, refuse such a service. In the case of any other illness, he argued, the sufferer could put an end to his misery if he so chose; but a mental illness reduced a man to a spine-less slave of fate. Otto had broken off the conversation in exaspera-tion. But in the course of the next few weeks Robert had reiterated his demand with such insistence and supported it with such calmly elucidated and entirely incontrovertible arguments that Otto had let the desired promise be wrested from him just to have done with the unwelcome subject. But even that didn't satisfy Robert. He wrote his brother a letter, a dry and businesslike document, confirming his reception of Otto's promise; and he enjoined Otto to preserve it so that he could show his irrevocable authorization for the perhaps nec-essary act to any potential accuser or doubter.

Having sent the letter, Robert felt calmer, and since then, as if by mutual agreement, not a word had been exchanged between the two brothers about it, nor was the slightest allusion made to it. But Robert felt as though he had been freed from a curse, as though the most dreadful of all the potential disasters that could threaten him had been destroyed once and for all. Even when he had felt obliged last spring to give up his occupation because of his failing memory; when he had withdrawn from social life because even the most ca-sual words irritated and pained him; when he even gave up his beloved piano playing because it would sometimes move him to tears, which then embarrassed him—even then he had not had the slightest fear of impending insanity. Nor had he been troubled by such a fear during his entire trip. It was clear to him, however, that last evening, just before falling asleep on the train, the fateful word had once more awakened to significance from its state of mere random, inert letters of the alphabet. But this only invested the contract between his brother and himself with new validity; and the document, which Otto surely had carefully preserved, had by now become a sort of IOU against whose mute inexorability there could be no protest at the hour when it threatened to fall due. Was there really a need for such a document? Wasn't Otto a man who would put a doomed man out of his misery even without such a binding contract absolving him of responsibility—simply out of humanitarian motives? Robert didn't doubt that honorable and perceptive physicians performed this kind of act much more often than was generally realized, even without a writ of authorization like the one he had given Otto.

But didn't doctors make mistakes too? Couldn't they themselves become insane and in consequence mistake a sane, healthy person for an insane one? And wasn't each one in either case delivered helplessly into the other's hands—the sane to the insane and the insane to the sane? At this point Robert forcibly pulled himself back. He wouldn't permit such morbid forebodings to drive him helplessly back into the dark land of a thousand uncertain possibilities where the highly probable and the hardly conceivable lived together in uncomfortably close proximity. He stole another hasty glance in the mirror. He could no longer see a difference between his left and his right eyelids. Both eyes looked rather dim and tired. As a matter of fact, he had been slightly nearsighted in his left eye from childhood and had acquired a habit of occasionally squinting. Besides, he had hardly slept last night. True, it was undeniable that he looked haggard and worn. For the time being he decided to put off his intended visit to Otto so that he would see him only after a good night's sleep—refreshed, in good spirits, and, if possible (and even this seemed not without importance to him), in altogether better, sunnier weather.

IV

Soon afterward he left the hotel and amused himself with the fantasy that he was a tourist walking around a strange city by deliberately having lunch in a little restaurant where he had never been before. Afterward he began to search for an apartment. He walked up and down the stairs of various houses for hours; he looked at dozens of vacant and occupied rooms—here interrupting a young lady at her piano, there a tutor giving lessons to two boys. He negotiated with obliging, indifferent, and surly landlords and caretakers and couldn't once convince even himself that he was doing all this in earnest and for a real purpose. At one point he found himself in a street where memories from a long-forgotten time flooded him—behind that corner window on the third floor he had spent many happy (or at least pleasant) hours many years ago. It was not really painful, more a minor unpleasantness, to realize that he was now even more alone in the world than he had been before. Thoughts of Alberta fleetingly crossed his mind but were immediately followed by a vivid and sharply delineated image of Fräulein Rolf, with whom he now felt more intimately connected because of that parting glance yesterday. He tried to recall her first name but didn't at first succeed. In any case, he knew very little about her and her family—only that mother and daughter, at home as well as on vacations, were seen about mostly without the father, a man who, though very much in demand as an attorney (and who was, indeed, almost famous), had an ambiguous reputation due to his unfortunate addiction to stock-market speculation. That was probably the reason why the only daughter, who must already be in her late twenties, was not yet married. Robert had a dim recollection of a rumor that she had been engaged to a famous musician, now dead. As he ruminated about her in this way, he became more and more moved by her image, which seemed to him to be surrounded by mystery.

That evening Robert went to a theatre in a suburb of Vienna. He followed the light operetta in a pleasant, somewhat tired and dreamy mood, and felt a childlike delight when the principal actor gave him a friendly nod from stage right in the middle of a couplet. After the theatre he went to the café near the city center where for years a small circle of his friends—with whom Robert had exchanged brief postcards, at least at the beginning of his trip—met nightly. When he walked in he saw Herr August Langer, a cousin of his late wife's, sitting in a corner. He was an agreeable, elderly gentleman and a high-level bank official who in his dress and behavior tried to emphasize his often-noted resemblance to an aristocrat very popular in sporting circles. Without getting up or putting down his newspaper, Langer waved to him from afar, and then cordially shook his hand, remarking with genuine pleasure on how well he looked. Rudolf Kunrich, a minor actor in the Hoftheater, came up and agreed with Herr Langer. Both Kunrich as well as Langer seemed to Robert to have aged many years in the six months of his absence. Leinbach's entry, which, because he was a family man and a very busy physician, was infrequent here, pleasantly surprised Robert. On seeing his friend, Leinbach immediately monopolized him and asked him the questions customarily directed at someone just back from a long journey. Finally he asked him whether he was going back to work right away.

Robert expressed doubt that he was sufficiently recovered to resume his duties.

Dr. Leinbach only smiled.

Robert persisted, "You forget the state of my nerves last spring before you sent me on my trip."

Leinbach shrugged his shoulders. "My dear friend, when a man is fortunate enough to be sent away on a trip, naturally we send him away. On the other hand, there are plenty of people who simply don't have the time to go crazy."

"Crazy?" Robert repeated to himself. Why does he say "crazy"? What if I told him about my eyelid? This might be just the right time. And carefully he began, "Actually, I was going to come to see you during your office hours tomorrow."

"Office hours? That takes two, my dear fellow! I would first have to take you on as a patient."

"I've noticed for some time now," Robert persisted, undeterred, "that my left arm is noticeably weaker than my right." This idea had just occurred to him at the moment. "All right, laugh, but it's true." He slowly lifted his left arm and let his fingers play awkwardly.

"Hmm," said Leinbach, with exaggerated gaiety. "Squeeze my wrist with your paralyzed left arm!"

Robert did so, and Leinbach let out a comic "Oww!" "Still," said Robert, "I assure you that this morning I felt as though I couldn't move my arm at all. Yes, my whole left side had this strange feeling. I also noticed a peculiar tiredness in the left half of my face, and—now he dared to reveal it—"I could hardly open my left eye." At the same time, seeing Leinbach scrutinize him with a certain professional keenness, he opened both eyes wide so as not to betray himself.

"Nonsense!" said Leinbach, "Everyone knows that one side is always weaker than the other. The alleged symmetry of the two halves of the body is just a myth, you know that. Anyway, where were you last? On the coast in the South, right? Maybe that wasn't quite the right thing, especially just before coming home. If I were you I would get a few days of mountain air before I started back on my job."

"You think . . . ?"

"Not that I think it's essential, not at all! But if one can . . ." He sighed. "As far as I'm concerned, you can stay here in Vienna without any problem."

Kahnberg the writer came up to the table and, to Robert's astonishment, greeted him like a long-lost, anxiously awaited friend. He pulled him over to a nearby table and told him the most recent installment of a romantic episode that Robert, to the best of his recollection, had never heard a word about. Leinbach asked him if a book that he had sent him some months ago had arrived properly. Robert remembered that he had received the volume, a drama in verse with a very warm inscription to him, and that he had read it. But he couldn't remember anything about its content. In his embarrassment he was wondering how to express belated appreciation for the gift and what to say about it, when everyone got up to spend the rest of the evening in a club. Robert happily went with them, and soon they were all sitting at little tables in a low-ceilinged, crowded, too brightly illuminated room, listening to a piano player who tirelessly turned out a medley of opera arias, dance music, and other songs that were beautifully harmonized, one after the other, with smooth and effortless transitions.

Robert especially listened with a kind of erudite delight, since his own talent was somewhat akin to that of this nighttime pianist who earned his living by day as a bank official. Dr. Leinbach attempted to explain his personal relationship to music in philosophical terms. He attributed a kind of amoral character to this art, and claimed that under the influence of beautiful sounds, he always felt inclined to exculpate himself for all errors and sins, past and future, now and forever. Robert remembered that he had last been in this club with Alberta, and he wondered where his former mistress was now. Had the young American with whom she had gone away really married her? He doubted it. The man might easily have been an adventurer and deserted her over there or even here in Europe. How unscrupulous it had been of him to give her up—not out of a sense of nobility but out of injured vanity—and to leave her to, even hand her over to, a total stranger.

More and more people crowded into the small room and squeezed between the tables and chairs. A very tall, unnaturally thin young woman in the company of two men stood very close to Robert for a while; she looked all around the room, and her arm brushed his. Since they couldn't find a table, she turned to leave again with her escorts, but at the door she looked back at Robert and smiled.

A fresh glass of champagne stood in front of him. He drank it down in one gulp—with pleasure, almost with greed. The pianist was improvising on some themes from Wagnerian operas in a mocking waltz-tempo. Something long forgotten ran through Robert's mind. Many years ago, when he was first married, he had once felt very amorous toward his young wife in a dark loge during a performance of *Tristan*. It seemed to him now, in retrospect, that he had loved her passionately then; he felt that many things in his life would have been different if she had not died so young. Despite this melancholy thought, however, he felt quite content and noticed that he was softly beating time to the piano music with his hand. He smiled or rather tried to smile, for he suddenly felt his lips twitch and tears come into his eyes; it was all he could do to keep from sobbing out loud. He clenched his teeth, looked around to see if anyone had noticed his moment of weakness, then laughed out loud, so boisterously and so shrilly that he attracted many an eye. Leinbach looked at him sharply.

"What's the matter with you?" he asked.

Robert shook his head. "I just thought of something funny."

"What?" asked Leinbach, apparently only out of idle curiosity.

"It would mean nothing to you, nothing at all," replied Robert. Then he covertly looked around and determined that he was not attracting further attention—that only one pair of eyes, those belonging to a young girl over in a corner, was still staring at him with scorn or perhaps with pity. He returned the look so harshly that the young girl averted her eyes and with exaggerated concentration continued to slurp her iced drink with a straw. But Robert told himself that he couldn't stay any longer, and he called for the waiter. I'm not going to be such an idiot as to give him a ten-gulden tip, he thought. It turned out that in the meantime, August Langer had already paid the whole bill. Robert thanked him with humorous exaggeration and took his leave. He deposited a gold ten-kronen coin into the plate on top of the piano, adding it to a mass of smaller coins already there. He immediately regretted it but didn't dare take it back. The pianist acknowledged his gift and without interrupting his playing, said, "You've been traveling, sir? We hope to have the pleasure of seeing you here again soon." How nice everyone is! thought Robert. All of them—Kahnberg, Langer, the pianist. Even the actor in the theatre personally acknowledged me from the stage. Only Leinbach is an insufferable fool, as usual. He suddenly hated him.

The streets were almost deserted. A tower clock struck two. It was good, he reflected, that he didn't have to keep office hours yet and could sleep in tomorrow. He walked rapidly and confidently, humming to himself. Finally he even began to sing in a beautiful deep voice that sounded foreign to him. Perhaps this isn't even my voice, he thought. Perhaps this isn't even me. Am I dreaming? Maybe I'm dreaming my last dream; maybe this is my deathbed dream!

He remembered an idea that Leinbach had expounded in all seriousness (in fact with a certain self importance) to a large gathering many years ago. He claimed he had found proof that there was no such thing as death. It was true beyond question, he had declared, that not only those who are drowning but all the dying live their entire lives over again in their last moments at a speed incomprehensible to the rest of us. Since, naturally, this remembered life also has a last moment, and that last moment again has a last moment, and so on, this meant that—in accordance with the mathematical formula of infinite limits—dying itself was at bottom eternity. Robert still remembered the bitterness with which Otto had rejected this as drivel. But Robert, without exactly declaring himself for Leinbach's theory, hadn't been able to find it totally absurd. If this explanation were correct, it wasn't possible to know how many times one had lived through any experience. And it didn't matter anyway since one was condemned to live through everything an infinite number of times. Oh, stuff and nonsense! A questionable figure, this Leinbach, and certainly not to be taken seriously as a doctor. It was easy to fool him on a whim—it was no trick at all. But it wasn't so easy to fool Otto. . . .

The hotel door opened before him. As he walked up the stairs, the walls about him were suddenly those of the quaint old *palais* they had been twenty years before; and the bleached-out red of the stair carpet now shone a deep purple under his feet. How many times had he gone up these stairs? A hundred, a thousand times? Again and again? How often had poor Höhnburg walked up them to his beloved actress? And was he still walking up, and would he have to walk up eternally? The devil take the absurd idea! At any rate, the staircase didn't seem to want to end—the end seemed to be shrouded in darkness. Suddenly the staircase lights went out. Robert started in fear. But he collected himself, struck a match, and so lit his way to his door. When he shut the door and turned on the light in the room, he drew a deep breath, as though he had escaped from some danger.

V

The next day, with a fully rigged sailboat and a battleship in his hands—both of which he had just bought at a toy store in grateful memory of his stay at the sea shore—he walked into the room of his two nephews, nine and six years old. They received their uncle and his gifts with delight. He was just explaining to the boys (without special technical knowledge but with considerable lay understanding) how the small models were constructed when their mother arrived laden with many small packages. She welcomed Robert warmly. With her characteristic slightly ironic, cheerful smile she asked him not to let himself be interrupted in his technical discourse. Soon afterward, as though he had had an intimation of Robert's visit, Otto came in earlier than usual, still in his overcoat and carrying his black leather instrument bag. His hair and his beard seemed to Robert to have become quite grey. "Well, here we are again," he said, a little dryly. He put down his bag, grasped his brother's hand, shook it, and, after a slight hesitation, embraced him, whereupon they were both somewhat embarrassed. Marianne nodded in approval.

"You're coming from the ministry today?" asked Otto.

"You're overestimating my zeal," said Robert. "My leave hasn't expired yet, and it's just possible that I may go up to the mountains for a few more days. Edmund, whom I ran into by chance at the café last night, advised me to do so."

He had used Leinbach's first name on purpose, in order to refer to him as his old friend rather than as a doctor, because Otto had always questioned his capacity in that profession. But Otto couldn't suppress an ironic smile despite that. For that reason, later at table, Robert was all the more at pains to praise Leinbach's human qualities—especially his amiability and good nature—with the intention of building a defense against a possible hostile attack. He spoke with animation, with a deliberate lightheartedness, and then talked about his recent trip in the same manner. He lingered with special warmth over the description of the balmy summerlike days at Lake Lucerne, deliberately not mentioning Alberta, and feeling thereby as though he were warding off a cloud of suspicion that hovered over him.

After lunch, since Otto had to hold office hours, Robert remained alone with his sister-in-law. He was smoking his cigar in silence when Marianne turned to him with the question, "How's your piano playing going?"

"My piano playing," he repeated with melancholy. "I really don't know myself. It's hard to get the opportunity to play while traveling. Sometimes I really missed it."

"So have we," Marianne said, smiling graciously.

It had been Robert's custom, after dinner, to sit down at the piano with a cigar between his lips and indulge in what Marianne called "musical coffee-and-Havana improvisations." So he got up now, went to the piano in the next room, and played a medley of serious and light classical and popular songs, similar to those the pianist in the nightclub had played the night before.

Suddenly he let his hands rest on the piano keys. He turned to Marianne, who had followed his playing as she sat in a corner of the sofa, busy with her knitting, and said, "Enough of that. It's not going well anyway." And when she protested, he said, "And it's high time for me to be going. I'm apartment hunting."

"Hadn't you better wait a little?" asked Marianne. "Since you're staying in a hotel for a while . . . perhaps you'll soon need a more spacious apartment than the one you're looking for now." Robert, not unaccustomed to such intimations from Marianne, shook his head. "For that, it's gradually become too late."

"Why?" she answered brightly. "It'll happen yet, one of these days. One fine day you'll surprise us with the announcement of your wedding."

Is she thinking of someone in particular? he asked himself. Of Fräulein Rolf perhaps? But I've only spoken to her maybe three times, if that. Have they found out about it here in Vienna already? Then he remembered that acquaintances had seen him with Alberta in various places in Switzerland, and that his relationship with her had been no secret to his brother and sister-in-law. Marianne had even sometimes commented appreciatively and with scarcely concealed admiration on Alberta's good taste and discretion when she had seen her with him in the theatre or somewhere else. As they had long ago ceased to measure Robert by bourgeois standards, and as he seemed calmer and happier to everyone since his relationship with Alberta than he had been for many years, he didn't doubt that the family would not have been displeased if he had married her. That he had been such an idiot as to relinquish the charming creature to another man without a contest, no one, not even Marianne, would suspect. And as for him—he could now understand it even less.

He tried to recall his last conversation with Alberta. He remembered his first joking remarks about the American, her strange silence, her smile, and finally her sudden, completely unexpected announcement that the foreigner had offered her his hand. He remembered quite clearly, too, that he had momentarily felt faint—as though he were going to fall to the floor unconscious or else hit Alberta in the face. But he had continued to play the part of the gay blade—the cool, superior one—and had, in a paternal and friendly manner, counseled her to accept the proposal, saying he didn't want to stand in the way of her future. In the end they had agreed that she would give the American her consent that very night, and that Robert would leave the next morning by himself without seeing her again. Robert also remembered very clearly paying his bill at six o'clock the next morning and driving down the mountain road to the seashore with a not unpleasant feeling of liberation, casting a last, scarcely nostalgic glance up to the window behind whose closed drapes Alberta was probably still sleeping.

What he couldn't remember now to save his life, however, was the moment when he had taken his final leave of Alberta. He could still see himself with her on the narrow trail which, after branching off from the broader walk, had led into the darkness of the forest; he also remembered that later he had sat on a tree stump in pitch darkness, overcome by heavy fatigue. But how he had found his way back to the hotel, what he had done in his room, how he had gone to bed, and how he had gotten up in the morning—he simply couldn't recall any of that. His memory began only with his paying of the bill in the hotel lobby, where the floor was just being swept. And suddenly, with a piercing shudder, he asked himself whether the conversation with Alberta after the seemingly calm farewell he remembered had not had a sequel of quite another sort which had entirely vanished from his memory. Had he, overwhelmed by a jealous fury, struck her down? Had he perhaps gone so far as to strangle her and bury her beneath the faded leaves, hiding her body? Only this much was certain: he had gone out into the woods with her and had come back without her. Whether she had later come back alone, he had never learned. If she had not come back, the hotel would certainly have noticed. But could he be sure that he had not perhaps invented some clever lies to cover up and explain her absence? If he had, as he suddenly felt was possible, murdered her in a somnambulistic state, all other things were likewise in the realm of possibility, especially all kinds of cunning tricks and treachery to conceal the crime.

He was aware that all these ideas and conjectures had rushed through his mind within the space of a few seconds. But now, when he saw Marianne's eyes on him with an unmistakable expression of concern, he became aware that he had become deadly pale, and said to himself that the most important thing now was not to give himself away. With a mighty effort of will he was able to compose his features; he asked Marianne to excuse him to his brother since he had to hurry away in order to have a second look at an apartment on the Wieden which was open for viewing only until a certain hour. "But I'm inviting myself to dinner with you again tomorrow." Then he added hastily, "If I don't drive up to Semmering for a couple of days."

"Restless spirit," Marianne called after him in parting.

As he went out the front door, he saw a man of questionable and suspicious elegance smoking a cigar and standing on the opposite side of the street in front of a large, reflecting window. The man averted his gaze with noticeable alacrity when Robert caught his eye. Has it gone as far as all that? he thought fleetingly. But then he laughed. That would be something novel, he said to himself, to be arrested and brought to justice because of a crazy idea. He was absolutely certain now that it had just been an absurd idea that had overwhelmed him earlier. But should he, just as a precaution, perhaps write the management of the Swiss hotel? If only in order to have on hand, against any possible suspicion, the confirmation that Alberta had come home that same evening and had left the next day in the company of another man? He cast an oblique glance sideways. The suspicious apparition of the elegant man was gone.

Robert continued on his way and forced himself to think about something trivial. He tried to recall the contents of his last report— statistical data on the public schools of lower Austria—and it reassured him to realize that now, with his mind rested, he could remember with great clarity many details that he hadn't thought about in months and which basically had never particularly interested him. At the same time he regretted, and not for the first time, that his collaboration had not been requested in another field in which he was much more at home—the matter of musical instruction in the schools. He knew that this was undoubtedly because Hofrat Palm took jealous care that no one who understood more about these matters than he did himself would be called upon to assist him. Robert felt nostalgic for his office—for his large desk, the comfortable, black leather armchair, the tall cabinets full of document files, even the yellowish walls with the maps and the charts. He longed for a sphere of activity in which he could accomplish something truly useful and also win the recognition of his superiors—perhaps even praise from the minister's own mouth, something that seemed important to him not only as a gratification of his ambitions but also for some other reason that wasn't immediately clear to him. And suddenly he discovered to his dismay that an absurd fear still lurked in the depths of his mind, as if the dark delusion that had left him could, independently of him, carry on its dangerous existence in other people, like a liberated evil spirit. But since, in looking around, he now found himself in a lively part of the Ringstrasse in an afternoon crowd, surrounded by others and quite unmolested, a harmless stroller among many, this last fantasy also evaporated into nothingness.

Involuntarily his eye fell upon a female figure sitting on a bench in a rather shabby, light brown coat with a black muff on her lap. Her face was pale, no longer young, and careworn. Now, looking up, she smiled almost imperceptibly and immediately looked down again. Robert kept on going and, attracted by a landscape painting, stopped in front of an art dealer's window, then saw in the mirrored glass the image of the same woman hurrying by, her eyes lowered. Robert turned toward her, and she went on without paying any attention to him. Both her hands were deep in her coat pockets, and the black muff protruded from one of its pockets. She walked erect, but her gait had an indefinable aura of apology about it. Her clinging coat, too tight and too long for her, revealed a pleasant, not overly thin figure. Robert followed her and wondered what sort of woman she might be. Wife of a bureaucrat? A bookkeeper? Because she had gradually slackened her pace, Robert was certain that she didn't mind being followed, and at a street corner, well into an outlying district of Vienna, he spoke to her straightforwardly.

"Would you take offense if I asked your permission to accompany you on your walk?"

She answered in a pleasant voice, neither surprised nor offended, "I'm not taking a walk; I'm going home." She hardly looked at him.

"But your permission," he said, "may I assume it's granted?"

She shrugged her shoulders, as if to say, "You really don't have to stand on all this ceremony with me," then for the first time she looked at him sideways. He spoke of how he had already noticed her on the Ringstrasse—how he had seen her sitting on the bench, her hands in her coat pockets, her muff in her lap, looking straight ahead, a pretty picture.

"Are you an artist?"

"Unfortunately I'm not," he replied. And since he had no reason to withhold his name from her, he introduced himself formally. She told him her name in an offhand manner, and in the conversation that flowed easily from then on she told him a good deal about her life without his having to urge her on. She gave piano lessons; her husband, a magistrate's clerk, had died three years ago; and now, widowed and childless, she lived on one of the nearby streets with the family of a skilled workman. Last summer, for the first time since her husband's death, she had taken a three-week vacation, which she had spent in a small, inexpensive summer resort near Vienna. "I got engaged again there," she added. "But nothing came of it. It's better that way," she concluded with a shrug of her shoulders, as if she were not accustomed to a better lot in life and didn't deserve anything more than she had.

An open one-horse carriage trotted by, and the coachman waved to them with his whip. Robert invited his companion for a little ride; they climbed in and drove through the outskirts of Vienna and then beneath the train viaduct into the Luxemburgerstrasse, which had a view of a chain of hills now bathed in evening twilight. Gradually they moved closer to one another. A train rushing past on a nearby track led Robert to tell her of his just-concluded travels; later he turned the conversation to the subject of music, which she joined without great interest—in her capacity as piano teacher she needed only the knowledge she had incidentally acquired in earlier years when she was in better circumstances than she was today.

The sun had gone down, and it had become decidedly chilly. Robert had the carriage turn back to the city. Neither of them talked any more, and when he took her hand she returned his grasp with unexpected warmth; a gleam of pleasure, almost of happiness, came over her tired features.

They stopped at a little inn that Robert knew from similar liaisons; they took a room and ordered dinner. While they waited for it, she sat on the blue velvet sofa with her hands folded in her lap as he, smoking a cigarette, walked back and forth in the modest but well-kept room. Over the bed hung two awful oil prints—gussied up Italian landscapes. On the right was Mount Vesuvius spreading smoke and fire over the Gulf of Naples; on the left was an *osteria* in the Roman countryside with coachmen and wide-mouthed, laughing girls dressed in red and blue in the foreground and an aqueduct with broken pillars in the background. She'll never know more of Italy, thought Robert, than what she gets to see in such pictures. And pityingly, with a sense of guilt, his gaze settled on her forehead. She was sitting motionless in her high-necked, somewhat wrinkled, blue-dotted linen blouse. Her hair was dark blonde and thick, her eyes large and bright. But in the yellowish light of the two-armed, hanging lamp her features looked even more faded than they had before and she said simply, almost dryly, "Don't think badly of me, but I'm really so alone."

Moved, he stepped closer to her, put his hands on her cheeks, and kissed her on the mouth.

Shortly after midnight, ready to go, she looked back at the table where the rest of their dinner still stood and said, "It's a shame to leave all that." "Oh," he said jokingly, "they'll warm it up tomorrow and serve it to somebody else." She replied, "Well, one could do that oneself. It's already all paid for." And in response to his disconcerted look, she said, "Do you object to that?" He said, with some embarrassment, "That really isn't necessary, my dear girl." And he added, "Forgive me for speaking of it, but if I can be . . . of assistance to you. . . ." She interrupted him with a decisive wave of her hand, without, however, acting offended. "Thanks," she said, and with a tired smile she added, "I don't want you to think that of me." She opened her music binder, which contained, besides some rather torn music books, a few sheets of legal-size paper. She wrapped the cold meat in one of them and put the package in the pocket of her raincoat. Then they went down the stairs. Robert lit the way with a little wax candle. On the street he took her arm. "Oh, you don't have to accompany me home," she said. "Of course I don't have to. But if I'd like to?" At the next corner stood a carriage. "Let's take it," he said. "Spendthrift," she replied in the same tired tone that she had used a few hours earlier when he had ordered a bottle of more expensive wine. But the coachman was already waiting. The young woman climbed in, and suddenly Robert felt not the slightest desire to accompany her. With hesitation, he remained standing next to the running board, her hand in his, and asked, "When are we going to see each other again, my dear girl?"

"I already told you where I live," she answered, "and if you ever want to see me again, just drop me a note. I'm always free."

"So much the better," he said. And slowly he added, "I thank you very much." And he kissed her hand while he said it. She was not wearing gloves, and her fingers were cool. When he looked up at her, he read in her eyes, "We'll certainly never see each other again. I know I haven't really pleased you—my poor, little, knotted body was not to your liking, nor were many other things that I just don't possess, things that you're used to. You won't write to me, I know." He read all of this so clearly in her look that he almost felt forced to deny it. But the carriage was already in motion. Once more she looked back at her lover of the past few hours and nodded a few times. Robert looked after the rolling carriage for a long time. Well, I certainly didn't murder her, he said to himself, and automatically looked around to see if there was anyone nearby who could testify that he had seen her get into the carriage and drive away, if he needed a witness. Then he laughed and shook off the absurd and intrusive thought. Perhaps I'll write to her sometime after all, he thought; and he made his way slowly through the darkened streets back to his hotel.

VI

The next day, a clear, late-autumn day, he went up to Semmering. Only after he had moved into a room with a view, over the tops of the fir trees, of the rocky cliffs of the Rax, now covered with newly fallen, glistening snow, did he write cheery postcards informing his brother, Dr. Leinbach, and also, without knowing quite why, Dr. Kahnberg, that he was going to spend a couple of days here recuperating from his long trip of the last few months. For hours on end, always alone, and with the bracing mountain air blowing on him, he wandered through cool forests and sunny meadows, conscious only of enjoying the air and the light. And he was able to ward off all his morbid broodings so successfully that even the continued weakness of his left eyelid didn't bother him any more. On the second day of his stay he wrote to the head of his office, department chief Baron Pranter, asking for a brief prolongation of his leave, and the friendly tone of the positive answer contributed to raising his good spirits even more.

It was on the third night, while a strong wind blew over the mountains, that Robert, lying in the dark and unable to sleep, once more tried to recall the details of his parting from Alberta. His inability to recall clearly the sequence of events tortured him more and more. He remembered certain scenes from the earliest days of their relationship, scenes in which a jealous rage had clouded his senses and he had restrained himself from physically attacking her only through a supreme effort of will. Since any image of whatever had followed the terrifying rage that had sprung up in him the last time he saw her had totally vanished from his memory, there was absolutely no proof that, in the end, he had not finally done what he had wanted to do on more than one occasion, and had really murdered her. The fact that no importance at all had been attached to her disappearance at the hotel was easily explained. Perhaps he himself had reported that she had left before he did; perhaps he had even named a place where her luggage should be sent. With the finesse of a born criminal he might have done other things to conceal the traces of what he had done beyond any possibility of discovery. All this was credible, yes, and more than that, it was probable. How else could he understand the inexplicable gap in his memory between the hour of his parting from Alberta in the evening and that of his own departure the next morning except by an unconscious and until now successful effort to repress the horrible deed whose memory he wasn't strong enough to bear?

Suddenly, with his heart standing still, he sat up in bed. Since the suspicion that Alberta had met death at his hand was forcing itself upon him ever more imperiously, perhaps she wasn't the only one who had met such a fate. More than ten years ago his young wife had died totally unexpectedly. One morning he had gone as usual into her bedroom to plant a kiss on her forehead before going to work, and had found her dead in bed. He remembered now with horror that at the time, at least in the first moment, he had felt no special shock, yes, hardly even a great surprise. The doctor had no doubt regarded the death of the young woman as somewhat strange but hardly puzzling in view of her not insignificant weight for one so young, and in light of certain heart problems that had appeared from time to time. Because not the slightest suspicion of suicide or murder had been raised, the body had been buried without further investigation.

The marriage had been considered a happy one throughout its three-year duration and Robert had always treated the loving, gentle, somewhat indolent creature if not exactly with great affection, at any rate with chivalrous gallantry, not only in public but also at home. Only he himself knew how much, from the very beginning, he had suffered precisely on account of her gentleness and good-heartedness; how often her sometimes silly remarks, her silences, her way of tolerating and expecting his kisses with pouted lips, sometimes just the mere fact of her presence, had filled him with a helpless, barely restrained, ill-humored impatience. But the worst thing about her had been her piano playing. Without sufficient talent but with a characteristic persistence, she had retained her childhood habit of practicing an hour every day; and her manner of thumping out Mozart and Beethoven sonatas with her childish, fat fingers had sometimes reduced him to a state of real despair as he sat in the next room smoking and reading after dinner. How often, when desire for other women had flared up in him and tempted him to new adventures, had he rebelled fruitlessly against the quiet coercion that Brigitte's touching dependency exerted on him? With what passion had he yearned for the irresponsibility of his young bachelor life, whose sweet freedom he had sacrificed for this mild, to be sure, yet still inescapable slavery? And if this longing, this impatience had become as overpowering then as he now felt it in mere memory, where was the proof that impatience and wish had not at some moment become will, and that will had not finally become deed? Where was the proof that Brigitte had really suffered a heart attack and not died from a cunningly given poison? How he might have procured such a poison, how he might have slipped it to her, whether he had mixed it in a drink one evening, or whether he had forced her to drink it—all that he could not of course explain now. But since it had become apparent that his existence included many hours of such completely repressed episodes, who was to say that he hadn't murdered Brigitte just as he had murdered Alberta? Just as he had murdered Alberta? What had Alberta to do with this?

He reached for the lamp near his bed and turned it on. As quickly as they had overcome him in the darkness, the terrifying thoughts now evaporated in the light of the room. He drew a breath of relief. What madness, he thought, to imagine that I poisoned Brigitte! That good, gentle creature that I still love even now! If I told my friend Leinbach about the ghosts of the night, what would he say? Probably, as a start, that he for his part had sometimes imagined having killed most of his now-dead acquaintances; then, perhaps he would say that in the end there wasn't much difference, philosophically speaking, between really killing someone and only wishing him dead—that we're all murderers, really, more or less; and that finally, for his part, he wouldn't hold it against me if I really had killed Alberta as well as Brigitte. Do I know you well, my friend Leinbach? But you won't have the opportunity to practice your wit on me! It's always safer in any case not to reveal these sorts of fantasies even to one's closest friends. I won't tell Otto about them either. No, no, I won't make it so easy for you two!

While the lamp still burned, sleep slowly overtook him.

VII

When he went out into the cool autumn air the next morning and saw the sky covered with dreary, turbulent clouds, he looked down morosely without noticing a young female figure in a white wool jacket sitting on the bench near the hotel entrance. But then he felt two eyes fastened on him, and when he turned around to look, he recognized Fräulein Rolf. "Is it possible!" he called out with an expression of surprise, even of delight, that he immediately felt to be exaggerated. "It most certainly is," answered Paula, giving him her hand. "Only yesterday, can you believe it, we arrived in Vienna and were immediately sent up here, Mama and I. But don't let me disturb you. Are you about to take a walk?"

"I'm not in a hurry. If you permit, I'll keep you company until your mother comes down."

"That might be too long for you," said Paula. "For me, too, in fact. I was just about to start out for a walk on my own."

Robert asked permission to join her. Paula had no objections; she walked out the door toward the middle of the street, pursed her lips, and gave a peculiar low, whistle, in response to which Frau Rolf became visible at the second-story window in a light blue robe. Paula called up to her, "I'm going on ahead, Mama, toward Kampalm, and the commissioner is going to come with me." Frau Rolf acknowledged Robert's silent greeting with a friendly smile. "How nice that you're here too, Commissioner. . . . but don't wait for me. I'll follow you shortly."

Paula immediately set out at a lively pace, and without paying attention to the interruption that had just taken place, she continued, "Papa always does this when he's very busy with especially difficult matters."

"What does he always do?"

"He sends us away. He can't stand to have anyone around, especially a member of the family."

"That's peculiar," said Robert.

"Why peculiar?" answered Paula. "I understand it completely." And she mentioned a famous trial that her father had pleaded three years ago, a trial in which he, contrary to general expectations, had secured freedom for a millionaire who had faked bankruptcy. He had sent his wife and daughter away on a trip at that time, too.

Robert silently wondered at this. It seemed to him that any task would be easier with an intelligent, clearheaded person such as Paula at one's side.

She asked about Robert's brother and sister-in-law, whom she had known casually some time before. She had for a while now given up almost all social life, as she got no pleasure from it. Robert thought he remembered that in previous years, musical evenings at the Rolfs had gained a certain reputation, and that Paula's presence had contributed to their success. He had never participated in such evenings himself, however. Paula for her part was able to remember that years ago she had heard the commissioner improvise on the piano—she no longer remembered in what company. "Do you still play often?" she asked. He gave a vague reply. And he remembered the rumor of her engagement with a famous composer, now dead.

They sat down on a bench on an overhanging bluff which offered a wide panorama of the winding trails, meadows, woods, bridges, and dawning plains below. Paula took a cigarette from her case and offered one to her companion. Her father had brought her the cigarette case from Moscow some time ago, she told him. Then she said she planned to take a trip to Japan next year.

"Alone?" asked Robert, as though concerned about her.

She smiled. "I'll probably have to go alone. Mama is much too afraid of getting seasick."

How wonderful it would be to travel around the world with her, thought Robert, knowing that she knew what he was thinking.

A light rain began, and they started back toward the hotel. In the woods they met Paula's mother, and they talked about the wonderful island where they had been neighbors for so many weeks without paying the slightest attention to each other. "You won't get away from us so easily here in the mountains," joked Paula.

At lunch the conversation turned to people they had all known in earlier years. To Robert, Paula's remarks seemed somewhat acerbic at times but always on target. In the course of the conversation Robert spoke of the nervous condition that had been the impetus for his trip, but which by now was as good as gone. It seemed to him that Paula was able to divine more than he saw fit to reveal. And he thought, I could confess crimes to her, had I committed any.

During his solitary walk in the afternoon he played with the question of whether he dared to woo Paula. He was very taken with her. The fact that she was not so young any more, perhaps already thirty, and in all probability had a serious affair of the heart behind her as well, only added to her charm. In the evening they sat together in the lobby for a long time and talked for so long like old friends that finally they asked one another why they had passed each other by like strangers back at the seaside—indeed, both confessed, at first even with a kind of antipathy.

"We have a lot to catch up on," said Robert, then added, "in the few days up here." For a while she looked straight ahead, but suddenly, with a rapid movement characteristic of her, she tossed her head and let the conversation continue innocently.

That night Robert dreamed about the poor piano teacher with whom he had spent his last night in Vienna. He was walking with her on a trail in the woods, the same one he had walked with Alberta when they parted. She kept her hands in the pockets of her long raincoat and spoke utterly incomprehensible words into space without even looking at Robert. Yet he knew somehow that this was not really a walk in the woods at all, but represented his life's path as it drew inexorably toward its end. And this recognition filled him with an emotion that was half amusement and half anger. When he awoke he felt, deep in his heart, only a vague tenderness, and he soon recognized that this tenderness, indeed, all his love, was for that poor piano teacher who was even lonelier than he. He got up and looked out the window. The windowpanes were clouded with ice from the light night frost, and the sky was wonderfully clear.

Since he was going out earlier than they were, he made an arrangement for the ladies to pick him up in a carriage on the newly constructed and well-built mountain road. In an almost lighthearted mood, such as he had not felt for a long time, he walked slowly and then energetically up the gently rising road beneath a bright, cool sky, as though purposefully setting out toward a distant goal. Sooner than he expected, he heard the rattle of wheels behind him. He waited at the roadside; the carriage stopped and both ladies invited him to get in, greeting him warmly. Thanking them, he took a seat facing them. Frau Rolf said she had not been able to fall asleep until early morning, which was characteristic of her while up in the mountains. Robert spoke of a strange observation he had made more than once—that in the mountains he not only dreamed more often but also quite differently than back home. In his dreams here, people or things didn't represent themselves but rather something completely different; indeed, they represented nothing concrete at all but rather concepts, abstractions. Instead of using his dream last night as an example, however, he mentioned one from a long time ago, in which he had seen something like a battle on a distant plain, but in such a dim light that he couldn't make out the participants either as individuals or as a group. Instead of the sun he had glimpsed a crooked chandelier in the sky; it flickered with a yellow light and was hung with organdy. And he had suddenly realized that it was this chandelier, and not the dim picture on the plain, that represented the battle. Paula put up the collar of her white jacket, and her face was rosy from the fresh air. Suddenly, with that same sudden toss of the head that Robert had already come to know and almost love, she turned to him and said, "Don't you think about yourself a little too much?" Disconcerted, Robert answered, "I don't think so. I'm just more open about it than others." And he asked himself, If I had met her sooner, would it have helped me? Would I have become a different man, a saner one, a better one, than I am today? Was my existence predetermined and mapped out from the beginning? Or did I once have a choice—a choice between weakness and strength, between health and sickness, between clarity and confusion? Had something already been decided? No. He suddenly knew, unquestionably, that he still had the choice to determine his fate—but, of course, not for long.

The carriage had turned around and was now rapidly heading downhill. Robert spoke of the official duties awaiting him, of his interest in the demands of his profession—so passionately, as if it were important to him to prove that he stood with both feet on solid ground and was by no means a dreamer or God knows what worse. And Paula's intelligent questions drew such incisive answers from his lips that during the conversation, which continued at table afterward with increasing seriousness, he felt an ever more genuine desire for work and activity. Paula's increasing attentiveness and her nods of approval became good omens for him. He carried away the pressure of her hand at parting, and her gentle, friendly look, like a promise.

He felt he was really recovering now. He believed he had found a new and reassuring explanation for the fantasies that had tortured him only a few days ago—actually, only yesterday. Left in the lurch, so to speak, by his own life, feeling the inner emptiness of his self, he had all too willingly—and indeed with a certain degree of self-satisfaction—begun to play a role which had then exerted a growing power over him and was gradually threatening to destroy his real self. But now he was proudly lifting his head up as though out of a gloomy fog and felt in himself the willpower and the strength to become healthy again, to become authentic at last.

The two women did not appear at dinner, and Robert assumed they had both felt tired and gone up to their room early. Nevertheless he didn't give up the hope that Paula would appear in the lobby later, and for quite a while he leafed through illustrated weeklies that he otherwise seldom looked at. But his expectation was not fulfilled; the lobby emptied, and there was nothing for Robert to do but go to bed like the other guests.

Before he did, however, he approached the desk clerk as though he wanted to ask about a letter. The concierge's characteristic way of forming a personal, indeed, a warm relationship with the hotel guests, which Robert had already experienced, allowed him to hope for some enlightenment about the Rolfs. And indeed, on handing him the room key, the clerk told him in a tone of light regret that the Rolf ladies had received a telegram and had left suddenly on the seven o'clock train. They had asked him to give their regards to the commissioner, the clerk added offhandedly as he diligently pasted stamps onto postcards.

"A telegram," repeated Robert absentmindedly. He remained standing for a moment, then composed himself and went up to his room. He turned on the light and paced back and forth. A telegram, he repeated to himself. What kind of telegram could it have been? And immediately he knew: they had been warned against him. The worried father had hastily called them back. "The ladies give their regards—?" A friendly invention of the clerk's. They had fled as fast as they could.

Apparently rumors about him were already circulating. But were they only rumors? Perhaps he was already being pursued, watched, and surrounded by detectives, and would be arrested early tomorrow morning. Even if he were innocent, how could he prove it? Alberta was in America or God knows where. Who would believe he hadn't killed her? Perhaps the suspicion that he had poisoned his wife had surfaced too. Would they exhume the body? Would they test for traces of poison? And even if none were found—what good would that do him after all this time? Suddenly he saw a picture of himself in his mind's eye, dressed in a guise in which he would never have allowed himself to be photographed in reality—in an overcoat, top hat, and cane, like those carelessly reproduced pictures in a newspaper—and beneath, in large letters, the caption, A NEW BLUEBEARD. He could smell the paper and the black print. Immediately afterward he saw himself standing before a judge as an accused criminal. He denied the charge. He swore to God that he had never killed anyone. "It's only a delusion of mine, gentlemen of the jury. How can you bring me to trial because of a delusion? I am ill, gentlemen of the jury, but I am no criminal. The circumstantial evidence is against me, yes. Do investigate everything, gentlemen. Alberta is married in America, and my wife had heart problems. She died a natural death." But then a shrill voice suddenly shouted, "How do you explain, defendant, that your mistress was found dead beneath fallen leaves in the forest?"

"She was found dead? Then somebody else killed her. The American did it!"

"You are entangling yourself in contradictions, defendant! Didn't you tell us yourself that this American courted your mistress and that you went walking with her in the woods while the American stayed behind in the hotel? Didn't you tell us, furthermore, that your wife's piano playing drove you to desperation and that you had long harbored murderous wishes against her?"

"I didn't tell you anything. You're attributing statements to me that I never made. I'm innocent. I wouldn't hurt a fly." Thunderous laughter went through the courtroom, rattling all the windows.

"Order!" shouted the judge. "This is not a theatre. I'll have the room cleared!"

Robert, who had been pacing ceaselessly back and forth in his room, stopped short, looked around, and, as usual when the thread of his thoughts became lost in the absurd and the tasteless, suddenly came to his senses. He said to himself that the departure of the ladies could not have had the slightest connection to his presence here. He knew that he was neither guilty of nor suspected of anything by anyone in the world. His nerves were still not in good shape, that was all. And Paula was the last person on earth to run away and leave him to his fate because of a vague and slanderous telegram. She would not have left without speaking to him; whatever she heard, she would try to get to the bottom of it with her own judgment. And even if he had really committed a crime, she was the woman who would understand and forgive. Anyway . . . all this was irrelevant. There were dozens of possible reasons for the women's departure. The father, or someone else in the family, was ill. Certainly it couldn't be anything grave or they wouldn't have remembered to send him their regrets. I'm not a murderer, and it didn't occur to anyone that I might be one. Tomorrow a letter will come from Paula—an apology, an explanation. And if not, I'll find out for myself. I'm a free man, after all; I'm not locked up, and Höhnburg has been dead a long time. Why am I thinking of Höhnburg now? My brother wouldn't dream of presenting that promissory note. I am not, nor am I suspected of being, guilty of anything . . . I have a choice to make. . . .

VIII

The next day Dr. Leinbach announced, via an amusing postcard, that he would visit him that same day. Robert, who had awakened feeling calm, decided to go to meet him. The two friends met on the wide forest road under the cool autumnal shade of fir trees through which a pale blue sky shimmered. Leinbach was dressed in mountaineer fashion with hobnail shoes, knee-length shorts, a walking stick, and a rucksack.

"What on earth are you planning to do?" asked Robert.

"Nothing much," answered Leinbach, "except to harmonize with the landscape and be prepared for all eventualities."

"Well," said Robert, "in any event, you'll have to do without my company if you plan to do any serious mountain climbing."

"I wouldn't dream of it, especially since I have to go back on the 5:20 train."

"So why the rucksack?"

"In case we want to eat outdoors."

"What did you bring with you?"

"Ham, cheese, bread, a bottle of wine, a volume of Goethe, and some bandages."

"Bandages?"

"They happened to be there from my last trip. I was going to take them out, but that would be tempting fate." He took Robert's arm. "So tell me, what've you been doing up here these last few days? You've had fine weather, haven't you?"

Robert said he had spent almost the whole of every day hiking about in the open air; he didn't mention the Rolfs. On the whole he had felt quite well, except that he had been dreaming a lot, every night and all night long—really wild things! Leinbach shrugged his shoulders. Whatever and however much Robert had dreamed, it couldn't compare to his own dreams. He had lived through years, even decades, in his sleep. Once, when he was still a Gymnasium student, he had experienced the whole of the Thirty Years War in an early morning hour before awakening.

"Surely not in great detail?" Robert asked, smiling. "Only an outline form, I take it?"

"All the same," answered Leinbach earnestly, "I got from 1618 to 1648."

They walked up a forest trail. "Formerly," said Leinbach, "my wife always accompanied me on Sunday outings like this. But now, ever since the fourth child, she's given it up. She lets me go by myself and devotes herself entirely to domesticity—or to whatever else she may be doing." Robert said nothing. He found his friend's remark as tasteless as it was ridiculous since he knew Frau Leinbach to be a thoroughly domestic, straightforward creature, wholly without charm. Indeed Leinbach, who hated emotional discomforts even more than bodily ones, would have taken care not to marry any other kind of woman.

When later, as they hiked ever higher and crossed an alpine meadow under a truly summery noon sun, Leinbach was prompted to compare the day to certain deceptive summer hours that occur in the autumnal days of human life but should not fool intelligent people.

"Why fool," parried Robert, rejecting the idea, "if it's really warm in such hours? Today, for example, we could lie down right here in the grass without the slightest danger. What do you think?" Leinbach agreed. They spread their coats on the ground, stretched themselves out on top of them, and looked down toward the valley, delighting in the same view that Robert had enjoyed with Paula from farther below. An intense feeling of well-being ran through him. I'm still young and healthy, he said to himself. Just what is it that overcomes me sometimes with such uncanny force? Well, who knows? Maybe similar ghosts haunt everyone. On the other hand, there are probably people who've actually committed a crime and have completely forgotten it. Didn't I recently read somewhere that in England alone almost a thousand people disappear every year without a trace? And it's quite possible that some of those thousand were killed by someone who afterward doesn't remember doing it, just like me. . . .

Uh-oh! He hurriedly collected himself and jumped up. He had been lying with his eyes closed and suddenly the landscape seemed too bright; it swayed and trembled before his eyes. Leinbach eyed him sideways with a peculiar blinking gaze. Hmm . . . why exactly had Leinbach come? Maybe he had been sent up here for quite specific reasons. Perhaps by Otto? Nonsense. At bottom Otto thought Leinbach a fool. And not totally without justification. "An intellectual fool," as he had expressed it recently. Nevertheless it was striking how quickly Leinbach averted his gaze and now looked up at the sky with seeming indifference. Robert began to whistle—why, he didn't quite know himself. Was it to test Leinbach, to annoy him, or to fool him? Suddenly he jumped up and suggested that they start back on the trail. Leinbach nodded and made rather elaborate preparations for the descent. When Robert hurried ahead a couple of steps, Leinbach remarked dryly, "Your paralysis seems to have cured itself."

Robert quickly turned to face him. But his friend's face wore only the usual expression of a faintly supercilious flippancy. "I never imagined I had a paralysis," Robert said. "I may be a hypochondriac, but I'm not an idiot. Besides, I've never felt as youthful and as refreshed as I do now."

"Yes," Leinbach sighed, "and who wouldn't feel that way if he could take six months' vacation! If one of us wanted his freedom for that long, he'd have to flee. By the way," he added, apparently without any connection, "what do you think of the Rolf affair?"

"The Rolf affair?" Robert's heart stood still. What could that mean, "the Rolf affair"? Was that a reference to him? Was he involved in some sort of scandal without suspecting it? Was Paula? They had both left yesterday, mother and daughter. He couldn't have killed Paula—it was completely impossible. Get hold of yourself! Quiet! What was that again? He had never killed anyone! That was certain, he knew it—never! "What kind of affair?" he asked calmly.

"Oh, I suppose you haven't seen the newspaper today yet. Dr. Rolf absconded. Misappropriated deposits, embezzled trust funds, and the like. People have long been whispering about him."

"So he fled. I haven't heard anything. Besides, I know him only very superficially. But I spoke with his family just yesterday. They were both here, the mother and the daughter. They left last night."

"So . . . they were here? It did say in the paper that they weren't in Vienna. . . . Yes . . . evidently he sent his family up here so that he could make his getaway undisturbed. Supposedly, he's been gone for thirty-six hours already. It's a pity. He was a very gifted man."

Robert couldn't help feeling that this was actually good news for him. The family's misfortune brought him closer to Paula; in a certain sense it meant that he now had a secret fellowship with her. He didn't say anything else to Leinbach about the matter, but instead of leaving the next morning as he had intended, he went back to Vienna with him that afternoon, to Leinbach's great satisfaction. True, Leinbach always claimed to love solitude, but actually he was, for the most part, quite unhappy without company.

His relationship to the Rolf family being what it was, Robert, much as he wanted to, couldn't think of going to their house and making inquiries in person. Driven by an irresistible longing however, he left his hotel late at night to wander past the Rolf house, where, to his astonishment, the windows were open and brightly illuminated. Only gradually did he remember that even the most extraordinary turn of fate doesn't express itself immediately in a decisive outward change; that Paula—even if at this moment she might, in the truest sense of the word, be poorer than that piano teacher who had taken home the remains of the dinner after a sorry one-night stand—would certainly continue to live for some time in a comfortable home, wear beautiful clothes, and, of course, never go hungry. He saw shadows moving back and forth and then observed the lights go out in one part of the house and go on again in another. Later a carriage drove up, and a distinguished-looking man appeared and vanished into the house. Robert began to feel that his walking back and forth in front of a house he couldn't really enter was pointless and ridiculous, and he began walking back home.

IX

The newspapers the next day treated the Rolf affair with conspicuous restraint. True, the matter had not yet been completely cleared up, but it was certainly no longer possible to speak of Rolf's having absconded—his whereabouts were known not only to his family but also to the authorities. Robert inferred from this both a desire to settle Rolf's entanglements out of court and the likelihood of doing so. But he did not feel as good about his conjecture as would have been natural under the circumstances.

In an ambivalent mood he went to his office, where his department head, Baron Prantner, greeted him cordially and surprised him with the news that Hofrat Palm would be allowed to take his pension at the beginning of the following year out of consideration for his health. "You, my dear sir," he added, "will very shortly assume a portion of Hofrat's duties. And Dr. Renthal, who has quite wonderfully carried out your duties during your absence, will continue to represent you in the office for the time being." Did they think I wouldn't come back? Robert fleetingly wondered. Then he remembered that Baron Prantner, who was dressed in mourning, had lost his wife in the course of the summer. Even though Robert had already expressed his condolences during his trip, he felt called upon to express his sympathy once more. The baron shook his hand and looked at the floor. Hmm, thought Robert, it is possible that he too killed his wife? Maybe that happens a lot more frequently than we think. It would be interesting to investigate. Maybe he suspects I did the same thing and that's the reason he's so overtly friendly to me now. Is there a kind of freemason's secret sign for us murderers? Strange, he's still holding on to my hand tightly. . . .

At that moment Hofrat Palm came in. Robert replied heartily to his welcome, and soon the three men were engaged in a professional conversation, in the course of which Robert took the opportunity to express his ideas about changing the system of musical instruction. They listened to him with interest. Afterward he went to visit several colleagues in their offices, and some of them congratulated him on his recovery in such a jocular manner that it seemed they had never really taken his illness seriously.

He went to lunch with Wegner, the ministerial secretary, who entertained him with all sorts of office gossip. Afterward they played a game of billiards, as they had been accustomed to do, so it was already late in the afternoon when Robert walked up the stairs of his brother's house. As his brother was still seeing patients in his office, Robert announced himself to Marianne and told her about his hike in the mountains with Dr. Leinbach. He exaggerated the doctor's gear in a humorous manner and made the contents of his ruck-sack seem ludicrous by inventing an array of extra cans of food and bottles of brandy. He played all sorts of games with the little boys, taking the younger one on his lap, and felt that this activity fore-shadowed his own bright and comfortable future. Otto came out of his office, heartily welcomed his brother, and invited him to come with him to Heitzing if he had nothing better to do. Robert accepted, and a few minutes later Otto's carriage was gliding through twilit streets toward the green suburbs of Vienna.

Robert talked with more than a little eagerness about the wonderful prospects opening up for him at the office. Then he talked about his stay in Semmering, and in doing so he could hardly avoid mentioning his meeting with the two Rolfs. Otto had no particular regard for them. In his opinion they weren't wholly blameless for the bad turn the attorney's affairs had recently taken. He added it was no wonder that the daughter, despite her charms, which, to be sure, were beginning to fade, had never found a husband.

The carriage stopped in front of a garden gate. A servant opened it, Otto went in, and Robert walked slowly up and down the quiet street between the now almost bare gardens on either side. Much as he tried to resist it, Otto's remarks about the Rolf family had affected him. Paula, only yesterday still the incarnation of his new hopes in life, now seemed strangely distant. When he tried to recollect her image, what he now saw was a person in an untidy morning robe, no longer young and a little faded, like the poor piano teacher; and he felt a dull resentment against her rise in him. He held it against her that she hadn't taken good enough care of her father, that she had fallen in love with an old musician, that she smoked cigarettes, and especially that she had left Semmering without a word of explanation. At the same time he was thoroughly aware of the injustice, indeed the absurdity, of all these accusations, which he clearly recognized for what they were—excuses for the early awakening of that hatred which had always gradually come to accompany his feelings of love. What he now experienced was only one more example of the incomprehensible seesaw of his emotions, which were capable of oscillating between self-sacrificing tenderness and consuming passion, and aversion, disgust, anger, rage, and murderous fantasies.

And, he asked himself, what really is the difference between wishing a person dead and actually killing him? Well, thoughts disappear, but actions are irreversible. But isn't that a malicious trick of providence? The emotion that makes an action possible could change into its complete opposite, but a deed remains done. Suppose the poison that I gave Brigitte had not worked. The next morning she would have awakened, would still be alive today, and no one would have any idea of what had happened—or, rather, what had been intended to happen. I myself wouldn't have any idea, either, because I would have repressed it. I did repress it. Did I really? No, I'm remembering it. . . .

"Have I kept you waiting long?" asked Otto, as the garden gate fell shut behind him.

"Oh, not at all!" answered Robert, composing himself quickly. "It was very pleasant to stroll up and down this quiet street."

They got into the carriage. Otto made a few jottings in his notebook. "Where should I have the carriage drop you?" he casually asked his brother.

"It doesn't matter. If you should happen to be going anywhere near my hotel . . ."

"That can be arranged. By the way, it's too bad you gave up your apartment. I never really understood why."

"I had to."

"Had to?"

"I didn't know whether I would ever be able to live in a big city again and resume my profession."

"How can you say that?" Otto replied, and put away his notebook.

"You don't seem to remember what a bad state I was in," replied Robert. "At the beginning of my trip"—he hesitated a moment—"I was still plagued by all sorts of stupid ideas."

Otto gave his brother an oblique look of friendly mockery. "What kind of ideas, if I may ask?"

"Not worth talking about . . . they were as absurd as obsessive ideas usually are."

"Come on," said Otto gently, "won't you tell me about them?"

"Well, let me think . . . ," began Robert, a little unsteadily. "For example, for a long time I couldn't get myself to drink the water that was put into my room in the evening, out of fear that someone, maybe one of the hotel servants or another guest, might have put some sort of harmful or even deadly substance into it."

"And so . . ."

"That went so far that many a night, when I couldn't manage to get something else to drink, I would suffer the most tormenting thirst rather than drink a drop of it."

"And?"

"Well, what else do you want to know? These fantasies, or delusions, vanished as completely as others had before them."

"Of course. But I ask you: Did you ever try to follow one of your suspicions to its logical conclusion? Did you ever—at least once—try to have one of those suspicious pitchers of water chemically analyzed? Was your suspicion occasionally directed at a specific person, and did you lodge a complaint?"

"No, I didn't. But that's not what matters."

"But of course it matters a great deal, my dear fellow, whether a so-called obsession has consequences, especially whether it's translated into compulsive acts or corrected in time. As long as one is capable of getting rid of a mental aberration before the point where it becomes dangerous to act on its logical implications, until that point, if you'll forgive my saying so, I don't have a real respect for it. For the same reason I'm not impressed by rage attacks in which the destructive urge targets only inanimate and, if possible, inexpensive objects. It may sound somewhat heretical, but I regard all craziness—to stick with the popular expression—over which the patient retains a degree of control and which he is able to turn off and on out of practical considerations, as a mere preference for make-believe, for play-acting; in short, as an unprincipled desire to escape from the real seriousness of life and to shirk uncomfortable responsibilities. Of course such a desire does, if you will, have something sick about it, but it certainly has nothing to do with real insanity."

Robert was silent for a while, embarrassed because somehow what Otto said coincided with ideas that had recently occurred to him as well. And then he asked, "And are you sure you can always draw the line between the two?"

"Of course I am. Otherwise I would have given up my profession a long time ago."

So he does remember, thought Robert. He wants to lull me into a false sense of security by making me believe that I'm not insane and therefore have nothing to fear from him. But how does he know that I'm not insane? I've just lied to him once more. I haven't said anything about my latest obsessions. Maybe he suspects them anyway. I can't stay silent for this long. True, he's looking out the carriage window into the street, but he's struck by my silence. He feels that I'm hiding something from him. It can't go on like this. I have to tell him the truth. If not today, then tomorrow. Everything between us has to be laid on the table.

"Actually," said Otto, suddenly turning toward his brother again, "we've gotten pretty far off the track. Don't you have any other complaints to tell me about?"

"What for," answered Robert in a similarly light tone, "since you only take me for a wretched actor because I haven't had all the hotel chambermaids of Switzerland arrested for trying to poison me?"

But Otto didn't take up the joke. "You know what I think?" he said in the serious, somewhat stern tone sometimes characteristic of him. "I think that regular work will be very good for you after such a long episode of loafing. And as for your twitching eyelid, you don't need to worry about it in the slightest."

Robert turned to him in consternation. "So you noticed it?"

Otto sighed. "What all have you been imagining . . . ?"

"You said my eyelid twitches. I . . . I didn't really know that. I had the impression of a . . . an incipient paralysis."

"Not in the least. It's your imagination. Because of your repeated efforts to test the mobility of your eyelid, you've now gotten in the habit of twitching. Don't think about it any more—then it will go away of its own accord."

The carriage stopped in front of the hotel. "Oh, we're here already," said Robert. "How about coming up to take a look at my room, Otto? It's very nice."

"Next time. I'd love to, but unfortunately I don't have any more time today. I'll see you again tomorrow, I hope. And . . . please . . . for once, be sensible! It's about time!" And he heartily shook hands with Robert in parting.

Robert felt as if a heavy load had been taken from him. For the moment, Otto's words, as if by magic, had freed him completely not only from the trivial and indeed nearly forgotten worry about his eyelid but also from all his other imaginary terrors.

X

A good period began for Robert. He took up his professional work with zeal, resumed a pleasantly entertaining social life with his old friends, and visited his brother's house every day for an hour or so, joking with the children and chatting with Marianne. Once, when she complained that Otto, despite his heavy clinical load, didn't give himself a moment's rest from his scientific research, Robert gladly seized the opportunity to give his brother some friendly advice about living in an unreasonable manner—advice that was listened to patiently but not followed in the least.

One evening, at the café, the subject of the Rolf affair happened to come up in Robert's presence. It was said that either no legal action had actually been brought against the fugitive attorney or that it had been withdrawn—though his magnificent house was already privately rented out for the coming season. At this news Robert was seized with an inordinate pity; he suddenly felt that it had been cruel of him, even reprehensible, to have paid no attention at all to the two women, who certainly had the right to expect some sign of life from him. Guilt over his neglect pursued him in his sleep, and the next morning he telephoned to ask when he might inquire after the two ladies in person. He recognized Paula's voice only when she, quite casually, asked him to call on them that very evening.

The large drawing room that he entered around six o'clock looked inhospitable, almost dreary. The furniture was covered with grey linen, and the chandeliers with white organdy cloth, reminding Robert of his recent dream about the battle. On top of the closed piano were all sorts of art objects made of glass, porcelain, and bronze, obviously assembled for packing. Nails protruded from the walls, and pictures were propped face down against them. Paula entered in a bright dress, clear-eyed and cheerful, and since Robert had been prepared to find her melancholy and somberly dressed, she appeared particularly radiant to him, so much so that his surprise was reflected in his features. She gave him her hand as straightforwardly as if there had been not the slightest change in her circumstances since their last meeting. "It doesn't look very attractive around here," she said simply, "but you probably know we're moving."

"Soon?" asked Robert. "Not before the New Year," she replied. "But before that we'd like to get rid of certain objects that we won't be needing anymore. But let's not talk about that. I'm glad you came. I almost wrote to you. But I like it better this way."

"If I had known that my visit . . ."

She didn't let him finish. "A lot has happened since we last talked, but it appears that certain events are being taken harder by those not directly involved than by those who are. The most awkward thing about misfortune is really always the embarrassment of others."

Robert was about to frame a reply when Frau Rolf came in, enveloped by an atmosphere of equanimity which apparently neither outer nor inner storms could disturb. She was really sorry, she remarked, that she hadn't been able to say goodbye to the commissioner personally. And somewhat hesitantly she added, "But you must have heard and read all kinds of things. . . ."

Paula, blushing lightly, interrupted her. "The newspapers have been full of all sorts of stupid and false stories." Robert tried to interject, but Paula continued. "The only thing that's true is that father has gone away and in all probability will not return. But there's nothing forcing him to stay away. It would just be awkward for him to continue to live here in such reduced circumstances. He's one of those people who can begin a new life only in a new environment. It's different with me . . . with us," she added, with an affectionate glance at her mother.

"I thank you for your confidence," replied Robert softly.

"And now," said Paula in a tone of final dismissal of the subject, "enough about us. How've you been?" She asked him how he had managed his return to his profession and his circle of friends after such a long leave. He welcomed the opportunity to express himself, and spoke with animation about his new work, which concerned the matter of musical instruction in the schools. While speaking, his glance fell involuntarily on the closed piano, and when Paula remarked that it had not been played for a long time, Robert walked over to it and struck a few chords, at first without sitting down. The chords sounded a little muffled, and the porcelain trembled softly in harmony. Paula began to clear the objects off the piano, and with Robert's help she put the cups, plates, clock, candlesticks, and vases on the floor. Robert then sat down at the open piano and began to improvise in his usual manner, changing from a dance tune he had drifted into unintentionally and found not quite suitable for the moment into a melancholy melody reminiscent of Chopin. The women were silent after he finished; he couldn't see them because they were sitting behind him in a corner of the room, but he could feel that they had liked his playing. Paula rose, walked over to him, and asked if he had a good piano at his disposal. "I had an excellent one," he answered, "but last spring I sold it, along with many other things. As soon as I have another place, I'll get a new one. For now I'm still staying in a hotel." A faint smile glimmered in Paula's eyes, and he knew what it meant. In the look that they exchanged afterward, their mutual understanding was clear beyond any doubt, and when he took his leave, Paula's handshake, even more clearly than her words, said, "Come again soon."

How is it possible, he asked himself when he was back in the street, that in the last few days I've only thought about her with complete indifference? That she's been drifting through my thoughts as if in disguise, and that I've contemplated her masked image almost with hostility? It's as though I had an unconscious reluctance, yes, a fear of approaching her again, evidently because deep inside me there is still the fear that if she were my mistress . . . my wife . . . the same thing might happen to her that happened to the others I've loved. To the others . . . ? And he immediately caught himself. What happened to the others? I didn't harm them—there's not the slightest doubt about that any more. Yet my thoughts keep on running in this direction without rhyme or reason, as if stuck on a broken track. On a broken track, he repeated. Yes, that's it. And this analogy almost calmed him.

Kahnberg had been waiting for him impatiently in the café. The writer, who had recently chosen Robert as the confidant for his amorous sorrows, drew him into a quiet corner and told him of the tormenting jealousy that raged in his heart. He declared that he couldn't answer for what might happen—he didn't know how it would all end. "Last night, as she lay sleeping at my side," he remarked in the indiscreet way that Robert detested, "I was so close to ending it all—everything, myself and her—that I hardly know what finally restrained me. There's an abyss in us, commissioner, an abyss. . . ."

"I'm not an expert in such matters," answered Robert, recoiling, "and I don't know why you are doing me the honor of telling me all this."

"That's very simple, commissioner. Because you, as is plainly written on your brow, are a man of great experience and therefore capable of understanding things that might make other people shudder."

"That's a mistake, Herr Kahnberg; I don't have the slightest understanding of any abyss. My mind is well ordered."

"I had no doubt about that," replied Kahnberg, a little offended.

"I also don't quite understand," Robert continued, more and more irritated, "how I came to have the honor of receiving your play on my trip, and with an all too flattering dedication. You won't succeed in making me your accomplice in this fashion! Do you understand me, Herr Kahnberg?"

"I'm listening with increasing astonishment, commissioner!"

"So I notice. But, if you'll excuse my saying so, I don't like your manner of listening."

"I regret that, commissioner."

"I don't like it at all, Herr Kahnberg," he repeated vehemently, and got up. "And if you wish to kill the Fräulein," he concluded hoarsely, "then please do it on your own account and at your own risk. With which, I have the honor. . . ." He took his hat and walking stick and left. He was hardly on the street when he said to himself that he had pursued the conversation in an idiotic way; indeed, in a manner designed to arouse suspicion, and he decided that for the next couple of days he had better avoid Kahnberg's company as well as that of the rest of the circle. Because on closer consideration it seemed to him by no means out of the question that Kahnberg had been deliberately selected to set a trap for him. Even if it was clear that he had not committed a murder, and also, fortunately, that he wasn't insane, there was another possibility that he couldn't dismiss out of hand—namely, that someone else, for example, his dead wife's cousin, Herr August Langer, who had recently looked at him across the card table in a most peculiar way, suspected him of murdering Brigitte. Nor was it out of the question that Alberta might be wasting away from some disease or other in America and that her lover or husband imagined that Robert had given the faithless woman a slow-acting poison out of revenge. And what good was it to be sane if the rest of the world was filled with insane people? Now all that was lacking was that the poor creature with whom he had spent a sorry evening of love a couple of weeks ago should become ill—or even die—from eating the remains of the dinner she had taken home. How could he clear himself of the suspicion of having poisoned her—especially if insane accusations of a similar nature were brought against him from other quarters?

A colleague from the ministry greeted him on the street, now enlivened by evening crowds, and cornered him for a while with trivial questions. Robert was able to make conversation and even joked about Baron Prantner, and when the colleague left, Robert looked around as though he had just awakened from a bad dream. Crowds of people walked by, electric lights gleamed to his left and right, and tall buildings towered up into the dark night sky from the harsh brightness around him. All at once a feeling of tremendous desolation overwhelmed Robert. Then suddenly—it was like a liberation—it occurred to him that Paula was there and that he wasn't all alone any more. Save me, he murmured to himself, with his hands involuntarily folded, as though in prayer to her. And he cast a glance upward, as though his absurd obsessions were fleeing up into the night sky, back into the nothingness from which they had come.

XI

He let three days elapse before he visited the Rolfs again. He was received as an old friend; he felt wonderfully at home, stayed for dinner, and before he left, he made a date to walk with Paula in Dornbacher Park the next day. There, under the bare trees, in the warm haze of a windless November day, Paula told him about her childhood and for the first time mentioned the name of the composer with whom rumor had linked her so intimately some years ago. She also told him about her parents, and Robert had the impression that nothing was more painful to her than her relationship with her father, whose reserved yet needy temperament she had not been able to penetrate despite all her childhood love.

The next evening the confidential tone of this conversation still resonated in them both. Paula took up her long-unused violin, and, accompanied by Robert, played a Beethoven sonata. Both were delighted with the success of their first attempt at a duet, to which her mother also listened with pleasure; and they decided to play music together every evening from then on.

Paula's mother didn't always have the time or the inclination to listen to them, and so the two of them were often left alone together. These were hours of the purest happiness in which they felt more and more intimately connected without saying as much in words. One evening, as the reverberation of the last chord had faded and Robert rose and closed the musical score, she looked at him earnestly and inquiringly, violin still in hand, whereupon he, as if answering, pressed a kiss upon her forehead and then upon her lips. They were silent for a long time. When he finally started to say something, she protested gently: "No more today, I beg you."

He left. As he walked out the front door, a window above him opened. He looked up. Paula, a white shawl wrapped snugly about her throat, stood in the darkness and waved him a farewell.

When he got back to his room, he found a letter waiting for him. It was from America. The address was in Alberta's handwriting. So she was alive! The feeling of joy, indeed, of liberation, that suddenly streamed through him made him aware that the delusion he thought he had overcome was still lurking in the depths of his mind. Alberta's letter was brief and matter-of-fact. It demonstrated once more that inability to be surprised at even the strangest turns of fate that she possessed to an even greater degree than most women. Her letter revealed that she was living in Chicago and was married, though not to the American in whose company she had traveled across the ocean but rather to a German merchant whom she had met in America. "Next summer," the letter continued, "we're planning to travel to Europe, and if we come to Vienna and you still remember me and want to see me, I have a lot to tell you." Then she asked him how he had been and whether he had, as she fervently hoped, found a sweet, loving wife who didn't make him as nervous as she unfortunately often had—through no fault of her own, of course.

Robert paced up and down his room in a state of elation. He felt that with this letter a dark and dangerous epoch of his life had closed once and for all. Even if he no longer needed a document of this sort in writing to reassure him, it was invaluable as evidence against accusations and suspicions of all kinds. He put the letter away very carefully before he went to bed.

XII

The engaged couple looked for a modest house in the suburbs of Vienna. For the immediate future they depended upon Robert's salary and on a small income Paula had inherited from her grandparents, and Paula sometimes raised the question of her contributing to their household maintenance by giving violin lessons. When once, during such a discussion, the name of the dead composer came up, Robert gave her a long and searching look that seemed to request, even demand, an explanation.

They were standing on the little balcony of the house they had just rented. It was late in the afternoon; the first winter snow was softly falling, and dusk was sinking into the small, bare, and leafless gardens below them that were separated from one another by low walls. Paula wrapped her dark fur boa more tightly around her neck and turned back into the bare, newly whitewashed room where the housekeeper waited with her ring of keys. She accompanied them down the narrow staircase, illuminated only dimly by bare light-bulbs, then outside through a hallway strewn with loose boards and glazed tiles. They were now walking silently through sparsely peopled streets, arm in arm, toward a still quieter district where small front gardens announced the beginning of the villa quarter. Here the snow lay on the ground, where a moment before it had dissolved into a dirty grey beneath their feet. Finally Paula began, "I understood your look up there. So you've also heard people talk about it?"

"How could I not have? The story was almost famous."

"Was it?" She smiled to herself.

"How long has he been dead?" he asked, gently.

"Seven years," she replied.

"Did you love him?"

"He meant a lot to me. But I didn't love him. I loved someone else. Naturally, people didn't talk about that—it wouldn't have been especially interesting. The other man was a completely unknown young attorney. Maybe you knew him." And she named a young man whom Robert had met briefly a few times in social gatherings.

"Quite a handsome young fellow," he remarked casually.

"Yes, that he was—and about twenty years younger than the other."

"And why did nothing come of that?"

"I don't really know myself. Probably because both things were going on at the same time, and my heart was torn between the two of them."

"Your heart . . . ," he repeated softly, and took her hand.

She clasped her hand around his. "You're right. It wasn't only a matter of my heart. But there was never a real danger on either side. Maybe because I didn't know what would become of me. And so, as you said earlier, nothing came of it—neither marriage nor anything else . . . nothing."

"And you don't regret . . . perhaps missing out on happiness?"

"Sometimes I do—I won't deny that. But you forget, my dear," and she smiled wanly, "that I come from a respectable family."

He didn't reply, and they strolled on through the softly falling snow. How pure is such a life, he thought to himself, how pure and faultless! Am I worthy of her? She knows I'm a man of experience. But she doesn't ask any questions. Well, yes, why should she be that curious? She has no inkling that anything in my past is any different from the usual experiences of young men. She has no inkling of the darkness of my soul, of the evil desires that still haunt me like ghosts, of the terror that seizes me in bad hours, of the letter that's in my brother's hands, the frightful letter that gives him power over my life.

Suddenly he felt a choking fear rise up in him, novel and yet familiar. What had reminded him of the letter just now? What did the letter mean at this point? It was only valid in a specific instance that didn't apply now and would never apply. He wasn't insane; he was sane. But what good was that if others thought him insane? What good would it do him if in the end even his own brother thought him insane? Wasn't it possible that it was precisely this recent wonderful change in his mental state, this feeling of elation, of ease, of happiness that might strike a jaundiced eye as a sign of an impending mental collapse? Only a few days ago Marianne had expressed to him her growing concern about her husband's pale and strained appearance—and when Robert had ventured a brotherly admonition to Otto, he had been struck by his disproportionate irritation, by the almost rude manner of his reply. As he remembered it now, it even seemed to him that Otto's manner and behavior toward him had strangely altered recently. Could he be more disturbed than I am? thought Robert. Otto the sick one? . . . Otto alone?

"What's wrong," asked Paula, "did I hurt your feelings in some way?"

He got hold of himself. "Darling," he whispered, and pressed her hand. But he could no longer subdue his inner unrest. He thought of the possibility of a malicious twist of fate—that just now, when he felt himself newly awakened to life and destined for a quiet happiness, his unfortunate brother should think himself justified and even obligated to exact the fulfillment of that fearful promise. In order to excuse his suddenly darkened mood, he thought it necessary to tell Paula that for weeks he had been tortured by a growing anxiety about his brother's health. Recently Otto was taking on more professional commitments than even the strongest constitution could long endure. He talked about him with love, even with passion, and in doing so felt his heart swell with a painful and burning compassion.

Moved, Paula listened. She knew Otto only superficially, but had always, from a distance, had a warm regard for him that was confirmed and justified last year by a chance meeting with him at the bedside of a sick friend. Robert's remark aroused her regard even more; she asked him not to postpone the visit they had been planning to pay him any longer, and so they made a date to see him the very next day.

XIII

This first visit to his brother's house went splendidly. The boys immediately took to the new aunt who brought them picture books and sweets. Marianne's cool politeness gradually warmed, and the friendly mocking banter that was characteristic of Otto in casual conversation made Paula feel like an old friend from the beginning. In this atmosphere of mutual goodwill, Robert's disquieting thoughts gradually lost their power. Many times he felt he was moving under newly auspicious stars and believed he could confidently look forward to the future.

But one night, after a sociable evening at his brother's house, Robert found himself unable to sleep for the first time in a long while. He heard the clock in the church steeple strike quarter-hour after quarter-hour, and tried to remember whether anything unpleasant or embarrassing had occurred in the course of the evening. At first he searched in vain for the probable cause of his growing discomfort. The evening had passed pleasantly enough. Robert and Paula had announced their engagement and had received hearty and unaffected congratulations from all sides; there had been a little music, and at the end, over coffee and cigars, the company had chatted in spontaneously changing small groups. One of Otto's close professional colleagues had drawn Robert into what seemed like an innocent conversation; he now remembered that at one point he had offered to light the professor's cigar and in the process had dropped the match. Evidently his hand had trembled slightly. He remembered that the professor had fixed him with a peculiar, searching gaze when this happened. Robert was also conscious of having spoken very rapidly and of having made a few slips of the tongue, as he was prone to do after two or three glasses of wine. It was certainly not unthinkable that all these trivialities, combined with a certain change in his manner and expression, particularly the undeniable, still present disparity of his eyelids, might have caught a practiced physician's eye. And he wondered whether Otto, not fully trusting his own sharp eye in this special case, had asked his colleague to observe Robert unobtrusively. One thing was certain: the two of them, Otto and the professor, had afterward carried on an intense conversation in a window nook. And at one point, Otto had fleetingly glanced at his brother and then quickly looked away.

Seized by a sudden disquiet, Robert turned on the light, sprang out of bed, and stepped in front of the mirror. The face that confronted him, with its wan cheeks, distended eyes, and disheveled hair, an unfamiliar expression around the lips, shocked him deeply. Was that really his face? Yes, of course it was, but it was a face that would be seen only by someone with the ability to look beneath the carefully groomed mask of everyday life to the genuine face below—the face on which the anxieties that had stalked him for half his life and had finally driven him away from home were engraved. Even if their power had diminished in the last few weeks, those around him could hardly know this, and it was reasonable to suppose that Otto, who for many years had feared he would suffer a serious mental illness, perhaps even an outbreak of insanity, would continue to observe him—and have him observed.

He had never seen this professor in his brother's house before; it couldn't be merely chance that he had been invited tonight. Obviously Otto was uneasy and worried about him—now, in these happier days, even more so than before. Just now, when Robert's outer and inner lives were beginning to take a turn for the better, when for the first time in twenty years he could face the future with his head held high, he had become more and more the object of his brother's suspicion. But couldn't the reason for this growing mistrust come just as well—in fact, wasn't it more likely to come—from Otto rather than from himself? Couldn't it be that Otto, recognizing the first signs of a mental disturbance in himself and shrinking away from acknowledging it, was satanically trying to ward disaster off his own person by projecting it onto another for whom in his opinion it was long predestined—his own brother? How many times had he heard and read that mad people believe others around them to be mad? That a completely sane person was declared mad and locked up in an asylum? And there was nothing more difficult to reverse than a mistake of this sort once attention had been focused on the wrong person.

Robert remembered court cases and newspaper accounts telling of accidental, frivolous, or criminal cases of this sort. And how likely such a mistake was in his case! All his life, at least since Höhnburg's breakdown, he had been plagued by all sorts of obsessive ideas and, worse, delusions. And he had not only confessed them to his brother but had practically begged him to do away with him if the ultimate horror should become reality—had not only begged him to do it but had forced a document upon him that obligated him to do it while absolving him of all responsibility. It might have been that cursed document that had planted the seeds of delusion in Otto in the first place. Wouldn't his delusion otherwise have developed in a completely different direction? Fortunately Otto didn't appear to be completely certain of his suspicions about Robert—otherwise he wouldn't have felt it necessary to look for allies to corroborate his diagnosis. Of course it was always easy to find allies, especially in a case of this sort, when the one with suspicions was a highly esteemed neurologist whom no one would suspect of having problems with his own nerves, and the suspect was the doctor's brother, a man who from childhood had been considered nervous, eccentric, and even actually crazy by many of those around him, and who, moreover, had just traveled around the continent for months on sick leave, unable to work.

But as alarming as matters seemed to be at this moment, as

much as he had to be on guard, all was not yet lost. There was no one right now who actually considered him insane in the literal sense of the word, with the exception perhaps of Otto. And if others, even the doctors, couldn't yet recognize Otto's serious disturbance—of course it wasn't actual insanity yet—then he, Robert, being the only one who saw matters clearly, had the right, indeed the duty, to warn Otto's closest associates about the threatening danger, and this by no means merely because he wanted to divert suspicion from himself. Of course he had to be careful. Since Otto had sought allies, there was nothing to prevent him from doing the same; in fact it was his duty and his responsibility to do so, for Otto's sake above all. He thought of Dr. Leinbach. Even if many of Leinbach's professional colleagues had doubts about his professional competence or perhaps even the sharpness of his mind, he had been close to Robert since childhood, was his friend, and even loved him in his own way. And it was precisely because he was not restricted to any one field and was very far from being a specialist of any sort that he was, in this case, the most incorruptible judge. He, more than anyone else, would be capable of grasping the uniqueness and the difficulty of Robert's position; he would be the one most likely to help him and stand by him. He needn't tell him everything at once, after all, and at first he wouldn't say any more than was urgently necessary. So Robert decided to talk to Leinbach the very next day but to take no one else, not even Paula, into his confidence.

This decision calmed him to the point that he smiled at his reflection in the mirror. When, naturally, it smiled back, he was pleased, though he knew this was absurd. He slept soundly the rest of the night and felt almost refreshed the next morning and able to perform his duties at work as usual, indeed even with heightened satisfaction, which further lifted his spirits. And when later that afternoon he walked into Paula's room, she wouldn't have noticed anything strange about him even if she hadn't been distracted by important news. Her father, she told her fiancé, was for the time being staying in an Italian port town waiting to hear from one of his boyhood friends in America. What he did next depended on what he heard from that source. It seemed there was a possibility that a new career might open up for him in journalism. And his letter showed an almost youthful hope and excitement, even a certain lust for travel and adventure that, Robert noticed with astonishment, seemed not only pardonable but also completely normal to his wife and daughter. Robert soon left with the remark that he had an appointment with Leinbach, whom he hadn't seen since his engagement to Paula.

He had asked his friend to meet him at the usual café, as he also wanted the opportunity to be seen by those of his social circle who might have found his long absence strange. They all congratulated him heartily on his engagement, though August Langer did so with a peculiar malicious twitch at the corner of his mouth—as though he wished to indicate that as far as he was concerned, he could fortunately afford to be completely indifferent to the fate of this new victim his former relation had found. Robert recognized immediately, however, that this interpretation, which for a split second he had been ready to attribute to a meaningless play of features, was merely the last flickering of an absurd and now long-abandoned delusion.

Dr. Leinbach seemed somewhat offended at having heard of the important event in his friend's life only by rumor. But he let himself be easily appeased by Robert's assurance that the public announcements of engagements had always seemed to him superfluous and indelicate. Leinbach took up and even enlarged upon Robert's view by maintaining that he was confident that in a more civilized epoch, wedding announcements and public wedding celebrations would be discontinued as barbaric customs. Robert let him continue for a while in order to put him into a good mood, but finally, when Leinbach threatened as usual to lose himself in an interminable philosophical discussion, he interrupted him with the comment that he had asked him to come here for a very specific and unfortunately very serious reason. Under pledge of complete secrecy he confided his worries about Otto's mental health to Leinbach and asked him whether Otto's restless gaze, exaggerated irritability, and odd manner of walking, had not recently struck him, too.

"I see him very seldom," said Dr. Leinbach, wrinkling his forehead.

"I also want to assure you," Robert continued, "that I'm not the only one who thinks Otto has changed. Marianne thinks so too. And if you saw him more often, you certainly wouldn't have failed to notice how much gloomier and more depressed he's become over the last year."

"Depressed?" repeated Leinbach in a self-important manner. "I should think so. Of course he's more depressed. How could it be any different? I'm also getting more depressed, even if it's less evident with me than with Otto. Maybe you notice it more with him than with me, since you're close to him. But believe me, if you ever meet a doctor who at a certain age, say between forty and fifty, is still lighthearted, he's either a butcher or a quack. Just think," and here Leinbach's voice quaked a little, "after all, in a certain sense we're destined to take upon ourselves the sufferings of all who bring their complaints to us, even if we aren't directly aware of doing so. It might be even worse if we were. The sentimental ones do better, to be sure; they're able to abreact their emotional tensions case by case. But with us, the strong, it accumulates. Naturally it isn't generally apparent, or we would present a truly tragic spectacle. Only those who love us notice what you quite rightly call depression. As a matter of fact, no one knows anything about any of us except the people who love us. We ourselves. . . ."

Robert gave up listening to him any further. He saw that he would get nothing from this quarter. He should have known better.

Why had he told his worries to this fatuous twit anyway? At the very least, it was careless of him.

August Langer and Kahnberg, who seemed to have completely forgotten the recent embarrassing scene, approached and invited Robert to join them in a card game. Robert gladly accepted the proposal and soon found himself so pleasantly entertained that he almost regretted having given up this innocent pastime for so long. Leinbach watched the game, at first in silence. But soon he couldn't resist tossing in comments of a general nature, especially on the topic of what was superficially called "luck" in gambling but which he, for his own part, had always recognized as an expression of hidden connections which of course were hidden from the player himself. Robert felt a growing irritation with him; suddenly he threw his cards on the table and angrily declared that he refused to listen to any more words of wisdom from this "philosophical busybody." Leinbach laughed, to be sure, but soon left and disappeared from the café without saying goodbye to Robert. Robert now regretted his vehemence all the more as his fellow card players gave him odd looks and exchanged significant glances with one another. He pulled himself together, went on with the game, and by the time they settled accounts an hour later, he had good reason to believe that they had completely forgotten his earlier outburst of temper. Nevertheless, as he went home he could not deceive himself that he—who after all had come to acquire an ally—was now even more alone if that were possible; and, what was even worse, even more of an object of suspicion.

XIV

The next morning, instead of going to his office, he set out on a walk that led him into a distant Prater neighborhood which was almost completely deserted at this time of year, especially on such a dreary, foggy day as this. No one would suspect that he was here. He had a feeling of complete safety; no danger threatened him from any quarter. Later he had a simple lunch in a well-heated cozy inn and suddenly realized with some surprise that he had not thought of his bride once in the course of the last few hours. Even now, as he evoked her image, she appeared to him not sharply delineated, as befitted her being the most important figure in his present life, but with blurred outlines, as though she already belonged to a period in his past. He saw her standing on the little balcony, snowflakes whirling about her, her hands propped on the railing and looking down. But there was nothing in the view below her that resembled in the slightest the suburban gardens they had just viewed; instead it was the Italian town softly blurred by a misty haze, where he had strolled about with his first wife on their honeymoon so many years ago. Yet he felt no yearning, either for the long-departed or for his present beloved. If there was anyone for whom he longed right now, he realized with a feeling of strangeness, it was none other than that pathetic and faded piano teacher he thought he had forgotten. He felt that of all persons now living, she was perhaps the only one who truly belonged with him and whose fate was mysteriously intertwined with his own. The fact that the lines of their destinies had crossed at a certain point, only in order to be flung ever farther and farther apart, seemed to him to have a hidden meaning, to be a prophecy of sorts. And the image of the pale woman gradually became so vivid that it seemed to him she was actually walking by outside the window of the inn, and slowly disappearing into the leafless pastures. He asked himself: Was this a warning sign, a premonition?

That the apparition had some meaning, even if it had only risen from his own mind to materialize in the winter fog of this day, he did not doubt. But what did it mean? Something good or something bad? To whom could he confide such things? he asked himself. No one would understand, and yet these things are perhaps the most meaningful of all that happen to us. That's why one is so alone.

In this little pub, in the dusk of an early December afternoon, where no one would ever expect him to be at this hour, he felt suddenly, strangely disconnected from all the human relationships to which he had felt attached as recently as this morning. All of them—his fiancée, his brother, and his friends—seemed like shadows of the past. And similarly, he felt that he was nothing but a faint image in their memory. At first this idea gave him a strange, almost sweet shudder, but gradually it changed into a mute dread. Finally an anxiety arose in him that drove him back into the city through deserted, damp and darkening streets, as though every step that brought him closer to the hustle and bustle of everyday life had the power to transform the faint image that dwelt in the hearts of those who cared about him into a sharp and vivid one.

And then he remembered once again that, indeed, there was a being in the world who was really there for him, who belonged to him forever—that he had a brother who remembered him and loved him, loved him perhaps even more than Paula did, loved him more than anyone else in the world had ever loved him; someone who in his love was prepared to do the unspeakable and the monstrous, and take upon himself the most profound measure of guilt in order to save him from a life of insanity.

He shuddered. Suddenly he became aware once again of the imminent danger that threatened him. The letter! Otto had in his hands the letter on which Robert's fate and very life depended! The letter had to be destroyed—this above all. There was nothing to do but to get it away from his brother—by bribery, command, or threat. He had to have a talk with Otto about it—about the letter and much else. . . . Whatever had developed between them, enigmatic and deep, perhaps even in early childhood, this interplay of understanding and misunderstanding, of brotherly love and alienation, of love and hate—all that had finally to be expressed. It still wasn't too late for them; once again he had his destiny in his own hands, just as his brother did. The time had come for Otto to decide between health and illness, between clarity and confusion, between life and death. As for him, he had already decided. His mind was clear; his sanity was saved. Now his brother, too, had the opportunity to choose for one last time.

As Robert entered, Otto looked up from the ledger in which he was writing. Robert read surprise, mistrust, and a slight alarm in his look. He felt a little like a student who has to take an important examination while insufficiently prepared and so is forced to rely completely on the inspiration of the moment for his answers. Robert assumed an exaggeratedly bright tone, which he felt immediately to be artificial.

"Yes, it's me," he said. "At a somewhat unusual hour for me, of course. Am I perhaps intruding?"

"Absolutely not," answered Otto, and looked at his watch. "Won't you sit down? How's your fiancée?"

"Fine, thanks. She has her hands full, as you can imagine. We've rented a place . . . you know, the one we recently told you about, overlooking the gardens. But not to detain you any longer than necessary . . . I've come for a very specific reason. As I told you recently, I'm trying to act in a manner appropriate to my present circumstances . . . ," he smiled as though embarrassed, which immediately seemed childish to him, " . . . and trying to get my old papers in order. Among them I found, among others, letters from our now long-dead friend Höhnburg." Otto nodded to indicate that he understood. "And in doing so," continued Robert, "it occurred to me that you must still have in your possession a rather ridiculous document from me that I'd like to have back."

"A ridiculous document?" Otto looked at him strangely.

"Don't you remember?" asked Robert. And, too rapidly, he immediately recognized, the explanatory words escaped him: "My death warrant." And he laughed.

"Your death warrant?" Otto repeated, apparently still without understanding. But immediately afterward a flash of comprehension in his eyes revealed that he understood.

"So you do remember?" Robert interrupted, as though he had caught his brother in some misdeed, and laughed again.

Otto grimaced in his mocking way. "I can't guarantee that I still have that document in my possession; I'm in the habit of cleaning out all of the stuff that accumulates over the course of time every few years, and it wouldn't be at all unlikely that your letter was consigned to the flames like a lot of other things. But if you think it's important, I'll have a look." He spoke with what seemed like studied ease.

"If you have time," said Robert quickly, "I'd be grateful because . . . I know you'll understand . . . I don't want it to fall into my nephews' hands one day and give them an occasion to make fun of their long-dead, crazy uncle."

"You're awfully concerned about your postmortem reputation," said Otto. "But it's possible that I've thought about it unconsciously already, and that the admittedly rather ridiculous document probably doesn't exist any more. In any case, I don't remember seeing it for years."

"I wouldn't have thought about it again either, naturally, but the new phase of life that I'm beginning . . . you understand, Otto, don't you? Well, one would like to leave everything reminiscent of the darker periods in one's life far behind; one would like to know that every trace of them had vanished from the world. . . . Unfortunately it isn't as easy with everything as it is with a piece of paper."

Otto had gotten up and with an uncharacteristically warm gesture now put his hands on his brother's shoulders as he sat in an armchair facing him. And with an altogether too friendly smile, he said, "Did you really ever seriously think I would make use of the power you so trustingly gave me?" And with a somewhat forced effort to make a joke, he added, "I would've had to do it a long time ago!"

"Naturally, I can't say you'd have been wrong," answered Robert, distressed, "but now everything is different, thank God. Yes, Otto, my finding Paula is a singular piece of good luck, completely undeserved." To his own astonishment he found he was able to speak to his brother more freely and more openly than ever before. He talked about how he had muddled along aimless and lost for so many years, how he had been dissatisfied with his official duties, how everything had bored him, how he had been harassed and driven time and time again by peculiar and absurd obsessions, and how the whole world had become brighter since Paula came into his life; how he was now finding unaccustomed pleasure even in his work, and most especially in music, since in that area, too, his fiancée was showing herself to be a true companion; and finally, how only now he felt that the heavy cloud that had always weighed on him had been lifted. But he was well aware that everything he said was meant not merely as a description of himself, was not only a kind of confession, but had the ulterior motive of appeasing his brother, distracting him from his delusion, and enlightening him.

"It's certainly fortunate," Otto interrupted his brother's copious flow of words, "that you've finally found the right woman, and you can be sure we all share your happiness. By the way, has the date of the wedding been set yet?"

What does he mean by asking me that? Robert asked himself. Is he giving me a reprieve until then? In the end, is his main concern that I don't bring blighted posterity into the world? But he was able to reply quite calmly, "We don't have an exact date yet. March, I think. We want to be able to go away on a honeymoon right away."

Otto smiled. "So you're only marrying in order to have an excuse to take another trip?"

"Not a long one, this time. I can't take another couple of months of leave again."

"Where do you two want to go?"

"To the Dalmatians. I want to show Paula Spalato, the palace of Diocletian, Ragusa. . . ."

Otto nodded. Years ago, as children, the two brothers had spent an Easter holiday with their parents in that region. Otto reminded Robert of many details of their vacation, and his voice sounded so warm, so intimate—especially as he then began to talk about other, long-forgotten things and finally also about their family home, a very old building in the city center, now long gone—that Robert began to have a wonderful feeling of security such as he had not felt in a long time. But it only lasted a short time. Suddenly he was ashamed of this feeling—as though he had been duped. He raised his head abruptly and looked his brother in the eye with such a cold and searching expression that Otto couldn't help being taken aback. And suddenly, with horror, Robert saw a face he knew. It was the same one that had stared out at him from the mirror that recent night—it was his own face, pale, with widely distended eyes, and an expression of deep suffering around the lips. The resemblance was so extraordinary, so compelling, that the thought struck him like lightning: had it actually been his brother's image, and not his own, that had stared back at him from the mirror, as a warning or a threat? Had it been the eternal power of blood that had asserted itself as a mysterious sign in a moment of significance?

It was only natural that Otto's expression changed at once, since he must have felt observed, yes, discovered. A smile that was close to a grimace appeared on his lips and he said, embarrassed, "Well, my dear boy, old times, old times. How long we could talk like this . . . ! But unfortunately . . ." He broke off, closed his ledger, arranged the books and papers on his desk, automatically felt for his appointment book in his breast pocket, then turned back to Robert, who had also gotten up. "By the way, have you already seen the children and Marianne?" Robert shook his head. Otto continued with too obvious eagerness, "Did I tell you that Marianne fairly raves about Paula?" He had rung and asked the entering servant whether Marianne was at home. She had gone out, so Robert accompanied his brother into the children's room, where they were just getting their supper and weren't happy that their uncle had come only to say good night and immediately afterward left again with their father, to whose hurrying they had become accustomed.

On the stairs Otto expressed his hope of seeing Robert and his fiancée again very soon at another informal evening at his house. "We'd be delighted," answered Robert. But to himself he thought, I'll do nothing of the kind! What for? In order to have myself observed by another so-called expert? "And I hope you two will occasionally play music together at our house, also," said Otto. "I hear that your fiancée plays the violin beautifully." From his carriage Otto gave another nod to his brother, who acknowledged his farewell with a bright smile.

It's high time to take precautions, thought Robert as he walked away. He's the famous doctor; no one will doubt the correctness of his diagnosis. By the time the truth comes out, it'll be too late. By that time I might long have gone really crazy in an insane asylum. Wouldn't it be the better part of valor to get out of Otto's sight for a while? It wouldn't be unthinkable that his delusion would then, so to speak, let go of me and fasten on someone else. I've experienced something like that myself, after all, when I still had obsessions. Out of sight, out of mind . . . out of sight, out of madness, I should perhaps say. But I won't go away by myself. No . . . I'll take Paula with me. Will she agree to come? Certainly! She'll agree to anything I want . . . I have only to say the word.

Paula had been anxiously awaiting him. "Where have you been all day?" she asked. He was surprised, for he had long since forgotten that he hadn't been to the office that day. Now Paula told him that this morning she had called him twice at his office in vain, had then asked for him at his hotel, and in the afternoon had twice called his brother to ask if he was expected there. Robert found it extremely strange that Otto hadn't even mentioned this, but immediately said to himself that it was important not to show either mistrust or embarrassment. So, humorously, he played the part of the sinner caught in the act; he confessed that he had felt an irresistible desire to play hooky just as he had in carefree childhood, and had driven out into the countryside early in the morning.

Paula seemed glad to let herself be convinced, and contented herself with small reproaches that he hadn't informed her of his intention and taken her with him to the countryside. They sat, as they were by now accustomed to, in Paula's charming girlhood room, done all in white, with a rosy light from a shaded ceiling lamp falling over the pictures and the carpets. Robert pulled Paula tenderly into his arms, but he was distracted. Vague plans of flight ran through his mind, and he tried in vain to give them a more substantive character. "What's the matter, dear?" asked Paula.

Just at this moment he had an inspiration that seemed to him particularly well suited to his purpose. He remarked as though incidentally, "Whom do you think I saw today? . . . The fiancé of the young woman I told you about a few days ago."

"Which young woman? . . . Despite your discretion, you've mentioned more than one."

"I'm talking about the one with whom I spent a few weeks in Switzerland last summer."

"Alberta? You ran into her?"

"Not into her, but her fiancé."

"The American?"

"Right, the American."

"Her husband then?"

"What? Oh, of course." He had completely forgotten that he hadn't told her anything about Alberta's last letter. But he recognized at once that he could use this fact to further his plan. And he said, "You're right. If he married her, as I assume he did, he must be her husband now. I didn't think of that at all."

"Then Alberta must be in Vienna too?"

"Possibly. I saw only him."

"Did you talk to him?"

"No, he didn't notice me at all. He was on the other side of the street." And quickly, as though he thought the meeting he had just invented was quite unimportant, he changed the subject and talked at length about the decoration of their future home and certain things they needed to get in order to set up house.

After dinner, with the help of Paula's mother, they drew up a detailed list of everything they needed and made a date to go shopping together downtown the next day. It was already late when Robert said goodbye in an apparently quite lighthearted mood, thinking that the last traces of uneasiness had vanished from Paula's mind too.

XV

As Robert left his room the next morning, he found his brother standing in front of his door. Robert felt himself turn pale but succeeded in hiding his shock. He exclaimed as though delighted, "It's you! It's really good to see you here. Won't you . . ."

"You're about to leave?" asked Otto. He stood in the doorway, both hands buried in the pockets of his fur coat, with an altogether too cheerful face.

"Oh, I'm not at all in a hurry. Do come in." And he closed the door behind Otto, who had followed him into the room.

"What I wanted to ask you," began Otto, "was whether you and Paula and her mother would like to come to dinner at our house this evening."

"We'd be delighted to! Very much so!"

"And at the same time I thought I would use this as an opportunity to have a look at your room, since you won't be here much longer."

He viewed the room from all angles. "Very attractive," he said. He walked over to the window and seemed lost in thought as he looked at the statue of the saint, whose stone folds were filled with frozen snow. Robert, also in his overcoat, and hat in hand, stood behind him and kept his eyes fastened on Otto's bowed grey head, which protruded from his fur collar and now seemed peculiarly alien to him, as though it were that of a tired old man he didn't recognize. What does this visit mean? he asked himself. What does he want here? Suddenly a question raced through his mind. Could Otto have brought along a poisonous powder that would spread through the room and have its dangerous effect later? Just in case, he resolved to open the window after Otto left. Suddenly Otto turned around. Robert assumed an expression of indifference and noticed that Otto's eyes seemed to blur slightly. Immediately afterwards Otto walked over quite close to him and said, smiling, "I hope you've come to your senses at last."

"At last?" repeated Robert, adopting the same jocular tone. "It's impossible to know that for sure, especially where I'm concerned. And is it so desirable, after all, to be sensible, completely sensible?"

"In my opinion, definitely yes," said Otto, sternly.

"Well, that remains to be proven," replied Robert, obstinately. "Maybe I really am crazy. I won't argue about it. But if I'm crazy, I'm feeling really good at the very same time. And that's the main thing, isn't it?" Suddenly he saw a new way to salvation. "I've never felt so good before," he repeated with emphasis. "So don't worry about me. I assure you, I wouldn't change places with anyone in the world."

Otto's face had remained impassive. "Well, then everything's in good shape," he said. He sounded distracted. And then, as though it had just now occurred to him, he took a folded piece of paper from the pocket of his overcoat. "Before I forget," he said casually, "here's your letter."

"What letter?" said Robert, really unable to remember at the moment.

"The one you requested yesterday. Luckily, I was able to find it. Here it is."

Robert gave a sigh of relief, as though he had received a merciful pardon. His eyes moistened, and he couldn't hold back his tears. Irresistibly drawn, he sank down sobbing onto his brother's chest. For a while he remained there, feeling Otto's kind, shy hands gently stroke his hair, so that he couldn't help but think of long-past childhood days and long-forgotten parental caresses. But suddenly—just as he was becoming conscious of this wonderful feeling of security—the thought ran through his head: What does this mean? Why did he search for the letter? Why did he bring it back to me? Is he trying to lull me into a false sense of security? Yes, that's it! He's taking on the responsibility of acting even without the letter! Other people must have seen it. Otto made a copy and had it certified by a notary. He doesn't need the original any more. Now he thinks I can't escape him any longer. Now he's lowering the boom on me. His hands are stroking my hair, but it's not a blessing, it's a farewell and a judgment. At the same time Robert knew that everything depended on his not betraying what he was thinking. And he remained hanging on his brother's neck until he had collected himself and composed his face into an expression of calm seriousness. Then he disengaged himself and looked cheerfully at his brother's face, which now wore a faint, masklike smile. Had Otto already resolved to do what the letter he had deceptively returned gave him the power to do?

Robert wasn't sure about it. He only knew that Otto's resolve, even if it were wavering at the moment, might in the next moment become irrevocable. There was only one thing left for him to do—to flee. Flee this very day! Because tomorrow it might already be too late. Where to? What difference did that make? The details could be settled once he left the city with Paula. His facial muscles obeyed him so well that they didn't reveal the slightest hint of what was going on inside him. He held the letter that Otto had given him in his hands, perused it fleetingly without actually reading it again, ripped it up into small pieces, and threw it into the fire with a little humorous smile to his brother. "And now it's ashes," said Otto dramatically, with a pathos that was unusual for him.

How clumsy, thought Robert, and kicked the door of the stove shut.

"But you probably should have been at the office long ago," said Otto in an exaggeratedly brisk tone. "May I offer you a ride?"

"Thanks, but I like to take a bit of a walk in the clear winter air before work." He opened the window as he had resolved to, and left the room with his brother.

"So we can definitely count on seeing both of you at our place this evening, all right?" Otto asked on the stairs.

Robert nodded. Everything was clear to him now. The deed was to be done this evening—a little powder in his wine or his coffee . . . and it was all over. And the explanation would be: he had had a heart attack. It was the simplest thing in the world; how often events of this sort might happen with no one the wiser.

At the door Otto shook hands once more with his brother, asked Robert to be punctual, climbed into his carriage, hastily took up a newspaper, and already seemed completely absorbed in it by the time the carriage moved away. Robert reflected that, in any event, the hours until eight this evening remained to him. Until then there was no threat of danger, and he could plan and prepare everything calmly. First he went to his office to put in an appearance so as not to arouse suspicion. Once at his desk he noticed with amazement that his work absorbed his interest completely, as though everything else in his life were in perfect order. He wrote down a few notes and some supplementary commentary, which he found so easy to do that he almost regretted not being able to finish the report for the present. He exhaustively discussed various details of his report with Baron Prantner, who had called him into his office around noon. Robert then asked for a short leave so that he could finish it undisturbed either at home or somewhere in the countryside. It occurred to him that he could actually take the manuscript with him wherever he went, finish it, and then send it back to the ministry as conclusive proof of his mental health.

"What's the matter?" he suddenly heard the baron's voice say, as though in a dream. And, rousing himself, he immediately asked himself whether he had betrayed his secret thoughts with his eyes or facial expression. The baron's frightened look led Robert to conclude that he already had suspicions about him. He remembered a series of petty incidents recently to which he, foolishly, hadn't attached any significance: peculiar, furtive looks from his colleagues, the sudden abrupt end of a conversation between the department head and the baron when he had come upon them unexpectedly. And he trembled with shame and anxiety at the thought that everyone around him had been warned about him as a mental case long ago. Yes, perhaps at this very hour Otto was with Paula, sowing the seeds of the most awful suspicion in her heart so as to appear justified to her and to others when he did the deed, to seem in fact to be Robert's helper, even his savior.

"What's the matter?" the baron asked again, putting his hand on Robert's shoulder.

A moment's reflection told Robert that he had better control himself outwardly in order to prevent a dangerous suspicion from turning into a mistaken certainty. He wiped his forehead and calmly answered, "Nothing, Herr Baron, nothing but a headache, a fleeting pain which sometimes overcomes me as though to remind me of my nervous condition last year. It's already gone."

Visibly relieved, the Baron sighed. "Well, that's good," he said. "Let's hope that even this last reminder will disappear for good in the countryside. . . ."

"Oh, I don't need any more rest, Herr Baron . . . not at all. The short leave, which you are so kindly granting me, really is for the purpose of enabling me finally to finish my report. I know I've already taxed your patience waiting for the final draft." And in a few terse sentences he finished explaining the details of his report. The baron nodded, satisfied, and when Robert finally left, the baron seemed to have completely forgotten the little incident.

XVI

The noon bells were ringing throughout the city when Robert hurried to Paula by the shortest route. She seemed astonished, even a little shocked, when she saw him enter her sunlit room at an hour so unusual for him. The cheerful expression that he had learned to assume visibly calmed her, and he recognized immediately that she, at least, had not yet been warned about him. Had that been the case, he had decided that he would tell her at once about the unhappy delusion that had taken over his brother's mind. Now that could wait, and he could even use the scenario he had invented yesterday for his own purposes again. He embraced her tenderly, and in a passionate tone, to which she was by now not unaccustomed, he asked her, "Could you decide to go away with me?"

"Go away?"

"Just for a few days. To the countryside."

"The countryside. With . . . with you, just you?"

"Yes, with me, just me, me alone." He drew her to him.

"Why, what's happened?" she asked with her eyes wide open.

"Nothing as yet. I told you yesterday that the American is here. Today I can tell you more. He's here because of me."

"Because of you? What does that mean?"

"Just that he's up to no good."

"No good . . . ? I don't understand you."

"Last night, just as I was about to open the door to my hotel, I saw him skulking about across the street in the shadow of the church. He was undoubtedly waiting for me. You ask: why? The matter couldn't be simpler. Jealousy. Jealousy after the fact."

"Why do you think that? Is Alberta here too?"

"Alberta? That . . . I don't know. I really don't think so. She probably stayed in America. Maybe he killed her long ago."

"Killed her?" She stared at him.

He answered in a matter-of-fact tone. "Why not? That sort of thing is often done without anybody's finding out or even suspecting it. Anyway, that's not our concern. Let's assume she's alive." He laughed. "For me, and I hope a little for you too, the only important thing is that he's here and has designs on me. Last night I managed to get away from him; I succeeded in slipping through the door without his noticing me. He walked up and down beneath my window half the night . . . maybe even longer, I don't know, for I was finally able to fall asleep."

"And this morning?"

"He was nowhere to be seen. For the time being. He probably thinks I can't escape him in the end. But he'll find he's wrong. I'm going away. And you're coming with me."

He looked her directly in the eye; she merely nodded. "I'll take care of everything once we're on the trip. It won't be particularly difficult. But I want to disappear for a few days or weeks, since it would be simply ridiculous just to hand myself over to a madman. Or do you think that's cowardice?"

"How can you say that?"

"And you've got to come with me, Paula, you've got to! Naturally, you can't tell your mother beforehand. You can write her a note from the train station, that'll be sufficient. Paula, why don't you answer me? Do you regret—?"

"What should I regret?"

"That you promised to go away with me? Just tell me. Confess! You're experiencing certain petty bourgeois reservations. . . ."

"How can you say that, Robert! I was just thinking . . ."

"Thinking what?"

"Whether it wouldn't be better . . . shouldn't you, I mean . . . try to settle the matter right here?"

"Settle it? How do you imagine that? I have no time to lose, and no one must find out a word of what I just confided to you—it could cost us both our lives. Yes, you too! Just trust me entirely. I've considered everything thoroughly. I'll wait for you at the Western train station. Our train leaves at six o'clock sharp. You don't need to take a lot of things. At ten in the evening we'll arrive at the place that I've picked as a refuge for the moment."

"What place?"

"Don't be upset if I don't tell you right now. In the confusion of the moment you might let it slip out. Maybe that's only superstition, but you must indulge me in this, Paula. Just swear you'll be at the station at the appointed time—otherwise all is lost. Without you I'm

lost. Totally lost! I know that for sure! If you're not there, everything
will be over. And . . . if you don't come alone, it's all over too. Do
you understand? So, you'll be at the station and won't breathe a
word of this to anyone. No one, Paula, no one."

He wanted to add: "not even my brother," but he refrained.
"So . . . will you be there?"

"Of course I'll be there." She stood before him, deadly pale,
with a tortured smile. But he didn't notice that her features had dras-
tically altered.

"Well, then everything's all right," he said. "And now I have to
go, darling."

"To go?" she repeated in a trembling voice.

"I have a lot of things to do," he said, "even though it's a matter
of a trip of only a few days. So you must excuse me." He got up, and
she held his hands tight.

"Don't you want me to come with you part of the way?"

"No thanks, sweetheart. It's better if you just stay home and use
the time to prepare your things. Naturally you won't need to take a
lot of things with you on the trip—our honeymoon trip," he added
softly, pulling her to him passionately. He felt her tremble a little in
his arms and took it to be bridal excitement. "Till then," he said. He
kissed her cool lips, and then, with a playful nod, as though the
whole thing had been a joke, he left the room.

He hurried down the stairs, dreading that she would call out
after him, and even when he was on the street he walked rapidly.
Will it really be just for a few days? he asked himself. Do I really
think it possible that Otto will come back to his senses simply by
my disappearance? Isn't it much more probable that he'll interpret
my leaving as a new sign of the correctness of his theory, that he'll
try to discover my whereabouts, follow me, or have me followed,
and in the end will find me? No, he won't! I'll be smarter than he is!
They won't find me! What if I pretended to commit suicide? Not a

bad idea. A double suicide! Paula and I. We'll leave a letter . . . as is usual in such cases. People wouldn't even be particularly surprised. No one. Certainly not Baron Prantner. Nor Herr Kahnberg. Otto least of all. He would only find his *idée fixe* corroborated. I would merely have saved him the trouble. That's how he would interpret the matter. And he would be the winner. The winner? Is this a duel then? Do we really wish to trump each other? I've got to do it differently. I've got to prove—yes, prove—his insanity. Yes. That's the important thing. Otherwise I won't have any peace on this earth. We can't hide our whole lives, Paula and I, though that would of course be the best thing. To disappear, to begin a new life somewhere else, under another name if possible, to be somebody else! Oh, if only that were possible!

He stood in front of the bank where what was left of his modest assets were secured; he entered, withdrew a sizable sum, and talked to the officer, whom he knew personally, in a humorous and mysterious manner about a financial transaction that he was thinking of undertaking. He pocketed the money, hastily ate his lunch in a small bistro that he had never been in before, and was back at his hotel before two o'clock in the afternoon. The concierge told him that a gentleman had asked for him but had not left a card. The superficial description seemed to fit August Langer best; what was striking, however, was that, according to the concierge's report, another gentleman had waited in a carriage at some distance. So it had come to this! He hurried up the stairs to his room. He had no doubt that preparations were being made to take him to a mental asylum for observation. Naturally that would seal his fate. In any case, it would be stupid to waste another quarter of an hour here where he was no longer sure of his freedom, perhaps even of his life. He had to leave the hotel immediately, as though he were going for a walk, and take an earlier train than the one he had agreed on with Paula. He put his most important documents in his pockets, locked his cabinets, and left his room ten minutes after he had entered it. At the hotel entrance he lit a cigarette and strolled down the street deliberately.

In a street some distance away he hired a carriage, bought everything he needed for the next few days on the way to the train, including a suitcase in which he packed his purchases, and arrived at the train station a quarter of an hour before the departure of the three o'clock train. In the waiting room he hastily wrote a few lines to Paula. For reasons he could only tell her later in person, he had left a few hours earlier. But she should still leave Vienna at the previously agreed upon time. He would be waiting for her at ten o'clock in the evening at the station which he now named and which, at the risk of her life, she was not to reveal to anyone. He closed with these words, "I don't have time to write more. You know everything. Don't let me wait in vain. Darling, I beg you, don't reveal anything. My life—our lives—are at stake." He had the coachman who had taken him to the station take the letter to Paula. And a few minutes later he was sitting in the train.

XVII

Darkness was falling early on this hazy grey December day. Hardly was the train past the outskirts of Vienna and the small enclaves of villas when snow began to fall, at first lightly, then gradually becoming heavier and heavier so that the forest, the hills, the highways, and the rooftops soon shimmered with a soft, soothing whiteness. Robert had bought a few newspapers, and alone in his compartment he immersed himself in foreign and domestic news of so little interest to him that he soon fell asleep over it.

When he awoke again, the train was gliding through a narrow valley between two rocky bluffs. The snowflakes had stopped, and the frozen snow clinging to the gentler slopes and the fir trees illuminated the evening wonderfully. Soon the bluffs drew so close together that the roaring of the Ache River from the gorge below was amplified many times. Farther on, where the bluffs drew apart again, he could see a wide expanse of starry blue winter sky. When the train stopped at a station for a few minutes, Robert opened the window. The air was cold and refreshing, the stillness consoling and soothing. Robert became conscious of the strangeness of his journey. Could it, in the end, really be just a trip? Could what he had planned and undertaken as a flight be destined to end as a pleasure trip? For one last time hope stirred in him that perhaps he might have been wrong after all, that his brother was not insane, that all would turn out well, that he might even be in a position to tell Paula that the story of the jealous American had been merely a fairy tale, concocted for the purpose of luring her, his beloved, to agree to a premature honeymoon. But it didn't last long. He couldn't allow himself to be duped by the deceptive hope that he was sure came only from extreme nervous exhaustion. In reality it was only a sign of new danger. He remembered this morning's events, that last look in his brother's eye, and he knew that his was an authentic flight.

The train stopped at the little market town that Robert had chosen as a temporary refuge in memory of a few summer days he had spent there with Alberta. But now the town, which on his trip he had visualized as decked out in fresh green and summer colors, lay stretched out before him buried in winter snow, and he felt confronted by a completely different and alien place that he had never seen before. He gave his suitcase to a porter and followed him across a bridge over the roaring Ache and down a lane along the riverbank, which he remembered from that summer as a street with high, sheltering, overarching trees, and finally across a deserted square with a now silent fountain. They arrived at the country inn through an arched gate beneath which a faint, yellowish red light shimmered from a wrought iron street lantern. He was shown a large room with a high arched window that looked out on faintly shim-

mering mountains. On the wall above an old chest hung a life-size
oil print of the Madonna. At both sides of the broad bed hung modest cotton curtains. Robert said he would take the room and added
that his wife would arrive tonight with the next train, around ten
o'clock. The bulb hanging from the ceiling gave such a feeble light
that he felt it necessary to order some candles. They were put in two
brass candlesticks on the huge, rickety table, and then he was left
alone. For a while he looked out the window across rooftops, snow-
covered farmlands and wooded slopes to a bluff between whose
snow-covered fissures bare grey rock stared back at him, thin and
disembodied. As the wood in the green tile stove began to glow and
crackle, he seated himself, still in his fur coat, in the wide-armed
black leather armchair that had been drawn up beside the bed. Three
lonely hours lay ahead of him. He intended to use the time to write a
brief account of the circumstances that had impelled him to his sudden departure, indifferent to whether what he wrote would ever be
read by anyone or whether it would serve only to help him collect
his thoughts and regain his composure.

He sent for a few sheets of paper, sat down at the desk, and
with a surety of expression that he did not usually possess, wrote
down a sketch of his entire life from birth to the present, having in-
stinctively begun with the date of his birth and his earliest childhood
memories.

His pen flew across the paper for two hours, and the last sentences he wrote before stopping for the time being were: "Suspicion
of my own complicity in my brother's delusion. Are the two of us
perhaps split manifestations of one and the same divine idea? One of
us must go into the darkness. He was chosen, although formerly it
seemed to be my destiny." He locked what he had written into his
suitcase, left the room, and went outdoors.

Behind the frosted windows of the pub in the inn, a small circle
of villagers sat drinking beer; he could hear their boisterous talk in

the public square outside. He walked on and met only a few others, mostly peasants dressed in traditional garb. On a bench in the lane alongside the river a young couple sat in a tight embrace, mindless of the cold. Only then, with a rush of ardor, did he remember that he was waiting for his beloved. She'll be here in an hour, he said to himself, and until just now I didn't really think about her at all. How easy everything will be when she's with me again. Since I left her today at noon, everything has been like a dream. I've dreamt my whole life over in the meantime, and that's why it seems so infinitely long ago that I left Paula, almost longer than the day that I walked along this same riverbank with Alberta.

He crossed the bridge and soon afterward paced back and forth along the platform next to the train tracks. The dead-straight black train tracks, now covered in white, ran far, far into the darkness. The stationmaster went by and greeted him politely. From somewhere far away came a sound like that of humming wires. The nearby bluffs pierced the blue of the night. How peaceful it is here, thought Robert. Could there be a happy ending after all? Wouldn't even Otto recover in such peace and quiet? He had to recover! He had to! Would I ever have another peaceful hour, yes, could I even go on breathing if he were never to recover? And he knew that there was no one on earth who was dearer to him than Otto—felt once again that there was no relationship of such inner depth, more durable, and so ordained by nature itself, than that of brother to brother; that it was more deeply connected with the roots of being than the relationship to parents, children, and lovers; that he was resolved to master the fate that threatened to tear apart this most mysterious and at the same time strongest of all bonds between two human beings.

A distant whistle sounded and came ever closer; the roar of the oncoming train became stronger; then the train arrived at the station black and puffing. A man in a short hunting fur got off, then two peasants and an old woman. A porter came running and took the luggage from the man in the hunting fur with an obsequious greeting; there was a whistle, the train set in motion again, drove into the darkness, and disappeared.

Robert stood there and watched the train disappear, not quite understanding what was happening. After some time he left the train station, outwardly calm and, to his own amazement, inwardly not too disappointed. Slowly he went back to the inn and said to himself: I'll find a telegram waiting for me, or one will come within the next few hours. Either Paula missed the train or she has good reasons for taking a later one. Most probably she won't come now until tomorrow around noon, not at two in the morning. For that was the time the next train was scheduled to arrive.

There was no telegram. Robert entered the low-vaulted pub, where the same circle of local peasants was still sitting in a cloud of smoke in front of the window. At another table, all alone, sat an old man smoking a pipe and staring into a newspaper with tired eyes, obviously not reading. Robert, whom no one paid any attention to, sat down in a corner, ordered a supper that he greatly enjoyed, and thought things over. Soon he became convinced that his earlier assumptions had been nothing but self-deception. If Paula had really wanted to follow him, nothing could have prevented her from being there on time. But she hadn't wanted to; she hadn't come; she had left him in the lurch. And he knew why. His ridiculous story about the jealous American, his whole behavior today as he was leaving must have seemed peculiar and suspicious to her. With the crafty dissimulation of women, she hadn't let him notice anything; and, heedless of her promise, in her agitation she had done the very last thing on earth that she should have done—she had rushed to Otto and told him everything. Yes, that's what had happened. He was sure of it. Paula had betrayed him—had handed him over. And what would happen now? he asked himself. Otto now has new reasons for thinking me crazy; his own delusion finds more to feed on, and he won't have the slightest trouble convincing Paula and everyone else he pleases that his suspicions are justified. What stupidity to let Paula out of my sight and not immediately bring her with me! Now everything is worse than it was before. Otto knows where I am. He'll follow me. My flight has only served to put him on my trail. He thinks the time has come to keep his promise. I'm in the most terrible danger. The jig is up for me!

While he was weighing all this, he went on eating and drinking in apparently perfect tranquility and noticed with some surprise that his thoughts were coolly logical and not derailed by anxiety. Of course he had to do something. Logical deduction rather than fear made him realize he couldn't stay here, that he had to continue his flight. The only question was, where to? If his pursuers were not on his trail by tomorrow, they would be in a very few days, and even if he succeeded in leaving the country or even the continent and reaching the New World, there was no safety from a crazy person's *idée fixe.* In the end, the awareness of constant danger and endless pursuit could make him really lose his mind, so that he would succeed only in putting everyone else in the right, in playing into his brother's hands, so to speak, and—through a diabolic trick of fate— confirming his brother's delusion.

He left the pub and strolled up and down the snowy, deserted market square in a very leisurely fashion with a cigar in his mouth, so that any one who saw him would have taken him for a carefree winter tourist. Suddenly he thought of what he had written this evening. Couldn't I use it to help me in this struggle? he asked himself. Anyone who reads my biographical sketch can't possibly take me for insane. But I'll rewrite the whole piece entirely, in more detail, with more clarity. Tomorrow I'll take the first train out of town, then at some branch station along the way I'll take another train to someplace where no one would think to look for me, and there I'll carefully write down my accusation or my defense. Accusation or defense? Well, which was it? And he ruminated. Like a pale ghost, the image of that poor piano teacher with whom he had spent his last sorry night of love floated into his mind. And once again the strange doubt arose in him. Had not life posed him a question one last time in that encounter, a question that he had answered thoughtlessly, even cruelly? Once more he relived in memory the serious and melancholy expression with which the lonely creature had nodded to him from the carriage as it pulled away, and he remembered how he had returned her look stonily, with a cold heart. But he saw himself as completely different than he could have looked at that moment or indeed at any other. He saw himself, much too tall and thin, standing there in a black overcoat that blew around him, casting a long, thin shadow far out in front of him. But he was actually seeing this shadow in reality—he was just now walking past a lantern whose light glowed a dull yellow above the entrance of the inn.

He entered the inn and, just in case, asked once more whether a telegram had come for him. The proprietor explained that there was no telegraph service between seven o'clock in the evening and seven o'clock in the morning in the little village. At this news Robert fell back on his first assumption—that Paula might have missed the train—and he felt he could still entertain the possibility that she would arrive at two o'clock in the morning.

He went back to his room and, fully clothed, lay down on the bed. He thought he would rest for an hour, since it was already past midnight, and then go down to the station again. He didn't turn off the light and stared out at the darkness beyond the window across from his bed. He saw only the sky and a lonely, rocky peak over which a star glimmered. The church tower bells chimed half past midnight, and the notes echoed for so long that it seemed the night did not want to yield them up. They became louder, fuller, and finally swelled like the peal of an organ. Robert was strolling in an immense, totally deserted church with Dr. Leinbach, and seated at the organ—Robert didn't see him, but he knew it was him—was the pianist from the café, while Höhnburg worked the pedals and at the same time kept stretching his head far out over the choir railing and drawing it back in again like a jack-in-the-box. Leinbach explained that the man up there was not playing a Bach fugue at all, but rather setting his autobiography to music, as all talented pianists are known to do. Immediately afterward Robert, a red flag in his hand, was wandering between train tracks toward open countryside. He continuously waved it and finally planted it on a mound of earth, under which Alberta lay buried. Then he walked along a narrow mountain ridge with gorges on both sides, through a wondrous blue winter night. Finally, refreshed, with cool cheeks and looking forward to his work, he was just sitting down at his desk when suddenly there was a violent knocking at the door. He knew this could be none other than Alberta's husband, come to demand a reckoning with him. But he was determined not to open the door. Instead he left the room by means of the opposite door and dashed through a long row of rooms. In each room there was a table; at each table sat a writer whose fountain pen flew over paper with tremendous speed while with his left hand he threw sheets of paper into a suitcase that opened and shut automatically on its own, like crocodile jaws. At the same time the knocking continued and appeared to become even stronger and more insistent. Automatically Robert reached for his revolver, which he had put on his dressing stand as was his custom when traveling; he got up quickly, put the weapon in his jacket pocket, realized that he had just awakened, and thought: a telegram. And he asked, "Who is it?"

"It's me, Robert," a voice answered.

His blood froze. It was Otto's voice. So he had followed him immediately! He was here to fulfill his dreadful task. Luckily the door was locked.

"May I come in?" asked Otto. Before Robert was able to answer, the door opened. Robert had forgotten to lock it.

"What do you want?" asked Robert with his eyes widely distended and staring, simultaneously tormented by the knowledge that both of his eyelids were equally wide open.

Otto stood in the doorway in his fur coat with a thick scarf wrapped around his neck, facing him. He spoke hastily, "They told me below that you wanted to go to the train station at two, but you overslept. Still, I wouldn't have come up if I hadn't seen a light on in your room."

"Where's Paula?" asked Robert, hoarsely.

"Paula is coming tomorrow. For the present you'll have to content yourself with her greetings." All the while he had a frozen smile around his lips.

"What do you want here? Why are you here?" Robert sat up in the bed and was aware of the fierceness and threat in his look.

"Why did I come? Well . . . ," and there was a suppressed sob in Otto's voice, "well, damn it, I came because I wanted to. What are you thinking of, Robert? What have you got into your head now?"

"Why are you here? What do you want with me? Take . . . take your hands out of your fur coat!"

Otto stared at him. At first he didn't seem to understand. But then, with an exaggerated gesture, he drew both hands out of his coat pockets; he shook his head and moved his mouth as if trying to laugh, then bit his lips and said, "Evidently, you . . . you seem to be still dreaming. Come to your senses! It's me, Robert—your brother, your friend. What are you imagining? Your brother, Robert! It's not possible that . . . you can't believe in all seriousness that . . . you couldn't really . . . think . . ."

Words failed him. In his eyes was an expression of anxiety, compassion, and infinite love. But to his brother, the glistening of tears in them signified malice, menace, and death. Otto, shaken to the depths by the expression of terror in his brother's face, could restrain himself no longer and moved closer to Robert in order to embrace him and thus reassure him of his brotherly love through an un-reserved and warm gesture of intimacy. But Robert, feeling his brother's cool hands around his neck, now no longer doubted that the dreaded moment, the moment of acute and terrible danger, had arrived—a moment against which he was entitled to defend himself by any means possible, as all laws, both human and divine, permit-ted, indeed, commanded. With his hand in his jacket pocket he cau-tiously cocked the trigger of his revolver, and, while his brother hung around his neck, he thrust its muzzle against Otto's chest. Otto only now recognized what was happening. But at the instant he real-ized it and tried to seize the barrel of the weapon, to step out of the way and call out, the bullet pierced his heart, and he sank to the floor without a sound.

Robert, who had not yet become fully aware of what he had done, only now began to have an inkling of the horrible, irreversible deed that had taken place. In a dull fear of recognizing what had taken place on this spot, he stumbled by his brother's body, through the dark hallway, down the stairs, across the corridor, through the still open door of the inn, and across the deserted market square. He ran along the village road into the open countryside through deep snow, threw off the overcoat that hampered his flight, and rushed headlong on and on, farther and farther, with nothing else in his mind except the firm resolve never to come to his senses again, through a resonating blue night that would never end for him. And he knew that he had rushed along this same road a thousand times before, that he was destined to flee down it a thousand times more through all eternity, through endless, echoing blue nights.

Not less than seven hours from the village he had fled, on a stony overhang that led down to the nearly frozen Ache, with his head hanging down, with bruised hand and dried blood on his fore-head and scalp, Robert's lifeless body was found three days later.

The notes that were found in his suitcase were handed over to the courts and extracts were published. The case, in all its melancholy, was as clear as it could be: paranoia. Who could doubt it? Dr. Leinbach of course had his own ideas about it, which he didn't hesitate to confide to his carefully kept diary. "My poor friend," he wrote, "suffered from the *idée fixe,* as it's called, that he was destined to die at his brother's hand—and the course of events proved him right in the end. How it was to come about—that, of course, he couldn't have foreseen. But he had a premonition of it—that can't be disputed. And what are premonitions? Nothing but trains of thought in the unconscious, using the logic of the metaphysical, one might say. But we speak of obsessions! Whether we have the right to call them that, or whether this term, like so many others, is not really an evasion—a flight into systemization away from the unsettling complexity of individual cases—that is another question. And a case like that of my poor friend. . . ."

Dying

DUSK WAS APPROACHING as Marie rose from the park bench on which she had been sitting for half an hour, first reading a book but then fixing her eyes on the park entrance that Felix usually used. Normally he didn't keep her waiting long. It had turned a little colder, but the air still held the warmth of the waning May day.

Not too many people remained in the Augarten, and the remaining strollers went in the direction of the gate that would soon be closed. Marie had almost reached the exit when she caught sight of Felix. Although he was late, he walked slowly, and only when his eyes met hers did he speed up a little. She stopped and waited for him, and when he, smiling, grasped the hand she extended nonchalantly, she asked him in a slightly irritated tone of voice, "So you had to work till now?" He offered her his arm but did not reply. "Well?" she asked. "Yes, dear, I did," he finally said. "and I completely forgot to look at the clock." She gave him an oblique glance. He seemed paler than usual. "Don't you think," she said affectionately, "it would be better if you devoted yourself a little more to your Marie? Stop working so hard for a while. Let's take more walks together, all right? From now on you'll always leave the house with me."

"Well . . ."

"Yes, Felix, from now on I'll never leave you alone any more."

He gave her a quick, almost frightened, look. "What's wrong?" she asked.

"Nothing!"

They had reached the park exit, and the evening street life swirled gaily around them. The city seemed suffused with something of that universal, scarcely conscious happiness that spring usually brings. "You know what we could do?" he asked.

"What?"

"Go to the Prater."

"Oh no, it was so cold down there the other day!"

"But look! It's practically sweltering here on the street. We could come back soon. Let's go!" He spoke in a halting, absent-minded way.

"Tell me, why are you talking that way, Felix?"

"What way?"

"What are you thinking about? Remember, you're with me, your girl!"

He stared at her with a vacant look.

"Felix!" she cried in alarm and clutched his arm more tightly.

"All right, all right," he said, collecting himself. "It's really sweltering. But I'm not absentminded! Even if I were, you shouldn't take offense." They started to walk toward the Prater. Felix was even more taciturn than usual. The streetlamps were already lit.

"Did you go to see Alfred today?" she asked suddenly.

"Why?"

"Well, you were planning to."

"What makes you think that?"

"You felt so fatigued last night."

"True."

"So you didn't go see Alfred?"

"No."

"Now look, yesterday you were still sick, and now you want to go to the Prater, where it's still damp. That's really careless of you."

"Oh, it doesn't matter anyway."

"Don't talk like that. You're going to ruin your health completely."

"Please!" he said in an almost tearful voice, "let's go . . . let's just go. I really want to go to the Prater. Let's go where it was so beautiful the other day. You know, the garden café. It's not that cold there."

"All right, all right."

"Really it isn't! And anyway, it's warm today. We can't go home. It's too early. And I don't want to have dinner in town because I don't feel like sitting between the four walls of a restaurant. And the smoke there isn't good for me either. Besides, I don't want to be with a lot of people; I can't stand the noise. . . ." At first he had talked rapidly and more loudly than usual. But now he let the last words trail off. Marie clung to his arm more tightly. She was worried and had stopped talking because she felt tears choking her throat. His longing for the quiet restaurant in the Prater, for a spring evening in the green tranquility of the outdoors, had gotten through to her. After they had been silent for a while she noticed a slow, wan smile on his lips; but when he turned back to her he tried to give his smile an expression of cheerfulness. She, who knew him well, recognized immediately that the smile was forced.

They had reached the Prater. The first tree-lined street that branched off the boulevard, now almost lost in the darkness, had led them to their destination. There was the simple restaurant. Its large garden was only dimly lit, the tables were not set, and the chairs leaned against them. Near the tables, dim red lights flickered in round globes on slender green posts. A few customers were sitting with the innkeeper. Marie and Felix walked past them, and the innkeeper stood up and raised his hat. They opened the door to the garden terrace in which a few low gas flames were hissing. A young waiter dozed in a corner. He quickly got up, hurried to turn up the gas jets, and helped the customers with their coats. They sat down in a far corner, dimly lit and cozy, and moved their chairs close together. They ordered something to eat and drink without much deliberation and were now alone. Only the dim red lights at the entrance blinked. The corners of the room almost dissolved in the semi-darkness.

They both remained silent until Marie, tormented, began in trembling words, "So please tell me what's wrong, Felix! I beg you, please tell me."

Again that smile appeared on his lips. "Nothing, sweetheart," he said. "Don't ask. You know my moods . . . or don't you know them yet?"

"Of course I know your moods. But you're not in a bad mood, you're upset about something, I can tell. There must be a reason for it. Please, what's wrong? Tell me, please!"

The waiter was just now bringing their order, and Felix scowled. And when she implored him again, "Tell me, tell me," he looked at the boy and made a gesture of annoyance. The boy left. "Now we're alone," said Marie. She moved closer to him and took both of his hands in hers. "What's the matter? What's wrong? I have to know. Don't you love me any more?" He remained silent. She kissed his hand. He slowly withdrew it. "Well? Well?" He looked around as though he were seeking help. "Please, I beg you, leave me alone. Don't ask me. Don't torture me." She let go of his hand and looked him squarely in the face. "I want to know." He stood up and took a deep breath. Then he grasped his head between his hands and said, "You're driving me crazy! Don't ask." And for a long time he remained standing with a fixed expression on his face. She anxiously followed his gaze as it stared into space. Then he sat down and breathed more calmly as a weary gentleness spread over his face. A few seconds later all the terror seemed to have drained from him, and he said to Marie softly, tenderly, "Go ahead, eat, drink."

She obediently took her knife and fork and asked anxiously, "And you?" "All right, all right," he answered, but remained sitting motionless and didn't touch his food. "Then I can't eat either," she said. So he began to eat and drink. But soon he silently put down his knife and fork, propped his head on his hand, and turned his eyes away from Marie. She looked at him a little while with pursed lips, then pulled away the arm that concealed his face from hers. And then she saw how his eyes were glistening, and at the very moment that she cried out, "Felix! Felix!" he began to cry and sob bitterly. She drew his head to her breast, stroked his hair, kissed his forehead, and attempted to kiss away his tears. "Felix! Felix!" His sobbing became quieter and quieter. "What's the matter, darling? Please, darling, please tell me!" With his head still pressed to her breast so that his words sounded heavy and muffled he answered, "Marie, Marie, I didn't want to tell you. One more year, and then it's all over." And now he cried vehemently and loudly. But she, with her eyes wide open and her face deathly pale, didn't understand, didn't want to understand. Something cold and terrifying choked her throat until she suddenly cried out, "Felix! Felix!" And she flung herself down in front of him and looked up at his tear-stained, distorted face, now sunk down upon his chest. He saw her kneeling in front of him and whispered, "Get up, get up." She stood up, mechanically obeying his words, and seated herself opposite him. She was unable to talk, unable to ask him anything. And then, after a few seconds of utter silence, he suddenly burst out again in a loud wail. His gaze was directed upward as though something incomprehensible were weighing him down. "The horror! the horror!"

She found her voice again. "Let's go, let's go!" But she

couldn't say anything else. "Yes, let's go," he said, gesturing as if shaking something off. He called the waiter, paid the bill, and they left the room quickly.

Outdoors, the spring night silently enveloped them. On the dark street Marie stopped and grasped her lover's hand. "But now do tell me . . ."

He had calmed down completely, and what he now told her sounded so straightforward and matter-of-fact that it really didn't seem to be anything so unusual. He freed his hands and stroked her cheeks. It was so dark they could hardly see each other.

"You needn't get upset, Mitzi, because a year is a long, long time! You see, I've got only a year to live!"

She cried out, "What! But . . . that's crazy, that's crazy!"

"It's awful of me to tell you at all—stupid in fact. But you know, to keep it all to myself and to walk around alone with the thought all the time—I probably couldn't have endured it for very long. Maybe it's good for you to get used to it. But come on, why are we standing here? I'm already getting accustomed to the idea, Marie. I haven't believed Alfred for a long time."

"Then you didn't go to see Alfred? But what do other doctors know?"

"You see, sweetheart, in the last few weeks I've suffered so much from the uncertainty of not knowing. At least now I know the truth. I consulted Professor Bernard, and he told me the truth."

"But no, no, he didn't tell you the truth! He just wanted to scare you so you'd take better care of yourself."

"Look, my dear girl, I had a very serious talk with the man. I had to know for sure. For your sake too."

"Felix! Felix!" she cried, and embraced him with both arms. "What are you saying? Without you I can't go on living, not a day, not an hour!"

"Come on," he said quietly, "calm down." They had reached the exit of the Prater. It had become livelier and brighter around them—noisy carriages rattled in the streets, trams whistled, bells rang, and a steam train rolled heavily over the bridge above them. Marie started in pain—all this life around her suddenly had something mocking and hostile about it, and it hurt her. She pulled him along so that instead of reaching the wide boulevard they went home by way of quiet side streets.

For a moment it occurred to her that he should take a carriage, but she hesitated to say anything. They could walk slowly.

"You're not going to die, no, no," she said in a barely audible voice, leaning her head against his shoulder. "Without you I can't go on living either."

"My dear girl, you'll change your mind. I've thought it through. Yes, you know, when this boundary line was suddenly drawn so precisely, I saw everything clearly."

"There isn't any boundary line."

"Yes there is, sweetheart. Of course it's impossible to believe. I don't believe it myself right now. It's something completely incomprehensible, isn't it? Just think, in another year, I, I who am walking at your side now and talking, speaking words you can hear, will be lying in the ground, cold, perhaps already decomposed."

"Stop it! Stop it!"

"And you, you'll look just as you do now. Just like this, maybe still a little pale from crying, but then there'll come an evening and many other evenings, a summer and a fall and a winter, and then another spring, and by that time I'll already be dead and cold a whole year. Yes! What's the matter?"

She was crying bitterly. Tears rolled down her cheeks and her neck.

At this, a despairing smile spread over his face, and he whispered hoarsely and harshly from between his clenched teeth, "Forgive me."

She kept on sobbing as they continued walking, and he fell silent. Their route led past the Stadtpark through dark and silent side streets. A soft and melancholy scent of lilacs wafted over from the trees in the park. Slowly they walked on. On the other side of the street there were monotonous tall grey and yellow houses. The mighty dome of the Karlskirche, rising into the blue night sky, came into sight. They turned into another side street and soon reached the house where they lived. Slowly they walked up the dimly lit stairs and heard the servant girls gossiping and laughing behind the corridor windows and doors. A few minutes later they had closed the door behind them. The window was open, and a pair of dark red roses standing in a simple vase on the night table filled the room with their aroma. A soft buzz floated up from the street. They walked over to the window together. The house across the street was silent and dark. Then he sat down on the sofa, and she closed the shutters and lowered the curtains. She lit a candle and placed it on the table. He didn't see any of this but sat absorbed in his thoughts. She approached him. "Felix!" she cried out. He looked up and smiled. "What is it, sweetheart?" he asked. As he said these words in a soft and gentle voice, a feeling of boundless fear gripped her. No, she didn't want to lose him. Never! Never! Never! It wasn't true! It just wasn't possible! She tried to talk, wanting to tell him this. She flung herself down in front of him but couldn't find the strength to speak. She put her head on his lap and cried. His hands rested on her hair. "Don't cry," he whispered tenderly. "Don't cry any more, Mitzi." She lifted her head, and a feeling akin to hope came over her. "It isn't true, is it? Tell me it isn't true!" He kissed her lips, long and passionately. Then he said almost harshly, "It's true," and stood up. He went over to the window and stood there completely in shadow. Only his feet were illuminated by candlelight. After a while he began to talk.

"You'll have to get used to the idea. Simply imagine that we've broken up. You don't even have to know that I'm no longer alive."

She didn't seem to be listening to him. She had hidden her face in the sofa cushions. He continued, "If you think about it philosophically, it's not so terrible. We still have lots of time to be happy, don't we, Mitzi?"

Suddenly she looked up at him with large, tearless eyes. Then she rushed over to him, clung to him, and pressed him to her with both arms. She whispered, "I'll die with you." He smiled. "That's childishness. I'm not as petty as you think. And I don't have the right to take you with me anyway."

"I can't live without you."

"How long were you without me? I was already doomed when I met you a year ago. I didn't know it then, but I already suspected it."

"You don't know it today either."

"Yes, I do know it, and that's why I'm giving you your freedom today."

She clung to him more tightly. "Take it, take it!" he said. She didn't answer but looked up at him as though she didn't understand.

"You're so beautiful and oh so healthy! What a glorious right to life you have! Leave me alone."

She cried out, "I've lived with you, I'll die with you!"

He kissed her on the forehead. "No, you won't. I forbid it. Get that idea out of your head."

"I swear to you . . ."

"Don't swear. Some day you'll beg me to absolve you from your oath!"

"So that's how much faith you have in me?"

"Oh, I know you love me. You won't leave me until . . ."

"I'll never, ever, leave you!" He shook his head. She nestled close to him, took his hands, and kissed them.

"You're so good to me," he said, "and that makes me very sad."

"Don't be sad. Whatever comes, we'll share the same fate."

"No," he said gravely and firmly. "Stop that. I'm not like other men and I don't want to be. I understand what's happening . . . it would be contemptible for me to listen to you any longer; contemptible if I let myself be intoxicated by your words, which are inspired by the first moment of pain. I have to go, and you have to stay."

She had begun to cry again. He caressed and kissed her to calm her down, and they remained standing by the window without saying anything else. The minutes passed and the candle burned lower.

After a while Felix sat down on the sofa. A great fatigue had overcome him. Marie came closer and sat down beside him. She gently took his hand and put it against her shoulder. He looked at her affectionately and closed his eyes. Then he fell asleep.

The next morning crept in pale and cool. Felix woke with his head still on her breast. But she was fast asleep. He quietly disentangled himself from her and tiptoed over to the window and looked down to the street, now deserted in the dawn. He shuddered with a sudden chill. A few minutes later he stretched himself out fully clothed on the bed and stared at the ceiling.

It was bright daylight when he awoke. Marie was sitting on the edge of the bed; she had kissed him awake. They both smiled. Hadn't it all been a bad dream? He now felt better, quite healthy and refreshed. And outdoors the sun was laughing. Noises echoed from the street, and everything was full of life. The windows were open in the house across the street, and there on the table, breakfast was ready, just as it was every morning. The room was bright—daylight flooded every nook and cranny. Beams of sunlight flashed here and there, and everywhere, everywhere, there was hope, hope, hope!

II

The doctor was smoking his afternoon cigar when a woman was announced. It was before his office hours, and Alfred was annoyed. "Marie!" he cried out, surprised, when she entered.

"Don't be angry at me for disturbing you so early in the morning. Oh, please go on smoking."

"If you don't mind . . . but what's the matter? What's wrong?"

She stood before him with one hand propped on his desk and the other holding a parasol. "Is it true," she blurted out, "that Felix is so ill? Ah, you're turning pale. Why haven't you told me? Why?"

"What are you talking about?" He walked back and forth across the room. "You're being silly. Please, sit down."

"Answer me."

"Of course he's not well. That's not news to you."

"He's beyond hope!" she shouted.

"Come, come!"

"I know it. He does too. Yesterday he consulted with Professor Bernard, who told him."

"Even professors make mistakes."

"You've examined him many times. Tell me the truth."

"In these matters there's no such thing as absolute truth."

"Yes, you say that because he's your friend. You just don't want to say it, isn't that it? But I can tell the truth by looking at you! So it's true, it's true! Oh God! Oh my God!"

"My dear girl, please calm yourself."

She looked up at him with a quick look. "Is it true?"

"Well, yes, he's ill. But you know that."

"Oh . . ."

"But why did they tell him this? So now . . ."

"What now? But please, don't give me any hope if there isn't any."

"No one can predict this kind of thing with certainty. It can go on for a long time."

"I know. A year."

Alfred bit his lip. "Hmm . . . tell me, why did he go to another doctor anyway?"

"Well, because he knew that you would never tell him the truth. It's as simple as that."

"That's really ridiculous," the doctor snapped, "really ridiculous. I don't understand it. As if it were so absolutely necessary to tell a person . . ."

At that moment the door opened and Felix came in.

"I thought so," he said as he caught sight of Marie.

"What kind of foolishness have you been up to?" the doctor demanded. "Really, Felix, honestly!"

"Save your breath, my dear Alfred," answered Felix. "I thank you heartily for your good will. You've acted like a friend. You've behaved well."

Marie interrupted, "He says that the professor surely—"

"Never mind," Felix interrupted. "As long as it was possible, you had a right to keep the truth from me. But now it's a tasteless farce."

"You're being childish," said Alfred. "There are lots of people running around Vienna who twenty years ago were told by their doctors that they would be dead in a year."

"But most of them are dead and buried anyway!"

Alfred paced up and down in the room. "First of all, nothing has changed since yesterday. You'll take better care of yourself, that's all. Yes, and you'll follow my advice better than you did before—that's the good part. Why, just a week ago a fifty-year-old man came to see me—"

"I know, I know," interrupted Felix. "He's the fifty-year-old man whom the doctors thought would die at twenty, and now he's the very picture of health and the father of eight healthy children."

"Such things do happen, no doubt about it," Alfred interjected.

"You know," said Felix, "I'm not the sort of person to whom miracles happen."

"Miracles?" exclaimed Alfred. "These events are all entirely natural."

"And just look at him," said Marie to the doctor. "I think he looks better now than he did this winter."

"He just has to be careful, that's all," said Alfred, and he stopped in front of his friend. "You're going to go up to the mountains and do nothing but loaf around, understand?"

"When should we leave?" asked Marie eagerly.

"That's all useless nonsense," said Felix.

"And in the fall you'll go south."

"And next spring?" Felix asked sarcastically.

"You'll have recovered by then, I hope!"

"Yes, recovered," laughed Felix. "Well! At least I won't be suffering any more."

"As I always say, these famous clinicians are bad psychologists, every one of them," exclaimed the doctor.

"Because they don't comprehend that we can't tolerate the truth?" interjected Felix.

"There are no truths, I say. The man merely thought he had to give you a good scare so that you wouldn't be so careless. That's what his reasoning was. That way, if you get well despite his prognosis, he won't be disgraced. He just warned you, after all."

"Let's cut out all this childish talk," interrupted Felix. "I had a very serious conversation with the man. I was able to make him see that I had to know the truth. Family concerns! That always impresses people. And I have to admit honestly that the uncertainty was too agonizing."

"As if you knew the truth now!" Alfred flared up.

"Yes, I know the truth now. Your efforts are futile. Now it's only a matter of living out the year I have left as fully as I can. You'll see, my dear Alfred, that I'm a man who'll leave this world with a smile. Oh, don't cry, Mitzi. You have no idea how beautiful this world will still seem to you even without me. Alfred, don't you agree?"

"Come on! You're torturing the poor girl quite needlessly."

"It's true. It would be better to make a quick end of it. Leave me, Mitzi! Go away! Let me die by myself!"

"Give me some poison!" Marie suddenly screamed.

"You're both crazy!"

"Poison! I don't want to live a second longer than he does, and I want to prove it to him. He doesn't believe me. Why doesn't he? Why doesn't he?"

"Listen, Mitzi, let me tell you something. If you mention this nonsense once more, just once more, I'll vanish from your sight and you'll never see me again. I have no right to tie your fate to mine, and I don't want that responsibility!"

"You know, my dear Felix," began the doctor, "do me the favor of starting your trip right away. Today is better than tomorrow! This can't go on. I'll take you both to the station this evening. The bracing air and the peace and quiet will hopefully bring both of you back to your senses."

"I have absolutely no objection to that," said Felix, "it doesn't matter to me where—"

"All right, all right," Alfred interrupted. "For the time being there isn't the slightest reason to despair, and you can spare me all these pathetic remarks."

Marie dried her tears and gave the doctor a grateful look.

"A great psychologist!" smiled Felix. "When a doctor is rude, one immediately feels healthy!"

"I'm first and foremost your friend. You know that."

"We leave tomorrow for the mountains!"

"Yes, that's what we agreed on."

"Well, in any case, thank you very much," said Felix, shaking his friend's hand. "And now let's go. Someone's already clearing his throat outside. Come on, Mitzi!"

"Thank you, doctor," said Marie in parting.

"No need to thank me. Just be sensible and take good care of him. Auf Wiedersehen, then."

On the staircase Felix suddenly said, "He's a wonderful man, this doctor, isn't he?"

"Oh yes."

"And he's young and in good health and probably has another forty good years left. Maybe a hundred."

They were back on the street, surrounded by people who walked and talked and laughed and lived and didn't think about death.

III

They moved into a little house right on the lake. It stood on the outskirts of the village, one of the last stragglers in the string of houses that faced the water. Behind the house a meadow undulated gently upward, and still higher there were fields of blooming summer wildflowers. Far behind the house and only visible at times were the blurred outlines of distant mountains. When they walked out of the house and onto the terrace that jutted out of the clear depths of the water on four damp brown posts, a long chain of bare cliffs, on whose heights the cold gleam of the silent sky rested, faced them on the opposite shore.

During the first days of their stay, a wonderful sense of tranquility came over them, a tranquility they scarcely understood themselves. It was as if fate had power over them only in their familiar surroundings. Here in their new milieu, the doom that had been pronounced in that other world was no longer valid. In all their time together, they had never enjoyed such rejuvenating solitude. True, they sometimes looked at each other as if some small incident had occurred between them, perhaps a quarrel or a slight misunderstanding that couldn't be mentioned. But Felix felt so well on these beautiful summer days that he wanted to resume his work soon after his arrival. Marie wouldn't permit it. "You're still not quite well enough," she said with a smile. The sunbeams danced on the little table on which Felix had heaped his books and papers. Soft, caressing breezes, oblivious to all the world's unhappiness, came from the lake through the open window.

One evening they hired an old farmer to row them out into the lake, as had become their custom. They found themselves in a sturdy wide boat with a cushioned seat on which Marie could sit while Felix lay at her feet, wrapped in a warm grey blanket that served as both mattress and blanket. He rested his head on her knees. Light mists floated on the broad, calm surface of the water, and it seemed as though dusk were rising slowly from the lake toward the shores. Today Felix dared to smoke a cigar, and he looked blankly over the water across the waves toward the bluffs whose tops were bathed in faint yellow sunlight.

"Tell me, Mitzi," he began, "do you dare to look up?"

"Where?"

He pointed to the sky. "There, straight up, into the deep blue. Because I can't. It scares me."

She looked up and fastened her gaze on the sky for a few seconds. "Actually, if anything, it makes me feel good."

"Really? When the sky is as clear as it is today, I can't deal with it at all. This remoteness, this terrifying remoteness! When there are clouds, I don't feel so uncomfortable. When I look at them I feel I'm looking at something that still belongs to our world."

"It'll probably rain tomorrow," the oarsman interjected, "the mountains seem too close today." And he stopped rowing, so that the boat glided soundlessly and ever more slowly over the waves.

Felix cleared his throat. "Strange, the cigar still doesn't really agree with me."

"So throw it away then!"

Felix twisted the glowing cigar between his fingers a few times, then threw it into the water. Without turning toward Marie, he said, "So, does this mean that I'm still not quite well?"

"Come on," she answered with a gesture of denial, and gently stroked his hair with her hand.

"What are we going to do if it starts to rain? Then you'll have to let me work after all."

"You're not allowed to."

She bent down to him and looked into his eyes. It struck her that his cheeks were flushed. "I'll drive your black thoughts away in short order! But shouldn't we be going home now? It's beginning to cool off."

"Cool off? I'm not cold."

"Well, you've got that thick blanket."

"Oh!" he exclaimed. "I'm such an egotist, I completely forgot that you're wearing a summer dress." He turned to the oarsman. "Home, please." After several hundred strokes of the oars, they were near their house. Then Marie noticed that Felix was clasping his left wrist with his right hand. "What's wrong?"

"Mitzi, I really don't feel well."

"Oh, Felix!"

"I have a fever. Hmm . . . it's too stupid!"

"I'm sure you're wrong," said Marie, worried. "I'll go get the doctor right away."

"Oh sure, that's all I need!"

They had tied up at the pier and climbed ashore. Their rooms were almost completely dark but still held the warmth of the day. While Marie prepared supper, Felix sat quietly in the armchair.

"Listen," he said suddenly, "our first week is already over."

She quickly walked over to him from the table she had been setting and embraced him. "What's the matter now?"

He shook her off. "Let me be." He stood up, then went to the table and sat down. She followed him. He drummed on the tabletop with his fingers. "I feel so defenseless. It suddenly overcomes me."

"But Felix, Felix." She moved her chair close to his.

He looked around the room with his eyes wide open. Then he shook his head angrily, as though he couldn't comprehend something, and hissed from between clenched teeth, "Powerless! Powerless! No one can help me. The thing itself is not so terrible . . . but this powerlessness!"

"Felix, please, you're upsetting yourself. I'm sure it's nothing. Do you want me—just for your peace of mind—to get a doctor?"

"Oh, please, spare me that! Forgive me for entertaining you with my illness again!"

"But . . ."

"It won't happen again. Go on, get me something to drink. Yes, yes, get me something to drink! Thanks! Well, why don't you say something?"

"What do you want me to say?"

"Anything. Read to me if you can't think of anything to say. Excuse me . . . after the meal, of course. Go ahead, eat. . . . I'm eating too." He helped himself. "I even have an appetite . . . this food's rather good."

"Well good," said Marie with a forced smile.

And they both ate and drank.

IV

The following days brought a warm rain. Sometimes they sat in their room, sometimes on their terrace, for the entire day, until nightfall. They read or looked out the window, or he watched her as she sewed. Sometimes they played cards, and he even taught her the rudiments of chess. At other times he lay down on the sofa and she sat beside him and read to him. These were quiet days and evenings, and Felix actually felt quite well. He was pleased that the bad weather wasn't harming him. The fever didn't return either.

One afternoon, when the sky seemed to clear for the first time after the long rain, they were sitting on the balcony again when Felix abruptly, without reference to any previous conversation, said, "Actually, everyone is walking around under sentence of death."

Marie looked up from her sewing.

"Why yes," he continued. "Imagine, for example, that someone said to you, 'My dear lady, you will die on May 1, 1970.' You'd then spend your entire life in a nameless fear of May 1, 1970, though today you certainly don't seriously expect that you'll live to be a hundred years old."

She didn't answer him.

He continued talking while looking across the lake, which was beginning to glitter with the sunbeams that were just now breaking through the clouds.

"On the other hand, there are some who are walking around proud and healthy today who'll be carried off by an absurd accident in a few weeks. But they're not thinking about death at all, are they?"

"Look," said Marie, "let those silly thoughts go. Surely you yourself now realize that you'll recover."

He smirked.

"Well, yes!" she said. "You're one of those who'll get well."

He laughed out loud. "My dear girl, do you really believe that I'll trick fate? Do you think I'm fooled for one minute by this apparent well-being with which nature now favors me? It happens that I know where I stand, and the thought of my imminent death makes me a philosopher, just as it has other great men."

"Oh, stop it, will you!"

"So, my Fräulein, I have to die and you're not even to suffer the small displeasure of hearing me talk about it?"

She threw her sewing aside and walked over to him. "I really feel," she said with a tone of sincere conviction, "that you'll stay with me. You yourself can't judge how much better you are. You've just got to stop thinking about it, and then this horrible shadow will be gone from our life."

He looked at her for a long time. "You really don't understand, do you? You have to see it in front of your eyes. Look at this." He picked up a newspaper. "What does it say here?"

"June 12, 1890."

"Yes, 1890. And now imagine that instead of the zero there is a one. By that time, everything will be long over. Well, do you understand it now?"

She took the newspaper out of his hand and threw it angrily on the floor.

"It's not the newspaper's fault," he said calmly. Then he got up energetically and suddenly seemed to toss these thoughts far away. He exclaimed, "Look! Look how beautiful everything is! The way the sun is lying on the water! And over there"—he bent over the side of the terrace and looked across to the opposite shore, where the land was flat—"how the grass is waving in the wind! I'd like to go out for a while."

"Won't it be too damp?"

"Come on, I have to get outdoors into the open air."

She didn't dare oppose him.

They both took their hats, threw on their coats, and set out on the road toward the meadows. The sky had almost completely cleared. White clouds in various shapes moved over the distant mountain range. It was as though the green of the meadow had lost itself in the golden whiteness that bordered the landscape. Soon they arrived in the middle of a wheat field where they had to walk single file as the stalks rustled against the edges of their coats. They turned off onto a side path that led into a moderately dense forest with well-tended trails and many benches for sitting. There they walked arm in arm.

"Isn't it beautiful here!" Felix exclaimed. "And this scent!"

"Don't you think that now just after the rain . . . ," interrupted Marie, without finishing her sentence.

He shook his head impatiently. "Forget it. What does it matter? It's so unpleasant to be reminded of it all the time!"

As they walked on, the forest gradually thinned. The lake glittered through the foliage. They were barely a hundred steps away from it, on a narrow splinter of land where the forest ended and only a few sparse hedges jutted out into the water. At its edge were a few pine benches and tables, and a wooden fence stretched along the shore. A gentle evening breeze had sprung up and was driving the waves against the shore. And now the wind was blowing further inland across the hedges and the trees, so that the wet leaves began to drip again. The faint sheen of the parting day lay on the water.

"I never knew that all this was so beautiful!" said Felix.

"Yes, it's lovely."

"But you don't really understand," exclaimed Felix. "You can't really understand, since you don't have to take your leave of it." And slowly he walked forward a few more steps and propped both his arms up on the thin fence whose narrow posts were lapped by the water. For a long time he looked over the shimmering surface of the lake. Then he turned around. Marie was standing behind him, her eyes sad with suppressed tears.

"Don't you see," said Felix in a bantering tone of voice, "that I'm leaving you all this? Yes, yes, for it belongs to me. That's the secret of what I feel now—I have such a powerful feeling of infinite ownership. I could do whatever I wanted to with all these things. I could make flowers bloom on the bare rock over there, and I could chase those white clouds from the sky. I'm not doing it, only because everything is so beautiful just as it is. My dear girl, only when you're alone without me will you understand this. Yes, you'll definitely feel that you've inherited all this."

He took her by the hand and pulled her close. Then he stretched out his other arm as though he wanted to show her all the splendor around them. "All this, all this," he said. But because she was still silent and still had those wide-open, tearless eyes, he abruptly broke off and said, "Let's go home now."

Dusk was approaching. They took the trail that ran along the shore and soon reached their lodging. "All the same, that was a beautiful walk," said Felix.

She nodded mutely.

"Let's do it again, Mitzi."

"Yes," she said.

"And," he added in a tone of disdainful pity, "I won't torture you any more."

V

On one of the following afternoons he decided to take up his work again. As he was about to put pencil to paper for the first time in a long time, he looked over at Marie with a certain malicious curiosity, wondering whether she would stop him. She said nothing. But soon he threw the paper and pencil aside and picked up a random book to read. Reading was a better distraction. He was still incapable of working. He would first have to struggle through to a feeling of utter disdain for life before he would be able to look eternity in the face calmly enough to compose his last will and testament like a wise man. That's what he wanted to do. Not the kind of will that ordinary people write, which always betrays a secret fear of dying. This document would not be about things that can be seen and touched, things which in the end would have to perish in time after him. His last will would be a poem—a quiet, smiling farewell to a world he had transcended. He said nothing about it to Marie. She wouldn't have understood. He felt so different from her. It was with a certain pride that he sat across from her on those long afternoons when, as often happened, she had dozed off over her book with her loosened curls circling her forehead. His self-esteem grew when he realized how much he could hide from her. He felt autonomous, exalted.

On one such afternoon, when her eyelids had once more fallen shut, he silently crept away. He took a walk in the woods. The stillness of the sultry summer afternoon surrounded him. Suddenly it struck him: it could happen today. He drew a deep breath. He felt light, free. He walked on beneath the heavy shade of the trees. The filtered daylight flowed gently over him. He experienced everything—the shade, the silence, the soft, warm air—with profound joy. He enjoyed it all. He felt no pain in the awareness that he would soon lose all this sweetness. "Lose it, lose it," he muttered under his breath. He took a deep breath, and as the warm air flowed so deliciously and easily into his lungs, he suddenly could not believe that he was sick at all. But he was sick, terminally ill, a condemned man. He had a sudden epiphany: he didn't really believe it! That was it; that was why he felt so free and so well; that was why it had seemed to him to be the right time today. He hadn't overcome his lust for life at all, he had merely lost his fear of death—because he no longer believed in death. He knew, yes, knew, that he would recover. He felt as though something that had lain dormant in a hidden corner of his soul was reawakening. He felt the need to open his eyes wider, to walk forward with longer strides, to breathe more deeply. The day grew brighter and life became more vivid. So that's what it was, so that was it! But why? Why did he suddenly have to become so drunk with hope again? Ah, hope! But it was more than hope. It was a certainty. As recently as this morning he had felt tortured, strangled, and now, now he was well, he was healthy. He exclaimed the word out loud, "Healthy!"

He was standing at the edge of the forest. Before him was the lake with its dark blue sheen. He sat down on a bench with a feeling of great comfort and with his gaze directed at the water. He thought about how strange it was that the joy of recovery had masqueraded itself as the feeling of a proud farewell.

He heard a small noise behind him. He hardly had time to turn around. It was Marie. Her eyes shone and her face was slightly flushed.

"What's the matter?"

"Why did you leave? Why did you leave me alone? I got very frightened."

"Oh, come on," he said and drew her down next to him. He smiled at her and kissed her. She had such warm, full lips. "Come," he said softly and pulled her onto his lap. She nestled close to him and put her arms around his neck. How beautiful she was! A sultry scent wafted from her blonde hair, and an infinite tenderness for this soft, sweet-smelling creature arose in him. Tears came into his eyes, and he grasped her hands and kissed them. How much he loved her!

A faint, hissing sound came from out on the lake. They looked up, rose, and approached the shore arm in arm. The steamboat could be seen in the distance. They let it get just close enough for them to make out the outlines of the people on the deck, then turned around and walked home through the woods. They walked arm in arm, slowly, smiling at each other now and then. Old words came to them again—the words of their first days of love. Once again they exchanged the sweet, teasing questions of love unsure of itself and the heartfelt words of flattering reassurance. They were cheerful and like children again, and they were happy.

VI

A heavy and scorching summer with hot, blistering days and warm, sensual nights had arrived. Every day was like the one before, every night like the one just past. Time stood still, and they were alone. They concentrated only on each other, and the forest, the lake, and the small house was their world. A sultry sensuousness enveloped them, and they forgot to think. Carefree, happy nights and lazy days of loving affection flew by.

On one of these nights, when the candle burned late, Marie, who was lying in bed awake, sat up. She looked down at her lover's face, which wore the peace of deep sleep. She listened to his breathing. It was as good as certain—every hour was bringing him closer to recovery. An inexpressible love filled her, and she bent over him with the desire to feel the touch of his breath on her cheeks. Oh, how beautiful it was to be alive after all! And he, only he, was her whole life. Oh, he was hers again, he was hers again, he was hers forever!

Suddenly she was startled by the sound of the sleeping man's breathing. One breath sounded different from the others—it was a soft, labored moan. On his lips, which had opened slightly, she saw an expression of pain, and with horror she became aware of the drops of sweat on his forehead. He turned his head slightly, but then his lips closed again. The peaceful expression on his face returned, and after a few labored breaths his breathing became regular again, almost soundless. But Marie suddenly felt gripped by a tormenting anxiety. She wanted to wake him and nestle close to him, to feel his warmth, his life, his essence. A strange awareness of guilt overcame her, and her joyous belief in his recovery suddenly seemed presumptuous. She tried to persuade herself that it had not been a firm belief; no, only a slight, grateful hope, for which she surely shouldn't be so harshly punished. She vowed never again to be so unselfconsciously happy. Suddenly their time of giddy rapture seemed to her a time of mindless sin for which they must atone. Of course! But then, what might be a sin under other circumstances . . . wasn't it different with them? A love that might work a miracle? And couldn't it be these last delicious nights that could give his health back to him?

A terrifying moan came from Felix's mouth. Still half asleep, he had sat up in bed. His eyes were opened wide in fear, and he stared into space. Marie screamed out loud and he awakened fully. "What is it, what is it?" he gasped. Marie was speechless. "Did you scream, Marie? I heard screaming." He was breathing very rapidly. "I felt as though I were choking. I dreamed something too, but I don't remember what."

"I was so frightened," she stammered.

"You know, Marie, I'm having chills too."

"Naturally," she answered, "when you have bad dreams . . ."

"Oh cut it out," he said and looked up angrily. "I've got a fever again, that's what it is." His teeth chattered, and he lay down and pulled the blanket up over himself.

She looked around in desperation. "Should I . . . do you want . . . ?"

"I don't want anything. Just go back to sleep. I'm tired. I'll go back to sleep too. Leave the light burning." He closed his eyes and pulled the blanket up over his mouth. Marie didn't dare ask him anything else. She knew that pity embittered him when he didn't feel well. After a few minutes he fell asleep again, but she couldn't sleep any longer. Soon the first grey bands of daylight began to creep into the room. These first, faint signs of morning made Marie feel better. She felt that something friendly and smiling was coming to visit her and she had a strange desire to go out to greet the morning. Very quietly she climbed out of bed, quickly put on her robe, and slipped out onto the terrace. The sky, the mountains, the lake—everything was still merged in a dark, uncertain grey. It gave her particular pleasure to strain her eyes to make out their shapes more distinctly. She sat down in the armchair and let her gaze penetrate the dawn. An inexpressible sense of well-being flowed through her as she leaned out over the terrace into the profound stillness of the dawning summer morning. Everything around her was so peaceful, so warm and soft, so eternal. It was beautiful to be alone for a while in the middle of this great stillness, wonderful to be out of the narrow, stuffy room. And suddenly she felt a flash of recognition: she had gladly left his side, was glad to be here, glad to be all by herself, alone!

VII

All day long the thoughts she had had during the night kept returning. They were less tormenting and disturbing than they had been in the darkness, but they were much clearer now and pointed the way toward the decisions she had to make. The most important one was that she must ward off the ardor of his love as much as possible. She couldn't understand why she hadn't realized this all along. Oh, she would be so gentle and clever that it wouldn't seem like a rejection—more like a new and better love.

But she didn't need any particular cleverness and gentleness. Since that night, the ardor of his passion seemed to cool. He treated Marie with a weary tenderness that soothed her at first but in the end alienated her. During the day he either read a great deal or just pretended to read—often enough she saw that he stared blankly into space over his book. Their conversations touched on a thousand everyday matters and on nothing of importance, but without giving Marie the impression that he had stopped sharing his secret thoughts with her. Everything happened in an entirely natural way, as if the muted indifference in his manner was merely the cheery weariness of the convalescent. In the morning he would stay in bed for a long time while she rushed outdoors at the first sign of daybreak. She

would either remain sitting on the terrace or she would go down to
the lake to sit in a boat without leaving the shore, allowing herself to
be rocked by the gently moving waves. Sometimes she took a walk
in the woods, and usually she had already returned from her morning outing when she came into the room to awaken him. She was
happy that he slept so soundly, interpreting this as a good sign. She
didn't know how often he awoke during the night, and she didn't see
the look of infinite sadness that rested upon her face as she enjoyed
the deep sleep of healthy youth.

One morning she had once again climbed into the boat as the
day cast its first golden sparks over the lake, when she was seized by
a desire to venture out farther on the sparkling bright water. She
went out a good distance, and because she was not very practiced in
rowing, she overexerted herself, though this only increased her
pleasure. It was apparent that even at such an early hour it was impossible to be all alone on the water. Several boats passed Marie's,
and it seemed to her that some of them came close to hers rather deliberately. A small, elegant keelboat rowed by two young men
passed right next to hers very rapidly. The two men pulled in their
oars, raised their caps, and greeted her politely with a smile.

Marie gave them both a surprised look and automatically said,
"Good morning." Then she turned around to look at the two young
men without being quite aware of doing so. They too had turned
around and were greeting her again. Then she suddenly became conscious that she had done something wrong, and she rowed back to
her lodgings as quickly as her modest skill allowed. It took her almost half an hour to return, and she arrived quite heated, with her
hair disheveled. She had already seen Felix sitting on the terrace
from the water, and now she rushed hastily into the house. Quite
confused, as though feeling guilty, she rushed to the balcony, embraced Felix from behind, and asked jokingly, with an exaggerated
cheerfulness, "Guess who?"

He slowly detached himself from her and gave her a calm, side-long glance. "What's the matter with you? Why are you so jolly?"

"Because I have you back."

"Why are you so hot? You're burning up!"

"Oh, God! I'm so happy, so happy, so happy!" In these high spirits, she pushed the blanket from his knees and sat on his lap. She was annoyed at her own embarrassment as well as his peevish expression. Then she kissed him on the lips.

"What are you so happy about?"

"Don't I have reason to be? I'm so happy . . . ," she stopped and then continued, "that it's been taken away from you."

"What?" There was something like suspicion in his question.

She had to keep on talking. There was no way out. "Well, the fear."

"The fear of death, you mean?"

"Don't say it out loud!"

"Why do you say, 'taken from me?' Taken from you, you mean?" As he said this, a searching and almost malicious look came into his eyes. And when she, instead of answering, burrowed into his hair with her hands and brought her lips close to his forehead, he leaned his head back a little and continued, pitiless and cold: "Wasn't it your intention once that my fate be your fate, too?"

"And it will be too," she interjected gaily.

"No, it won't," he interrupted, quite serious now. "Why are we fooling ourselves? It hasn't been taken from me. It is coming closer and closer; I can feel it."

"But . . ." she had imperceptibly moved away from him and was now leaning against the railing of the terrace. He stood up and started pacing up and down.

"Yes, I can feel it. I think it's my obligation to tell you. If it were to happen suddenly, it would probably scare you too much. That's why I'm reminding you that almost a quarter of my time is up. Maybe I'm only deluding myself to think that I have to tell you . . . perhaps it's really only cowardice that's causing me to do it."

"Are you upset that I left you alone?" she asked anxiously.

"Nonsense!" he replied quickly. "I like to see you in a good mood. I know myself well enough to know that I'll face that particular day with reasonable humor too. But for you to be gay—to tell you the truth, that's a little much for me. That's why I want you to feel free to separate your fate from mine within the next few days."

"Felix!" She tried to stop him from pacing. Again he freed himself from her.

"The worst is beginning now. Up to now I've been the interesting patient—a little pale, a little cough, a little melancholy. A woman can still find that sort of thing rather attractive. But what's coming now, my dear girl—spare yourself! It could poison your memory of me."

She sought in vain for an answer. She stared at him helplessly.

"You think it's hard to accept what I say? You think it's unloving, maybe even cruel? I tell you there's no question of that; on the contrary, you'll be doing me and my vanity a very special service if you accept my proposal. Because the very last thing I want is you remembering me with sorrow, you crying real tears for me. What I certainly don't want is you bending over my bed for days and nights on end, thinking 'If only it were already over, since it has to be over some day,' and feeling liberated when I leave you."

She fought to find something to say. Finally she managed to say, "I'll stay with you forever."

He paid no attention to her. "Let's not talk about it any more. In a week, I think, I'll go back to Vienna. I have to put a number of things in order. Before we leave this house, I'll ask you my question—no, make my request—once more."

"Felix! I—"

He interrupted her vehemently. "I forbid you to say another word on the subject until the time comes." He left the balcony and turned toward the room. She wanted to follow him. "Let me be," he said, very gently. "I want to be alone for a while."

She remained on the balcony and stared dry-eyed at the glistening surface of the lake. Felix had gone into the bedroom and flung himself down on his bed. He stared up at the ceiling for a long time. Then he bit his lip and clenched his fists. And with a sneer he whispered, "Surrender! Surrender!"

VIII

From that moment on something alien stood between them, and yet they had an anxious need to talk to each other constantly. They handled everyday matters with great thoroughness, but as soon as they stopped talking, they became nervous. They asked each other where the grey clouds that covered the mountains came from, what the weather would be like tomorrow, why the water was a different color at different times of the day—they had long conversations about such things. When they went walking, they left the immediate vicinity of their house and walked toward the more populated shore more often. This gave them many opportunities to exchange remarks about the people they encountered. When it happened that young men crossed their path, Marie showed particular reserve. And when Felix made a remark about the summer get-up of some rower or mountain climber, Marie would go so far as to claim, with scarcely conscious insincerity, that she hadn't noticed these people at all, and it was only with great effort that she was induced to notice them when they happened to encounter them again. The gaze that she felt fastened upon her on such occasions made her uncomfortable. At other times they would walk side by side in silence for a quarter of an hour. Sometimes they would also sit together in silence on their balcony, until Marie came up with the idea (without being able to conceal its purpose) of reading to him from the newspaper. She continued to read even when she noticed that he was no longer listening, glad at the sound of her own voice, glad that there wasn't total silence between them. And yet, despite all these strenuous efforts, both of them were absorbed exclusively in their own thoughts.

Felix admitted to himself that he had recently put on a ridiculous act for Marie. If he were really serious about his wish to spare her the upcoming misery, the best thing he could do would be simply to disappear. He could easily find a quiet place to die in peace. He was surprised that he could think about this kind of thing with complete equanimity. But when he began to think seriously about how he would carry out such a plan—when, during one horribly long, sleepless night, he imagined the details of how the actual event would take place, how he would get up and leave at dawn the very next day, without a farewell, and go into loneliness and approaching death, leaving her behind in the midst of a sunny, gay life that was lost to him—then he felt his helplessness, felt deep down that he couldn't do it, could never, ever do it. What then . . . what? The day was coming inexorably. It was coming ever closer—the day he would have to go and leave her behind. His whole existence was consumed by waiting for that day. It was nothing but a tortured respite, worse than death itself. If only, when he was younger, he had not learned to be so self-observant. He could easily have overlooked all the symptoms of his illness, or at least not taken them so seriously. He recalled people he had known who had been consumed by the same fatal illness as his, people who, only weeks before death, had happily and hopefully looked toward the future. How he cursed the hour when his uncertainty had led him to that doctor, the one whom he had pestered with lies and false pride until he was told the full, merciless truth. And so here he now lay, damned a hundred times over, no better off than a condemned man who could be approached any morning by the executioner for removal to his place of execution. He understood that he could never fathom the full horror of his existence. In some corner of his heart there lurked a deceitful and seductive hope that would never completely leave him. But his intellect was stronger, and it gave him clear, cold advice, gave it to him again and again. He heard it ten and a hundred and a thousand times during those endless nights when he lay sleepless; during all those unvarying days, which still passed all too quickly. There was only one way out and only one deliverance for him—to wait no longer, not an hour, not a second, and to end his life himself—that would be less pathetic. It was almost a consolation that nothing forced him to wait. He could put an end to his life any time he wanted.

But she, she! Especially during the day, when she walked next to him or read to him, it often seemed to him that it wouldn't be so hard for him to part from this creature. She was no more to him than a fixture of his daily life. She belonged not to him but to the life he would have to leave. At other moments, however, especially at night, when she lay beside him in her youthful beauty, fast asleep with her eyes shut tight, then he loved her beyond measure. The more deeply she slept, the more secluded from the world her slumber was, and the more remote her dreaming soul seemed to be from his wakeful torment, the more passionately did he adore her. And once—it was the night before they were to leave the lake—he could barely overcome his desire to shake her awake from her delicious sleep which now seemed to him to be a spiteful betrayal, and to scream into her ear: "If you love me, die with me! Let's die right now!" But he let her sleep on. Tomorrow he would tell her. Yes, to-morrow . . . maybe.

More often than he suspected, she felt his eyes upon her in those nights. More often than he suspected, she only pretended to sleep because a paralyzing fear kept her from fully opening the eye-

lids through which she had sometimes peered into the semi-darkness
of the bedroom at his figure sitting straight up in bed. The memory
of that last, serious conversation would not leave her, and she
dreaded the day when he would ask her the question again. But why
did she shudder at the thought of it? The answer was clear to her.
She would stay with him to the very last second; she would not
leave his side; she would kiss every sigh from his lips, every tear of
pain from his eyelashes. Didn't he trust her? Was any other answer
possible? Which one? Perhaps this one: "You're right, I'll leave you.
I want only to remember you as the interesting patient. I'm leaving
you now in order to love you better in memory." And then? She was
forced to imagine what would happen after such an answer. She
could see him before her, cool and smiling. He would extend his
hand to her and say, "I thank you." Then he would turn away from
her and she would rush away. It would be a summer morning,
sparkling with a thousand burgeoning joys. And she would rush ever
further into the golden morning, to escape from him as quickly as
possible. And then all at once the spell would be lifted from her. She
would be alone again, freed from pity. She would no longer feel the
sad, questioning, dying gaze that had so frightfully tormented her
these last months resting on her. She belonged to joy and to life; she
would be allowed to be young again. She would rush away, and the
morning breezes would chase gaily after her.

How doubly miserable she was when this image of her confused dreams faded! She suffered from the very fact that it had appeared at all.

How her pity for him gnawed at her heart, how she shuddered
when she thought of his awareness of his condition, his hopeless-
ness! How she loved him, how she loved him more and more the
closer the day came when she would have to lose him. Oh, there
could be no doubt about her answer. To stay at his side, to suffer
with him—that was the least she could do. To watch him wait for

death, to endure with him these long months of fear, how little was that really! She resolved to do more for him; to do her very best, her utmost. If she promised him that she would kill herself at his grave, he would die doubting whether she would really do it. She would die with him . . . no, before him. When he asked her the question again, she would have the strength to say, "Let's put an end to this suffering! Let's die together, right now." And as she became intoxicated with this idea, that woman whose image she had only just now seen—the one who ran through the green meadows, caressed by the morning breeze, rushing toward life and joy, and who was herself—seemed to her wretched and contemptible.

IX

The day of their departure dawned. It was a wonderfully warm morning, as though spring were coming back. Marie was already sitting on the terrace and breakfast was ready when Felix came out of the living room. He drew a deep breath. "Ah, what a glorious day!"

"Isn't it?"

"I have something to tell you, Marie."

"What?" And she continued quickly, as though she wanted to prevent him from answering: "We're staying here longer?"

"No, not that, but let's not go back to Vienna right away. I'm feeling pretty good today, not bad at all. Let's stop somewhere along the way."

"As you wish, darling." Suddenly she felt so good inside, better than she had in a long time. He hadn't spoken so naturally for many weeks.

"Let's stop in Salzburg, sweetheart."

"Whatever you say."

"We'll get back to Vienna soon enough, don't you think? And the train trip is too long for me anyway."

"Sure," said Marie brightly, "we're not in a hurry anyway."

"Everything is packed, isn't it, Marie?"

"Yes. We could leave right away."

"Let's take a carriage. It's only a four- to five-hour drive, and much pleasanter than the train. Yesterday's heat is probably still lingering in the train compartments."

"Just as you like, darling." She urged him to drink his glass of milk, and then she drew his attention to the beautiful silvery sheen on the crests of the waves. She talked a lot and a little too brightly. He answered in a friendly and innocuous manner. Finally she offered to order the carriage in which they would leave for Salzburg at noon. He accepted with a smile. She hurriedly put on her broad straw hat, gave Felix a couple of kisses, and ran out into the street.

He hadn't asked—and he wasn't going to ask. That was clearly written on his now cheerful face. Nor was there anything lurking underneath his friendliness today, as there sometimes had been before, when he had intentionally cut off a harmless conversation with a harsh word. She always knew when something of that sort was in the offing, but now she felt as though he had done her a great favor. In his gentleness there had been something generous and conciliatory.

When she returned to the balcony, she found him reading a newspaper that had arrived while she was out.

"Marie," he exclaimed, motioning her closer, "something strange, something really strange, happened."

"What is it?"

"Here, read! The man . . . well, Professor Bernard—died."

"Who?"

"Well, the man who . . . you know the one I . . . oh, the doctor who gave me such a bleak diagnosis."

She took the newspaper out of his hand. "What? Professor

Bernard?" She was about to say, "Serves him right," but she didn't say it out loud. They both felt that this event had great significance for them. Yes, he, the man who with the arrogant wisdom of robust health had taken away all his hope, the man to whom he had come for help, had himself been carried off within a few days. Only at that moment did Felix realize how much he had hated the man—it seemed a good omen that the vengeance of fate had overpowered him. He felt as though a sinister ghost had vanished from his world. Marie threw the newspaper down and said, "Goes to show you— what do we human beings know about the future anyway?"

He seized on her words eagerly. "What do we know about to-morrow? We know nothing, nothing!" After a short pause he abruptly changed topics. "Did you order the carriage?"

"Yes," she said, "for eleven o'clock."

"Then we can walk down to the water for a little while, can't we?" She took his arm, and they walked at a leisurely pace toward the boathouse. They felt as if they had received a well-deserved favor.

X

In the late afternoon they drove into Salzburg. To their surprise, they found most of the houses in the city flying flags. The people they encountered wore holiday clothes, and some wore rosettes made of ribbons on their hats. In the hotel where they stopped and rented a room with a view of the Moenchsberg Mountain, they were told that a big choral festival was being held in town. They were offered tickets to the concert that was to take place at eight o'clock in the Kurpark, which was to be magnificently illuminated by electric lighting. Their room was on the second floor, and the Salzach River flowed right beneath their window. They had both napped a good deal on their journey and now felt so refreshed that they stayed at the hotel only briefly and went out into the street even before twilight.

Excitement pervaded the whole town. All of the residents seemed to be out in the street, and the singers, decorated with their crests, strolled among them in lighthearted groups. Many tourists were also in evidence, and many peasants, in town from the surrounding villages and dressed in their Sunday best, weaved in and out of the crowd. In the central part of town, flags bearing the town colors flew from gabled rooftops. There were flower-bedecked triumphal arches and a restless stream of people surging through the streets, which were bathed in the comfortable, warm air of a fragrant summer evening.

Starting out from the bank of the Salzach, where they had been surrounded by luxurious silence, Felix and Marie joined the hustle and bustle of the city. After having spent such an uneventful time on their quiet lake they found that the unaccustomed noise made their heads reel. But they soon regained the *savoir faire* of the seasoned urbanites they were and found that they were able to take the teeming crowds around them in stride. Felix didn't much like the boisterousness of a crowd; he never had. But Marie soon felt that she was in her element, and like a child she stopped to gawk—now at a few women wearing Salzburger folk costumes, now at some tall singers, decorated with sashes, who sauntered past. Sometimes she would look up and admire the especially magnificent decoration of some building. At other times she would turn to Felix, who walked at her side without paying much attention, and exclaim, "Look there, how pretty!" without receiving any answer except a silent nod.

"Tell me honestly," she said finally, "aren't we lucky to have come here now?"

He gave her a look that she couldn't quite decipher. Finally he said, "I suppose you'd really like to go to the concert in the Kurpark."

She only smiled. Then she replied, "Well, we don't have to overdo it right away."

Her smile annoyed him. "You'd really be capable of demanding that I go!"

"Whatever do you mean?" she said, quite taken aback, just as her gaze fell on an elegant and good-looking couple on the other side of the street. They looked as though they were honeymooners, walking by in happy conversation. Marie strolled along next to Felix, but without taking his arm. Not infrequently the crowd separated them for a few moments; then she would find him skulking next to the wall of a house, obviously unwilling to come into physical contact with so many people. Meanwhile it grew darker; the street lights were lit, and in various places throughout the city, especially along the triumphal arches, colored lanterns that had been hung up especially for the occasion glowed. A stream of people moved in the direction of the Kurpark. The hour of the concert was approaching. At first Felix and Marie were pulled along by the crowd, but then he suddenly took her arm. After turning into a narrow side street, they were soon in a quieter and less brightly illuminated part of town. After a few minutes of silent strolling they found themselves above a remote bank of the Salzach where the constant roar of the water below reached their ears.

"What are we looking for here?" she asked.

"Silence," he said, almost imperiously. And when she made no reply, he continued in a tone of nervous irritability. "We don't belong there. The colorful lights and the gay singing and the laughing young people are not for us any longer. This is the place for us, here, where we can't hear any of the jubilation, where we're alone. We belong here." Then, as his voice fell from an anguished tone into one of cold scorn, he added, "At least I do."

As he was saying this, she realized that she was no longer as deeply moved by his words as she once had been. She rationalized that she had heard him say this many times by now, and that he was obviously exaggerating. She answered him in a soothing tone, "I really don't deserve this."

He replied, as he had so often, in a malicious tone of voice, "I'm sorry." And she continued, grasping his arm tightly and holding it close to her, ". . . and neither of us belongs here."

"Yes, we do!" he almost shouted.

"No," she answered gently, "though I don't really want to go back into that noisy crowd either. I don't like it any more than you do. But what reason do we have to flee as though we were outcasts?"

At that moment the full sound of the orchestra wafted toward them through the pure, still, windless air. They could hear almost every note clearly. There were festive trumpet fanfares and a festival overture which marked the beginning of the concert.

"Let's go," said Felix suddenly, after stopping with her to listen for a while. "Hearing music from a distance makes me sadder than anything else in the world."

"Yes," she agreed, "it sounds very melancholy."

They quickly walked toward the city center. Here the music was less clearly audible than it had been down by the river bank, and when they were again in the illuminated streets teeming with life, Marie felt the return of the old, tender pity she felt for her beloved. Once more she understood, and she forgave him everything. "Shall we go home?" she asked.

"No, why should we? Are you sleepy?"

"Oh no!"

"Let's stay outdoors a little longer then, all right?"

"All right . . . as you wish . . . but isn't it too cool for you?"

"No, it's humid. It's positively hot," he answered nervously. "Let's eat dinner outdoors."

"I'd love to."

They had reached the vicinity of the Kurpark. The orchestra

had finished its overture, and now, from the brightly illuminated park, they heard the multifaceted sound of a crowd of people talking and enjoying themselves. A few people who still wanted to go to the concert hurried by. Two singers who were late also rushed by quickly. Marie followed them with her eyes and immediately afterward, as though she wanted to atone for some wrong, looked anxiously at Felix. He was gnawing on his lips and wore on his forehead an expression of anger held back with great effort. She thought he was going to say something, but he remained silent. He averted his gloomy gaze from her and looked again at the two men who were just now disappearing from view at the park entrance. He knew what he was feeling—that here, walking before him, was the thing he hated most, a fragment of what would still be here when he wasn't here any more, something that would still be alive and young and laughing when he could no longer laugh and cry. And at his side, now pressing his arm more tightly than before because of a guilty conscience, was another fragment of that laughing, living youthfulness that unconsciously felt its kinship with the rest. He knew this, and it burrowed into him with excruciating pain. For a long time neither of them spoke. Finally a deep sigh escaped from his mouth. She wanted to look in his face, but he had turned away. All of a sudden he said, "This is fine here." She didn't know at first what he meant. "What?" she asked.

They were standing in front of an outdoor restaurant right next to the Kurpark. It had tall trees with tops that spread out over white-clad tables and dimly glowing lanterns. There were not many customers right now so they had their pick of tables and finally sat down in a corner of the garden. In all, scarcely twenty people were there. The elegant young couple they had encountered earlier that day sat nearby; Marie recognized them immediately. In the park beyond, the chorus began to sing. The voices that reached them were a little faint but utterly melodious, and it was as though the very leaves of the trees around them moved in time with the powerful sound of the bright voices. Felix had ordered a good Rhine wine and sat there with his eyes half closed, letting the wine melt on his tongue and surrendering to the magic of the music without much thought about where it came from. Marie had moved closer to him, and he felt the warmth of her knee next to his. After the dreadful agitation of the last few moments, a soothing indifference suddenly came over him, and he was pleased that he had been able to break through to such a feeling by an act of will. As soon as they sat down at the table, he had staunchly decided to overcome his piercing pain. He was too exhausted now to inquire more closely as to how much his willpower had contributed to this victory, but he was reassured by a few thoughts: that he had interpreted Marie's gaze more negatively than it deserved, that perhaps she would have looked at anyone the same way, and that she looked at the pair of strangers at the next table no differently than she had looked at the singers earlier.

The wine was good, the music seductive, the summer evening intoxicatingly warm, and when Felix looked over at Marie he saw a look of infinite compassion and love in her eyes. He wanted to immerse his entire being in this moment. He made one last demand on his willpower—to be free of both past and future. He wanted to be happy, or at least a little intoxicated. And suddenly a new and totally unexpected sensation came over him, a feeling that had something wonderfully liberating about it: namely, that it wouldn't take very much for him to decide to take his own life right now. Yes, right away, now. And he would be free to do so at any time. He could readily re-create an atmosphere just like this one—music, light intoxication, and a lovely girl at his side. Oh yes, it was Marie. He reflected. Any girl like her would perhaps be just as welcome to him now. She too was sipping the wine with great pleasure, and Felix soon had to order a new bottle. He was more contented than he had been in a long time. He explained this to himself by thinking that this contentment originated merely in a little more alcohol than he was used to. But what difference did that make? As long as something like this existed! Really, death did not frighten him any more. Oh, nothing mattered anyway.

"Don't you think, Mitzi . . . ?" he asked.

She nestled close to him.

"Don't I think what?"

"Nothing really matters. Don't you agree?"

"Yes, nothing," she replied, "except that I love you forever and ever."

It struck him as very strange that she said this so seriously—her individual identity was now almost a matter of indifference to him. She was merged with everything else. Yes, that was it, that was the way one had to deal with things. But no, it wasn't the wine that conjured this up; wine only relieves us of that which usually makes us awkward and cowardly—it takes away the importance of individuals and things. Now to have a little white powder and to put it into the glass—how simple that would be! And all the while he felt tears welling up in his eyes. He was moved by his own fate.

The chorus in the distance stopped singing. They heard applause and shouts of "Bravo!" then muffled noises, and soon the orchestra began again with the solemn gaiety of a *polonaise*. Felix kept time with his hand. The thought ran through his head: I want to live the little bit of time I have left as fully as I can. There was nothing horrifying to him about this idea now; if anything, there was something proud, even regal in it. Should he anxiously await the final breath, which is, after all, what's in store for everyone? Should he spoil his days and nights with empty brooding when he still felt in his bones that he was sound and vigorous enough for many pleasures, that the wine was delicious, and that, most of all, he could take this radiant girl into his lap and cover her with kisses? No, it was still too early to let his mood be spoiled. And when the time came when he no longer felt any enthusiasm or desire—then a quick end by his own hand, proud and regal! He took Marie's hand and held it in his for a long time. He let his breath slowly caress her.

"Oh yes," whispered Marie with an expression of contentment.

He gave her a long look. She was beautiful, beautiful! "Let's go," he said.

She answered artlessly, "Don't we want to listen to one more song?"

"Yes, we do," he said. "We'll open our window and let the wind carry it into our room."

"Are you tired?" she asked, a little worried.

He playfully caressed her hair and laughed, "Yes, I am."

"Let's go then."

They arose and left the garden. She took his arm firmly and leaned her cheek against his shoulder. On the way back to their lodging they were accompanied by the sound of the singers growing ever fainter. It was a bright melody in waltz tempo, with a joyful refrain that made them take lighter and looser steps. The hotel was just a few minutes away. Walking up the stairs, they couldn't hear the music any more, but as soon as they walked into their room they heard the refrain of the waltz resounding again in all its exuberance.

They found the window wide open and the blue moonlit night flooding the room in soft waves. Opposite them, the outline of the Mönchsberg and its castle was clearly visible. It wasn't necessary to light a lamp—a wide band of silver moonlight lay on the floor, and only the corners of the room remained in darkness. In one of them, near the window, was an armchair. Felix threw himself on it and pulled Marie passionately to him. He kissed her and she kissed him back. In the park outside the song ended, but there was so much applause that the chorus repeated the whole piece from the beginning. Suddenly Marie rose and rushed to the window. Felix followed her. "What's the matter with you?" he asked.

"No! no!" Marie cried.

He stamped his foot on the floor. "Why not?"

"Felix!" she folded her hands imploringly.

"No?" he said with clenched teeth. "No? I should be making dignified preparations for death instead?"

"But Felix!" And she flung herself down in front of him and clasped his knees.

He pulled her up. "You're just a child," he whispered. And then in her ear, "I love you, don't you know that? Let's be happy as long as there's still a little life left. I'll give up a year of misery and fear; I only want a few more weeks, a few days and nights. But I want to live them, I don't want to deny myself anything, not anything, and then, if you want, I'll disappear into that. . . . And with one arm he pointed out the window to the river that flowed beneath them as with the other he held her tight. The singers had finished their song, and now they heard only the soft murmur of the river.

Marie didn't answer. She had embraced him tightly with both arms. Felix drank in the fragrance of her hair. How he adored her! Yes, a few more days of happiness and then . . .

XI

Silence had fallen around them, and Marie had fallen asleep beside him. The concert had ended long ago, but the last of the festival's stragglers were still strolling beneath the window, talking and laughing loudly. Felix reflected how strange it was that these noisy people were the same ones whose singing had so deeply moved him. Finally the last voices faded, and now he could hear only the plaintive murmur of the river. Yes, a few more days and nights, and then. . . . But she enjoyed life too much. Would she ever dare to do it? But she needn't dare anything; she needn't know anything. One day she would fall asleep in his arms just as she had now—and not wake up again. And when he was entirely certain of that, then yes, he could go too. But he wouldn't say anything to her; she loved life too much. She would grow frightened of him, and in the end he would have to go alone. How awful! It would be best to do it right away—she was sleeping so soundly! A firm pressure here on her neck, and it would be done. No, that would be stupid! He still had many hours of happiness ahead of him; he would know when his last hour had come. He looked at Marie and felt as though he held his sleeping slave in his arms.

XII

The decision he had finally made calmed him down. A spiteful smile played around his lips when, as he strolled through the streets with Marie over the next few days, he occasionally saw a man give her an admiring glance. And when they took a carriage ride together, when they sat in a garden in the evenings, when at night he held her in his arms, he had a proud feeling of possession such as he had never had before. Only one thing sometimes disturbed him—that she wouldn't be going with him of her own free will. But there were indications that he would succeed in this as well: she no longer dared resist his tempestuous desires and she had never been so full of dreamy surrender as she had been in the last few nights. With tremulous joy he saw the moment approach when he would dare to say, "Today we'll die." But he postponed that moment. In the meantime he fantasized a romantic scenario in which he plunged a dagger into her heart as she, breathing her last sigh, kissed his beloved hand. He asked himself constantly if she had already reached that point. But he always had reason to doubt it.

When Marie awoke one morning she had a terrible fright—Felix was not at her side. She sat up in bed and saw him sitting in the armchair by the window, deathly pale, his head sunk down on his chest and his nightshirt open. Gripped by a violent fear, she rushed to him. "Felix!"

He opened his eyes. "What? What is it?" He touched his chest and moaned.

"Why didn't you wake me up?" she cried, wringing her hands.

"It's all right now," he said. She hurried over to the bed, removed the blanket, and spread it over his knees. "Tell me, for heaven's sake, how did you get here?"

"I don't know. I must have been dreaming. Something seized me by the throat. I couldn't breathe. I didn't think about you at all! Here by the window I felt better."

Marie had quickly pulled on a dress and closed the window. An unpleasant wind had risen, and now a fine rain began to drizzle from the grey sky, bringing a life-threatening dampness into the room. The room suddenly lost all the coziness of the summer night and was now alien and grey. A bleak fall morning had dawned all at once, mocking all the magic they had conjured up.

Felix was completely calm. "Why are you acting so frightened? What's wrong, anyway? I had bad dreams even when I was still in good health."

She wouldn't calm down. "I beg you, Felix, let's go back, let's go back to Vienna."

"But . . ."

"Summer's over now anyway. Just look out there at how bleak, how cheerless it is! It's also dangerous now that it's turning cold."

He listened to her attentively. To his astonishment, he felt completely well at that moment, like an exhausted but recovered convalescent. He breathed easily, and in the weariness that enveloped him there was something sweet and lulling. It made perfect sense to him that they should leave town. In fact, the thought of changing location was rather attractive. He looked forward to lying in the railway compartment on this cool, rainy day with his head on Marie's breast.

"Fine," he said, "let's go."

"Right now?"

"Yes, today. On the noontime express train if you like."

"But won't that tire you out too much?"

"Oh, why do you say that? It's not a strenuous trip, is it? And you'll take care of everything I dislike about traveling, won't you?"

She was infinitely glad that she had convinced him to leave so easily. She immediately set about packing. She took care of the hotel bill, ordered the carriage, and reserved a train compartment for them. Felix was soon dressed, but he didn't leave the room. He spent the whole morning stretched out on the sofa observing Marie rushing busily around the room and smiling occasionally. Most of the time, though, he dozed. He was so tired, so very tired. And when he looked at her, he was glad she was going to stay with him everywhere he went; that they would soon rest together, too. All this went dreamily through his mind. "Soon, soon," he thought. And yet the moment had never seemed so distant.

XIII

And so, just as he had imagined it that morning, Felix was comfortably stretched out in the train compartment in the afternoon. He was covered with the plaid blanket, and his head rested on Marie's breast. He stared into the grey day outside through the closed window, saw the rain trickle down, and occasionally glimpsed nearby hills and houses emerging out of the fog. Telegraph poles with dancing wires shot past, and occasionally the train stopped at a station, although from his position Felix could not see anyone standing on the platform—he heard the footsteps, the voices, the ringing of bells, and the bugle calls only in a dreamy, indistinct way. At first he had Marie read to him from the newspaper, but she strained her voice and soon they gave up. They were both glad to be going home.

It was getting dark and the rain drizzled. Felix felt a need to think clearly, but his thoughts refused to come into focus. Well, he thought, here lies a seriously ill man . . . he has just been in the mountains because that's where seriously ill people go in the summer . . . and here is his sweetheart, who faithfully took good care of him, and is now tired of it. . . . She's very pale. Or is that only the light? Oh yes, the lamp up there is already lit. But it's not yet completely dark outdoors . . . autumn is coming . . . autumn is so sad and so quiet. . . . This evening we'll be in our room in Vienna again . . . there I'll feel as though I've never been away. . . . It's good that Marie is sleeping . . . I don't want to hear her talk now. . . . I wonder if anyone from the choral festival is on this train? I'm just tired . . . I'm not sick at all. There are others on this train who are a lot sicker than I am. Oh, how good it feels to be alone . . . how did we spend the day? Was it really just today that I lay on the sofa in Salzburg? It seems so long ago. . . . Yes, time and space, what do we know about them? The riddle of the universe . . . when we die, maybe we solve it then. . . . And now a melody sounded in his ear. He knew it was only the sound of the rolling train . . . but still it was a melody . . . a folksong . . . a Russian one . . . very beautiful. . . .

"Felix, Felix!"

"What is it now?" Marie was standing in front of him and stroking his cheeks.

"Did you sleep well, Felix?"

"What's happening?"

"We'll be in Vienna in half an hour."

"That's impossible!"

"You slept soundly. I'm sure it did you a lot of good."

She assembled their luggage, and the train hurtled through the night. At short intervals there was a prolonged, high-pitched whistle, and flashes of light appeared and faded rapidly outside the windows. They were traveling through the stations on the outskirts of Vienna.

Felix sat up. "All this lying down has made me feel more tired," he said. He sat down in a corner and looked out the window. He could see the shimmering streets of the city in the distance. The train slowed, and Marie opened the compartment window and leaned out. They were entering the station. Marie waved her hand out the window. Then she turned to Felix and cried, "There he is, there he is!"

"Who?"

"Alfred!"

"Alfred?"

She kept on waving. Felix stood up and looked over her shoulder. Alfred was rapidly approaching their compartment and extended his hand up to Marie.

"Greetings! Hello, Felix!"

"What are you doing here?"

"I telegraphed him," said Marie quickly, "about our arrival."

"A fine friend you are," said Alfred. "I suppose letter writing is an unknown invention to you. But come along now!"

"I slept so much," said Felix, "that I'm still quite groggy." He smiled as he climbed down the steps of the train carriage and wobbled a little.

Alfred took his arm, and Marie quickly grabbed his other one as if she merely wanted to link arms with him.

"I suppose you're both quite exhausted, aren't you?"

"I'm totally done in," said Marie. "Don't you agree, Felix, that these awful train rides are exhausting?"

They slowly descended the stairs. Marie sought Alfred's eyes; he avoided hers. Down on the street, Alfred hailed a carriage. "I'm so glad to have seen you, dear Felix," he said. "Tomorrow morning I'll come over for a longer chat."

"I'm really groggy," repeated Felix. Alfred tried to help him into the carriage. "Oh, it's not that bad, really it's not!" Felix protested. He climbed in and reached down to help Marie. "You see?" he said. Marie followed him.

"Till tomorrow then," she said to Alfred as she held out her hand through the carriage window. There was so much doubt and anxiety in her eyes that Alfred had to force himself to smile. "Yes, tomorrow," he cried, "I'll have breakfast with the two of you." The carriage drove away. For a while Alfred remained standing with a serious expression on his face.

"My poor friend!" he whispered to himself.

XIV

The next morning Alfred came very early, and Marie received him at the door. "I must talk to you," she said.

"Let me see him first. After I've examined him, everything we need to talk about will make more sense."

"I'd like to ask you for just one thing, Alfred! No matter how you find him, please don't tell him anything!"

"What are you thinking of? Surely it isn't that bad. Is he still asleep?"

"No, he's awake."

"How was the night?"

"He slept well until four in the morning. After that he was restless."

"Let me see him alone first. You've got to compose yourself. You can't go to him looking like this." He shook her hand with a smile and walked into the bedroom alone.

Felix had pulled the bedcover up over his chin and he nodded to his friend. Alfred sat down next to him on the bed and said, "So you're home again, safe and sound. You've had a wonderful vacation, and I hope you left your melancholy in the mountains."

"Oh yes!" said Felix, without changing his expression.

"Don't you want to sit up a bit? I make such early calls only in my role as a doctor."

"All right," said Felix, indifferently.

Alfred examined the patient and asked a few questions, which were answered curtly. Finally he said, "Well, so far, so good."

"Oh, stop this charade!" replied Felix, irritated.

"It would be better if you stopped with your silly notions. Let's tackle this thing vigorously now. You must have the will to get well, and you mustn't play the role of the person resigned to his fate. It doesn't really suit you very well."

"What do I have to do then?"

"First of all, you'll have to stay in bed for a few days. Understand?"

"I don't feel like getting up anyway."

"All the better."

Felix became more animated. "I just want to know one thing. What was the matter with me yesterday? Seriously, Alfred, you've got to explain that. It all seems like a murky dream—the train ride, the arrival, how I got up here and into this bed."

"What is there to explain? You're not a superman to begin with, and that's what happens when you're overtired!"

"No, Alfred. A fatigue like yesterday's is something completely new to me. I'm tired today too, but I can think clearly again. Yesterday wasn't actually all that unpleasant, but the memory of it horrifies me. When I think that something like it could strike me again . . ."

At that moment Marie came into the room.

"Thank Alfred," said Felix. "He's nominated you to be my nurse. I have to stay in bed from now on, and I herewith have the honor of introducing you to my deathbed."

Marie looked absolutely horrified.

"Don't let this clown turn your head," said Alfred. "He merely has to stay in bed for a few days, so please be so kind as to take care of him."

"Oh, if you only knew, Alfred," Felix said with ironic enthusiasm, "what an angel I have by my side."

Alfred then gave them detailed instructions about what Felix needed to do, and finally said, "I must explain to you, my dear Felix, that I'll make a doctor's visit only every other day. More than that isn't necessary. On the other days there'll be no talking about your condition; I'll come around to talk to you as usual."

"Oh God," cried Felix, "what a psychologist this man is! But save your tactics for your other patients, particularly the more simpleminded ones."

"My dear Felix, I'm talking to you man to man. Listen to me. It's true, you're sick. But this is also true: with the proper care you'll get well. I can say nothing more or less than that." And with that he stood up.

Felix's eyes followed him with a suspicious look. "One might almost be tempted to believe him."

"That's up to you, dear Felix," answered the doctor curtly.

"Well, Alfred, now you've spoiled it," said the patient. "This brusque tone with seriously ill patients—a well-known trick."

"Till tomorrow," said Alfred, turning to the door. Marie followed him and wanted to accompany him out. "Stay here," he whispered to her imperiously. She closed the door behind him.

"Come to me, sweetie!" said Felix, as she feigned a cheerful smile and busied herself with her sewing at the table. "Yes, come here. There, you're such a good, good, very good little girl." He spoke these tender words in a harsh, sharp tone of voice.

XV

Over the next few days Marie did not budge from his side and was full of kindness and devotion. At the same time she adopted a tone of calm and unaffected gaiety that was intended to do the patient good, and sometimes actually did. But more often her measured cheerfulness irritated him. And when she began to chatter on about some item that happened to be in the newspaper, or about how she noticed that he was looking better, or about the plans she was making for their future life together when he was fully recovered, he would sometimes interrupt her and beg her to please leave him in peace and spare him such talk. Alfred came every day, sometimes even twice, but hardly ever appeared to concern himself with his friend's physical condition. He spoke about mutual friends, told stories about the hospital, and carried on conversations about artistic and literary matters in such a way that Felix didn't have to say much. Both of them, his beloved and his friend, acted so naturally that Felix had trouble fending off the bold hopes that at times came crowding in on him. He told himself that it was merely their duty to put on the drama that had been staged for gravely ill patients since time immemorial and with varying success. But even when he thought he was only playing along with their act, he repeatedly caught himself talking about the world and people as if he were destined to have many more years to wander in the sunlight among the living. But then he remembered that it was exactly this odd feeling of well-being that was supposed to be a sign of imminent death in patients like him, and he bitterly rejected all hope. He even reached the point where he interpreted his vague feelings of anxiety and depression as good omens and came close to rejoicing in them. But then he realized how absurd this logic was—that in this realm there was neither knowledge nor certainty. He had resumed his reading but got no enjoyment from it. Novels bored him, and some of them, especially those that opened broad vistas into vibrant and eventful lives, deeply disturbed him. He turned to the philosophers and asked Marie to bring Schopenhauer and Nietzsche from the bookcase. But their wisdom brought him peace only briefly.

One evening Alfred found him just as Felix had allowed a volume of Schopenhauer to slip down onto his bedcover. He was staring gloomily into space. Marie was sitting next to him busy with some needlework.

"I want to tell you something, Alfred," he called toward his friend in an almost excited voice, "I'm going to start reading novels again after all."

"What's happened?"

"At least novels are honest fables—good, bad, by artists or hacks. But these gentlemen here . . ." and he indicated with his eyes the volume lying on his blanket, "are despicable poseurs."

"Oh!"

Felix sat up in bed. "To despise life when one is as healthy as a god and to look death calmly in the eye while riding around Italy, surrounded by life blooming in its brightest colors—that's what I call a pose. Take such a man and lock him in a room, condemn him to a fever, to a struggle for breath, tell him that he will be dead and buried between the first of January and the first of February the next year, and then let him philosophize for you."

"Come on!" said Alfred. "What kind of sophistry is this?"

"You don't understand. You can't understand! I find it downright disgusting. They're all poseurs!"

"And Socrates?"

"He was an actor. It's natural for a human being to fear the unknown; at best he can only conceal his fear. I'm going to be totally honest with you. Our understanding of the psychology of the dying is wrong because all of the greats of world history—the ones whose deaths we know about—felt an obligation to put on an act for posterity. And I? What am I doing? What indeed? When I talk calmly with you about all sorts of things that don't concern me any more in the least, what am I doing?

"Come on, don't talk so much, especially such nonsense."

"I too feel that I have to put on an act when in reality I feel a fear that is so boundless and frenzied that no healthy person can have any idea of it. And everyone has such a fear, even the heroes and the philosophers—it's just that they're the better actors!"

"Please, Felix, do calm yourself," begged Marie.

"I suppose you two also believe," continued the patient, "since you still haven't the faintest idea of what it really means, that you're looking eternity calmly in the eye. You have to be under a sentence of death like a criminal—or like me—then you can talk about it. The poor devil who walks up to the gallows with composure, the great sage who utters aphorisms after he's emptied the cup of hemlock, the captured freedom fighter who smiles when he sees the rifles aimed at his chest—they're all hypocrites. I know that their composure, their smiles, are all a charade. For they're all terrified of death, hideously afraid, because such a fear is as natural as death itself."

Alfred had calmly sat down on the bed, and when Felix finished, he said, "In the first place, it's not good for you to talk so much and so loudly. Second, you're being really maudlin, outrageous, and an awful hypochondriac to boot."

"And you're feeling so much better lately!" exclaimed Marie.

"Could she really believe that?" Felix asked, turning to Alfred. "Go ahead and finally enlighten her, won't you?"

"My dear friend," replied the doctor, "you're the one who needs enlightenment! But you're being difficult today, so I can't do it. In two or three days, provided you don't give any more long speeches, you'll be able to get up out of bed. Then we'll have a consultation about your emotional state as well."

"If only I weren't able to see through you so completely," sighed Felix.

"All right, all right," replied Alfred, "don't act so hurt." Then he said, turning to Marie, "One day even this gentleman here will come to his senses again. But now tell me, why isn't there a window open? It's the most beautiful autumn day imaginable outdoors."

Marie stood up and opened a window. It was just beginning to get dark, and the breeze that came in was so refreshing that Marie wanted to let it caress her a while longer. She remained standing by the window and leaned her head out. Suddenly she felt as though she had actually left the room. She felt she was out in the fresh air by herself. She hadn't had such a pleasant sensation in days. Now, when she turned her head back to the room again, the mustiness of the sickroom rushed at her and weighed heavily and oppressively on her. She saw Felix and Alfred talking; she couldn't quite make out their words, but she had no desire to take part in the conversation. Again she leaned out the window. The street was rather silent and empty; the only sound was the muffled rattle of carriages in the boulevard nearby. A few strollers were sauntering slowly down the opposite sidewalk. In front of the doorway across the street, a few servant girls stood chattering and laughing. A young woman in the house across the way was looking out of the window just as Marie was. At that moment, Marie couldn't comprehend why the woman wasn't out taking a walk. She envied everyone; everyone was happier than she was.

Soft and easy September days had arrived. Evening came early, but the air remained warm and calm.

Marie had developed the habit of moving her chair away from the invalid's bed and sitting by the open window as often as she could. She sat there for hours, especially when Felix was dozing. A profound weariness had overcome her, an inability to think clearly about her situation, even a downright aversion to thinking about it.

There were hours on end when she had neither memories nor future plans. She daydreamed with her eyes wide open and was content when a little fresh air from the street touched her forehead. Then again, when a soft moan reached her from the sickbed, she started. She realized that she had gradually lost the gift of empathy. She was capable of only a nervous overreaction, and her pain had turned into a mixture of fear and indifference. She surely had nothing to reproach herself for, and when the doctor called her an angel and meant it (as he had once recently), she had little reason to feel ashamed of herself. But she was tired, infinitely tired. She had not left the house in ten or twelve days now. Why not? Why? She had to think about it. She had a sudden flash of insight: because it would hurt Felix's feelings! And she liked to stay with him, yes she did. She still adored him, no less than she did before. She was just tired, and that, after all, was only human. Her longing for a few hours outdoors in the fresh air became ever more pressing. It was childish of her to deny herself the gratification of this desire. In the end even he would agree with that. It became clear to her once more that she must love him infinitely if she wished to spare him even the possibility of hurt feelings. She had let her sewing slide to the floor, and cast a glance toward the bed already in the shadow of the wall. It was dusk, and the patient had dozed off after a calmer day. She could leave now without his even becoming aware of it. Oh, yes, down the stairs here, around the corner there, and once again to be with other people; to go by the Stadtpark and the Ring Strasse and the Opera, where the electric lamps glowed; to be in the midst of teeming crowds—that was what she longed for. When would such a normal life come back? It could come back only if Felix got well. What, after all, did streets, parks, and other people mean to her, what did life mean to her without Felix!

She stayed home. She moved her chair closer to his bed. She took the sleeping man's hand and shed silent, sad tears upon it. She continued to cry long after her thoughts had strayed far from the person on whose pale hand her tears were falling.

XVI

When Alfred called on Felix the following afternoon, he found him more alert than he had been in the last few days. "If things continue this way," he said to Felix, "I'll let you get out of bed in a couple of days." As to everything else Alfred said, the sick man responded with distrust. He replied with an irritated "Yeah, yeah." Alfred turned to Marie, who was sitting by the window, and said, "You could look a little better yourself."

Even Felix, who took a closer look at Marie upon hearing these words, was struck by her extreme pallor. He was accustomed to warding off the thoughts he sometimes had about her self-sacrificing devotion. Sometimes her martyrdom seemed not quite genuine to him, and he was annoyed by the air of patience she displayed. He sometimes wished she would be impatient. He watched for the moment when she would betray herself with a word or a glance. Then he could maliciously throw it back to her that he was not deceived for a single moment, that her hypocrisy disgusted him, and that she ought to let him die in peace.

Now that Alfred had mentioned how pale she looked, she blushed a little and smiled. "I'm feeling quite well," she said.

Alfred walked over to her. "No, it's not as simple as that. Felix won't enjoy his recovery very much if in the process you get sick."

"But I really feel quite well."

"Tell me, do you ever get any fresh air?"

"I don't feel the need to."

"Tell me, Felix, does she never stir from your side?"

"Well, you know," said Felix, "she's an angel."

"Forgive me for saying so, Marie, but this is just plain stupid.

It's unnecessary and childish to wear yourself out this way. You have to get some fresh air. I'm prescribing it as a necessity."

"But what do you want from me?" said Marie with a weak smile. "I have absolutely no desire to go out."

"That doesn't matter. In fact, it's a bad sign that you have no desire to go out. You've got to get out this very day. Go and sit for an hour in the Stadtpark. Or, if you don't like that idea, hire a carriage and go for a ride . . . into the Prater, for example. It's beautiful out there now."

"But . . ."

"No buts. If you keep on like this, the complete angel, you'll ruin your health. Go and look in the mirror. You're destroying your health."

Felix felt a sharp pain in his breast as he heard Alfred say this. A grim rage gnawed at him. He thought he noticed an expression of conscious martyrdom that demanded pity in Marie's features, and like an incontrovertible truth that could not be challenged, it flashed through his mind that this woman was obligated to suffer and to die with him. She was ruining herself . . . well yes, of course. Did she intend to keep her rosy cheeks and bright eyes while he rushed to his end? And did Alfred really believe that this woman, his beloved, had the right to think beyond his last hour? And did she herself perhaps dare . . . ?

Consumed with rage, Felix studied the expression on Marie's face as the doctor repeated the things he had said before in an ill-humored way. Finally he made Marie promise that she would go out that very day. He explained to her that keeping this promise was just as much a part of her nursing duties as all the others. "Because I don't count any more at all," thought Felix. "Because he who is doomed in any case is left to rot by the wayside." When Alfred finally left, he shook hands with him very limply. He hated him.

Marie escorted the doctor only as far as the door and immediately returned to Felix. He lay there with pursed lips and a deep furrow of anger on his forehead. Marie understood; she understood him completely. She leaned over him and smiled. He took a deep breath. He wanted to speak, wanted to fling some outrageous insult into her face. It seemed to him that she deserved it. But she, stroking his hair with that patient, weary smile on her face, whispered tenderly very near his lips, "You know I'm not going to go."

He didn't answer. The whole evening long and until deep into the night she remained seated by his bed and finally fell asleep in her chair.

XVII

When Alfred came the next day, Marie tried to avoid talking with him. In fact, he didn't seem to take an interest in her appearance today and concerned himself only with Felix. But he said nothing about Felix's being able to get out of bed soon, and the sick man was reluctant to ask him. He felt weaker than he had on the preceding days. He felt more reluctant to talk than he ever had before and was glad when the doctor left. To Marie's questions, too, he gave short and sullen answers. And when, after hours of silence, she asked him again in the late afternoon, "How are you feeling now?" he said, "It doesn't matter." He had crossed his arms behind his head and had now closed his eyes and dozed off. Marie stayed at his side for some time, observing him; then her thoughts became blurred and she began to daydream. After some time she experienced a strange feeling of well-being flowing through her limbs, as though she were waking up from a healthy, sound sleep. She rose and pulled up the curtains. It was as though the fragrance of late-blooming flowers from the nearby park had strayed into the narrow street this evening. The air that now flooded the room had never before seemed as glorious to her. She turned to look at Felix; as before, he was lying there sleeping and breathing calmly. Usually in such moments she had been so moved that she was spellbound in the room, her whole being suffused by a lethargic melancholy. But today she remained calm, happy that Felix was sleeping. And she decided, without an inner battle and as if she had done this every day, to go outdoors for an hour. She tiptoed into the kitchen, instructed the servant to stay in the sickroom, quickly picked up her hat and umbrella, and fairly flew down the stairs. For a moment she stood there in the street. After a quick walk through a few quiet streets she came to the park and was glad to see hedges and trees and the deep blue sky for which she had long yearned. She sat down on a bench; next to her and on other nearby benches sat nannies and wet nurses. On the tree-lined trails small children were playing. But since it was beginning to get dark, all this activity was nearing its end; the nannies were calling the children, taking them by the hand and leaving the park. Soon Marie was almost alone. Only a few people were still walking by, and now and then a man turned around to look at her.

So now here she was, out in the fresh air. Well, how did things stand? It seemed to her that the time had come to survey her situation without flinching. She wanted to find the precise, accurate words for her thoughts, words she could say inwardly. I'm with him because I love him. I'm not making a sacrifice, because I can't help doing it. What's going to happen now? How long is it going to take? He can't be saved. And what then? What then? Once I wanted to die with him. Why are we such strangers to each other now? He thinks only of himself. Does he still want to die with me? And the certainty that he did pierced her. And the image that appeared to her now was not the image of the loving youth who wanted to sleep with her for all eternity. No, she felt as though he were pulling her down to him, selfishly, jealously, simply because she belonged to him, because she was his property.

A young man had sat down next to her on the bench and made a remark. She was so distracted that at first she asked, "What?" But then she stood up and quickly walked away. The glances of those she encountered in the park had begun to bother her. She walked out to the Ring Strasse, hailed a carriage, and let herself be taken for a ride. Dusk had fallen, and she leaned comfortably into a corner to enjoy the pleasant, effortless motion and the changing scenes, dipped in the golden light of the evening and the flickering gaslights. The beautiful September evening had lured a crowd of people out into the streets. As Marie rode past the Volksgarten, she heard bright sounds of military music, and she couldn't help but think of that evening in Salzburg. In vain she tried to persuade herself that all this teeming life around her was something empty and transitory, that it would be a matter of little consequence to leave it behind. But she couldn't banish the feeling of well-being that had begun to pervade her whole being. She just felt good. That the festive theatre was still there with its shining, white-arced lamps, that people still sauntered from the walkways of the Rathauspark out into the streets, that people still sat outdoors in front of that café, that there were still people whose cares she knew nothing about or who perhaps even had none, that a warm and mild air caressed her, that she would be allowed to experience many such evenings, a thousand more wonderful nights and days, that a feeling of life-affirming health was flowing through her veins—all of that did her good. What? Should she feel guilty that after countless hours of deadly exhaustion she finally had a minute to herself? Wasn't it her inalienable right to be aware that she was alive? After all, she was in good health, she was young, and, as if from everywhere, as if from a hundred springs at once, the joy of existence flooded her. This was as natural as breathing and the sky above. Was she supposed to be ashamed of it? She thought of Felix. If a miracle happened and he recovered, she would certainly go on living with him. She thought about him with gentle, conciliatory anguish. It was almost time to go back to him. Was he content when she was with him? Did he appreciate her tenderness? How harsh his words were! How piercing his looks! And his kiss! How long had it been since they had kissed? She thought of his lips, which were now always so pale and so dry. These days she only wanted to kiss him on the forehead. His forehead was cold and damp. How ugly illness was!

She leaned back in the carriage. She deliberately turned her thoughts away from Felix and his sickness. In order not to have to think about him, she eagerly looked into the street and observed everything intently as though she wanted to imprint it in her memory.

XVIII

Felix opened his eyes. A candle burned near his bed and cast a faint light. Next to him sat an old woman, her hands in her lap, indifferent. She started when the invalid demanded of her, "Where is she?" The woman explained to him that Marie had gone out but would be back very soon.

"You can go," answered Felix. And when the woman hesitated, he said, "Please go. I don't need you."

He remained alone. An agitation more agonizing than any he had ever felt overcame him.

Where was she, where was she? He could hardly stand to stay in bed, but he didn't dare get up. Suddenly the thought flashed through his mind: Maybe she's left! She wanted to leave him alone, forever alone. She couldn't tolerate life with him any longer. She was afraid of him. She had read his thoughts. Or he had talked in his sleep and said out loud what was always somewhere in his mind, even when for days on end he wasn't quite aware of it himself. She didn't want to die with him after all. Thoughts raced through his mind. He had a fever, the fever that came every evening. It had been so long since he had said a friendly word to her; maybe it was only that! He had tortured her with his moods, with his distrustful looks, with his bitter speeches, when what she needed was gratitude! No, no, only justice! Oh! If only she were here! He had to have her here! With a burning pain he realized that he couldn't do without her. He would beg her forgiveness if he had to. He would look at her tenderly again and find words of fervent intimacy once more. He wouldn't let one syllable betray his suffering. He would smile when his chest felt crushed. He would kiss her hand as he struggled for breath. He would tell her that he was dreaming nonsense, that what she heard him say in his sleep was nothing but delirium. And he would swear that he adored her, that he didn't begrudge her a long and happy life, but on the contrary, fervently wished for it. If only she would stay with him until the end, if only she would not stir from his bed, would not let him die alone. He would face the terrible hour with patience and peace if only he knew that she was with him! And that hour could come soon, yes, could come any day now. That's why she had to be with him always, because when he was without her he was afraid.

Where was she? Where was she? The blood whirled through his head, his vision grew dim, his breathing became labored, and no one was there. Oh, why had he sent the woman away? She was, after all, a human soul. Now he was helpless, helpless. He sat up in bed. He felt stronger than he thought he would, except for his breathing, his breathing. It was terrible the way it tormented him. He couldn't stand it any more. He jumped out of bed, barely clothed, and ran to the window. Here there was air, air! He drew a few deep breaths; how wonderful that felt! He put on the loose robe that hung over the bedpost, and sank into a chair. For a few minutes his thoughts were jumbled; then one question, always the same one, pierced through the rest: Where was she? Where was she? Had she often left him like

this as he slept? How would he know? Where did she go on such occasions? Did she want only to escape the stuffy air of the sickroom
for a few hours, or did she want to flee because he was sick? Was his
nearness repugnant to her? Was she afraid of the shadow of death
that already hovered in the room? Was she longing for life? Was she
looking for life? Did he no longer mean life to her? What did she
want? Where was she? Where was she?

And the racing thoughts became whispered syllables, then
moans and loud words. And he shouted and screamed: "Where is
she?" And he pictured to himself how she might have hurried down
the stairs with a smile of liberation on her lips, rushing off to somewhere, to anywhere where there was no sickness, no disgust, no
slow dying; rushing to somewhere unknown, somewhere where
there were perfume and flower blossoms. He saw her disappear and
vanish into a light fog that concealed her from him and through
which he could hear her ringing laughter, a laughter of happiness
and joy. And then the fog parted and he saw her dancing. She
whirled farther and farther away from him, and then she disappeared. And suddenly he heard a muffled rumbling coming closer
and closer and suddenly stopping. Where was she? He gave a start.
He hurried to the window. It had been the rolling of a carriage, and it
had stopped in front of the door. Yes, it was a carriage; he could see
it. And from the carriage . . . yes . . . it was Marie! It was Marie! He
had to go to meet her. He rushed headlong into the hall, now completely dark. He couldn't find the door handle. Then a key turned in
the lock, the door opened, and Marie entered, bathed in the faint
gaslight of the corridor. She bumped into him without seeing him
and screamed out loud. He grabbed her by the shoulders and
dragged her into the room. He opened his mouth but couldn't talk
at all.

"What's the matter with you?" she exclaimed in horror. "Have you gone mad?" She freed herself from his grasp. He remained standing. He seemed to be looming taller and taller. Finally he was able to say, "Where have you been? Where?"

"For God's sake, Felix, get hold of yourself! How could you! I beg you, at least sit down."

"Where have you been?" he said softly, as though everything were already lost. "Where? Where?" he whispered. She took his hands; they were burning hot. He willingly, almost unconsciously, allowed her to lead him and slowly press him down into a corner of the sofa. He looked around, as though he needed time to gradually regain his senses. Then he said again, quite audibly, but in the same monotone, "Where have you been?"

She had regained some of her composure, and she tossed her hat onto a chair behind her. She sat down next to him on the sofa and said cajolingly, "Darling, I only went out for an hour to get some fresh air. I'm afraid of getting sick myself. What good would I be to you if I did? I even took a carriage just so I could be back with you sooner."

He was lying in his corner, completely exhausted now. He glanced at her obliquely and didn't reply.

She continued, caressing his hot cheeks. "You aren't angry with me, are you? By the way, I did tell the servant to stay with you until I returned. Didn't you see her? Where is she, anyway?"

"I sent her away."

"But why, Felix? She was supposed to stay until I came back. I missed you so much! What good is the fresh air outdoors to me if I don't have you?"

"Mitzi, Mitzi!" he put his head against her breast like a sick child. As they had in earlier days, her lips touched his hair. He looked up at her with pleading eyes. "Mitzi," he said, "you must always stay with me, always. Will you?"

"Yes," she replied and kissed his tangled, damp hair. She was heartsick, absolutely heartsick! She wanted to cry, but in her feelings there was something dry and withered. There was no consolation for her anywhere, not even in her own pain. And she envied him when she saw tears flowing down his cheeks.

XIX

And so, for all the days and evenings that followed she sat by his bedside again, brought him his meals, and gave him his medicine. And when he was alert enough to request it, she read to him either from the newspaper or from a chapter of a novel. The morning after her walk it had begun to rain, and a premature autumn set in. Thin grey ribbons of rain dripped down the windowpanes for hours, for days, almost without stopping. Marie sometimes heard the invalid talk incoherently in his sleep. At such times she would stroke his forehead mechanically with her hands and whisper, "Sleep, Felix, sleep, Felix," the way one soothes a restless child. He grew weaker and weaker but didn't suffer much. And when the brief attacks of shortness of breath that vividly reminded him of his illness ended, he usually sank into a state of torpor that he could not explain even to himself. Only sometimes did it occur to him to wonder, "Why have I stopped caring about anything?" When he saw the rain drip down outside, he thought, "Oh, well, it's autumn," but he didn't pursue the thought further. Actually he no longer thought about change—not about the end, not about recovery. And in those days Marie too completely stopped hoping for any kind of improvement. Even Alfred's visits had become more or less routine. For him, of course, coming as he did from the outside and for whom life continued as usual, the sickroom appeared different every day. He gave up all hope. He noticed that for Felix as well as for Marie, a certain phase had now begun, a phase that sometimes sets in for people who have suffered extreme agitation—a phase in which there is neither hope nor fear, in which even the experience of the present is murky because it lacks a vision of the future and a memory of the past. He always entered the sickroom with a feeling of great discomfort and was pleased when he found the two of them just exactly as he had left them. For the time was bound to come when they would be compelled to think again about what was coming.

One day, when he had come up the stairs once more with such thoughts in his head, he found Marie standing in the hallway. Her cheeks were pale and she wrung her hands. "Come quickly, come quickly," she called out. He followed her hurriedly. Felix was sitting straight up in bed. He gave both of them a nasty look and cried out, "What are you two planning to do with me, anyway?"

Alfred quickly walked over to him. "What's the matter, Felix?" he said.

"What are you planning to do with me—that's what I want to know!"

"What kind of a silly question is that?"

"You're letting me rot, rot miserably!" cried Felix, almost screaming.

Alfred stepped close to him and reached for his hand. But the invalid withdrew it violently. "Leave me alone! And you, Marie, stop your hand-wringing. I want to know what you're planning to do with me. How long is this supposed to go on, that's what I want to know?"

"Things would go on much better," said Alfred calmly, "if you wouldn't get so needlessly worked up."

"Well, I've been lying here for how long, how long? You look on and let me lie here." He suddenly turned toward the doctor. "What are you planning to do with me anyway?"

"Oh, don't talk nonsense," Alfred replied.

"But nothing is being done for me, nothing at all! It's over-whelming me, and nobody is lifting a finger to fight it off!"

"Felix," said Alfred in an urgent tone of voice, as he sat down on the bed and again tried to take Felix's hand.

"Well, you're just giving up on me! You're letting me lie here and take morphine."

"You've got to be patient for a few more days."

"But you can see that lying here doesn't do me any good! I know, I can feel how things are with me! Why are you letting me fall apart so hopelessly? You can see that I'm dying here. I can't stand it any more! There must be something that can help me; there must be some possibility of help. Think hard, Alfred, you're a doctor, after all, and it's your duty."

"Of course there's something that can help," said Alfred.

"And if there's no remedy, then maybe there's a miracle. But a miracle won't happen here in this place. I have to get away. I want to get away from here."

"As soon as you get a little stronger, you'll be able to get out of bed."

"Alfred, I'm telling you, it's getting too late. Why should I stay in this awful room? I want to get away. I want to get out of town. I know what I need. I need spring. I need to go south, where the sun still shines. Then I'll get well."

"That all sounds very reasonable," said Alfred. "Of course you'll go south, but you've got to have a little patience. You can't travel today, or tomorrow either. As soon as you're able, you can go."

"I can travel today, I know it. Just as soon as I'm out of this horrible death chamber, I'll be a different person. Every day you keep me here is dangerous."

"My dear friend, you have to keep in mind that as your doctor I—"

"You're a doctor and therefore you make merely routine judgments. Patients know best what they need. It's thoughtless and inconsiderate of you to let me just lie here and die. In the south, miracles sometimes do happen. You shouldn't just twiddle your thumbs as long as there is any glimmer of hope left. And there is still some hope. It's inhumane to leave a person to his fate, as you two are doing with me. I want to go south. I want to go back to spring!"

"Yes, quite so, that's what you should do," said Alfred.

"We can leave tomorrow, then, can't we?" interjected Marie hastily.

"If Felix promises me he'll rest for three days, I'll let him go away. But today? Right now? That would be criminal! I can't permit that under any circumstances. Just look at this weather," he turned to Marie, "it's stormy and rainy. I wouldn't advise a person in the best of health to go traveling today."

"Then tomorrow!" cried Felix.

"If it clears up a bit," said the doctor. "In two or three days. I give you my word."

The invalid gave him an intense and searching look. Then he asked, "Your word of honor?"

"Yes!"

"Well, did you hear that?" exclaimed Marie.

"So you don't believe," said the invalid, turning to Alfred, "that there is still hope for me? You wanted to let me die here in my homeland? That's false humanitarianism. When one is about to die, there is no more homeland. The ability to live—that's the homeland. And I won't . . . I won't . . . die so defenselessly!"

"My dear Felix, you know very well that it's my intention to have you spend the whole winter in the south. But I can't let you leave in this weather."

"Marie," said the patient, "get everything ready." Marie looked at the doctor with anxious, questioning eyes.

"Well, all right," said the doctor, "there's no harm in that."

"Get everything ready. I want to get up in an hour. We'll leave as soon as the first ray of sunshine appears."

XX

Felix got up out of bed that afternoon. It seemed as if the very thought of a change of scene had a beneficial effect on him. He was awake and lying on the sofa, but he had neither the outbursts of despair nor the dull indifference of the preceding days. He took an interest in the preparations that Marie was making, gave advice and directions, pointed out the books from his library that he wanted to take along, and even took a big stack of manuscripts out of his desk. "I want to look at my old writings," he said to Marie. And later, as she tried to fit the manuscripts into the suitcase, he mentioned the topic again. "Who knows whether all this resting hasn't done my mind a lot of good! I feel that I've matured. Sometimes I feel a wonderful sense of clarity about all my ideas up to now."

The day after the rainstorm was a beautiful one. And the very next day it became so warm that the windows could be opened. Now the glow of a warm and friendly autumn afternoon lit up the room, and as Marie knelt in front of the suitcase, the sunbeams nestled in her wavy hair.

Alfred arrived just as Marie was putting the stacks of papers carefully into the suitcase, and as Felix, lying on the sofa, began to talk about his plans.

"I'm supposed to allow you that too?" asked Alfred, smiling. "Well, I hope you'll be careful not to start working too soon."

"Oh," said Felix, "it won't be any effort for me. A thousand new lights are now illuminating ideas that used to be in darkness."

"That's wonderful," Alfred said slowly as he watched the patient. Felix was staring into space with an empty gaze.

"Don't misunderstand me," continued Felix. "My ideas are not entirely clear, but it seems to me that something is brewing."

"Hmm . . ."

"You know, I feel as though I am hearing the instruments of an orchestra tuning—a sound that always made a deep impression on me. I feel that at any moment there will be pure harmonies and that all the instruments will come in correctly." And, suddenly changing the topic, he asked, "Did you reserve a compartment?"

"Yes," answered the doctor.

"So, tomorrow morning!" cried Marie in a good-humored way. She was continually busy as she went from the dresser to the suitcase, from there to the bookcase, then again to the suitcase, arranging and packing. Alfred felt especially moved. Was he in the company of carefree young people who were preparing for a pleasure trip? The atmosphere in the room now seemed as full of hope and almost as untroubled. When he left, Marie followed him out. "Oh God," she exclaimed, "what a good idea it is that we're going away! I'm so happy! And he's practically a changed person since it's become definite."

Alfred didn't know what to say. He shook hands with her and turned to go. But then, turning around again, he said to Marie, "Promise me . . ."

"Promise you what?"

"I mean . . . a friend is more than a doctor. You know that I'm always at your disposal. Just send me a wire."

Marie was quite frightened. "You think it might be necessary?"

"I'm telling you just in case." And with that he left.

She remained standing for a while, lost in thought. Then she went quickly into the room, fearful that Felix would be concerned about her extended absence. But he seemed to be awaiting her return only in order to continue his previous remarks.

"You know, Marie," he said, "the sun always does me good. When it gets colder, we'll go farther south still, to the Riviera. And after that . . . what do you say? . . . Africa! Yes! Below the equator I could surely manage to write a masterpiece."

So he chattered on until Marie finally walked over to him, patted his cheeks, and said with a smile, "Now enough of that. You overdo things right away. Besides, you have to go to bed, because tomorrow morning we've got to get up early." She saw that his cheeks were very red and that his eyes were almost glowing. And when she grasped his hands in order to help him up from the sofa, they were burning hot.

XXI

Felix awoke at the crack of dawn. He felt the joyful excitement of a child going on vacation. A full two hours before they were to leave for the train station, he was already sitting on the sofa ready to go. Marie too had long finished all her preparations. She wore her grey duster and the hat with the blue veil, and stood at the window watching for the arrival of the carriage she had ordered. Every five minutes Felix asked if it was already there. He became impatient. He was talking about sending for another one when Marie called out, "It's here, it's here!"

"Oh, Felix," she added immediately, "Alfred is here too."

Alfred had turned the corner at the same time as the carriage and was waving a friendly greeting to them. Almost immediately afterward he appeared in the room. "You're already ready!" he exclaimed. "What are you going to do at the station so early, especially since I see you've already had breakfast?"

"Felix is so impatient," said Marie. Alfred walked over to him, and the invalid gave him a cheerful smile. "Wonderful travel weather," he said.

"Oh yes, you'll have a wonderful time," said the doctor. He took a piece of toast from the table. "May I?"

"Don't tell me you haven't had your breakfast?" Marie exclaimed, quite surprised.

"Yes, yes, I have. I drank a glass of cognac."

"Wait, there's still some coffee in the pot." She insisted on pouring the rest of the coffee into a cup for him, and then she went out to give some instructions to a servant in the anteroom. Alfred held the cup to his lips for a long time. He was uneasy being alone with his friend and didn't know what to say. Marie returned to the room and announced that nothing stood in the way of their leaving the apartment. Felix stood up and was the first to walk to the door. He had put on a grey raincoat and a soft, dark hat, and carried a cane in his hand. He wanted to be the first to walk down the stairs, but he had hardly touched the banister when he began to reel. Alfred and Marie were right behind him and supported him. "I'm a little dizzy," said Felix.

"Well, that's only natural," said Alfred, "the first time out of bed after so many weeks." He took the patient by one arm, Marie took him by the other, and they led him downstairs. The coachman took off his hat when he saw the invalid.

At the windows of the houses opposite, a few sympathetic women's faces became visible. And when Alfred and Marie lifted the deadly pale man into the carriage, the doorman too rushed up to offer his help. As the carriage drove off, the doorman and the women exchanged knowing glances filled with emotion.

XXII

Standing on the steps of the train compartment, Alfred chatted with Marie until the last signal sounded. Felix sat in a corner and appeared apathetic; only when the whistle of the locomotive sounded did he seem to become alert again. He nodded a farewell to his friend. The train began to move. Alfred remained standing on the platform for a while and followed the train with his eyes. Then he slowly turned to leave. No sooner had the train left the station than Marie sat down close to Felix and asked him whether there was anything he wanted. Should she open the bottle of cognac for him, get him a book, read to him from the newspaper? He seemed grateful for all this kindness and squeezed her hand. Then he inquired, "When do we arrive in Merano?" Since she didn't know the exact time of their arrival, he asked that she read him all the important information from the train schedule in their compartment. He wanted to know where the lunch station was and where they would be at nightfall; he showed an interest in all kinds of details to which he usually paid no attention at all. He tried to figure out how many people were on the train and wondered if there were any newlyweds among them. After a while he asked for the cognac, but it made him cough so badly that he angrily told Marie never to give it to him again, even if he asked her to. Later he had her read to him the weather report from the newspaper and nodded contentedly when he heard the favorable forecast.

They were crossing the Semmering Mountains. He attentively watched the changing images that presented themselves but uttered no more than a soft "Nice, very nice," in a tone of voice completely devoid of enthusiasm. At lunch he ate some of the cold food they had brought along, and he became very angry when Marie denied him the cognac. She finally had to consent to give him some. It agreed with him fairly well, and he became more alert and began to show an interest in all sorts of things. But he soon reverted from talking about what flitted by outside the windows of their compartment and what he saw in the station to talking about himself. He said, "I've read about sleepwalkers who dreamed of a cure that no doctor had thought of and who were cured by taking it. A sick person should follow his desire, I say."

"Of course," replied Marie.

"The South! Southern air! They think the only difference is that it's warm there and that there are flowers all year and perhaps more ozone and no storms and no snow. Who knows what else is in that southern air? Mysterious elements that we don't even know about."

"You'll get well there for sure," said Marie, taking the invalid's hand between her own and pressing it to her lips.

He talked further about the many painters to be found in Italy, about the desire that had driven so many artists and kings to go to Rome; he talked about Venice, where he had once been long before he met Marie. Finally he grew tired and wanted to stretch out full length on the seats of the compartment. There he stayed, dozing in a light sleep, until evening.

She sat across from him and watched him. She felt calm, though she harbored a mild regret. He was so pale. And he had aged so much. How his handsome face had changed since spring! It was a different kind of pallor from the one that now touched her own cheeks—hers made her look younger, almost virginal. How much better off she was than he! Never had this idea come to her with such clarity. Why was her pain not more excruciating! Oh, it wasn't lack of sympathy; it was simply a profound fatigue that hadn't left her for days even if from time to time she seemed to feel more alert. She was glad she felt fatigue, because she dreaded the pain she would feel when she was no longer tired.

Marie suddenly started from the sleep into which she had sunk. She looked around; it was almost completely dark. She had put the veil of her hat over the lamp glimmering above, so that there was only a faint green shimmer of light in the compartment. Outside the windows was black night. Night! It seemed like they were going through a long tunnel. Why had she started up so violently? It was almost completely still around her; only the monotonous rattling of the wheels could be heard. Gradually she became accustomed to the dim light and could make out the invalid's features. Lying there motionless, he seemed to be sleeping calmly. But suddenly he sighed an unearthly, mournful moan. Her heart started pounding. He must have moaned this way before, and that was what had awakened her. But what was this? She looked at him more closely. He wasn't sleeping at all. He lay there with his eyes wide open, very wide; she could see this quite clearly now. She was afraid of those eyes staring into emptiness, into space, into darkness. And again there was a moan, more mournful than the one before. He moved, and now he sighed again, a sigh full of fury rather than pain. And suddenly he sat up; he propped his hands on the pillows, kicked the grey coat covering him to the floor, and tried to stand up. But the motion of the train was too much for him, and he sank back into the corner. Marie jumped up and tried to remove the green veil from the lamp. But suddenly she felt his arms clasp her, and now he pulled the trembling girl onto his knees. "Marie, Marie," he said in a hoarse voice.

She wanted to free herself, but she couldn't. All his strength seemed to have returned to him, and he pressed her to him violently. "Are you ready, Marie?" he whispered, his lips very close to her neck. She didn't understand; she felt only a boundless fear. She was defenseless; she wanted to scream. "Are you ready?" he asked again, holding her less convulsively, so that his lips, his breath, and his voice were farther away from her and she could breathe more freely.

"What do you want?" she asked anxiously.

"Don't you understand?" he replied.

"Let go of me, let go of me," she screamed, but her voice was drowned out by the noise of the rolling train.

He paid no attention but he let his hands fall, and she rose from his knees and sat down in the opposite corner.

"Don't you understand?" he asked again.

"What do you want?" she whispered from her corner.

"I want an answer," he replied.

She remained silent; she trembled; she longed for the dawn.

"The hour is near," he said softly, leaning forward so that she could hear his words more clearly. "I'm asking you whether you're ready."

"What hour?"

"Ours! Ours!"

She understood him. She felt as though she were suffocating.

"Don't you remember, Marie?" he continued, and now his voice took on a soft, almost supplicating tone. He took both her hands into his. "You gave me the right to ask this," he continued whispering. "Do you remember?"

She had by now regained some of her composure. Even though the words he spoke were terrifying, his eyes had lost their inhuman stare, and his voice had lost its menace. Now he seemed to be a supplicant. And once again he asked, almost sobbing now, "Don't you remember?" By now she had the strength to reply, though with trembling lips, "What a child you are, Felix."

He didn't seem to hear this at all. In a monotonous voice, as if something half forgotten was coming back to him with new clarity, he said, "The end is coming now, and we have to go, Marie. Our time is up." Though they were whispered softly, there was something spellbinding, unconditional, and inescapable in these words. If he had threatened her, she would have been better able to defend herself. For a moment, as he moved still closer to her, an enormous fear came over her—the fear that he would pounce on her and strangle her. She was preparing to flee to the other end of the compartment, smash the window, and call for help when at that very moment he let her hands fall from his and leaned back as though he had nothing further to say. Then she said:

"What kind of nonsense are you talking, Felix! Now, just when we're going south, where you're going to get completely well!" He was leaning on the other side of the compartment and seemed lost in thought. She stood up and quickly pushed her veil away from the lamp. Oh, how good that was! All of a sudden it was light. Her heart began to beat more slowly, and her fear vanished. She sat back down in her corner. He had been looking down, but now he raised his eyes again. Then he said slowly:

"Marie, I won't be deceived by the morning anymore, and not by the south either. Today I know."

Why is he talking so calmly now? thought Marie. Is he trying to make me think I'm safe? Is he afraid I'll try to save myself? And she resolved to be on her guard. She watched him constantly, hardly listening to his words, observing his every movement and look.

He said, "Of course you're free. Even your oath doesn't bind you. How could I force you? Won't you give me your hand?"

She gave him her hand, but in such a way that her hand lay on top of his.

"If only it were daytime!" he whispered.

"Let me tell you something, Felix," she said. "Do try to get a little more sleep! It will soon be morning, and in a few hours we'll be in Merano."

"I can't sleep any more," he replied and looked up. At that moment their eyes met, and he saw the mistrustful, watchful look in hers. At that instant everything became clear to him. She wanted him to sleep so that she could get off unnoticed and escape at the next station. "What are you planning to do?" he screamed.

She flinched. "Nothing."

He tried to stand up. She fled from her corner into another one, far away from him.

"Air!" he screamed. "Air!" He opened the window and leaned

his head out into the night air. Marie felt reassured—it was only his difficulty in breathing that had led him to get up so suddenly. She went to him and gently pulled him away from the window. "That can't be good for you," she said. He sank down into his corner again, breathing laboriously. She remained standing in front of him for a while with one hand propped on the window ledge, then took her seat opposite him once more. After a while his breathing became more normal, and a weak smile appeared on his lips.

"I'll close the window," she said. He nodded. "The dawn! The dawn!" he exclaimed. Reddish grey streaks had appeared on the horizon.

Now, for a long time, they sat silently across from each other. Finally, as that same smile played around his lips, he said, "You're not ready!" She was going to reply in her usual manner, saying that he was being childish or something of that sort. But she couldn't. That smile forbade any answer.

The train slowed. After a few minutes it arrived at the breakfast stop. Waiters ran up and down the platform with coffee and pastry. Many travelers left the train; there was shouting and calling out. The ordinariness of the station hubbub soothed her, and Marie felt as though she had awakened from a bad dream. With a feeling of complete serenity she got up and looked out on the platform. Finally she beckoned to a waiter and asked him to hand her a cup of coffee. Felix watched her sipping the coffee but shook his head when she offered him some.

Soon thereafter the train started moving again, and when they left the station it was bright daylight. And how beautiful it was! The mountains, bathed in early morning red, towered in the distance. Marie resolved never again to be afraid of the night. Felix looked out the window now and then; he seemed to want to avoid her eyes. She felt he must be a little ashamed of what had happened during the night.

The train stopped a few times at short intervals, and when they arrived at the Merano station it was a magnificent, warm summer morning. "Here we are!" exclaimed Marie. "Finally, finally!"

XXIII

They hired a carriage and drove around, house hunting. "We don't need to economize," said Felix. "I still have enough money for this." They asked the coachman to stop at various villas, and while Felix remained in the carriage, Marie looked at rooms and gardens. She soon found a suitable house. It was quite small, only one and a half stories high, and had a small garden. Marie asked the caretaker to come out to the carriage to explain the various merits of the villa to the young man sitting there. Felix declared himself satisfied with everything, and a few minutes later the pair moved in.

Felix withdrew to the bedroom without paying attention to Marie's busy interest in the rest of the house. He gave the room a cursory inspection. It was roomy and friendly, with light green wallpaper. It had a large open window, so that the whole room was filled with the fragrance of the garden. Felix was so exhausted that he threw himself lengthwise on one of the beds that stood opposite the window.

Meanwhile Marie had the caretaker show her around and was particularly happy about the small garden. It was enclosed by a high lattice fence and could be entered without having to go through the house, by way of a little door at the back. There was also a wide path that offered a shorter, more direct route to the train station.

When Marie returned to the room where she had left Felix, she found him lying on the bed. She called out to him, but he didn't answer. She came closer; he was even whiter than usual. She called out again. No answer—he didn't stir. A horrible fright came over her; she called the caretaker and sent for a doctor. No sooner had the woman left than Felix opened his eyes. At the very moment he was about to say something, he sat up with a face distorted by fear. He immediately sank back down again and rasped. Blood trickled from his lips. Marie bent over him helplessly, despairing. She rushed back to the door to see if the doctor was coming, only to rush back to Felix and call his name. If only Alfred were here! she thought.

Finally the doctor came—an elderly gentleman with grey whiskers. "Help him, help him!" Marie cried out. Given her state of agitation, she told him as much about the patient as she could. The doctor looked at the invalid, felt for his pulse, and declared that he couldn't examine him right after a hemorrhage. He gave orders for what had to be done. Marie accompanied him out the door and asked what she could expect. "I can't tell yet," said the doctor. "Have a little patience! Let's hope for the best." He promised to return that evening. He waved to Marie, who had remained in the house, in such a friendly and unaffected way that it seemed he had just paid her a social call.

Marie stood there helplessly for only a second; the very next moment she had an idea that seemed to promise deliverance—she rushed to the post office to send Alfred a telegram. After she had sent it off, she felt relieved. She thanked the woman who had taken care of the patient while she was gone, and begged her to excuse the trouble they had caused her on their very first day. She promised they would show her their appreciation handsomely.

Felix was still lying fully clothed and comatose on the bed, but his breathing was now more regular. While Marie sat at the head of the bed, the woman consoled her; she told her about the many gravely ill persons who had recovered in Merano; that she herself had been very ill in her youth and had—as was obvious—made a wonderful recovery despite all the bad luck that had befallen her. Her husband had died after two years of marriage; her sons had gone away into the world. Yes, everything could have been different, but now she was very happy to have a position in this house. She couldn't really complain about the owner, since he came from Bolzano only twice a month at the most to check on everything. She rattled on and was full of an overflowing friendliness. She offered to unpack the suitcases, an offer that Marie gratefully accepted, and later she brought them lunch to their room. The milk for the patient was ready, and his subtle stirring seemed to signal that he would soon awaken.

Finally Felix regained consciousness. He looked around a few times and fixed his gaze on Marie, who was bending over him. At that he smiled and squeezed her hand weakly. "What happened to me?" he asked. The doctor, who came again in the afternoon, found him much better and permitted him to be undressed and put to bed. Felix submitted to everything with equanimity.

Marie did not stir from the sickbed. What an endless afternoon it was! Through the window, which was left open upon explicit orders from the doctor, came the gentle odors of the garden. And it was so quiet! Marie mechanically followed the dance of the sunbeams on the floor. Felix held her hand almost without interruption. His own was cool and moist and gave Marie an unpleasant sensation. Sometimes she interrupted the silence with a few words that she forced herself to say: "You're feeling better, aren't you? Well, you see . . . don't talk . . . the day after tomorrow you'll be able to go into the garden!" And he nodded and smiled. Then Marie tried to calculate when Alfred would arrive. Tomorrow, in the evening, he might be here. So only one more night and one more day. If only he were here!

It seemed that the afternoon would never, ever end. The sun disappeared and dusk fell upon the room, but when Marie looked out into the garden she could still see yellow sunbeams gliding over the white gravel paths and the fence posts in the distance. Suddenly, while looking out, she heard the patient's voice: "Marie." She quickly turned her head toward him.

"I'm feeling much better now," he said quite loudly.

"You shouldn't talk so loudly," she admonished him gently.

"Much better," he whispered. "It went well this time. Maybe it was the crisis."

"It must have been," she heartily agreed.

"I'm hopeful about the good air. But it can't happen again—otherwise I'm lost."

"It won't! You see, you're already feeling stronger."

"You're good-hearted, Marie. I'm grateful to you. But take good care of me. Be careful, be careful!"

"Do you have to tell me that?" she replied with a gentle reproach.

But he continued whispering, "Because if I have to go, I'll take you with me."

A cold dread shot through her when he said this. But why? He wasn't dangerous now. He was much too weak to be violent. She was ten times stronger than he was now. What could he be thinking of? What was he looking for with his eyes fixed in the air, on the wall, on empty space? He couldn't even get up and had no weapons on him. Poison maybe? Could he have obtained poison? Maybe he carried it with him and wanted to put some drops in her glass. But where could he be hiding it? She herself had helped him undress. Maybe he had a powder in his wallet. But that was in his jacket. No, no, no! The fever made him say these words—that and the desire to torment her, nothing else. But if the fever could cause such words and such thoughts, why couldn't it cause him to act as well? Maybe he would use a moment when she was asleep to simply strangle her. That didn't take much strength. She would immediately become unconscious, and then she would be defenseless. No, she wouldn't sleep that night. . . . And tomorrow Alfred would be here!

The evening progressed and night came. Felix had not uttered another word, and the smile had completely vanished from his lips.

He stared into space with a uniformly gloomy seriousness. When it grew dark, the woman brought in lighted candles and prepared to make up the bed next to Felix's. Marie motioned to her that this wasn't necessary. Felix noticed. "Why not?" he asked, and immediately he added, "You're too good to me, Marie. You should get some sleep. I'm feeling much better." It seemed to her that there was mockery in his words. She didn't go to sleep. She spent the long, silent night next to his bed without shutting an eye. Felix lay there quietly for the most part. Once in a while she suspected he might be only pretending to sleep in order to lull her into thinking she was safe. She took a closer look at him, but the wavering light of the candle simulated twitching movements around his lips and eyes, which only confused her. At one point she went to the window and looked out into the garden. It was bathed in a dull blue-grey. When she leaned out a little and looked up, she could see the moon floating right above the trees. Not a breeze was stirring, and in the infinite stillness that enveloped her it seemed to her that the fence posts, which she could see quite clearly, were moving slowly forward and then stopping again. After midnight Felix awoke. Marie arranged his pillows for him, and, obeying a sudden impulse, she took the opportunity to probe between the pillows to see if he had hidden anything there. His words rang in her ears: "I'll take you with me! I'll take you with me!" But would he have said this if he had meant it seriously? If he were at all capable of formulating a plan he would take care not to give himself away. She was being really childish to let herself be frightened by the disorganized fantasies of a sick man. She grew sleepy and moved her chair far from his bed . . . just in case. She couldn't fall asleep, but her thoughts began nevertheless to lose their clarity, and from the clear consciousness of the day they fluttered into the grey twilight of dreams. Memories welled up. Memories of days and nights of radiant happiness. Memories of hours in which he had held her in his arms as the breath of early spring moved through the room. She had an indistinct sensation that the fragrance of the garden wouldn't dare enter here, that she had to go to the window again in order to drink it in. From the patient's damp hair came a sweetish, stale odor that permeated the room with the smell of sickness. What now? If only it were over! yes, over! She no longer shrank from the thought, and she remembered the words that turned the most horrific of thoughts into a hypocritical empathy: If only he were released! And what then? She could see herself sitting on a bench beneath a tall tree in the garden outside, pale and tear-stained. But these signs of mourning were only on her face. Into her soul had crept a blissful peace she had not known for a long, long time. And then she saw her own figure arise, go out into the street, and walk slowly away. Because now she was free to go wherever she wanted.

But in the midst of these daydreams she remained sufficiently alert to listen for the invalid's moaning breath. Finally the morning hesitantly approached. At the crack of dawn the caretaker appeared at the door and kindly offered to sit with the patient for the next few hours. Marie accepted with genuine joy. After a brief, final glance at Felix, she left the room and went into the adjoining room where a sofa beckoned her to a comfortable rest. Ah! How wonderful that felt! She threw herself onto it fully clothed and closed her eyes.

XXIV

She didn't wake up for many hours. A pleasant semi-darkness enveloped her. Only narrow strips of sunlight fell through the crevices of the closed shutters. She quickly got up and immediately grasped the situation clearly. Today Alfred was bound to come! The thought enabled her to face the gloom of the coming hours with more courage. Without hesitating she went into the next room. When she opened the door, she was dazzled for a moment by the white cover that had been spread over the invalid's bed. Then she caught sight of the caretaker, who put a finger to her mouth, got up from her chair, and tiptoed toward Marie. "He's fast asleep," she whispered. Then she recounted that he had lain awake with a high fever until an hour ago and had asked after her a couple of times. The doctor had been there early in the morning and found the patient's condition unchanged. She had wanted to wake the lady, but the doctor wouldn't allow it. He said he would come back sometime that afternoon anyway.

Marie listened attentively to the old woman, thanked her for her solicitude, and then took her place.

It was a warm, almost sultry day, nearly noon. A silent, heavy sunshine lay over the garden. When Marie looked over at the bed, she saw the invalid's narrow hands, sometimes lightly twitching, lying on top of the blanket. His chin had sunk low, his face was deathly pale, and his lips were slightly open. His breathing stopped for seconds on end and was followed by shallow wheezing. "Perhaps he'll die before Alfred comes after all," Marie thought. The way Felix lay there now, his face had again taken on the expression of a suffering youth; it had a limpness about it as after an unspeakable pain, a surrender as after a hopeless battle. Marie suddenly realized what it was that had changed his features so horribly: it was the bitterness that had been etched in his face when he looked at her. But there was no bitterness in his face now and no hatred in his dreams. He was handsome again. She wished he would wake up. As she looked at him now she was filled with an unspeakable grief and a consuming fear. Once again it was her lover whom she saw dying. Suddenly she understood again what that meant. The whole misery of his inescapable and horrifying fate came over her, and once again she understood it all, all—that he had been her happiness and her life, that she had wanted to die with him, that now the moment when everything would be gone was terrifyingly close. And the rigid cold-

ness that had weighed on her heart, the indifference of whole days
and nights now seemed to her altogether incomprehensible. And yet
now, now everything was still all right. He was still alive after all; he
was breathing, perhaps dreaming. But soon he would lie there stiff,
dead; they would bury him, and he would rest deep in the earth in a
quiet cemetery where the days would pass uninterrupted as he de-
cayed. And she would live and be with others, all the time aware of a
silent grave out there where he rested—he, he whom she had loved!
Her tears flowed without stopping; finally she sobbed out loud. He
stirred, and as she quickly dried her cheeks with a handkerchief, he
opened his eyes and gave her a long questioning look. He said nothing. After a few minutes he whispered, "Come!" She rose from her
chair, bent over him, and he lifted his arms as though he wanted to
embrace her. But he dropped his arms again and asked, "Were you
crying?"

"No," she answered quickly, brushing her hair from her forehead.

He gave her a long and solemn look, and then turned away. He
appeared to be pondering something.

Marie wondered if she should tell him about her telegram to
Alfred. Should she prepare him for it? No. What for? It would be
best if she pretended to be surprised herself at Alfred's arrival. The
rest of the day passed in the dull tension of expectation. Outward
events moved past her as if in a fog. The physician's call was soon
over. He found the invalid totally apathetic, waking only infrequently from a moaning half sleep to ask trivial questions and express trivial wishes. He asked what time it was; he wanted water; the
caretaker came in and out. Marie was with him in the room the entire time, usually sitting in a chair next to him. Once in a while she
stood at the foot of the bed, propping herself against the footboard;
sometimes she went to the window and looked down into the garden, where she saw the shadows of the trees slowly lengthen as dusk

crept over the meadows and the paths. It had become a sultry evening, and the light of the candle on the night table at the head of the patient's bed scarcely flickered. Only when it was completely dark and the moon appeared over the blue-grey mountains in the distance did a light breeze begin to stir. Marie felt quite refreshed when it blew about her forehead, and it seemed to do the invalid good too. He moved his head and turned his wide-open eyes toward the window. And finally he drew a deep, deep breath. "Ah!"

Marie took his hand, which hung down beside his pillow. "Do you want anything?" she asked.

He slowly withdrew his hand from hers and said, "Marie, come!"

She moved closer to him and put her head very close to his pillow. He put his hand on her hair as though to bless her and let it rest there. Then he said softly, "I thank you for all your love." She let her head rest on his pillow and now felt her tears flow again. The room became very quiet. Only the whistling of a train sounded in the distance. The stillness of the sultry summer evening was heavy, sweet, and incomprehensible. Suddenly Felix sat upright in his bed, so quickly, so violently that Marie was frightened. She lifted her head from the pillow and stared into his face. He grabbed Marie's head with both hands, as he had often done in the heat of wild passion. "Marie!" he cried, "I want to remind you now."

"Of what?" she asked, and tried to wrest her head from his hands. But he seemed to have regained his strength and held her tightly.

"I want to remind you of your promise," he said hastily, "of your promise to die with me." He was quite close to her as he said these words. She felt his breath move over her mouth and could not draw back. He was so close that it was as if he wanted her to drink his words in with her lips. "I'll take you along. I don't want to go alone! I love you, and I won't leave you here!"

She was almost paralyzed with fear. A hoarse scream, so muffled that she could hardly hear it herself, came from her throat. Her head was pinned between his hands; he squeezed her temples and her cheeks convulsively. He talked on and on, singeing her with his hot, moist breath.

"Together, together! That was what you wanted, wasn't it? I'm afraid of dying alone! Will you? Will you?"

She kicked the chair from underneath her and finally, as though freeing herself from an iron vise, she wrested her head from his grip. He continued holding his hands in the air, as though her head were still between them. He stared at her as though he couldn't comprehend what had happened.

"No, no!" she screamed, "I won't!" And she ran to the door. He rose as though he wanted to jump out of bed. But now his strength gave out, and he sank back onto the bed with a dull thud. But she didn't see this any more; she had flung the door open and was running through the adjoining room and into the hall. She didn't know what she was doing. He had tried to strangle her! She could still feel his fingers gliding down her temples, down her cheeks, to her throat. She rushed out the front door. No one was there. She remembered that the woman had gone out to get some supper. What should she do? She rushed back through the hallway and into the garden. As though she were being pursued, she ran across the trail and the grass until she came to the other end.

At that point she turned around and could see the open window of the room from which she had just come. She saw the candlelight flicker, but otherwise she saw nothing. What happened? What happened? she kept saying to herself. She didn't know what to do. She walked aimlessly up and down the walkway next to the fence. Suddenly she remembered—Alfred! He was coming. He had to be coming by now! She looked between the fence posts to the moonlit path that led to the train station. She rushed to the garden door and opened it. There was the path, white, deserted. Maybe he was taking the other road? No, no . . . there, there, a shadow was approaching, coming closer and closer, faster and faster, the figure of a man. Was it him? Was it him? She hurried a few steps toward him. "Alfred!" "Is that you, Marie?" It was him! She could have cried for joy. When he reached her, she tried to kiss his hand. "What's going on?" he asked. And she pulled him along without answering.

Felix had lain there motionless for only a moment, and then had sat up and looked around. She was gone. He was alone! A suffocating fear choked him. Only one thing was clear to him: that he had to have her near him. Here, with him. With one leap he was out of bed. But he couldn't stay upright, and he fell backward onto the bed. He felt a buzzing and a roaring in his head. He leaned on the chair and managed to move forward by pushing it ahead of him. "Marie, Marie," he mumbled, "I don't want to die alone. I can't!" Where was she? Where could she be? Pushing his chair in front of him, he had reached the window. There was the garden and the bluish gleam of the sultry night. How it shimmered and whirled! How the grasses and the trees were dancing! Oh, this was the kind of spring that would heal him. This air, this air! With such air surrounding him, he had to recover! Ah! There! What was that over there? And in front of the fence that seemed far below him as though it were in a deep abyss he saw a female figure enveloped by the blue glow of the moon coming over the white, shimmering gravel path. How she floated! How she flew! And yet she was still no closer! Marie! Marie! And right behind her was a man. A man with Marie, enormously large. Now the fence began to dance. It danced behind them, and so did the black sky and everything, everything danced behind them. And there were sounds and the ringing of bells and voices from afar . . . beautiful, so beautiful! And then it grew dark.

Marie and Alfred came running up together. Arriving at the open window, Marie stopped and peered anxiously into the room.

"He isn't here!" she screamed. "The bed is empty!" Suddenly she let out a scream and sank into Alfred's arms. While gently pushing her away, Alfred leaned over the railing outside the window and saw his friend lying inside on the floor of the room. He wore his white nightshirt, he was stretched out with his legs spread far apart, and next to him was an overturned chair whose back he clasped with one hand. A ribbon of blood trickled from his mouth and down his chin. His lips and his eyelids seemed to be twitching; but as Alfred took a closer look, he saw that it was only the deceitful moonlight playing over his pale face.

Fräulein Else

YOU REALLY don't want to play anymore, Else?

No, Paul, I can't play any more. Adieu. Goodbye, madam.

But Else, do call me Frau Cissy—or even better, just plain Cissy.

Goodbye, Frau Cissy.

Why are you going so soon, Else? It's still almost two whole hours till dinner.

Just go ahead and play singles with Paul, Frau Cissy. It's really no fun playing with me today.

Let her be, madam. She's in one of her moods today. By the way, you look wonderful when you're in a bad mood, Else—especially in that red sweater.

I hope you'll find me better disposed toward you in blue, Paul. Adieu.

That was rather well said. I hope the two of them don't think I'm jealous. I swear there's something going on between cousin Paul and Cissy Mohr. I couldn't care less. Maybe I'll turn around and wave to them again. Wave and smile. Do I look gracious enough? Oh God, they're already playing again.—Actually, I play better than Cissy Mohr, and Paul isn't exactly a matador. But he does look handsome—with his open collar and his bad-little-boy look. If only he weren't so affected. Don't worry, Aunt Emma. . . .

What a gorgeous evening! Today would have been the perfect weather for the trip to the Rosetta chalet. How gloriously the Cimone towers up into the sky!—We would have started out at around five in the morning. Oh, I'd have felt awful at first, as usual, but that soon gets better. Nothing is more divine than hiking at daybreak.— That one-eyed American at the Rosetta looked like a boxer. Maybe someone knocked his eye out in a fight. I'd rather like being married in America, but not to an American. Or maybe I could marry an American, but then live in Europe. A villa on the Riviera. Marble steps going down into the sea. I'm lying naked on the marble.— How long has it been since we were in Mentone? Seven or eight years. I was thirteen or fourteen at the time. Ah yes, we were better off in those days.—It really was stupid to postpone the outing. We'd have been back by now in any case.—Around four, when I went out to play tennis, the express letter Mama telegraphed me about hadn't arrived yet. It might not be here even now. I could easily have played another set after all.—Why are those two young men greeting me? I don't even know them. They've been at the hotel since yesterday and take their meals on the left side of the dining room by the window, where those Dutch people used to sit. Did I thank them ungraciously? Or even haughtily? I'm really not like that at all. What did Fred say on the way home from *Coriolanus*? High spirited. No, high-minded. *You're high-minded, Else, but not haughty.*— A fine word, high-minded. He always comes up with the right word.—Why am I walking so slowly? Can it be that I'm afraid of Mama's letter after all? Well, it won't contain anything pleasant, that's for sure. Special delivery! I'll probably have to go back home. Oh dear. What a life—notwithstanding the red silk sweater and the silk stockings. Three pair! The poor relative, invited by her rich aunt. I'm sure she already regrets it. Should I put it in writing, dear aunt, that I wouldn't dream of going after Paul? Oh, I don't dream about anybody. I'm not in love. Not with anyone. And I've never

been in love. Not even with Albert, although for a whole week I
imagined I was. I don't think I'm really capable of falling in love.
That's odd, really. Because I'm a sensual person, that's for sure. But
at the same time high-minded and ungracious, thank God. Maybe at
thirteen I really was in love. With Van Dyck, the tenor—no, the
Abbé Des Grieux—and with Marie Renard, the soprano.—Well, no,
that wasn't anything. Why am I reminiscing like this? I'm not writing my memoirs. I don't even keep a diary like Bertha. I like Fred,
but that's all. Maybe if he had more style. I really am a snob. Papa
thinks so too and laughs at me. Oh, dear Papa, you worry me so
much. I wonder whether he's ever deceived Mama? Of course he
has! Often. Mama is really rather stupid. She doesn't understand me
at all. Neither does anyone else. Fred? Yes, but only a little.—What
a heavenly evening! How festive the hotel looks! So many prosper-
ous, carefree people. Like me, for instance. Ha ha! Wouldn't that be
nice! Too bad.—There's a red glow over the Cimone now. Paul
would say "Alpine glow." But it's not an Alpine glow yet. It's beautiful enough to make you cry. Oh, why do I ever have to go back to
the city!

Good evening, Fräulein Else.

How do you do, madam?

Back from tennis?

Well, it's obvious. Why does she ask? *Yes, madam. We played
almost three hours. And you, madam, you're taking a walk?*

*Yes, I'm taking my usual evening walk. Down the Rolleweg. It
runs so beautifully through the meadows. In the daytime it's almost
too sunny.*

*Yes, the meadows here are magnificent. Especially by moon-
light from my window.*

Good evening, Fräulein Else. How do you do, madam?

Good evening, Herr von Dorsday.

Back from tennis, Fräulein Else?

How observant you are, Herr von Dorsday.

Don't make fun of me, Else.

Why doesn't he call me "Fräulein" Else?

Anyone who looks as good as you do with a tennis racket is permitted to carry it merely for decoration.

The ass! I'm not even going to reply to that. *We played the whole afternoon. Unfortunately, there were only four of us—Paul, Frau Mohr, and I.*

I used to be a serious tennis player.

And you aren't any more?

I'm too old for that now.

Too old? Come, come. In Marienlyst there was a sixty-five-year-old Swede who played every evening from six to eight. And the year before that he played an entire tournament.

Well, thank God I'm not sixty-five yet. But I'm also unfortunately not a Swede.

Why unfortunately? I suppose he thinks that's funny. The best thing for me to do is to smile politely and leave. *How do you do, madam? Adieu, Herr von Dorsday.*

What a deep bow he's making and how he's eyeing me! I wonder if I insulted him by the story of the sixty-five-year-old Swede? Well, it doesn't matter. Frau Winawer must be an unhappy woman. She's nearly fifty, I'm sure. Those bags under her eyes—as though she had cried a lot. Oh, how awful it must be to be so old! Herr von Dorsday is walking toward her. There he is, walking at her side. He still looks pretty good with his greyish Van Dyck beard. But I don't like him. He's just an artful social climber. A first-class tailor isn't enough, Herr von Dorsday! Dorsday! I'm sure your name used to be something else.—Here comes Cissy's sweet little girl with her Fräulein. *Hello, Fritzi. Bonsoir, mademoiselle. Vous allez bien?*

Merci, mademoiselle. Et vous?
What do I see, Fritzi? Yes, you're carrying an Alpine stick! Are
you planning to climb to the top of the Cimone?
Of course not. I'm not allowed to go that high.
Next year you will be. Bye, Fritzi. À bientôt, mademoiselle.
Bonsoir, mademoiselle.

An attractive person. I wonder why she became a governess? Especially for Cissy! A bitter fate. Oh God, that could still happen to me too. No, I'd do something better. Better?—What an exquisite evening! *The air is like champagne.* That's what Dr. Waldberg said yesterday. The day before yesterday somebody else said it too. Why do people stay indoors in wonderful weather like this? It's incomprehensible. Or are they all waiting for an express letter? The porter has just seen me. But if there were an express letter for me, he'd have brought it over immediately. So it couldn't have arrived yet. Thank God. I'll lie down for a while before dinner. Why does Cissy say *diner* in French? That's such a stupid affectation. They're suited to each other, Cissy and Paul.—Oh, I wish the letter were here already. It'll probably show up during *diner.* And if it doesn't show up, I'll have a restless night. I slept so badly last night. Of course it's because it's almost that time of the month. That's also why I have cramps in my legs. Today's the third of September. So probably on the sixth. I'll take some Veronal tonight. Oh, I won't become addicted to it. No, my dear Fred, you don't have to worry about that. In my thoughts I always address him with the intimate *du.*—One should try everything—even hashish. I think that Ensign Brandel brought some with him from China. Is one supposed to drink or smoke hashish? It's supposed to give you marvelous visions. Brandel invited me to drink—or smoke—hashish with him.—A brazen fellow. But handsome.

If you please, Fräulein, a letter for you.
The porter! So it arrived after all.—I'll turn around quite casu-

ally. After all, it could be a letter from Caroline or from Bertha or Fred or Miss Jackson.—*Thank you.* It's from Mama after all. Express. Why didn't he tell me right away when it's clearly an express letter? *Oh, an express letter?* I won't open it until I get to my room and can read it in peace.—The marchesa. How young she looks in the twilight! I bet she's forty-five. Where will I be when I'm forty-five? Maybe dead already. I hope so. She's smiling at me very sweetly, as usual. I'll let her pass and nod a little—not that I take it as a special honor that a marchesa smiles at me.

Buona sera. She's greeting me with *buona sera.* Now I'll have to nod after all. Was that too deep? She is so much older than I am, after all. How beautifully she walks. Is she divorced? My way of walking is also beautiful. But—I'm aware of it, yes, that's the difference.—An Italian would be dangerous for me. Too bad that dark and handsome one with the Roman head is already gone. Paul would say that he looks like a playboy, what the French call a *filou.* Oh God! I've got nothing against *filous.* On the contrary.—So here I am. Number seventy-seven. A lucky number really. Nice room. Pine. There's my virginal bed.—Now the sunset really has become an Alpine glow. But I won't admit it to Paul. Actually, Paul is really shy. A doctor. A gynecologist! Maybe that's why. The day before yesterday, when we were so far ahead of everyone else in the woods, he could have made a pass at me. It wouldn't have done him any good, to be sure. Actually, no one has ever made a real pass at me. Oh, possibly three years ago while swimming in the Wörthersee. Did he make a pass at me? No, he was just plain indecent. But handsome. Belvedere Apollo. Actually, I didn't quite understand it then. Well, I was only sixteen. My heavenly meadow! Mine! If only I could carry it back to Vienna with me. A soft haze. Already autumn? Well, it's the third of September and high in the mountains.

Well now, Fräulein Else, when are you going to make up your mind to read the letter? Maybe it doesn't have anything to do with

Papa. Maybe it's something about my brother? Maybe he's gotten engaged to one of his old flames. To a chorus girl or a glove sales-girl. Oh no, he's too smart for that. Actually, I don't know him very well. When I was sixteen and he was twenty-one, we were really close for a time. He told me a lot about a certain Lotte. Then sud-denly he stopped. This Lotte must have done something to him. Since then he hasn't told me anything.—Well, now the letter's open, and I didn't even notice that I'd opened it. I'll sit on the window ledge and read it. Got to be careful that I don't fall out. According to sources from San Martino today, a lamentable accident occurred today at the Hotel Fratazza: Fräulein Else T., a beautiful nineteen-year-old girl, the daughter of a well-known attorney. . . . Of course they'll say I killed myself over an unhappy love affair or because I was pregnant. Unhappy love affair! Unfortunately not.

My dear girl—I'll look at the end first.—*So once more, don't be upset with us, my dear, sweet girl. And a thousand . . .*—Oh God, they haven't killed themselves! No—if they had, there'd be a telegram from Rudi.—*My dear girl, you can't imagine how sorry I am to have to interrupt your beautiful vacation*—as though I weren't always on vacation, unfortunately—*with such unpleasant news.*—Mama always writes in such an awful style.—*But after con-siderable reflection I really can't do anything else. Not to beat about the bush, the situation with Papa has become desperate. I don't know what to do or how to help.*—Why so many words?—*It's a matter of a rather ridiculously small sum—thirty thousand gulden—*That's ridiculously small?—*which we have to have within three days, or it's all over.*—For God's sake, what does that mean?—*Just think, my dear girl, Baron Höhning*—Who, the district attorney?—*summoned Papa to his office this morning. You know how the baron thinks the world of Papa—is really very fond of him. A year and a half ago, when things were also hanging by a hair, he talked to the chief creditors personally and put everything in order at the last* *minute. But this time absolutely nothing can be done if the money isn't forthcoming. Aside from the fact that we'll all be ruined, there will be a scandal the likes of which has never before been seen. Think of it, an attorney, a famous attorney, who—no, I can't even write it down. I'm constantly on the verge of tears. You know, child (for you're perceptive), that we've been, God help us, in a similar situation several times before, but that the family has always helped us out. Last time a hundred and twenty thousand were involved. But that time Papa had to sign an agreement that we would never approach a relative again, especially not Uncle Bernhard.*—Well, go on, go on. What's the point? What can I do about it?—*The only one we could think of as a last resort this time is Uncle Victor, but he, unfortunately, is on a trip to the North Cape or to Scotland*—Yes, he's got a cushy life, the miserable wretch.—*and is absolutely unreachable, at least for the moment. Going to one of Papa's colleagues, specifically to Dr. Sch., who has often helped Papa in the past*—Oh God, what kind of reputation do we have?—*is unthinkable now that he's married again*—Well, what then? What then? What do you want from me?—*And then your letter came, my dear girl, the letter in which you mentioned that Dorsday is also staying at Fratazza, and that seemed to us like a stroke of fate. You know how often Dorsday used to come and visit us in former years.*—Well, it wasn't so often.—*It's just sheer accident that we haven't seen very much of him for two or three years; he's supposed to be deeply entangled—and just between you and me, nothing very high class.*—Why "between you and me"?—*Papa still plays whist with him every Thursday at the Residenz Club, and last winter he saved him a pretty piece of money in a suit against another art dealer. Furthermore—why shouldn't you know it?—he came to Papa's assistance once before.*—I thought so.—*At that time only a mere trifle was involved, only eight thousand gulden. But after all, thirty thousand is not very much to Dorsday either. So I wondered whether you could do us the*

*favor of speaking to Dorsday.—*What?*—He's always been especially fond of you.—*I never noticed that. True, he stroked my cheeks
when I was twelve or thirteen: "Becoming quite a young lady, aren't
we?"*—And since Papa, fortunately, hasn't approached him since
the eight thousand, he won't refuse us this favor. He's supposed to
have made eighty thousand the other day on just a single Rubens
that he sold to an American. Of course, you can't mention that.—*Do
you think I'm an idiot, Mama?*—But otherwise you can talk to him
quite frankly. If the occasion arises, you can also mention that
Baron Höhning sent for your father. And that with the thirty thousand the worst really will be averted, not just for the time being, but,
God willing, forever,—*Do you really believe that, Mama?*—because
the Erbesheimer case, which is going brilliantly, will surely bring
Papa a hundred thousand. Naturally he can't demand anything from
the Erbesheimers at this point. So, I beg you, my dear girl, talk to
Dorsday. I assure you there's nothing to it. True, Papa could just
have telegraphed him—we considered that seriously—but there's
nothing like talking to someone in person. The money must be here
at noon on the sixth. Dr. F.—*Who is Doctor F.? Oh yes, Fiala—*is
implacable. Of course there's also personal rancor in the matter. But
since, unfortunately, it involves trust funds—*Oh God! Papa, what
have you done?*—nothing can be done. And if the money isn't in
Fiala's hands by twelve noon on the fifth, an arrest warrant will be
ordered. Baron Höhning will restrain himself until then. So Dorsday
would have to wire the money to Dr. F. by telegraph through his
bank. Then we'll be saved. Otherwise, God knows what will happen.
Believe me, you'll have nothing to reproach yourself for, dear child.
Papa had reservations about asking you at first. He even asked two
other people. But he came home in despair.—*Is it possible that Papa
can be in despair?*—Perhaps not so much because of the money, but
because people are treating him so shamefully. One of them was
once Papa's best friend. You can guess whom I mean.—*I can't

guess. Papa has had so many best friends, and in reality, none at all. Maybe Warnsdorf?—*Papa didn't come home until one o'clock in the morning, and right now it's four o'clock. He's finally sleeping, thank God.*—It might be better for him if he never woke up.—*I'm taking this letter to the post office myself first thing in the morning— express, so you should have it by the morning of the third.*—How did mother think it would get here by then? She never knows how to do anything.—*So talk to Dorsday immediately, I beg you, and telegraph us at once about how it turned out. Do not, for God's sake, let Aunt Emma find out; it's sad enough that in a case like this one can't turn to one's own sister. But one might as well talk to a stone as to her. My dear, dear girl, I'm so sorry that you have to be involved in things like this at your young age, but believe me, Papa is only the least little bit at fault in all this.*—So whose fault is it then, Mama?—*Well, let's hope to God that the Erbesheimer case will, in all respects, mark a decisive change in our lives. We just have to get past these next few weeks. Wouldn't it be an irony if a catastrophe occurred over thirty thousand gulden?*—She doesn't seriously mean that Papa would commit . . . but wouldn't . . . the other thing . . . be even worse?—*I'll close now, my dear child, and hope that, no matter what*—No matter what?—*you'll be able to stay in San Martino through the holidays, at least until the ninth or the tenth. You won't need to come back because of us, in any case. Say hello to your aunt for me; continue to be nice to her. Again, don't be upset with us, my dear, sweet child, and a thousand . . .*—Yes, I know that already.

So, I'm supposed to solicit Herr Dorsday . . . that's insane. How does Mama imagine that? Why didn't Papa just board a train and come here?—He would have arrived just as fast as the express letter. But maybe they would have held him at the station on suspicion of flight.—Horrible! Horrible! Even thirty thousand won't save us. Always the same story! For seven years! No—longer. Who would believe it to look at me? No one. And they wouldn't believe it to look at Papa either. And yet everyone knows it. It's a miracle we can hold our heads up. How one gets accustomed to things! As a matter of fact, we're living quite well at the same time. Mama really is an artist. That dinner last New Year's for fourteen people—unbelievable. But the two pairs of evening gloves for me were a big crisis. And when Rudi recently needed three hundred gulden, Mama almost cried. Yet Papa is always in a good mood despite all this. Always? No, oh no. Recently, during *Figaro* at the opera, an expression came over his face—it became suddenly quite vacant—and I was frightened. He was like someone else. But afterward when we had dinner at the Grand Hotel, he was in just as good a mood as ever.

And now I'm holding this letter in my hand. The letter's crazy. I should talk to Dorsday? I would just die of shame.—Shame? Me? Why? It's not my fault.—What if I talked to Aunt Emma after all? Ridiculous. She probably doesn't have that much money at her disposal anyway. And uncle is a tightwad. Oh God, why don't I have any money? Why haven't I ever earned anything? Why didn't I ever learn anything?—Oh, I have learned some things! Who dares to say I haven't learned anything? I play the piano. I can speak French, English, and a little Italian, I've attended lectures in art history—ha ha! And even if I had learned something more useful, what good would that do me now? I could never have saved thirty thousand gulden in any case!

The Alpine glow has faded. The evening is no longer gorgeous. The whole place seems dreary. No, it's not the place. It's life itself. And I'm sitting here calmly on the windowsill. Papa is to be locked up. No. Never, never. He mustn't be. I'll save him. Yes, Papa, I'll save you. It's very easy, after all. Just a few nonchalant words—I'm good at that. I'm "high-minded."—Ha ha, I'll treat Herr Dorsday as if it were an honor for him to send us money. It is an honor!—*Herr von Dorsday, might you have a few minutes for me? I've just* received a letter from Mama; she's temporarily embarrassed— actually, it's Papa.—*But of course, my dear Fräulein, with great pleasure. How much is involved?*—If only I didn't find him so disagreeable. And his manner of looking at me! *No, Herr Dorsday, I'm not taken in by your elegance, or by your monocle, or by your air of nobility. You might just as well be dealing in old clothes as in old paintings.*—But Else! Else, what are you saying?—Oh, I can say it. No one can tell by looking at me. I'm even a blonde, a strawberry blonde, and Rudi looks absolutely like an aristocrat. Of course it's obvious with Mama, at least when she talks. But it's not with Papa. Really, they should notice it. I don't deny it at all, and certainly Rudi doesn't. Just the opposite. What would Rudi do if Papa were put in jail? Would he shoot himself? What nonsense! Shootings and jail— these kind of things don't happen to us; they only happen in the newspapers.

The air is like champagne. Dinner, the *diner,* is in an hour. I can't stand Cissy. She doesn't care about her little girl at all. What am I going to wear? The blue or the black? The black is perhaps right for tonight. Too low cut? *Toilette de circonstance* they call it in French novels. In any case, I've got to look ravishing when I talk to Dorsday. After dinner, nonchalantly. His eyes will fasten on my décolletage. Repulsive man. I hate him. I hate everybody. Why does it have to be Dorsday, of all people? Is there really only one Dorsday in the world who has thirty thousand gulden? What if I talked to Paul? If he told aunt that he had gambling debts, I bet she'd be able to come up with the money.

It's almost dark. Night. Death. I wish I were dead.—Oh, that's not true. What if I went down right now and talked to Dorsday before dinner? Oh, how awful!—Paul, if you give me the thirty thousand, you can have anything you want from me. No, that's right out of a novel again. The noble daughter sells herself for her beloved father, and in the end really enjoys it. Ugh, disgusting! No, Paul, even for thirty thousand you can't have me. No one can. But for a million?—For a palace? For a string of pearls? If I marry some day, I'll probably do it for less. Is that really so bad? Fanny as much as sold herself in the end. She told me herself that her husband makes her shudder. Well, how about it, Papa? What if I just auctioned myself off this evening? To save you from prison? What a sensation! I have a fever, I'm sure of it. Or am I getting my period already? No, I have a fever. Maybe from the air. Like champagne.—If Fred were here, could he give me advice? I don't need advice. There's no advice to give. I'll talk to Herr Dorsday, the Vicomte von Eperjes, and will solicit money from him. I, the high-minded Else, the aristocrat, the marchesa, the beggar maid, the embezzler's daughter. How have I come to this? No one can climb mountains better than I can. No one has as much spunk—a sporting girl, as the English say. I should have been born in England, or as a countess.

Here are the clothes in the armoire. Is the green loden one actually paid for, Mama? Only one installment, I think. I'll wear the black. They all stared at me yesterday. Even the pale little man with the golden pince-nez. I'm not really beautiful, but I look interesting. I should have gone on stage. Bertha's already had three lovers and no one thinks the less of her for that. . . . In Düsseldorf it was the director. In Hamburg it was a married man, and she lived in the Atlantic Hotel. Suite with a bathroom. I think she's almost proud of it. Stupid, they're all so stupid. I'll have a hundred lovers, a thousand. Why not? My décolletage is not low enough. If I were married, it could be lower.—*How fortunate that I meet you here, Herr von Dorsday. I've just received a letter from Vienna.* . . . I'll take the letter with me in any case. Should I ring for the chambermaid? No, I'll dress myself. I don't need anyone to help me with the black dress. If I were rich, I'd never travel without a chambermaid.

I'd better turn on the light. It's getting cold. Close the window. Curtain down?—Not necessary. No one's standing on the mountain over there with a telescope. Too bad.—*I've just gotten a letter, Herr von Dorsday.*—Maybe it would be better after dinner after all. Everyone's in a better mood then. Dorsday too.—And I could have a glass of wine first. But if I were done with the whole business before dinner, I'd enjoy it more. *Pudding à la merveille, fromage, et fruits divers.* And what if Herr von Dorsday says no?—Or what if he makes a pass at me? Ah no, no one's ever made a pass at me. Well, Marine Lieutenant Brandl, but he wasn't serious.—I've gotten a little thinner again. It suits me.—The twilight is staring in at me. It's staring at me like a ghost. Like a hundred ghosts. Ghosts are rising from my meadow. How far is Vienna? How long have I been gone? How lonely I am here! I have no girlfriends. I have no boyfriends either. Where are they all? When will I get married? Who will marry the daughter of an embezzler?—*I've just received a letter, Herr von Dorsday.*—*Really, don't mention it, Fräulein Else. I just sold a Rembrandt yesterday. You're embarrassing me by even asking, Fräulein Else.*—And now he's tearing a page out of his checkbook and signing it with his gold fountain pen. And tomorrow morning I'll go to Vienna with it. No matter what. Even without a check. I'm not going to stay here any longer. I just couldn't. I shouldn't. I'm living here like an elegant young lady, and Papa has one foot in the grave—no, in prison. The next-to-last pair of silk stockings. Nobody will notice this little rip just under the knee. Nobody? Who knows? Don't be frivolous, Else.—Bertha's nothing but a tramp. But is Christine the least bit better? Her future husband will be very happy. I'm sure Mama's always been a faithful wife. I won't be faithful. I'm highminded, but I won't be faithful. I'm too attracted to *filous.* I'm sure the marchesa has a *filou* for a lover. If Fred knew what I'm really like, his respect for me would disappear at once.—*You could have been all sorts of things, Fräulein—a pianist, a bookkeeper, an actress. There's no end of things you could have been. But you've always been too well-off.* Too well-off!—Ha ha! Fred overestimates me. In reality I have no talent for anything.—Who knows? I could have gone as far as Bertha, though. But I don't have enough ambition. A young lady from a good family. Good family, ha. Her father embezzles trust funds. Why did you do this to me, Papa? If only you had something to show for it! But it's gambled away in the stock market! Is it worth the trouble? And the thirty thousand won't help you either. For a few months maybe. But in the end he'll have to flee anyway. A year and a half ago the situation was almost the same. Then, help arrived just in time, but there'll be a time when you won't be able to get help. And what will become of us then? Rudi will go the Vanderhulst Bank in Rotterdam. But what about me? Wealthy match. Oh, if only I had the ambition to do that! I'm really beautiful today. That's probably because I'm so nervous. Who am I beautiful for? Would I be happier if Fred were here? Oh, in the end Fred isn't the right man for me. He isn't a *filou*! But I'd take him if he had money. And then a *filou* would come along—and the *malheur* would begin. You'd like to be a *filou*, Herr von Dorsday, wouldn't you?—From a distance you sometimes look the part. Like a dissipated vicomte or an overage Don Juan with your stupid monocle and your white flannel suit. But really you're a long way from being a *filou*.—Do I have everything? Ready for *diner*?—But what am I going to do for an hour if I don't run across Dorsday? What if he's out walking with that miserable Frau Winawer? Oh, she isn't unhappy at all—she isn't the one who needs thirty thousand gulden. Well, I'll just sit in the lobby, look magnificent in a leather armchair, leaf through the *Illustrated News* and the *Vie Parisienne,* and cross my legs. No one will notice the rip under my knee. Perhaps a billionaire has just arrived.—*It's you over there, Fräulein Else, you, or no one.*—I'll take the white shawl. It looks so becoming. I'll throw it carelessly around my gorgeous shoulders. What do I have them for, these gorgeous shoulders? I could make some man very happy. If only the right man were here. But I don't want to have any children. I'm not maternal. Marie Weil is maternal. Mama is maternal. Aunt Irene is maternal. I have a noble brow and a beautiful figure.— *If only I could paint you as I really want to, Fräulein Else.*—Yes, I'm sure you'd like that. I don't even remember his name anymore. I know it wasn't Titian, so it was an affront.—*I've just received a letter, Herr von Dorsday.*—A little more powder on my throat and my neck, a drop of *verveine* on my handkerchief. Lock the armoire, open the window again—oh, how glorious! Too beautiful for tears! I'm nervous. Well, don't I have the right to be nervous under such circumstances? I have the box of Veronal with my underwear. I also need new underwear. That'll be another big crisis. Oh God.

Uncanny, that enormous Cimone, as though it wanted to fall on me. There's not a star in the sky yet. The air is like champagne. And the perfume from the meadows! I'll live in the country. I'll marry a landowner and have children. Dr. Froriep is perhaps the only one with whom I might have been happy. How wonderful those two evenings were, the first one at Kniep's and the other at the artists' ball. Why did he suddenly disappear—at least as far as I was concerned? Maybe because of Papa? I bet that's it. I'd like to blow a kiss up into the air before I go downstairs to the rabble again. But to whom should the kiss go? I'm all alone. No one can imagine how alone I am. Hello, lover! Who? Hello, bridegroom! Who? Hello, suitor. Who, Fred? Hardly. So the window will stay open. Even if it gets cold. Turn off the light. So—yes, right, the letter. I've got to take it with me in any case. The book on the night table. So. I'm going to read further in *Notre Coeur* no matter what happens. Good evening, most beautiful Fräulein in the mirror. Remember me. Farewell. . . .

Why am I locking the door? Nothing ever gets stolen here. I wonder if Cissy leaves her door open at night? Or does she open it only when he knocks? Is that really true? But of course. Then they'll lie together in bed. Unappetizing. I won't share a bedroom with my husband and with my thousand lovers.—The stairs are completely empty! Always at this hour. My footsteps are echoing. I've been here for three weeks now. I left Gmunden on the twelfth of August. Gmunden was boring. How did Papa get the money to send Mama and me to the countryside? And even Rudi spent four whole weeks traveling God knows where. He hasn't written twice the whole time. I just can't understand how we get by. Of course Mama doesn't have any jewelry any more.—Why did Fred spend only two days in Gmunden? I'm sure he has a mistress too! To be sure, I can't imagine it. I can't imagine anything at all. It's been a week since he's written to me. He writes beautiful letters.—Who's sitting over there at the little table? No, it's not Dorsday, thank God, I couldn't talk to him now, before dinner.—Why does the porter look at me so strangely? Could he have read Mama's express letter? I think I'm crazy. I have to tip him again soon.—The blonde over there is already dressed for dinner too. How can anybody be so fat!—I'll go out in front of the hotel and walk up and down a bit. Or into the music room. Isn't somebody playing in there? A Beethoven sonata! How can anyone play a Beethoven sonata here? I've been neglecting my piano playing. When I get back to Vienna I'll practice regularly again. Begin a completely new life. We'll all have to. This can't go on. I'll have a serious talk with Papa—if there's still time for that. There will be, there will be. Why haven't I done it before? Everything at home is settled by joking, but no one's really lighthearted. Everyone is basically afraid of everyone else. Everyone is all alone. Mama is alone because she isn't bright enough and doesn't understand anything about anyone—not about me, not about Rudi, and not about Papa. But she isn't aware of it, and neither is Rudi. He's a nice, elegant fellow, true. But he had more promise at twenty-one than he does now. It'll be good for him to go to Holland. But where will I go? I'd like to go away and do what I want. If Papa runs off to America I'll go with him. I'm all confused. The porter will think I'm insane, sitting here on the bench and staring into space. I'll light a cigarette. Where's my cigarette case? Upstairs. But where? I've got the Veronal underneath the underwear. But where did I put the cigarette case? Here come Cissy and Paul. Yes, she has to change for *diner*; otherwise they would have kept on playing in the dark.—They don't see me. What's he saying to her? Why is she laughing so inanely? It would be fun to write an anonymous letter to her husband in Vienna. Could I do such a thing? Never. Who knows? They've just seen me. I'll nod to them. She's upset that I'm looking so good. She looks almost embarrassed.

Hello, Else. Ready for dinner already?

Why is she now saying dinner and not *diner*? She can't even be consistent. *As you see, Frau Cissy.*

You look absolutely ravishing, Else. I have a great desire to pay court to you.

Save yourself the trouble, Paul. Just give me a cigarette.

With great pleasure.

Thank you. How did your singles match turn out?

Frau Cissy beat me three times in a row.

That's because he was distracted. By the way, Else, do you know that the crown prince of Greece is coming here tomorrow?

What do I care about the crown prince of Greece? *Really!* Oh God—Dorsday with Frau Winawer! They're waving at me. They're going on. I waved back at them too formally. Not as I usually do. Oh, what kind of person am I?

Your cigarette isn't lit, Else.

Well, give me another match. Thanks.

Your shawl is very pretty, Else. It goes very well with that black dress. Come to think of it, I must go and change too.

I'd rather she stayed. I'm afraid of Dorsday.

I've ordered the hairdresser for seven. She's excellent. Spends the winter in Milano. Well, adieu, Else. Adieu, Paul.

Goodbye, madam.

Adieu Frau Cissy. She's gone. Good. At least Paul is staying.

May I sit with you a minute, Else? Or am I disturbing your dreams?

Why my dreams? Perhaps my realities. Actually, that doesn't mean anything. I'd rather he left. I have to talk to Dorsday, after all. There he is, still standing with the unhappy Frau Winawer. He's bored. I can see he'd rather come over to me.

Are there realities in which you don't want to be disturbed?

What's he saying? He can go to hell. Why am I smiling at him so flirtatiously? It's not meant for him at all. Dorsday is eyeing me. Where am I? Where am I?

What's the matter with you today, Else?

Why? Is there something the matter with me today?

You're being mysterious, devilish, seductive.

Don't talk nonsense, Paul.

One could go mad looking at you.

What's he trying to do? Why is he talking to me that way? He's good-looking, that's true. My cigarette smoke is catching in his hair. But I have no use for him now.

You're looking past me in such a peculiar way. Why, Else?

I'm not going to answer him. I have no use for him now. I'll be as disagreeable as possible. I just can't have a conversation now.

Your mind is somewhere else.

That's quite possible. He's nothing to me. Does Dorsday recognize that I'm waiting for him? I'm not looking his way but I know he's looking at me.

Well, then—goodbye, Else.

Thank God! He's kissing my hand. He doesn't usually do that.

Adieu, Paul. Where did I get that dripping voice? There he goes, the hypocrite. Probably still has to arrange details about tonight with Cissy. I hope he enjoys himself. I'm going to draw the shawl over my shoulders, get up, and go out in front of the hotel. It'll probably be a little cool there already. Too bad that my coat—oh yes, I hung it in the porter's office this morning. I can feel Dorsday's gaze on the nape of my neck, piercing through the shawl. Frau Winawer is going up to her room now. How do I know that? Telepathy. *Excuse me, porter.*

Does Fräulein wish her coat?

Yes, please.

It's already a little cold in the evening now, Fräulein. It comes on so suddenly here.

Thank you. Should I really go out to the front of the hotel? Of course—what else? In any case, I'll go to the door. Now they're coming out, one after the other. The man with the gold pince-nez. The tall blond with the green vest. They're all looking at me. The little woman from Geneva is quite pretty. No, she's from Lausanne. It's really not so cold.

Good evening, Fräulein Else. For God's sake, it's him. I won't say anything about Papa. Not a word. Not 'till after dinner. Or I'll go back to Vienna tomorrow. I'll go to Dr. Fiala myself. Why didn't I think of that right away? I'm going to turn around and pretend I didn't know who was standing behind me.

Ah, Herr von Dorsday!

Are you still planning to take a little walk?

Well, not exactly a real walk. I just want to stroll a little before dinner.

It's still almost an hour till dinner.

Really? It's not actually so cold. The mountains are blue. It would be quite amusing if he suddenly asked for my hand.

There certainly is no more beautiful spot on earth than this one.

Do you really think so, Herr von Dorsday? Please don't tell me that the air is like champagne.

No, Fräulein Else, I say that only at two thousand meters. Here we're only sixteen hundred and fifty meters above sea level.

Does that make such a big difference?

But of course! Have you ever been to the Engadine?

No, never. I take it that the air there really is like champagne?

You could almost say so. Although champagne is not my favorite drink. I prefer this region. If only because of the wonderful forests.

How boring he is. Doesn't he realize it? He obviously doesn't quite know what he should say to me. It would be simpler with a married woman. A slightly off-color remark and the conversation is under way.

Are you staying here in San Martino for a while, Fräulein Else?

Idiotic. Why am I looking at him so flirtatiously? He's already smiling that way. I can't believe how stupid men are.

That depends partially on my aunt. That's not true at all. I could go back to Vienna alone. *Probably until the tenth.*

Your mother is still in Gmunden?

No, Herr Dorsday. She's back in Vienna already. She's been back for three weeks. Papa's back in Vienna too. He took barely a week's vacation this year. I think the Erbesheimer case is making a lot of work for him.

I can believe that. But your father is probably the only person who can save Erbesheimer. . . . Success is already indicated in the fact that it's become a civil suit.

That's good, that's good. *I'm pleased to hear that you have such a favorable premonition too.*

Premonition? About what?

Well, that Papa is going to win the Erbesheimer case.
I wouldn't go so far as to say that with great confidence.
So, he's retreating already? I'm not going to let him. *Oh, I be-*
lieve in premonitions and signs. Just think, Herr von Dorsday, today
I received a letter from home. That wasn't very well done. He's
making a rather astonished face. Just go on, don't swallow. He's a
good old friend of Papa's. Go on. Go on. Now or never. *Herr von*
Dorsday, you've just spoken so well of Papa that it would be down-
right wrong of me if I weren't totally frank with you. What kind of
stupid eyes is he making at me? Oh my God, he notices I'm up to
something. Go on. Go on. *For the letter mentioned you, Herr von*
Dorsday. It's a letter from my mother.
   Yes?
   Actually, it's a very sad letter. You know our circumstances,
Herr von Dorsday. Oh God, I actually have tears in my voice. Go
on, go on, there's no retreating now. *In short, Herr von Dorsday, it*
seems we're once again in the same position. Now he'd like to dis-
appear if he could. *It's about—a bagatelle. Really only a bagatelle,*
Herr von Dorsday. And yet, according to Mama, everything depends
on it. I'm rambling on like a stupid cow.
   Indeed? But please—please calm yourself, Fräulein Else.
   He said that nicely. But he needn't pet my arm on that account.
   So what's the trouble, Fräulein Else? What's in that sad letter
from your mother?
   Herr von Dorsday, Papa—my knees are trembling—*Mama*
writes that Papa . . .
   For heaven's sake, Else, what's the matter? Wouldn't you
rather—here is a bench. May I put your coat about you? It's gotten a
little cold.
   Thank you, Herr von Dorsday. Oh, it's nothing, nothing at all.
But suddenly I'm sitting on a bench. Who is that lady passing by?
Don't know her. If only I didn't have to keep talking. The way he's

staring at me! How could you ask this of me, Papa? It wasn't right of you, Papa. But now it's done. I should have waited till after dinner. *Well now, Fräulein Else?*

His monocle is dangling. It looks so stupid. Should I answer him? I have to. Quickly now, get it over with. What can happen to me, anyway? He's Papa's friend, after all. *Oh Lord, Herr von Dorsday, you're such an old friend of the family.* I said that very well. *And it probably won't surprise you if I tell you that Papa once again finds himself in a very awkward position.* How strange my voice sounds! Is that really me talking? Am I dreaming? I must look different from the way I usually do.

Indeed, it doesn't greatly surprise me—you're right about that, dear Fräulein Else—even though I regret hearing it.

Why am I looking at him so imploringly? Smile! Smile! It'll be all right.

I feel the most sincere friendship for your father, for you all.

He shouldn't look at me that way. It's indecent. I'll talk to him in a different way and stop smiling. I've got to act more dignified. *Well, Herr von Dorsday, you now have the opportunity to demonstrate your friendship for my father.* Thank God, I have my old voice back again. *It appears, Herr von Dorsday, that all of our relatives and friends—most of them aren't in Vienna right now. Otherwise my mother would never have thought of it—Well, just recently in a letter to Mama I happened to mention your presence here in Martino—among others, of course—*

I take it for granted, Fräulein Else, that I wasn't the exclusive theme of your correspondence with your Mama.

Why is he pressing his knee against mine while he's standing there in front of me? Oh well, I'll just put up with it. What's the difference? Once you've sunk so low . . . *The situation is this: it's Dr. Fiala who appears to be giving Papa particular trouble this time.*

Oh, Dr. Fiala.

He evidently knows what kind of person this Fiala is. *Yes, Dr. Fiala. And the amount involved is supposed to be there on the fifth. That's the day after tomorrow, at twelve o'clock noon—or rather, it has to be in his hands by then. Otherwise Baron Höhning—Yes, can you believe it? The baron summoned Papa to him personally, he's so fond of him.*—Why am I going on about Höhning? That isn't necessary at all.

Are you trying to say, Else, that otherwise an arrest is inevitable?

Why does he say that so bluntly? I'm not going to answer anything. I'll just nod. *Yes.* Now I've said it anyway.

Hmm, that is—really unfortunate, that is truly very—that greatly gifted, brilliant man. How much money is actually involved, Fräulein Else?

Why is he smiling? He finds it unfortunate and yet he's smiling. What does his smile mean? That it doesn't matter how much it is? And what if he says no! I'll kill myself if he says no. So—I have to tell him the amount. *What, Herr von Dorsday? I didn't say how much is involved? A million.* Why did I say that? This is no time for joking. But when I tell him how much less is really involved, he'll be pleased. The look on his face! Does he really think that Papa would ask him for a million?—*Pardon me, Herr von Dorsday, for joking at a time like this. In truth, I'm not in a joking mood at all.*— Yes, yes, press your knees to mine, you can take that liberty. *Of course it isn't a matter of a million. All in all, the sum runs to thirty thousand, Herr von Dorsday. That's the amount that has to be in Dr. Fiala's hands by the day after tomorrow at twelve o'clock noon. Yes, Mama wrote that Papa made all possible efforts, but, as I said, the relatives we might have turned to are not in Vienna right now.*—Oh, God, how I'm debasing myself.—*Otherwise, Papa obviously would never have thought of turning to you, Herr von Dorsday; that is, of asking me to turn*—Why is he silent? Why doesn't he have any expression? Why doesn't he say yes? Where are the checkbook and the fountain pen? Oh my God, he isn't going to say no, is he? Should I throw myself on my knees in front of him? Oh God! Oh God!

On the fifth, did you say, Fräulein Else?

Thank God, at least he's saying something. *Yes, the day after tomorrow, Herr von Dorsday, at twelve noon. It would therefore be necessary—I don't think there's enough time to do it by letter—*

Of course not, Fräulein Else. We'd have to telegraph.

We—that's good, that's very good.

Well, that would be the least of the problem. How much did you say it was, Else?

He's heard me say it already; why is he torturing me? *Thirty thousand, Herr Dorsday. Really a ridiculously small sum.* Why did I say that? How stupid! But he's smiling. Silly girl, he's thinking. He's smiling quite amiably. Papa is saved! He'd have loaned him fifty thousand too, and we could all have bought ourselves all sorts of things. I'd have bought myself new underwear. How contemptible I am! Well, one gets that way.—

Not quite so ridiculously small, my dear girl—Why does he say "dear girl"? Is that good or bad?—*as you imagine; even thirty thousand gulden have to be earned.*

Forgive me, Herr von Dorsday, I didn't mean it that way. I was only thinking of how sad it is that because of such a sum, Papa—because of such a bagatelle—Oh God, I'm bungling it again. *You can't imagine, Herr von Dorsday—even if you have some idea of our circumstances—how terrible this is for me, and especially for Mama.* He's putting a foot on the bench. Is that supposed to be elegant—or what?—

Oh, I can imagine it easily, dear Else.

How strange his voice sounds, completely changed, peculiar.

And I've often thought myself: it's such a pity, such a pity that this talented man—

Why does he say "such a pity"? Won't he give us the money? No, he's only generalizing. Why doesn't he say yes, once and for all? Or is he taking that for granted? How he's looking at me! Why doesn't he go on talking? Oh, because the two Hungarian women are passing by. At least now he's assumed a more respectable stance. His foot is no longer on the bench. His cravat is too bright for an older man. Did his mistress select it for him? Nothing very high class—"between us," Mama wrote. Thirty thousand gulden! But I'm smiling at him. Why am I smiling at him? Oh, I'm such a coward.

If one could at least assume that this sum would really make a difference. But—you're such a clever creature, Else. What would thirty thousand gulden be? A drop of water on a hot stove.

Oh my God, he doesn't want to give us the money. I mustn't look so scared. Everything's at stake. Now I've got to say something intelligent and convincing. *Oh no, Herr von Dorsday, this time it wouldn't be just a drop on a hot stove. The Erbesheimer case is at hand, don't forget that, Herr von Dorsday, and it's already as good as won. You sensed that yourself, Herr von Dorsday. And Papa has other cases too. And furthermore I intend—don't laugh, Herr von Dorsday—to talk to Papa very seriously. He takes me seriously. I can say that if there's one person capable of having some influence on him, it's me!*

You really are a touching, delightful creature, Fräulein Else.

His voice has that tone again. I can't stand it when men get that tone in their voice. I don't even like it in Fred.

A delightful creature, upon my word.

Why does he say "upon my word"? That's fatuous. They only say that at the Burgtheater.

But as much as I would like to share your optimism—once the cart has gone so far astray—

It hasn't, Herr von Dorsday. If I didn't believe in Papa, if I weren't completely convinced that these thirty thousand gulden—I don't know what else to say. I can't just literally beg him. He's thinking it over, apparently. Perhaps he doesn't know Fiala's address. Nonsense. The situation is impossible. I'm sitting here like a poor wretch. He's standing in front of me, grinding his monocle into my face, and saying nothing. I'm going to stand up, that's the best thing. I'm not going to let myself be treated like this. Papa can kill himself. I'll kill myself too. It's a disgrace, such a life. It would be best just to jump from that cliff over there right away and get it over with. It would serve you right, all of you. I'm getting up.

Fräulein Else.

Pardon me, Herr von Dorsday, for having bothered you at all under these circumstances. Naturally, I completely understand your inclination to refuse. So, I'm finished. I'm going.

Stay, Fräulein Else.

Stay, he's saying? Why should I stay? He's going to give us the money. Yes. Of course. He has to! But I won't sit down again. I'll remain standing, as though I were going in half a minute. I'm a little taller than he is.

You didn't wait for my answer, Else. Once before—forgive me if I mention it in this context, Else,—he shouldn't say Else so often—*I've once before been in the position of helping your father out of an embarrassment of this sort. To be sure, that was an even more laughable sum than this one, and I didn't flatter myself with the hope of ever seeing the money again. And so there's no real reason for my refusing my assistance this time. Especially when a young girl like you, Else, comes in person as an intermediary—*

What's he getting at? His voice no longer has that tone. Or does it? The way he's looking at me! He'd better watch out!!

And so, Else, I'm prepared—Dr. Fiala will have the thirty thousand gulden at twelve noon by the day after tomorrow—on one condition—

He shouldn't say anything more; he shouldn't. *Herr von Dors-*

day, I, I personally, will guarantee that my father will pay you back the money as soon as he receives Erbesheimer's fee. So far, there's not even a retainer—Mama told me so herself.

Let it be, Else. One should never guarantee another's actions— not even one's own.

What does he want? His voice has that tone again. Never has anyone looked at me in that way. I can guess where this is going. He'd better watch out!

I wouldn't have thought it possible even an hour ago that I would ever even consider setting a condition in a situation like this. And now I'm doing it. Yes, Else, I'm only a man after all. And it's not my fault that you're so beautiful, Else.

What does he want? What does he want?

Perhaps I would have asked you for the same thing today or to-morrow, even if you hadn't sought a million—pardon me, thirty thousand—gulden from me. But of course, under normal circum-stances you would never have given me the opportunity of speaking with you alone for so long.

Oh, but I've really taken up too much of your time already, Herr von Dorsday. That was well said. Fred would be pleased. What's this? He's reaching for my hand? How dare he!

Haven't you known it for a long time now, Else?

He should let go of my hand! Thank God, he's letting it go. Not so close, not so close!

You wouldn't be a woman, Else, if you weren't aware of it.—Je vous désire.

The Herr Vicomte could have said that in German too.

Must I say more?

You've already said too much, Herr Dorsday. But I'm still standing here. Why? I'll leave. I'll leave without a word.

Else! Else!

Now he's next to me again.

Forgive me, Else. I was also merely joking, just as you were earlier about the one million. My demand, too, isn't as great as you may have feared—as I must unfortunately put it—so that the lesser one will perhaps pleasantly surprise you. Please stay, Else.

I'm actually staying here. Why? Here we are standing face to face. Shouldn't I have just slapped him in the face? Isn't there still time for that? The two Englishmen are walking by right now. This would be the right moment. Now, right now. So why am I not doing it? I'm a coward; I'm ruined; I'm humiliated. What does he want instead of the million? A kiss maybe? I would consider that. A million is to thirty thousand as—there are some funny comparisons.

If you should ever really need a million, Else—though I'm not a rich man—we'll see what we can do. But this time I'll be modest, like you. This time I don't want anything, Else, except—to see you.

Is he crazy? He's seeing me already!—Uh oh, so that's what he means. So that's it! Why aren't I slapping him in the face, the lecher! Did I turn red or white? So you want to see me naked? So would many others! I'm beautiful when I'm naked. Why don't I just slap him in the face?—His face is enormous. Why are you so close, you beast! I don't want to feel your breath on my face. Why don't I just leave him standing here? Am I trapped in his gaze? We're locked eye to eye, like mortal enemies. I'd like to call him a beast to his face, but I can't. Or is it that I don't want to?

You're looking at me as though I were crazy, Else. Perhaps I am, a little, because you exercise a spell that perhaps you aren't aware of yourself, Else. You must understand, Else, that my request is not an insult. Yes, I say "request," even if it seems despairingly like extortion. But I'm not an extortionist; I'm just a man who has learned many things from experience—among them this: that everything in the world has its price and that anyone who gives his money away when he is in a position to get something for it is a consummate fool. And—what I want to buy now, Else, as valuable as it is, won't make you any poorer if you sell it. And that it would remain a secret between you and me, this I swear to you, Else, by—by all the charms whose revelation will make me happy.

Where did he learn to talk that way? It sounds like something out of a book.

And I also swear that I—that I won't take any advantage of the situation except for that which is agreed to in our contract. I ask no more of you than to be allowed to stand for a quarter of an hour in reverance of your beauty. My room is on the same floor as yours, Else. Number sixty-five, easy to remember. The Swedish tennis player you spoke of today—wasn't he precisely sixty-five years old?

He's crazy! Why am I letting him continue? I feel paralyzed.

But if for any reason you don't want to visit me in room sixty-five, then I suggest a little stroll after dinner. There is a clearing in the woods—I discovered it by chance just the other day, barely five minutes from our hotel. It will be a wonderful summer night tonight, almost warm, and the starlight will clothe you divinely.

He talks to me as he would to a slave. I'll spit in his face.

Please don't answer me immediately, Else. Think it over. After dinner, kindly announce your decision to me.

Why does he say "announce"? What a stupid word: announce.

Think about it calmly, and take your time. Perhaps you'll real-ize that it isn't merely a business transaction that I'm suggesting to you.

What is it then, you repulsive crook!

Perhaps you'll come to realize that a man is speaking to you, a man who is rather lonely and not particularly happy and who per-haps deserves a little pity.

Pretentious hypocrite! Talks like a bad actor. His manicured fingers look like claws. No, no, I won't. Why don't I tell him so? Kill yourself, Papa! What does he want with my hand? My arm is quite limp. He's drawing my hand to his lips. What hot lips. Phew!

My hand is cold. I'd like to knock his hat off. Ha! That would be funny. Are you done kissing yet, you lecher?—The lamps in front of the hotel are lit. Two windows are open on the third floor. The one where the curtain is moving is mine. Something's shining on top of the armoire. There's nothing on it. It's only the brass ornament.

So, auf Wiedersehen, Else.

I'm not going to say anything. I'm just standing here motionless. He's looking me right in the eye. My face is blank. He doesn't know anything at all. He doesn't know whether I'll come or not. Neither do I. I only know that everything's over. I'm half dead. There he goes. A little bent. Swine! He's feeling my gaze on his neck. Whom is he greeting now? Two women. He greets them as though he were a count. Paul ought to challenge him and shoot him dead. Or Rudi. How does he dare! Shameless swine! Never, never! There's nothing else for you to do, Papa—you have to kill yourself. Those two over there are evidently coming back from an outing. Good-looking, both of them. Do they still have time to change their clothes before dinner? They're obviously on their honeymoon or maybe they aren't married at all. I'll never go on a honeymoon. Thirty thousand gulden. No, no, no! There must be thirty thousand gulden somewhere in the world! I'll go to Fiala myself. I'd still get there on time. Mercy, have mercy, Herr Dr. Fiala. With pleasure, my dear Fräulein. Go into my bedroom—Do me a favor, will you, Paul, and ask your father for thirty thousand gulden? Tell him you have gambling debts and that otherwise you'll have to shoot yourself. Gladly, my dear cousin. I'm in room number so and so; I'll expect you at midnight. Oh, Herr von Dorsday, how modest you are. For the time being. Now he's changing his clothes. Dinner jacket. So let's decide. A clearing in the moonlight or room number sixty-five? Will he accompany me into the woods in his dinner jacket?

There's still time before dinner. A little walk. Have to think the whole thing over calmly. I'm a lonely old man, ha ha. Heavenly air, like champagne. Not cold any more at all. Thirty thousand, thirty thousand—I must look very good against this wide expanse. Too bad there's no one else out here. The man at the edge of the woods over there obviously finds me very attractive. Oh, my dear sir, I'm even more beautiful naked, and the price is laughable, only thirty thousand gulden. Perhaps you can bring friends with you; then it'll be cheaper for each of you. I hope you have many handsome friends, better looking and younger than Herr von Dorsday. Do you know Herr von Dorsday? He's a beast—an affected beast. . . .

So, let me think, let me think. . . . A human life is at stake. Papa's life. But no, he won't kill himself; he'd rather go to jail. Three years at hard labor, or five. He's been living in terror of this for five or ten years already. . . . Trust funds. . . . And Mama too. And me too.—For whom will I have to strip next time? Or should I make permanent arrangements with Herr Dorsday for simplicity's sake? His present mistress is nothing very high class, "between us." He'd certainly prefer me. But am I really more high class? Don't give yourself airs, Fräulein Else, I could tell tales about you . . . a certain dream, for example, which you've had three times already and which you haven't even told your friend Bertha, who wouldn't take offense. And what was that episode a little while ago in Gmunden, on the balcony at six o'clock in the morning, my high-class Fräulein Else? Didn't you see the two young men in a boat who were staring at you? Of course they couldn't really make out my face from the sea, but they couldn't help noticing that I was in my underwear. And I enjoyed it. Oh, more than enjoyed it. I was almost intoxicated. I ran my hands over my hips and acted as though I didn't know that anyone saw me. And the boat didn't move from the spot. Yes, I'm like that, I'm like that. I'm a slut. Yes, everyone knows it. Even Paul knows it. Naturally—he's a gynecologist after all. And the Navy lieutenant also knew it, and the painter too. Only Fred, the dummy, doesn't know it. That's why he loves me. But I don't want to be naked in front of him, never, never. I wouldn't enjoy it at all. But in front of that *filou* with the Roman head—gladly! In front of him most of all. Even if I had to die the next minute. But it isn't necessary to die right afterward. One gets over such things. Bertha has gotten over more than that. I just know that Cissy lies there naked when Paul sneaks to her through the hotel corridors, just as I'll sneak tonight to Herr von Dorsday.

No, no. I won't. I would to anyone else—but not to him. To Paul, for all I care. Or I'll pick out someone at dinner tonight. It doesn't matter who. But I can't tell everyone that I want thirty thousand gulden for it! Then I'd be like a whore from the Kärntnerstrasse. No, I won't sell myself. Never. I'll never sell myself. I'll give myself away. Yes, if I find the right man, I'll give myself away. But I won't sell myself. I'll be a wanton, but not a whore. You miscalculated, Herr von Dorsday. And Papa did too. Yes, he miscalculated. He must have foreseen this. After all, he knows how people are. He knows Herr von Dorsday. He must have guessed that Herr Dorsday wouldn't do it for nothing—otherwise he would have telegraphed or come here himself. But it's easier and more convenient this way, isn't it, Papa? When one has such a pretty daughter, why should one have to march off to prison? And Mama, stupid as always, just sits right down and writes the letter. Papa didn't dare. If he had written it, I would have known it immediately. But you won't succeed. No, you counted too much on my childish affection, Papa; you were too certain I'd rather bear any indignity than let you suffer the consequences of your criminal carelessness. You're a genius. Herr von Dorsday said it; they all say it. But how does that help me? Fiala is a nobody, but he doesn't embezzle trust funds; even Waldheim can't be mentioned in the same breath with you. Who said that? Dr. Froriep. *Your Papa is a genius.*—And I've only heard him speak once!—Last year in the jury room—for the one and only time. Glorious! Tears ran down my cheeks. And the miserable creature he defended was acquitted. Maybe he wasn't even a miserable creature. He only stole something; he didn't embezzle trust funds in order to play baccarat and speculate on the stock market. And now it'll be Papa himself who will be tried before the jury. It'll be in all the newspapers. The second day of the trial, the third; the attorney for the defense stood up to reply. Who will defend him? Not a genius. Nothing will help him. Unanimous guilty verdict. Sentenced to five years. Stein Prison, uniform, cropped hair. Visitors permitted once a month. I'll go there with Mama, third class. For we'll have no money. No one will give us a loan. A small place in the Lerchenfelderstrasse, like the one I saw our seamstress in ten years ago. We're bringing him something to eat. How? We don't have anything ourselves. Uncle Victor will give us a small pension. Three hundred gulden per month. Rudi will be in Holland at Vanderhulst—if they take him. The children of a convict! Novel by Temme in three volumes. Papa receives us in a striped prison uniform. He doesn't look angry, just sad.—Oh, he'll be thinking, Else, if you had gotten me the money that time—but he won't say anything. He won't have the heart to reproach me. He's so good-hearted; he's just irresponsible. His undoing is his passion for gambling. He can't help it; it's a kind of insanity. Maybe they'll acquit him for reason of insanity. He didn't give enough thought to the letter either. Maybe it never even occurred to him that Dorsday would use the situation to demand such an indecency from me. He's a good friend of the family; he loaned Papa eight thousand gulden once before. How could he suspect the man would do a thing like that? Papa certainly tried everything else first. What must he have gone through to resort to having Mama write that letter? He must have run from one friend to the other, from Warsdorf to Burin, from Burin to Wertheimstein to God knows who. I know he went to Uncle Karl. And they all abandoned him. All his so-called friends. And now Dorsday is his last hope, his only hope. And if the money doesn't come, he'll kill himself. Of course he'll kill himself. He won't let himself be imprisoned. Arrest, trial, jury verdict, jail, convict's clothes. No, no! When the arrest warrant comes, he'll hang himself. He'll hang himself from the crossbar of the window. Word will come from the house across the street, the locksmith will have to open the door, and it'll all be my fault. And right now he's sitting with Mama, smoking a Havana cigar in the same room in which he'll hang himself the day after tomorrow. Where does he keep on getting the Havana cigars? I can hear him talking, soothing Mama. *Depend on it—Dorsday will wire the money. Don't forget, I saved him a large sum of money this winter through my intervention. And now there's the Erbesheimer case.* . . . Really, I hear him talking. Telepathy! Strange. I'm also seeing Fred at this moment. He's passing by the Kursalon in the Stadtpark with a girl. She's wearing a pale blue blouse and light shoes and is a little hoarse. I'm sure of it! When I get back to Vienna, I'm going to ask Fred if he was with his mistress on the third of September between 7:30 and 8:00 o'clock.

Where to go now? What's the matter with me? It's almost completely dark. How beautiful and peaceful it is! There's no one about, near or far. They're all at dinner now. Telepathy? No, that's not telepathy. I heard the dinner gong a little while ago. *Where is Else?* Paul will wonder. Everyone will notice if I'm not there for the first course. They'll send up for me. *What's wrong with Else? She's usually so punctual.* The two men at the window will also wonder: *Where on earth is that beautiful young girl with the reddish blonde hair today?* And Herr von Dorsday will get worried. He's a coward, that's certain. Calm yourself, Herr von Dorsday, nothing will happen to you. I despise you far too much. If I wanted it, you'd be a dead man tomorrow night.—I'm convinced that Paul would challenge you if I told him the story. I'm making you a gift of your life, Herr von Dorsday.

How enormously wide the meadows are and how deep the

black of the mountains. Almost no stars. Yes there are—three, four—more will soon be out. And the woods behind me are so silent. It's beautiful, sitting here on a bench at the edge of the woods. The hotel's so distant, so far away, and its lights seem like fairy-tale lights. But what scoundrels are sitting inside! Ah, no—just people, poor people; I feel sorry for all of them. I even feel sorry for the marchesa. I don't know why. And for Frau Winawer and the governess for Cissy's little girl. She's not sitting at the table; she had to eat earlier with Fritzi. *What's going on with Else?* Cissy's asking. *What, she isn't in her room either?* They're all worried about me, I'm sure. I'm the only one who's not worried. I'm in Martino di Castrozza, sitting on a bench at the edge of the woods and the air is like champagne and it seems that I'm crying. Why am I crying? There's no reason to cry. It's just nerves. I've got to get hold of myself. I can't let myself go to pieces like this. But crying isn't unpleasant at all. Crying always does me good. When I visited our old French nurse in the hospital—the one who later died—I cried. And at grandma's funeral, and when Bertha went to Nuremberg, and when Agatha's baby died, and in the theatre when the lady of *La Dame aux Camélias* died, I cried. Who will cry when I die? Oh how beautiful it would be to be dead. I'm lying on a bier in the salon; candles are burning around me. Long candles. Twelve long candles. The hearse is already waiting downstairs. People are standing at the door. *How old was she? Only nineteen. Really only nineteen?—Just think, her father is in prison. Why did she kill herself? Because of an unhappy love for a* filou. *No, what are you talking about? She was going to have a baby. No, she fell from the Cimone. It was an accident. Good afternoon, Herr Dorsday. You are paying your last respects to little Else too?* Little Else, the old lady calls me—But why?—*Naturally, I have to pay her my last respects; I was the first to disgrace her. Oh, it was worth the trouble, Frau Winawer—I've never seen such a beautiful body. It cost me only thirty million. One*

Rubens costs three times as much. She overdosed on hashish. She only wanted to have beautiful visions, but she took too much and didn't wake up again. Why does he have a red monocle, that Herr Dorsday? Who is he waving his handkerchief at? Mama is coming down the stairs and is kissing his hand. Ugh. Now they're whispering together. I can't understand a word because I'm lying in state on a bier. The wreath of violets around my forehead is from Paul. Ribbons stream all the way to the floor. Nobody dares to come into the room. I'd rather get up and look out the window. What a great, blue sea! A hundred ships with yellow sails. The waves are glistening. So much sun. A regatta. The men are wearing rowing tanks. The women are in bathing suits. That's indecent. They think I'm naked. How stupid they are! I'm wearing black mourning clothes because I'm dead. I'll prove it to you. I'm going to lie down on the bier again. Where did it go? It's gone. They've taken it away. They've embezzled it. That's why Papa's in prison. But they've freed him on three years probation after all. Fiala bribed all the jurors. I'll go to the cemetery on foot; that way Mama will save the expense of a burial. We have to economize. I'm walking so fast that no one can follow me. Oh, how fast I can walk! They're all stopping to stare at me on the street. How dare they stare that way at someone who's dead? That's indecent. I'd rather walk across the field; it's all blue with forget-me-nots and violets. The Navy officers stand with swords raised. Good morning, gentlemen. Open the gate, Herr Matador. Don't you recognize me? I'm the girl who just died . . . you don't have to kiss my hand just because of that. . . . Where is my crypt? Did they embezzle that too? Oh, thank God, it isn't a cemetery at all! It's the park in Menton. Papa will be so happy that I'm not dead and buried. I'm not afraid of snakes. If they don't bite me in the foot. Oh no!

What's going on? Where am I? Did I fall asleep? Yes, I fell asleep. I must've been dreaming. I've got such cold feet. My right foot is very cold. Why? There's another little rip in my stocking by my ankle. Why am I still sitting in the woods? They must have rung for dinner long ago. *Diner.*

Oh God, where have I been? I was so far away. What did I dream? I think I dreamt I was dead. And I had no worries and didn't have to rack my brain about anything. Thirty thousand, thirty thousand . . . I don't have it yet. I have to earn it first. And here I am sitting alone at the edge of the woods. I can see the hotel gleaming all the way from here. I have to go back. It's horrible that I have to go back. There's no time to lose. Herr von Dorsday is waiting for my decision. Decision. Decision! *No, no, Herr von Dorsday. In short— no. You were joking, Herr von Dorsday.* Of course. Yes, that's what I'll say. Oh, that's excellent. *Your joke wasn't very delicate, Herr von Dorsday, but I'll forgive you. I'll telegraph Papa tomorrow morning that the money will be in Dr. Fiala's hands punctually, Herr von Dorsday.* Wonderful. That's what I'll say. Then he must send the money. Must? Must? Why must he? And even if he did, he'd take revenge in some way. He'd arrange it so that the money arrived too late. Or he would send the money and then tell everyone that he'd had me. But he's not going to send the money at all. *No, Fräulein Else, that wasn't our bargain. Telegraph your papa whatever you want; I'm not sending the money. Don't allow yourself to believe that I'm going to let myself be outwitted by a little girl like you, Fräulein Else, I, the Vicomte von Eperjes.*

I have to walk carefully. The path is so totally dark. Strange, I feel better than I did before. Nothing at all has changed, but I feel better. What did I dream about? A matador? What kind of matador? It's farther to the hotel than I remember. I'm sure they're still at dinner. I'll just sit down quietly at the table, say that I had a migraine, and ask to be served. Herr von Dorsday will personally come over afterward and tell me that the whole thing was just a joke. *Forgive me, Fräulein Else, forgive me the bad joke. I've already telegraphed my bank.* But he won't say that. He hasn't telegraphed. Everything is exactly as it was before. He's waiting. Herr von Dorsday is waiting. No, I don't want to see him. I can't see him again. I don't want to see anyone. I don't want to go back to the hotel; I don't want to go back home; I don't want to go back to Vienna; I don't want to see anyone, not Papa, not Mama, not Rudi, not Fred, not Bertha, and not Aunt Irene. She's still the best of the lot; she's the only one who'd understand. But I won't have anything more to do with her, or with anyone else. If I were a magician, I'd be someplace else in the world entirely. On some glorious ship in the Mediterranean, for example, but not alone. With Paul perhaps. Oh yes, I can imagine that very well. Or I'd be living in a villa by the sea and we'd lie on the marble steps that lead into the water, and he would hold me close in his arms and nibble my lips the way Albert did two years ago at the piano, the shameless fellow. No. I'd like to lie on the beach by myself and wait. And finally, a man—no, several men—would come, and I'd take my pick. And the rest, the ones I rejected, would all throw themselves into the sea in despair. Or they'd have to be patient until the next day. Oh, what a marvelous life that would be! Why do I have gorgeous shoulders and beautiful slim legs? What am I alive for, after all? It would serve them right, every one of them; they've raised me only to sell myself, one way or another. They wouldn't hear of my going into the theatre. They laughed at me. Last year they would have liked to marry me off to Dr. Wilomitzer, who's almost fifty. True, they didn't try to persuade me. In the end, Papa was too embarrassed after all. But Mama dropped some very clear hints.

How huge the hotel is—like an enormous, brightly lit, magic castle. Everything is so enormous. The mountains too. It's scary. They've never been so black. There is no moon yet. It will rise only for the performance—the grand performance on the meadow, when Herr von Dorsday bids his slave to dance naked. What is Herr Dorsday to me? Oh, Mademoiselle Else, why are you making all this fuss? A minute ago you were prepared to run away, to become the lover of strange men, one after the other. And the trifle that Herr von Dorsday demands of you—that bothers you? You're prepared to sell yourself for a string of pearls, for beautiful clothes, for a villa by the sea. But your father's life isn't worth as much? It would be just the right beginning. It would justify everything else to follow. It was you, I could say, you who brought me to this. All of you are guilty for my having turned out this way, not only Papa and Mama. Rudi is also guilty and Fred and all of you, all of you, every one, because no one really cares about anyone else. A little caress when you look especially pretty, a bit of anxiety when you have a fever, and then they send you away to school. And when you're at home you study piano and French, and in the summer you go to the countryside, and for your birthday you get presents, and at dinner they talk about all kinds of trivia. But about what was going on inside me? What worried me and what tormented me? Did you ever care about that? Sometimes I could see by Papa's look that he had some idea of what I felt, but it passed quickly. There was always his career, his worries, and his stock market deals—and probably some woman or other in secret, "nothing very classy, between us"—and I was alone again. Well, what would you do, Papa, what would you do if I didn't exist?

Here I am, here I am, standing right in front of the hotel.—Horrible, horrible, that I have to go in, have to see them all—Herr von Dorsday, my aunt, Cissy. How beautiful it was earlier on the bench at the edge of the woods when I was already dead. A matador—if only I could remember what it really was.—It was a regatta, right? And I was watching from my window. But who was the matador?— If only I weren't so tired, so horribly exhausted. And now I'm supposed to stay up till midnight and then sneak quietly into Herr von Dorsday's room? Maybe I'll meet Cissy in the hallway. Does she have anything on under her robe when she goes to see him? It's so difficult when one doesn't have any practice in these matters. Should I ask Cissy for advice? Naturally I wouldn't say that it has to do with Dorsday; I'd let her think I have a nighttime rendezvous with one of the handsome young men here in the hotel. For instance, that tall blond man with the shining eyes. But he isn't here anymore. He suddenly vanished. I never even thought about him until this minute. But unfortunately it isn't the tall blond man with the shining eyes. It isn't even Paul. It's Herr von Dorsday. So how should I do it? What will I tell him? Just "yes"? But I really can't go to Herr Dorsday's room. Of course he'll have all sorts of elegant bottles on his washstand, and the room will smell like French perfume. No, I won't go to his room—not for anything in the world. Better outdoors. He won't matter to me there. The sky is so vast and the meadow is so huge. I won't have to think about Herr Dorsday at all. I don't even have to look at him. If he dares to touch me, I'll kick him with my bare feet. Oh, if only it were some other man, any other! Anyone else could have anything he wanted from me tonight; anyone could, just not Dorsday. Why does it have to be him! Him! How his eyes will stab and pierce me! He'll stand there with his monocle and smirk. But no, he won't smirk. He'll look dignified, refined. For he's used to this kind of thing. How many women has he seen naked? A hundred? A thousand? But were any of them like me? No, certainly not. I'll tell him that he's not the first to see me naked. I'll tell him I have a lover. But only after he's sent the thirty thousand gulden to Fiala. Then I'll tell him what a fool he was; that he could have had me for the same amount. That I've already had ten lovers, twenty, a hundred.—But he won't believe that.—And even if he did believe me, what good would that do me? If only I could spoil his pleasure in it somehow. What if someone else were to be there? Why not? He didn't stipulate that he had to be alone with me. Oh, Herr von Dorsday, I'm so afraid of you. Won't you please do me the favor of letting me bring a mutual friend? Oh, that's not at all contrary to our agreement, Herr von Dorsday. If I wanted to, I could invite the whole hotel and you would still be obligated to send the thirty thousand gulden. But I'll be content just to bring my cousin Paul. Or would you prefer someone else? The tall blond is unfortunately not here at the moment, and the Italian *filou* with the Roman head is not either. But I'll easily find someone else. You fear a scandal? That's neither here nor there. I don't care about discretion. When you've sunk as low as I have, nothing matters anymore. Today's just the beginning. Or do you think that after this adventure I'll go back home as a decent girl from a good family? No, neither a good family nor a decent young girl. All that's finished. From now on I'll stand on my own two legs. I have beautiful legs, Herr von Dorsday, as you and the other participants in this festival will soon have occasion to learn. So everything's arranged, Herr von Dorsday. Around ten o'clock, when everyone is still sitting in the lobby, we'll wander across the meadow in the moonlight, then through the woods to that famous glade you've discovered. In any event, you'll bring the telegram for the bank with you. Because I'm entitled to demand some sort of security from a shady character like you. And at midnight you can go back home and I'll stay in the moonlight with my cousin or whoever it is in the meadow. You have no objections to that, do you, Herr von Dorsday? You're not allowed to have any. And if by chance I should be found dead tomorrow morning, don't be too surprised. In that event, Paul will send the telegram. He'll take care of it. But don't think even for a minute, for God's sake, that you, you miserable wretch, drove me to my death. I've long known I'd end up this way. Just ask my friend Fred if I haven't told him so time and time again. Fred—that's Herr Friedrich Wenkheim, the only decent person, incidentally, that I've ever known in my entire life. The only one I might have loved if only he had been a little less decent. Yes, that's the kind of depraved creature I am. I'm not cut out for a bourgeois life, but I don't have any talents either. It would be better for our family if our line died out. Sooner or later there will also be some catastrophe with Rudi. He'll get himself into debt over some Dutch chorus girl and then embezzle from Vanderhulst. It runs in the family. My father's youngest brother shot himself when he was fifteen. No one knows why. I didn't know him. Ask them to show you his photograph, Herr von Dorsday. We have it in an album . . . I'm supposed to look like him. No one knows why he killed himself. And nobody will know why I did either. But it won't be because of you, Herr von Dorsday! I wouldn't do you the honor. Whether at nineteen or at twenty-one, it doesn't make any difference. Or should I become a children's nanny or a telephone operator? Or marry a Herr Wilomitzer or let myself be kept by you? It's all equally disgusting, and I'm never going out into the meadow with you either. No, that's all much too much of an effort, and too stupid, and too revolting. When I'm dead you'll be so good as to send the thirty thousand gulden for Papa, because it would be too dreary if he were to be arrested on the same day my body is taken to Vienna. But I'll leave a letter behind with a will: Herr von Dorsday has the right to see my corpse. My beautiful, naked young girl's corpse. So you can't complain that I cheated you, Herr von Dorsday. You're getting something for your money. Our contract didn't specify that I had to be alive. Oh no. That's not in our contract. So—to the art dealer Dorsday I bequeath a view of my naked corpse; and to Herr Fred Wenkheim I bequeath my diary up to my seventeenth year—I didn't get any further—and to the Fräulein who works for Cissy I bequeath the five twenty-franc pieces I brought from Switzerland years ago. They're in my desk next to my letters. And to Bertha I leave my black evening dress. And to Agatha my books. And to my cousin Paul I bequeath a kiss on my pale lips. And to Cissy I leave my tennis racket, because I'm generous. And I want to be buried here in the beautiful little cemetery of San Martino de Castrozza. I don't want to go home. Not even as a corpse. And Papa and Mama shouldn't grieve too much; I'm better off than they are. And I forgive them. I'm not a great loss. Ha ha, what a funny testament! I'm really touched. When I think that tomorrow when the others are sitting down to dinner, I'll already be dead! Of course Aunt Emma won't come down to dinner and neither will Paul. They'll order room service. I'm curious as to how Cissy will react. Only I won't know, unfortunately. I won't know about anything anymore. Or is one still aware of everything as long as one isn't buried yet? Maybe in the end I'll only seem dead but not really be dead. And when Herr Dorsday approaches my body, I'll wake up and open my eyes, and he'll be so shocked he'll drop his monocle.

But unfortunately none of this is true. I won't just seem dead, and I won't be really dead, either. I won't kill myself at all; I'm much too much of a coward for that. Even though I'm a courageous mountain climber, I'm still a coward. And perhaps I don't even have enough Veronal. How many packets does one need? Six I think. But ten is safer. I think I still have ten. Yes, that should be enough.

How many times have I walked around the hotel by now? Well, now what? I'm standing in front of the door. No one's in the lobby yet. Naturally—they're all still at dinner. The lobby looks odd when it's so completely deserted. On the armchair over there is a hat, a Tyrolean hat, very smart. Pretty tuft of chamois hair on it. Over there in the leather armchair is an old gentleman. He probably doesn't have much of an appetite any more. He's reading the paper. He's well off. Doesn't have any worries. He's reading the newspaper peacefully, and I have to rack my brains to figure out how to get Papa thirty thousand gulden. But no. I know how to get them. After all, it's so terribly simple. But what do I want to do? What do I want to do? What am I doing here in the lobby? They'll be coming back from dinner any minute. What should I do? Herr von Dorsday must be on pins and needles. *Where is she?* he's thinking. *Did she kill herself in the end? Or did she hire someone to kill me? Or is she inciting her cousin Paul against me?* Don't worry, Herr von Dorsday, I'm not such a dangerous person. I'm just a little slut, nothing more. You'll be rewarded for all this anxiety. Twelve o'clock, room number sixty-five. It'll be too cold for me outdoors, after all. And from your room, Herr von Dorsday, I'm going to go directly to my cousin Paul's. You don't object to that, do you, Herr von Dorsday?

Else! Else!

What? Who? That's Paul's voice. Is dinner over already?

Else!

Oh, hello, Paul! What's wrong, Paul? I'll act innocent.

Where in the world have you been, Else?

Where would I have been? I just went for a walk.

Just now, during dinner?

Well, why not? After all, it's the best time for a walk. I'm talking nonsense.

Mama's been imagining all sorts of things. I stopped by your door and knocked.

I didn't hear anything.

Seriously, Else, how could you cause us such worry! You could at least have told Mama that you weren't coming down for dinner.

You're right, Paul, but if you only knew what a headache I've had. I said that very seductively. Oh, what a slut I am!

Is it better now at least?

I can't really say so.

Well, I just want to go tell Mama—

Wait, Paul, wait, not yet. Make my apologies to aunt, but let me go up to my room for a few minutes so that I can freshen up. Then I'll come right down and order a little something to eat.

Why are you so pale, Else? Should I send Mama up to you?

Oh don't make such a fuss about me, Paul. And don't look at me like that. Haven't you ever seen a woman with a headache before? I promise I'll come down again. In ten minutes at the most. I'll see you then, Paul.

All right, auf Wiedersehen, Else.

Thank God, he's going. Stupid boy, but sweet. What does the porter want with me? What, a telegram? *Thank you. When did this arrive?*

Fifteen minutes ago, Fräulein.

Why is he looking at me that way, so—pityingly? God in heaven, what could this be about? I'll wait until I'm upstairs to open it, otherwise I might faint. In the end, did Papa really . . . ? If Papa's dead, then everything's all right; I don't have to go out to the meadow with Herr von Dorsday. . . . Oh, what a worthless person I am! Dear God, please let there be nothing horrible in this telegram. Dear God, please let Papa be alive! Arrested, all right, but not dead. If there's no bad news in it, I'll make a sacrifice. I'll become a governess; I'll take a position in an office. Don't be dead, Papa. I'm ready; I'm ready to do anything you ask. . . .

Thank God I made it upstairs. Turn on the light, turn on the light. It's gotten cold in here. The window was open for too long. *Courage. Courage.* Oh, maybe it will say that the matter's been settled. Maybe Uncle Bernhard gave him the money and they're telegraphing me: *No need to talk to Dorsday.* I'll know right away. But if I'm looking at the ceiling, naturally I can't read what's in the message. Tra la, tra la. *Courage.* I've got to read it. *Repeat urgently: ask Dorsday. Sum not thirty, but fifty. Anything less is useless. Address remains Fiala.* But fifty. Anything less is useless. Tra la, tra la. Fifty. Address remains Fiala. Well, fine, whether it's fifty or thirty doesn't make much difference one way or the other. Especially to Herr von Dorsday. The Veronal is beneath the underwear, in case of emergency. Why didn't I ask for fifty in the first place? I even thought of doing it! Anything less is useless. So, go downstairs.

Hurry up. Don't just sit here on the bed. A little mistake, Herr von Dorsday, forgive me. Not thirty, but fifty; anything less is useless. Address remains Fiala.—*Do you take me for a fool, Fräulein Else? Not at all, Lord Vicomte, how could I? But for fifty I'd have to ask proportionately more, Fräulein.* Anything less is useless. Address remains Fiala. As you wish, Herr von Dorsday. Pray command me. But first of all, write the telegram to your bank. Otherwise I don't have any security.—

Yes, that's how I'll do it. I'll go to see him in his room, and only after he's written the telegram before my eyes—then I'll undress. And I'll hold the telegram in my hands. Ha, how unappetizing! And where am I supposed to put my clothes? No, no, I'll undress here and wrap myself in the big black coat that reaches down to my ankles. That's the most convenient way to do it. For both of us. Address remains Fiala. My teeth are chattering. The window is still open. Close it. Outdoors? I would die of the cold there. Beast! Fifty thousand. He can't say no. Room sixty-five. But before I go, I'll tell Paul to wait for me in his room. I'll go directly from Dorsday to Paul and tell him everything. Then Paul will challenge him. Yes, this very evening. An eventful program for the evening! And then the Veronal. No. What for? Why should I die? I won't. Have fun, have fun; life is only just beginning now. You'll get what you want. You'll be proud of your little daughter. I'll become a strumpet such as the world has never seen. Address remains Fiala. You'll have your fifty thousand gulden, Papa. But with the next fifty I earn I'll buy myself new nightgowns, with lace, completely transparent, and expensive silk stockings. You only live once. What's the point of looking as beautiful as I do? Turn on the light.—I'll turn on the lamp above the mirror. How beautiful my reddish blonde hair is, and my shoulders, too; my eyes aren't bad either. Huh, how big they are. It would be a pity to waste all this. There's always time for Veronal.—But I've got to go down at once. Way down. Herr

Dorsday is waiting, and he doesn't even know that meanwhile it's gone up to fifty thousand. Yes, I've gone up in price, Herr von Dorsday. I'll have to show him the telegram, otherwise he won't really believe me and will think I'm trying to make a profit off the transaction. I'll send the telegram to his room and write something to go with it. To my great regret, it's now become fifty thousand, Herr von Dorsday, but I'm sure it's all the same to you. And I'm convinced the compensation you asked for wasn't seriously meant. After all, you're a vicomte and a gentleman. I know that tomorrow morning you'll send the fifty thousand on which my father's life depends to Fiala without delay. I'm counting on you—*Of course, my dear Fräulein, I'll send one hundred thousand just in case, without asking for any compensation, and on top of that I pledge myself to take care of your whole family's financial needs, to pay your father's stock market losses, and to make good all the embezzled trust funds.* Address remains Fiala. Ha ha ha! Yes, that's the Vicomte von Eperjes all right! What nonsense! What can I do? I have to do it; I've just got to do it; I've got to do everything Herr von Dorsday demands, so that Papa will have the money tomorrow—so that he won't be arrested, so that he won't kill himself. And I'll do it. Yes, I'll do it, even though in the end it will all be for nothing. In half a year we'll be in exactly the same situation that we're in today! In four weeks! But then it won't be my concern any more. I'll make this one sacrifice—and no more after that. Never, never, never again. Yes, I'll tell Papa this as soon as I get to Vienna. And then I'll leave—I don't care to where. I'll discuss it with Fred. He's the only one who really cares for me. But I'm not at that point yet. I'm not in Vienna; I'm still in Martino di Castrozza. Nothing's happened yet. So how, how, what? That's the telegram I'm holding in my hand. What am I doing with it? I know what I wanted to do: send it to his room. But what else? I have to write something on it. Well, yes, but what should I write? Expect me at twelve. No, no, no! He can't have that triumph. I won't—won't—won't do it! Thank God I have the Veronal. That's the only way out. Oh God, they haven't been stolen? No, here they are. There, in the box. Are they all still here? Yes, they are. One, two, three, four, five, six. I just want to look at them, the precious powders. That doesn't commit me to anything. Even pouring them into the glass doesn't commit me to anything. One, two—but I won't kill myself. I'm certain of that. Wouldn't think of it. Three, four, five—that won't really kill anybody by a long shot. It would be terrible if I didn't have the Veronal with me. Then I'd have to throw myself from the window, and I wouldn't have the courage to do that. But with Veronal—you slowly go to sleep and just don't wake up anymore; no agony, no trouble. You lie down in bed, drink the whole thing in one gulp, dream, and then everything's over. The day before yesterday I took one packet, and the other day I even took two. Shh, shush, don't tell anybody. Today it will just be a little more. It's only if I have to. Only if it revolts me too much. But why should it? If he touches me, I'll just spit in his face. That's all there is to it.

But how can I get the letter to him? I can't send it to Herr von Dorsday with the chambermaid. The best thing is to go downstairs and talk to him and show him the telegram. I have to go downstairs in any case. I can't just stay in my room. I couldn't stand it for three whole hours—until the moment comes. I have to go downstairs, if only for my aunt's sake. Ha! What's my aunt to me? What are all these people to me? Look, ladies and gentlemen, here's the glass with the Veronal. So, now I'm taking it into my hand. So, now I'm raising it to my lips. Yes, any minute I can be on the other side where there are no aunts and no Dorsday and no father who embezzles trust funds. . . .

But I won't kill myself. I don't have to do that. I'm not going to go to Herr von Dorsday's room, either. Wouldn't think of it. I'll be damned if I'll stand naked in front of an old lecher for fifty thousand gulden in order to save a good-for-nothing from jail. No, no, neither for the one nor for the other. How did Herr von Dorsday come into the picture? Why does it have to be him? If he gets to see me, then everybody should get to see me. Yes—wonderful idea!—Everybody will get to see me. The whole world will get to see me. And then the Veronal. No, not the Veronal—what for? Next will be the villa with the marble steps and the handsome young men and freedom and the whole wide world. *Good evening, Fräulein Else, I like you this way.* Downstairs they'll think I've gone crazy. But I was never saner. For the first time in my life, I'm really sane. All of them, everyone, will get to see me.—After that there will be no return, no going back home to Papa and Mama, uncles and aunts. I'll no longer be the same Fräulein Else that they wanted to marry off to some old Director Wilomitzer or other; I'll make fools of them all—especially that swine Dorsday—and I'll be born into the world a second time. . . . Anything less is useless. Address remains Fiala. Ha ha!

There's no time to lose. Don't become cowardly again. Off with the dress. Who'll be the first? Will it be you, Cousin Paul? Lucky for you that the Roman head isn't here anymore. Are you going to kiss these beautiful breasts tonight? Oh, how beautiful I am. Bertha has a black silk camisole. Sexy! I'll be sexier. What a wonderful life! Off with these stockings; that would be indecent. I'll be naked, completely naked. How Cissy will envy me! And the others too. But they won't dare do anything. They'd all love to do it! Go ahead, take me for an example, everyone! I, the virgin, I dare to do it. I'll laugh myself to death over Dorsday. Here I am, Herr von Dorsday. Quick—to the post office. Fifty thousand. Surely it's worth that much?

Beautiful, I'm beautiful! Look at me, Night! Look at me, Mountains! Sky, look at me, look how beautiful I am! But you're all blind. What do I get from you? It's the people downstairs who have eyes. Should I undo my hair and let it down? No. Then I'll look like a madwoman. But I don't want you all to think I'm crazy. Only shameless. A prankster. Where is the telegram? For God's sake, where did I put the telegram? There it is, lying peacefully next to the Veronal. *Repeat urgently—fifty thousand—anything less is useless. Address remains Fiala.* Yes, that's the telegram. It's a piece of paper, and there are words on it. Sent from Vienna at 4:30. No, I'm not dreaming; it's all true. And at home they're waiting for the fifty thousand. And Herr von Dorsday is also waiting. Let him wait. There's plenty of time. Oh, how pleasant it is to walk up and down the room naked. Am I really as beautiful as I look in the mirror? Oh, won't you please come closer, beautiful Fräulein? I want to kiss your blood-red lips. I want to press your breasts against mine. Too bad there's this glass between us, this cold glass. We'd get along together so well, don't you think? We wouldn't need anyone else. Maybe there isn't anyone else. There are telegrams and hotels and mountains and train stations and forests, but no other people. We merely dream them. Only Dr. Fiala exists with his address. It always remains the same. Oh, I'm not at all crazy. I'm a little agitated, that's all. That's quite natural right before you're reborn. For the earlier Else has already died. Yes, I'm dead for sure. The Veronal isn't even necessary. Maybe I should pour it out? The chambermaid might drink it by mistake. I'll leave a note here and write on it: P-O-I-S-O-N; no, better, MEDICINE—so that nothing will happen to the chambermaid. I'm so noble! So. MEDICINE!!! underlined twice and three exclamation marks. Now nothing can happen accidentally. And then when I come back up afterward and don't feel like killing myself and just want to go to sleep, I won't drink the whole glass, but just a quarter of it or less. Very simple. Everything's ready. The easiest thing would be to run downstairs just as I am, down the corridors and down the stairs. But no—if I did that, someone might stop me before I got there—and I've got to be sure that Herr von Dorsday is there! Otherwise, of course, he won't send the money, the dirty crook.—But I have to write to him. That's the most important thing of all. Oh, the back of the armchair is cold, but it feels good. When I have my villa on the Italian seacoast I'll always walk around my park naked. . . . I'll leave the fountain pen to Fred when I die. But for the time being I've got something better to do than to die. *Most honored Herr Vicomte*—be sensible, Else, no salutation. Neither "most honored" nor "most despised." *Your condition, Herr von Dorsday, has been fulfilled—at the moment that you're reading these lines, Herr von Dorsday, your condition has been fulfilled, though perhaps not in the manner that you intended*—My, how well that girl writes, Papa would say.—*And so I'm depending on you to keep your part of the bargain and have the fifty thousand gulden telegraphed to that well-known address without delay. Else.* No, not Else. No signature at all. So. My beautiful yellow stationery! Got it for Christmas. It's a pity. So—and now telegram and letter into the envelope—Herr von Dorsday, room number sixty-five. Why the number? I'll just put the letter in front of his door as I walk by. But I don't have to. I don't have to do anything. If I felt like it, I could just go to bed and sleep and not worry about a thing. Not about Herr von Dorsday and not about Papa. A striped prison uniform can be really stylish. And many people have killed themselves. We all have to die.

But you don't have to do any of that for the time being, Papa. You have a daughter who grew up to be a beauty, and the address remains Fiala. I'll take up a collection. I'll go around with the plate. Why should Herr von Dorsday be the only one to pay? That would be unfair. Each according to his means. How much will Paul put in the plate? And the gentleman with the gold pince-nez, how much? But don't expect the fun to last long. I'll soon cover myself up again, run up the stairs to my room, lock myself in, and, if I feel like it, I'll drink the whole glass in one gulp. But I won't feel like it. That would just be cowardice. They don't deserve such an honor, the swine. Ashamed in front of you? I, be ashamed in front of anyone? I really don't need to be. Just let me look into your eyes again, beautiful Else. What enormous eyes you have close up. I wish someone would kiss my eyes, my blood-red mouth. My coat barely covers my ankles. They'll see that my feet are naked. So what. Later they'll see so much more! But I'm not obligated to do it. I can turn around right now, even before I've gone downstairs. I can turn around on the first floor. I don't have to go downstairs at all. But I want to. I'm looking forward to it! Haven't I wanted to do something like this all my life?

What am I waiting for? I'm ready, after all. The performance can begin. Don't forget the letter. An aristocratic handwriting, Fred insists. Goodbye, Else. You're beautiful in that coat. Florentine ladies used to have their portraits painted this way. Their portraits hang in galleries and it's an honor.—They can't see anything when I have my coat on. Well, the feet, just the feet. I'll wear the black patent leather shoes; then they'll just think I'm wearing flesh-colored stockings. I'll go through the lobby dressed like this, and no one will suspect that there's nothing beneath the coat except me, just me. And then I can still go back upstairs—Who's playing the piano so beautifully down there? Chopin?—Herr von Dorsday must be quite nervous. Maybe he's afraid of Paul. Patience, patience; everything will be all right. I don't even know myself what's going to happen; I'm in terrible suspense. Turn out the light! Is my room in order? So long, Veronal, see you later. So long, dearly beloved image in the mirror. How you gleam in the darkness! I'm already quite used to being naked underneath the coat. It feels rather nice. Who knows if there aren't many other women sitting in the lobby like this without anyone knowing it? Who knows how many women go to the theatre and sit in their loges like this—for fun or for other reasons.

Should I lock the door? What for? Nothing gets stolen around here. And even if—I won't need anything anymore anyway. . . . So, that's it. . . . Where's number sixty-five? There's nobody in the hallway. They're all still downstairs at dinner. Sixty-one . . . sixty-two . . . those are really huge hiking boots in front of that door. Here's a pair of trousers hanging on a hook. How coarse. Sixty-four, sixty-five. So. That's where he's staying, the vicomte. . . . I'll leave the letter leaning against the door here. That way he can't help but see it right away. Nobody will steal it, will they? So, there it is . . . it doesn't matter . . . I can still do whatever I want. I've just made a fool of him . . . if only I don't meet him on the steps now. Here he comes . . . no, it's not him! . . . He's much handsomer than Herr von Dorsday, very elegant, with a small black mustache. When did he arrive? I could do a little rehearsal—just lift the coat a little bit. I'm really tempted to. Yes, take a good look at me, my dear sir; you have no idea what you're passing by. Too bad that you're coming upstairs right now. Why don't you stay in the lobby? You're going to miss something. A grand performance. Why don't you stop me? My fate lies in your hands. If you greet me, I'm turning right back. So please greet me. I'm giving you such a charming look. . . . He's not greeting me. He's gone. He's turning around; I can feel it. Call me! Greet me! Save me! Maybe you'll be responsible for my death, my dear sir! But you'll never know it. Address remains Fiala. . . .

Where am I? Is this the lobby already? How did I get here? So few people and so many strangers. Or is my eyesight bad? Where is Dorsday? He's not here. Is that a stroke of fate? I want to go back upstairs. I'll write a different letter to Dorsday. I'll be waiting for you in my room at midnight. Bring the dispatch to your bank with you. No. He could see that as a trap. It might be one too. I could have Paul hidden with me, and he could force him to hand the dispatch over to us at gunpoint. Extortion. A pair of criminals. Where's Dorsday? Dorsday, where are you? Maybe he's killed himself out of remorse over my death? He's probably in the card room. Yes, that's where he is. He'll be sitting at a card table. If he is, I'll signal him from the doorway with my eyes. He'll get up immediately. *Here I am, my dear Fräulein.* His voice will have that tone. *Shall we take a little walk, Herr Dorsday? As you wish, Fräulein Else.* We'll take the Marienweg to the woods. We'll be alone. I'll open the coat. The fifty thousand are due. The air is cold; I'm going to get pneumonia and die. Why are these two women looking at me? Do they notice anything? Why am I here? Am I crazy? I'll go back to my room, quickly get dressed, the blue one, then the coat over it like it is now, but open. Then nobody will believe that I didn't have anything on before. . . . I can't go back. And I don't want to go back. Where's Paul? Where's Aunt Emma? Where's Cissy? Where is everybody? No one will see anything. . . . It's impossible to see anything. Who's playing so beautifully? Chopin? No, Schumann.

I'm flitting about the lobby like a bat. Fifty thousand! Time is running out. I've got to find that damned Herr von Dorsday. No, I have to go back to my room . . . I'll drink the Veronal. Just a little swallow, then I'll be able to sleep well. . . . After work well done, sleep comes easily. . . . But the work isn't done yet. . . . If the waiter serves that black coffee to that old gentleman over there, everything will be fine. If he brings it to the newlyweds in the corner, everything's lost. Why am I saying that? What does that mean? He's bringing the coffee to the old gentleman. Triumph! Everything will be fine. Aha, Cissy and Paul! They're walking up and down in front of the hotel. They're chatting together quite happily. He doesn't seem very concerned about my headache. Hypocrite! Cissy's breasts aren't as beautiful as mine. Of course not, she's had a child. . . . What are those two talking about? If only I could hear them! What do I care about what they're talking about? But I could also go outside to the front of the hotel, wish them a good evening, and then flit farther, farther over the meadow, into the woods, climbing, higher and higher, all the way to the top of the Cimone, lie down, fall asleep, freeze to death. *Mysterious Suicide of a Young lady of Vien-*

nese Society. *Dressed only in a black evening coat, the beautiful girl was found dead in an inaccessible location behind the Cimone della Pala.* . . . But perhaps they won't find me . . . or not till next year. Or even later. Decomposed. A skeleton. No, it's better to stay here in the warm lobby and not freeze to death. Well, Herr von Dorsday, where are you hiding? Am I obligated to wait for you? You have to find me, not I you. I'm going to look in the card room. If he isn't there, he's lost his right to see me. And I'll write to him: *You were not to be found, Herr von Dorsday, so you've voluntarily given up your right; but that doesn't free you from the obligation to send the money immediately.* The money. What money? What concern is that of mine? I don't care whether he sends it or not. I don't feel the slightest sympathy for Papa any more. I don't feel any sympathy for anyone. Not for myself, either. My heart is dead. I don't think it's beating any more. Perhaps I've already taken the Veronal. . . . Why is the Dutch family looking at me like that? It's really impossible to see anything. The porter is also looking at me suspiciously. Has another message arrived perhaps? Eighty thousand? A hundred thousand? Address remains Fiala. If there were a message, he'd tell me. He's looking at me most respectfully. He doesn't know that I'm not wearing anything under my coat. No one does. I'm going back to my room. Back, back, back! If I tripped on the stairs now—that would be a pretty picture. Three years ago at the Wörthersee there was a woman who went swimming in the nude. But she left that same afternoon. Mama told me the woman was an operetta singer from Berlin. Schumann? Yes, "Carnival." He or she plays very well. But the card room is to the left. Last chance, Herr von Dorsday. If he's there, I'll signal to him with my eyes to come over to me and I'll tell him, *I'll be with you at midnight, you dirty old man.*—No, I won't call him a dirty old man. But I'll call him that afterward. . . . Someone is walking behind me. I'm not going to turn around. No, no.—

Else!

Oh no, for God's sake, it's my aunt! Just keep going! Keep going!

Else!

I've got to turn around, there's no way out. *Oh, good evening, aunt.*

Else, what on earth is the matter with you? I was just going to look in on you upstairs. Paul told me—My God, how strange you look!

Do I look strange, aunt? I'm feeling fine again. I've also had a little something to eat. She sees something; she sees something.

Else—you're not—wearing any stockings!

What did you say, aunt? Oh my goodness, you're right. I don't have any stockings on. No!

Aren't you feeling well, Else? Your eyes—you must have a fever—

Fever? I don't think so. It's just that I've had the worst headache ever.

You must go to bed immediately, child, you're deathly white.

That's on account of the lighting, aunt. Everybody looks white here in the lobby. She's looking me up and down so strangely. Does she see something? I've got to keep my head now. Papa will be lost if I don't keep my head. I've got to say something. *Do you know what happened to me recently in Vienna, aunt? I went out into the street wearing one yellow and one black shoe.* Not a word of it is true. I've got to keep on talking. What can I say? *You know, aunt, after a migraine I sometimes get so disoriented. Mama used to have that too.* Not a word of it is true.

I'm going to send for a doctor, just in case.

But please, aunt, there isn't one in the hotel. They'd have to get him to come from another town. He'd laugh if we fetched him because I'm not wearing stockings. Ha ha! I shouldn't laugh so loudly.

My aunt's face is full of anxiety. She finds the whole thing bizarre. Her eyes are popping out of her head.

Tell me, Else, did you see Paul by any chance.

Ah, she's looking for help. Keep calm; everything depends on it. *I think he's walking up and down in front of the hotel with Cissy Mohr, if I'm not mistaken.*

In front of the hotel? I'll bring them both in. We'll have a little tea, all right?

With pleasure. What a stupid face she's making. I'm nodding to her in a very friendly and innocent way. Now she's gone. I'll go to my room now. No, what would I do in my room? It's high time, it's high time. Fifty thousand, fifty thousand. Why am I running around so much? Slowly. Slowly. . . . What am I trying to do? What's the man's name? Herr von Dorsday, funny name . . . there's the card room. Green curtain over the door. Can't see anything. I'm going to stand on tiptoe. A game of whist. They play every evening. Two men are playing chess over there. Herr von Dorsday isn't here. Victory! Saved! Why am I saying that? I've got to keep on looking. I'm condemned to look for Herr von Dorsday for the rest of my life. No doubt he's looking for me too. We always miss each other. Perhaps he's looking for me upstairs. We'll meet on the stairs. Those Dutch people are looking at me again. The daughter is quite pretty. The old gentleman has a pair of glasses, glasses, glasses. . . . Fifty thousand. It isn't really so much. Fifty thousand, Herr von Dorsday. Schumann? Yes, "Carnival." . . . I studied it once myself. She plays beautifully.

Why she? Perhaps it's a he. Perhaps it's a woman virtuoso? I'll take a look in the music room.

Yes, there's the door.—Dorsday! I'm going to faint. Dorsday! There he is standing at the window, listening. How is that possible?

I'm tormenting myself—I'm going crazy—I'm dead—and he's listening to a strange lady play the piano. There on the sofa are two gentlemen. The blond one just arrived today. I saw him get out of the carriage. The lady is no longer young. She's already been here for a few days. I didn't know that she could play the piano that well.

She's well off. Everyone's well off . . . only I'm cursed. . . . Dorsday! Dorsday! Is it really him? He doesn't see me. At the moment he looks like a decent man. He's listening. Fifty thousand. It's now or never. Open the door quietly. Here I am, Herr von Dorsday! He doesn't see me.

I'll just signal to him once with my eyes, then I'll lift my coat a little, that will be enough. After all, I'm a young girl. A decent young girl from a good family. I'm not a prostitute. . . . I want to go away. I want to take Veronal and go to sleep. You've made a mistake, Herr von Dorsday; I'm not a prostitute. Adieu, adieu! Aha, he's looking up. Here I am, Herr von Dorsday. How he's looking at me! His lips are trembling. His eyes are burning into my forehead. He doesn't suspect that I'm naked beneath my coat. Let me go, let me go! His eyes are burning. His eyes are threatening. What do you want from me? You're a beast. No one sees me except him. They're all listening. So come, Herr von Dorsday! Don't you see anything? There, in the leather armchair—my God, in the leather armchair—there's the *filou!* Thank heaven! He's back again; he's back again. He was only away on an outing! Now he's back. The Roman head is back. My bridegroom, my lover. But he doesn't see me. He mustn't see me, either. What do you want, Herr von Dorsday? You're looking at me as though I were your slave. I'm not your slave. Fifty thousand! Are we sticking to our agreement, Herr von Dorsday? I'm ready. Here I am. I'm perfectly calm. I'm smiling. Do you understand my look? His eyes say: come to me! His eyes say: I want to see you naked. Well, you swine, I am naked! What more do you want? Send the telegram . . . immediately. . . . Chills are running up and down my skin. The woman keeps on playing. It's giving me wonderful chills up and down my body. How wonderful it is to be naked. The woman keeps on playing.

She doesn't know what's happening. No one does. No one else has noticed yet. *Filou, Filou!* I'm standing here naked! Dorsday is opening his eyes wide. Now he finally believes it. The *filou* is standing up. His eyes are gleaming. You understand me, handsome fellow!

Ha ha! The woman has stopped playing. Papa is saved. Fifty thousand. Address remains Fiala. *Ha ha ha!* Who's laughing here? Is it me? *Ha ha ha!* Who are all those faces around me? *Ha ha ha!* Too stupid, this laughing. I don't want to laugh, no, I don't want to! *Ha ha!*

Else!

Who's calling *Else?* It's Paul. He must be behind me. I feel a breath of air on my naked back. My ears are ringing. Perhaps I'm already dead? What do you want, Herr von Dorsday? Why are you so enormous and stumbling toward me? *Ha ha ha!*

What have I done? What have I done? What have I done? I'm collapsing. It's all over. Why has the music stopped? An arm is slipping around the nape of my neck. It's Paul. Where's the *filou?* I'm lying here on the floor. *Ha ha ha!* My coat is floating down toward me. And I'm lying here. They think I've fainted. No, I'm not unconscious. I'm fully conscious. I'm a hundred times awake; I'm a thousand times awake. I just can't stop laughing. *Ha ha ha!* Now you've had your wish, Herr von Dorsday; now you've got to send the money for Papa. Immediately. *Haaaah!* I don't want to scream, but I can't stop. Why do I have to scream?—My eyes are shut. No one can see me. Papa is saved.

Else!

That's my aunt.

Else! Else!

A doctor, a doctor!

Quickly, go get the porter!

What's happened?

That's impossible.

The poor child.

What are they talking about? What are they whispering? I'm not a poor child. I'm happy. The *filou* saw me naked. Oh, I'm so ashamed. What have I done? I'm never going to open my eyes again.

Please, close the door.

Why should the door be closed? What a murmur. There must be a thousand people around me. They all think I've fainted. I haven't fainted. I'm just dreaming.

Try to calm yourself, madam.

Has the doctor been sent for?

It's a fainting spell.

How far away they all are. They're all talking from the top of the Cimone.

We can't let her lie there on the floor.

Here's a throw.

A blanket.

A throw or a blanket, it doesn't make any difference.

Quiet, please.

On the sofa.

Will somebody please close the door!

Don't get so nervous. It's already closed.

Else! Else!

If my aunt would only be quiet!

Can you hear me, Else?

You can see she's unconscious, Mama.

Yes, thank God you think I'm unconscious. And I'll stay unconscious, too.

We have to take her up to her room.

What's happened here? Oh my God!

Cissy. How does Cissy happen to be in the meadow? Oh, this isn't the meadow.

Else!

Quiet, please.

254 · ARTHUR SCHNITZLER

Step back, please.

Hands, hands under me. What do they want? How heavy I am. Paul's hands. Go away; go away. The *filou* is near; I can feel it. And Dorsday's gone. They've got to look for him. He can't kill himself before he's sent off the fifty thousand. Ladies and gentlemen, he owes me money. Arrest him.

Do you have any idea who sent the telegram, Paul?

Good evening, ladies and gentlemen.

Else, can you hear me?

Let her be, Frau Cissy.

Oh, Paul.

The manager says it could be four hours before the doctor arrives.

She looks like she's sleeping.

I'm lying on the sofa. Paul is holding my hand; he's feeling for my pulse. Right; he's a doctor, after all.

There isn't any danger, Mama. It's a—a fit.

I'm not staying in this hotel another day.

Please, Mama.

We're leaving tomorrow morning.

Let's just take her up by way of the servant staircase; the stretcher will be here right away.

Stretcher? Haven't I already been on a stretcher today? Wasn't I already dead? Do I have to die again?

Won't you please see that everyone stands clear of the door, Herr Direktor?

Don't get so upset, Mama.

It's so inconsiderate of everyone.

Why are they all whispering? Like in a funeral home. The bier will be here any minute. Open the gate, Herr Matador!

The hallway is clear.

People might at least have some consideration.

Please, Mama, calm yourself.

Please, madam.

Won't you look after my mother for a while, Frau Cissy?

She's his mistress, but she's not as beautiful as I am. Now what? What's happening now? They're bringing the stretcher. I can see it with my eyes closed. That's the stretcher they put the injured on. It's the same one they carried Dr. Zigmondi on when he fell off the Cimone. And now I'll be lying on the same stretcher. I fell down too. Ha! No, I don't want to scream again. They're whispering. Who's that bending over my face? There's a nice smell of cigarettes. His hand is under my head. Hands under my back, hands under my legs. Go away, go away, don't touch me. I'm naked, after all. Ugh! What do you want from me? Leave me alone. It was only for Papa.

Please be careful. Slowly. Slowly.

The throw?

Yes, thank you, Frau Cissy.

Why does he thank her? What did she do? What's going to happen to me? Oh, how wonderful this feels, how wonderful. I'm floating. I'm floating. I'm floating to the other side. They're carrying me, they're carrying me, they're carrying me to my grave.

But I'm used to this, Herr Doctor. I've carried much heavier people on this stretcher! Last fall there were two at the same time.

Shhh, shhh.

Be so good as go to ahead, Frau Cissy, and make sure that everything in Else's room is ready.

What right does Cissy have to go into my room? The Veronal, the Veronal! If only they don't pour it out! If they do, I'll have to jump out the window after all.

Thank you very much, Herr Direktor, don't bother any further.

I'll take the liberty of inquiring again later.

The steps are creaking; the bearers are wearing heavy hiking boots. Where are my patent leather shoes? Back in the music room. They'll be stolen. I wanted to bequeath them to Agatha. Fred gets my fountain pen. They're carrying me; they're carrying me. Funeral procession. Where is Dorsday the murderer? He's gone. The *filou* has gone too. He's gone back to his hiking. He only came back to see my white breasts. And now he's gone again. He's walking on a dangerous trail between cliffs and gorges. Farewell, farewell. I'm floating, I'm floating. Let them just keep on carrying me up, farther and farther, up to the roof, up to heaven. That would be so convenient!

I saw it coming, Paul.

What did my aunt see coming?

I saw something like this coming for the past few days. She really isn't normal at all. Of course she has to go into an asylum.

But Mama, this isn't the moment to talk about that.

Asylum? Asylum?

You don't imagine, Paul, that I'm going back to Vienna in the same compartment with this creature? A lot of things could happen.

Nothing whatsoever will happen, Mama. I guarantee it. You won't have the slightest embarrassment.

How can you guarantee that?

No, aunt, you won't have any embarrassments. No one will have any embarrassments. Not even Herr von Dorsday. Where are we anyway? We're stopping. We're on the third floor. I'll just open my eyes for a second. Cissy's standing in the doorway talking to Paul.

Over here, please. Yes. Yes. Here. Thanks. Please move the stretcher close to the bed.

They're lifting the stretcher up. They're carrying me. How wonderful! Now I'm back home again. Aah!

Thanks. Yes, that's good. Please close the door. If you'll be so good as to help me, Cissy—

Oh, with pleasure, Herr Doctor.

Slowly, please. Here, Cissy, please take her there. There, underneath her legs. Careful. And now—Else? Can you hear me, Else?

Of course I can hear you, Paul. I can hear everything. What

business is that of yours? It's so wonderful to be unconscious. Oh, go ahead and do what you want.

Paul!

Madam?

Do you really think she's unconscious, dear?

"Dear"? She calls him "dear." I've caught you! She calls him "dear"!

Yes, she's completely unconscious. That's typical of such an attack.

I could die laughing when you act so grown up playing doctor.

I've found you out, you hypocrites! I've found you out!

Be quiet, Cissy.

Why, if she can't hear anything.

What's happened? I'm lying here naked beneath the bed covers. How did they do that?

Well, how is she? Better?

That's my aunt. What does she want?

Still unconscious?

She's creeping up to me on tiptoe. She can go to the devil. I'm not going to let myself be taken to an asylum. I'm not insane.

Isn't there a way of waking her up?

She'll come to soon, Mama. Right now she just needs some peace and quiet. So do you, Mama. Why don't you go to bed? There is absolutely no danger. I'll keep a night watch here with Frau Cissy.

Yes, madam, I'll be the chaperone. Or Else will be, depending on how you look at it.

Miserable creature! I'm lying here unconscious and she's joking.

And I can depend on you, Paul—you'll wake me just as soon as the doctor arrives?

Yes, Mama, but he won't come before tomorrow morning.

She looks as though she's sleeping. Her breathing is regular.

As a matter of fact, Mama, it is a kind of sleep.

I still can't get hold of myself, Paul. Such a scandal! You'll see; it'll be in the newspaper.

Mama!

But she can't hear anything if she's unconscious. We're talking very quietly.

In this condition the senses are sometimes unusually acute.

You have such a learned son, madam.

Please, Mama, go to bed now.

Tomorrow we'll leave here no matter what. And in Bolzano we'll get an attendant for Else.

What? An attendant? You're fooling yourself there.

We'll talk about all of that tomorrow, Mama. Good night, Mama.

I'll have a cup of tea brought to my room, and in a quarter of an hour I'll look in here once more.

That's absolutely unnecessary, Mama.

No, it's not necessary. Just go to the devil. Where is the Veronal? I'll have to wait. They're walking my aunt to the door. Now nobody can see me. It's got to be on the night table, the glass with the Veronal. If I drink all of it down, it's all over. I'll drink it right away. My aunt has left. Paul and Cissy are still standing in the doorway. Ha. She's kissing him. She's kissing him. And I'm lying naked under the covers. Aren't you two ashamed of yourselves? She's kissing him again. Aren't you ashamed of yourselves?

Look, Paul, now I know she's really unconscious—otherwise she would have jumped up and grabbed my throat for sure!

Won't you please do me the favor of being quiet, Cissy?

What's the matter with you, Paul? Either she's really unconscious and can't hear or see anything. Or she's making fools of us. In which case it serves her right.

Someone's knocking, Cissy.

I thought so too.

I'll open the door quietly and see who it is.—Good evening, Herr von Dorsday.

Excuse me, I just wanted to ask how the patient—

Dorsday! Dorsday! Does he really dare! How beastly. Where is he? I hear them whispering behind the door. Paul and Dorsday. Cissy is standing in front of the mirror. What are you doing in front of the mirror? It's my mirror. Isn't my image still in it? What are they saying behind the door, Paul and Dorsday? I feel Cissy's gaze. She's looking at me from the mirror. What does she want? Why is she coming closer? Help! Help! I'm screaming, but no one hears me. What do you want at my bed, Cissy? Why are you bending over me? Do you want to strangle me? I can't move.

Else!

What does she want?

Else! Can you hear me, Else?

I can hear you, but I can't talk. I'm unconscious; I can't talk.

Else, you've given us quite a fright.

She's talking to me. She's talking to me as though I were awake. What does she want?

Do you know what you did, Else? Just think, you came into the music room dressed only in your coat and suddenly you stood there naked in front of everyone and then you fainted. An hysterical attack, everyone says. I don't believe a word of it. I don't believe you're really unconscious, either. I bet you can hear every word I'm saying.

Yes, I can hear her. Yes, yes, yes. But she can't hear my "yes." Why not? I can't move my lips. That's why she can't hear me. I can't move at all. What's wrong with me? Am I dead? Do I just look like I'm dead? Am I dreaming? Where's the Veronal? I want to drink my Veronal. But I can't stretch out my arm. Go away, Cissy. Why are you bending over me? Go away, go away! She'll never know I heard her. No one will ever know. I'll never talk to anyone again. I'll never wake up again. She's going to the door. She's turning around once more. She's opening the door. Dorsday! There he stands. I can see him with my eyes closed. No, I'm really seeing him. My eyes are open after all. The door is ajar. Cissy is out there, too. They're all whispering now. I'm alone. If only I could move now.

Ha! I can, I can! Yes! I'm moving my hand, I'm moving my fingers, I'm stretching out my arm, I'm opening my eyes wide. I can see, I can see! There's my glass. Quick, before they come back into the room. Are there enough packets of Veronal in it? I can't ever wake up again. I've done what I had to do in the world. Papa is saved. I'd never be able to go out and be in the company of others again. Paul is peering through a crack in the doorway. He thinks I'm still unconscious. He doesn't see that I've almost extended my arm all the way. Now they're standing outside the door again, the murderers!—They're all murderers. Dorsday and Cissy and Paul; even Fred is a murderer and Mama is a murderess. They've all murdered me and don't want to admit it. She killed herself, they'll say. You've killed me, all of you, all of you. Do I finally have a hold of it? Quickly, quickly! I've got to! Can't spill a drop. Yes. Quickly. It tastes good. Go on; go on. It isn't a poison at all. Nothing has ever tasted so good to me. If you only knew how good death tastes! Good night, my glass.—Clink, clink.—What's that? The glass is lying on the floor. Down below. Good night.

Else, Else!

What do you want?

Else!

You're here again? Good morning. Here I am lying unconscious with my eyes closed. You'll never see my eyes again.

She must have moved, Paul. How else could it have fallen?

An involuntary movement—that's possible.

If she isn't really awake after all.

What are you saying, Cissy? Just look at her.

I drank the Veronal. I'll die! But everything is just the same as it was before. Maybe it wasn't enough. . . . Paul is holding my hand.

Her pulse is steady. But don't laugh, Cissy. The poor child.

Would you call me a poor child, too, if I had appeared naked in the music room?

Please be quiet, Cissy.

Just as you wish, sir. Maybe I should go and leave you alone with your naked Fräulein. But please don't be embarrassed. Act as though I weren't here.

I drank the Veronal. That's good. Now I'll die. Thank God.

Anyway, you know what I think? That this Herr von Dorsday is in love with the naked Fräulein. He was very upset—as if he took it all personally.

Dorsday, Dorsday! Why that's the—fifty thousand! Is he going to send it? Oh God, what if he doesn't send it? I have to tell them everything. They'll have to force him. Oh God, what if everything was in vain? I can still be saved right now. Paul! Cissy! Why don't you hear me? Don't you know I'm dying? I don't feel anything. I'm just tired. Paul! I'm so tired. Can't you hear me? I'm tired, Paul. I can't open my mouth. I can't move my tongue, but I'm not dead yet. It's the Veronal. Where are you? Soon I'll go to sleep. Then it'll be too late! I can't even hear them talking. They're talking, but I don't know what they're saying. Their voices buzz so. Oh Paul, help me, help me! My tongue feels so heavy.

I think she'll wake up soon, Cissy. It looks as though she were trying to open her eyes. Cissy, what are you doing?

I'm only putting my arms around you. Why not? She didn't have any sense of shame either!

No, I didn't have any sense of shame. I stood there naked in front of everyone. If only I could talk, you would understand why.

Paul! Paul! I want you to hear me. I've taken Veronal, Paul. Ten packets, a hundred. I didn't want to. I was crazy. I don't want to die. You have to save me, Paul. You're a doctor, aren't you? Save me!

Now she seems to be quite calm again. Her pulse—her pulse is almost regular.

Save me, Paul. I beg you. Don't let me die! There's still time. But soon I'll fall asleep and you won't know anything about it. I don't want to die. Save me, please! It was only because of Papa. Dorsday insisted on it. Paul! Paul!

Look here, Cissy, doesn't it seem to you that she's smiling?

How could she not be smiling, Paul, when you're tenderly holding her hand all the time?

Cissy, Cissy, what have I ever done to you that you're so cruel to me? Keep your Paul—but don't let me die. I'm still so young! Mama will grieve so. I want to climb many more mountains. I want to dance. And I'll marry someday too. I want to travel. Tomorrow we'll take that hike up the Cimone. Tomorrow will be a lovely day. The *filou* will come along. I'll humbly invite him. Run after him, Paul. He's hiking on such a dangerous trail. He'll meet Papa. Address remains Fiala, don't forget. It's only fifty thousand and then everything will be all right. Look there, they're all marching in convict's clothes and singing. Open the gate, Herr Matador! It's all just a dream after all. There goes Fred with his husky-voiced Fräulein and the piano is standing outdoors underneath the open sky. The piano tuner lives in the Bartensteinstrasse, Mama! *Why didn't you write to him, child? You forget everything. You should practice your scales more often, Else. A girl of thirteen should be more industrious.*—Rudi went to a masked ball and didn't come home until eight in the morning. *What did you bring me, Papa?* Thirty thousand dolls. I'll need my own house for all of them. But they can also take a walk in the garden. Or go to the masked ball with Rudi. *Hello,*

*Else. Oh, Bertha, are you back again from Naples? Yes, from Sicily.
I want you to meet my husband, Else. Enchanté, monsieur.*

   Else, can you hear me, Else? It's me, Paul.

   Ha ha, Paul. Why are you sitting on that giraffe on the merry-go-round?

   Else, Else!

   Don't ride away from me. You can't hear me if you ride so fast through the main boulevard. You're supposed to save me. I took Veronal. It feels like ants running over my legs, both of them. Yes, just catch him, that Herr von Dorsday. There he goes. Don't you see him? He's jumping over the pond there. He's murdered Papa. So run after him. I'll come along. They've strapped the stretcher on my back, but I'll run along with you. Where are you, Paul? Fred, where are you? Mama, where are you? Cissy? Why are you all letting me run alone through the desert? I'm so afraid all alone. I'd rather fly. I knew that I could fly.

   Else!

   Else!

   Where are you? I can hear you, but I can't see you.

   Else!

   Else!

   Else!

   What's that? A whole chorus? And an organ too? I'll sing along. What kind of song is it? Everybody's singing along. The woods too, and the mountains and the stars. I've never heard anything more beautiful. Give me your hand, Papa. We'll fly together. The world is so beautiful when you can fly. Please don't kiss my hand. After all, I'm your daughter, Papa.

   Else! Else!

   They're calling from so far away. What do you want from me? Don't wake me up. I'm sleeping so well. Tomorrow morning. I'm dreaming and flying. I'm flying ... flying ... flying ... sleeping and dreaming ... and flying ... don't wake me ... tomorrow morning ...

El ...

I'm flying ... I'm dreaming ... I'm sleeping ... I'm drea ... drea ... I'm flying ...

IVAN R. DEE PAPERBACKS

Literature, Arts, and Letters
Brooke Allen, *Twentieth-Century Attitudes*
Roger Angell, *Once More Around the Park*
Walter Bagehot, *Physics and Politics*
Sybille Bedford, *Aldous Huxley*
Stephen Vincent Benét, *John Brown's Body*
Ira Berkow, *The Minority Quarterback*
Isaiah Berlin, *The Hedgehog and the Fox*
F. Bordewijk, *Character*
Robert Brustein, *Cultural Calisthenics*
Robert Brustein, *Dumbocracy in America*
Robert Brustein, *The Siege of the Arts*
Anthony Burgess, *Shakespeare*
Philip Callow, *Chekhov*
Philip Callow, *From Noon to Starry Night*
Philip Callow, *Son and Lover: The Young D. H. Lawrence*
Anton Chekhov, *The Comic Stories*
Bruce Cole, *The Informed Eye*
James Gould Cozzens, *Castaway*
James Gould Cozzens, *Men and Brethren*
Theodore Dalrymple, *Life at the Bottom*
Clarence Darrow, *Verdicts Out of Court*
Floyd Dell, *Intellectual Vagabondage*
Theodore Dreiser, *Best Short Stories*
Joseph Epstein, *Ambition*
Robert Thomas Fallon, *A Theatergoer's Guide to Shakespeare*
André Gide, *Madeleine*
Gerald Graff, *Literature Against Itself*
John Gross, *The Rise and Fall of the Man of Letters*
Olivia Gude and Jeff Huebner, *Urban Art Chicago*
Raul Hilberg, *The Politics of Memory*
Irving Howe, *Politics and the Novel*
Irving Howe, *William Faulkner*
Aldous Huxley, *After Many a Summer Dies the Swan*
Aldous Huxley, *Ape and Essence*
Aldous Huxley, *Collected Short Stories*
Vladimir Kataev, *If Only We Could Know!*
Roger Kimball, *Art's Prospect*
Roger Kimball, *Experiments Against Reality*
Roger Kimball, *Lives of the Mind*
Roger Kimball, *Tenured Radicals*
Hilton Kramer, *The Twilight of the Intellectuals*
Hilton Kramer and Roger Kimball, eds., *Against the Grain*
Hilton Kramer and Roger Kimball, eds., *The Survival of Culture*
F. R. Leavis, *Revaluation*
F. R. Leavis, *The Living Principle*
F. R. Leavis, *The Critic as Anti-Philosopher*
Marie-Anne Lescourret, *Rubens: A Double Life*
Primo Levi, *The Search for Roots*
Sinclair Lewis, *Selected Short Stories*
Lynne Munson, *Exhibitionism*
Joseph Parisi and Stephen Young, ed., *The Poetry Anthology*
Carl Rollyson, *Reading Susan Sontag*
Carl Sandburg, *Poems for the People*
Richard Schickel, *Woody Allen*
Arthur Schnitzler, *Desire and Delusion*
Arthur Schnitzler, *Night Games*
Budd Schulberg, *The Harder They Fall*
Budd Schulberg, *Moving Pictures*
Ramón J. Sender, *Seven Red Sundays*
Karl Shapiro, *Creative Glut*

Peter Shaw, *Recovering American Literature*
James B. Simpson, ed., *Veil and Cowl*
Tess Slesinger, *On Being Told That Her Second Husband Has Taken His First Lover, and Other Stories*
Red Smith, *Red Smith on Baseball*
Donald Thomas, *Swinburne*
B. Traven, *The Bridge in the Jungle*
B. Traven, *The Carreta*
B. Traven, *The Cotton-Pickers*
B. Traven, *General from the Jungle*
B. Traven, *Government*
B. Traven, *March to the Montería*
B. Traven, *The Night Visitor and Other Stories*
B. Traven, *The Rebellion of the Hanged*
B. Traven, *Trozas*
Anthony Trollope, *Trollope the Traveller*
Ivan Turgenev, *Literary Reminiscences*
John Tytell, *Ezra Pound*
Rex Warner, *The Aerodrome*
Rebecca West, *A Train of Powder*
Wilhelm Worringer, *Abstraction and Empathy*